He was screaming. Chazia felt his heart clenching and twitching in her hand. Shoving the blood hard round his body. He was working his lungs fast and deep. Too fast. Too deep.

It didn't matter. Not any more. She squeezed.

When she had killed him, she withdrew her hand from his chest, wiped it carefully on a clean part of his shirt and went back round to her side of the desk. Turned the knob on the intercom box. Pulled the microphone towards her mouth.

"Iliodor?"

"Yes. Commander." The voice crackled in the small speaker.

"There is a mess in my office. Have it cleared away. And I need you to find someone for me. A woman. Shaumian. Maroussia Shaumian. There is a file. Find her for me now, Iliodor. Find her today and bring her to me."

Also by Peter Higgins

Wolfhound Century
Truth and Fear
Radiant State

TRUTH AND FEAR

PETER HIGGINS

www.orbitbooks.net

Orbit
Hachette Book Group
1290 Avenue of the Americas, New York, NY 10104
HachetteBookGroup.com

First US Edition: March 2014
First trade edition: March 2015

Orbit is an imprint of Hachette Book Group, Inc. The Orbit name and logo are trademarks of Little, Brown Book Group Limited.

Library of Congress Control Number: 2014931637

ISBN: 978-0-316-21971-6 (paperback)

10 9 8 7 6 5 4 3 2 1

RRD-C

Printed in the United States of America

The salt stars melt in the barrel –
The ice-water turns coal-black –
Death is getting purer, hard times saltier,
The planet edging closer to truth and to fear

OSIP MANDELSTAM (1891–1938)

Part One

1

In the debatable borderland between night and day, the city of Mirgorod softens. A greyness that is not yet dawn settles on rooftops and gathers in wide empty avenues and squares. Yellow lamp-lit windows grow bleak and drab. Things move in the city, but surreptitiously, in the margins, with a muted, echoless quietness of speech. Mud-footed night-shapes pad away down alleys. A boatman winces at the raw gunning of his barge engine. A waiter eases the iron shutters of the Restaurant Hotel Aikhenvald carefully open so they will not clatter.

Low on the city's eastern horizon, a gap opens in the growing milky bruise of morning and a surprising sliver of sun, a solar squint, spills watery light. The River Mir that has flowed black through the night kindles suddenly to a wide and wind-scuffed green. An exhalation of water vapour, too thin to be called a mist, rises off the surface. The breath of the river quickens and stirs, and on its island between the Mir and the Yekaterina Canal, moored against the embankment of the Square of the Piteous Angel, the Lodka condenses out of the subsiding night, blacker and blacker against the green-tinged yellowing sky. Its cliff-dark walls seem to belly outwards like the sides of a momentous swollen vessel. The jumbled geometry of its roofscape is forested with a hundred flagpoles, and from every pole a red flag edged with black hangs at half mast, draped and inert. Banners hang limply from parapets and window ledges: repetitious, identical fabrics of blood and black, the officious, unwavering, requiring stare of collective mourning.

Within the walls of the Lodka, the unending work of the Vlast goes on. Its skeleton crew, the three thousand watchkeepers of the night – civil servants, diplomats, secret police – are completing their reports and tidying their desks. First light is falling grey through the grimed glass dome onto the still-empty galleries of the Central Registry, where the great wheel of the Gaukh Engine stands motionless but expectant. On hundreds of yards of unlit shelving, the incoming files – the accusations and denunciations, the surveillance records, the intercepted communications – await the archivists of the new day. The stone slabs of the execution yards are being scrubbed and scoured with ammonia, and in the basement mortuary the new arrivals' slabbed cadavers seep and chill.

In the Square of the Piteous Angel the morning light loses its first bright softness and grows complacent, ordinary and cold. Along the embankment the whale-oil tapers, burning in pearl globes in the mouths of cast-iron leaping fish, are bleached almost invisible, though their subtle reek still fumes the dampness of the air. The iron fish have heavy heads and bulging eyes and scales thick-edged like fifty-kopek coins. Their lamps are overdue for dousing. The gulls have risen from their night-roosts: they wheel low in silence and turn west for the shore.

And on the edge of the widening clarity of the square's early emptiness, the observer of the coming day stands alone, in the form of a man, tall and narrow-shouldered in a dark woollen suit and grey astrakhan hat. His name is Antoninu Florian. He takes from his pocket a pair of wire-framed spectacles, polishes with the end of his silk burgundy scarf the circular pieces of glass that are not lenses, and puts them on.

It is more than two hundred years since Antoninu Florian first watched a morning open across Mirgorod. Half as old as the city, he sees it for what it is. Its foundations are shallow. Through the soles of his shoes on the cobbles he feels the slow seep and settle of ancient mud, the deep residuum of the city-crusted delta of old Mir: the estuarial mud on which the Lodka is beached.

The river's breath touches Florian's face, intimate and sharing. Cold moisture-nets gather around him: a sifting connectedness; gentle, subtle water-synapses alert with soft intelligence. Crowding presences move across the empty square and tall buildings not yet there cluster against the skyline. The translucence of a half-mile tower that is merely the plinth for the behemoth statue of a man. Antoninu Florian has seen these things before. He knows they are possible. He has returned to the city and found them waiting still.

But today is a different day. Florian tastes it on the breath of the river. It is the day he has come back for. The long equilibrium is shifting: flimsy tissue-layers are peeling away, the might-be making way for the true and the is. And in Florian's hot belly there is a feeling of continuous inward empty falling, a slow stumble that never hits the floor: he recognises it as quiet, uneasy fear. The breath of the river brings him the scent of new things coming. It tugs at him. Urges him. Come, it says, come. Follow. The woman who matters is coming today.

Florian hesitates. What he fears is decision. Choices are approaching and he is unsure. He does not know what to do. Not yet.

The curiosity of a man's gaze rakes the side of his face. A gendarme is watching him from the bridge on the other side of the square. Florian feels the involuntary needle-sharpening of teeth inside his mouth, the responsive ache of his jaw to lengthen, the muscles of neck and throat to bunch and bulk. His human form feels suddenly awkward, inadequate, a hobbling constraint. But he forces it back into place and turns, hands in pockets, narrow shoulders hunched against the cold he does not feel, walking away down Founder's Prospect.

The gendarme does not follow.

2

In her office high in the Lodka, on the other side of the Square of the Piteous Angel, Commander Lavrentina Chazia, chief of the Mirgorod Secret Police, put down her pen and closed the file.

'We are living in great days, Teslom,' she said. 'Critical times. History is taking shape. The future is being made, here and now, in Mirgorod. Do you feel this? Do you taste it in the air, as I do?'

The man across the desk from her said nothing. His head was slumped forward, his chin on his chest. He was breathing in shallow ragged breaths. His wrists were bound to the arms of his chair with leather straps. His legs, broken at the knees, were tied by the ankles. His dark blue suit jacket was unbuttoned, his soft white shirt open at the neck: blood had flowed from his nose, soaking the front of it. He was a small, neat man with rimless circular glasses and a flop of rich brown hair, glossy when he was taken, but matted now with sweat and drying blood. Not a physical man. Unused to enduring pain. Unused to endurance of any kind.

'Of course you feel it too,' Chazia continued. 'You're a learned fellow. You read. You watch. You study. You understand. The Novozhd is dead. Our beloved leader cruelly blown apart by an anarchist's bomb. I was there, Teslom. I saw it. It was a terrible shock. We are all stricken with grief.'

The man in the chair groaned quietly. He raised his head to look at her. His eyes behind their lenses were wide and glassy.

'I've told you,' he said. 'A hundred times … a thousand … I know nothing of this. Nothing. I … I am … a librarian. An archivist. I keep books. I am the curator of Lezarye. Only that. Nothing more.'

'Of course. Of course. But the fact remains. The Novozhd is dead. So now there is a question.'

The man did not reply. He was staring desperately at the heavy black telephone on the desk, as if its sudden bell could ring salvation for him. Let him stare. Commander Chazia stood up and crossed to the window. Mirgorod spread away below her towards the horizon under the grey morning sky. The recent floods were subsiding, barges moving again on the river.

There had been rumours that when the recent storms were at their height sentient beasts made of rain had been seen in the city streets. Dogs and wolves of rain. Rain bears, walking. Militia patrols had been attacked. Gendarmes ripped to a bloody mess, their throats torn out by hard teeth of rain. And rusalkas had risen from the flooded canals and rivers. Lipless mouths, broad muscular backs and chalk-white flesh. With expressionless faces they reached up and pulled men down to drown in the muddied waters. The rumours were probably true. Chazia had made sure that the witnesses and the story-spreaders were quietly shot in the basement cells of the Lodka. It was good that people were afraid, so long as they feared her more.

She had left Teslom long enough. She turned from the window and walked round behind his chair. Rested her hand on his shoulder. Felt his muscles quiver at her gentle touch.

'Who will rule, Teslom? Who will have power? Who will govern now that the Novozhd is dead? That's the question here. And you can help me with that.'

'Please ...' said Teslom. His voice was almost too quiet to hear. 'Please—'

'I just need your help, darling. Just a little. Then you can rest.'

'I ...' He raised his head and tried to turn towards her. 'I ... I can't ...'

Chazia leaned closer to hear him.

'Let's go over it again. Tell me,' she said. 'Tell me about the Pollandore.'

'The Pollandore ... ? A story. Only a story. Not a real thing ... not something that exists ... I've told you—'

'This is a feeble game, Teslom. I'm not looking for it. It isn't lost. It's here. It's in this building. I have it.'

He jerked his head round. Stared at her.

'Do you want to see it?' said Chazia. 'It would interest you. OK, let's do that, shall we? Maybe later. When we can be friends again. But first—'

'If you already have it, then …'

'The future is coming, Teslom. But who will shape it? Tell me about the Pollandore.'

'I will tell you *nothing*. You … you and all your … you … you can all *fuck off*.'

Chazia unbuttoned her uniform tunic, took it off and hung it on the back of Teslom's chair. He was staring at the telephone again.

'Do you know me, Teslom?' she said gently.

'What?'

'I think you do not. Not yet.'

She rolled the sleeves of her shirt above the elbow. The smooth dark stone-like patches on her hands were growing larger. Spreading up her arms. The skin at the edges was puckered, red and sore and angry. The itching was with her always.

'Let's come at this from a different direction,' she said. 'A visitor came to the House on the Purfas. An emissary from the eastern forest. A thing that was not human. An organic artefact of communication. You're surprised that I know this? You shouldn't be. Your staff were regular and thorough in their reports. But I'm curious. Tell me about this visitor.'

She was stroking him now. Standing behind him, she smoothed his matted brown hair. He jerked his head away.

'No,' he said hoarsely. 'I choose death. I choose to die.'

'That's nothing, Teslom.' She bent her head down close to his. She could smell the sourness of his fear. 'Everyone dies,' she breathed in his ear. 'Just not you. Not yet.'

As she spoke she slid her stone-stained hand across his shoulder and down the side of his neck inside his bloodied shirt, feeling his smooth skin, his sternum, the start of his ribs. She felt the beating of his heart and rested her hand there. Closing her eyes and feeling with her mind for the place. She had done this before, but it was not easy. It needed concentration. She let her fingers rest a moment on the gap in his ribs over his heart. Teslom was still. Scarcely breathing. He could not have moved if he wanted to: with her other hand she was pressing against his back, using the angel-flesh in her fingers to probe his spinal cord, immobilising him.

She had found the place above his heart. She dug the tips of her fingers into the rib-gap, opening a way. It needed technique more than strength, the angel-substance in her hand did the work. Teslom's quiet moan of horror was distracting, but she did it right. She reached inside and cupped his beating heart in her palm. And squeezed.

His eyes widened in panic. He could see her hand deep in his chest. He could see there was no blood. No wound. It was not possible. But it was in there.

'Are you listening to me, Teslom?'

He was weak. Cold sweat on the dull white skin of his face, livid blotches over his cheekbones. Chazia released the pressure a little. Let his heart beat again.

'Are you listening to me?'

He shifted his head almost imperceptibly to the left. An attempt at a nod.

'Good. So. This strange living artefact, this marvellous emissary from the forest. Why did it come? What did it want? Did it concern the Pollandore?'

'It ... I can't ...'

Chazia adjusted her grip on his heart.

'There,' she said. 'Is that better? Can you talk now?'

'Yes. Yes. Oh please. Get it out. Get it out. Stop.'

'So tell me.'

'What?'

'The messenger. From the forest.'

'It ... addressed the Inner Committee.'

'And what did it say?'

'It said ... it said there was an angel.'

'An angel?'

'A *living* angel. It had fallen in the forest and it was trapped there. It was foul and doing great damage. Oh. Please. Don't ...'

Chazia waited. *Give him time. Let him speak. Patience.* But his head had sunk down again and there was a congested bubbling in his chest. Perhaps she had been too harsh. Overestimated his strength. The silence lengthened. She lessened the pressure on his heart but kept her hand in place. It was the horror of seeing it in there, as much as anything, that made them speak.

'Teslom?' she said at last. 'Tell me more. The forest is afraid of this living angel? Afraid it will do terrible things?'

'Yes.'

'And so? This emissary. Why did the forest send it? Was it the Pollandore?'

'Of course. Yes. Open the Pollandore, it said. Now. Now is the time. Before it's too late.'

'Too late? For what?'

'The Pollandore is breaking. It is failing, or leaking, or waking, or … something. I don't know. I didn't understand. It wasn't clear … I can't … I need to stop now … rest … please … for fuck's sake …'

He coughed sour-smelling fluid out of his mouth. Viscous spittle stained with flecks of red and pink. It spilled on her forearm. It was warm.

'You're doing fine, Teslom. Good. Very good. Soon it will be over. Just a few more questions. Then you can rest.'

He struggled for breath, trying to bring his hands up to push her off. But his hands were strapped to the chair.

Chazia sensed his strength giving out. He was on the edge of death. She tried to hold him there, but she didn't have complete control. There was a margin of uncertainty. But they had come to the crisis. The brink of gold. Crouching down beside him, she rested her head on his shoulder, her cheek against his.

'Just tell me, darling,' she said quietly. '*How* was the Pollandore to be opened?'

'There was a key.' He was barely whispering. 'The paluba – the messenger – it brought a key.'

'What kind of key?'

'I don't know. I didn't see it. I wasn't there. I heard. Only heard. Not a key. Not exactly. Not like an iron thing for a lock. But a thing that opens. A recognition thing. An identifier. I don't know. The paluba offered it to the Inner Committee. Oh shit. Stop. Please.'

'And what did the Inner Committee do?'

'*Nothing.*'

'Nothing?'

'They refused the message. They were afraid. What *could* they do? They didn't *have* the Pollandore. They lost it. The useless fuckers lost it long ago. Please—'

'So?'

'So they sent it away. The paluba. They sent it away.'

'What happened then? What did the paluba do? Where did it go? What happened to the *key*?'

He closed his eyes. His head sank forward again. She was losing him.

'Your daughter, Teslom. You have a daughter. You should think of her.'

'What?'

'She is pregnant.'

'No ... not her ... Leave her alone!'

'If you fail me now, I will reach inside your daughter's belly for her feeble little unborn child – it's a girl, Teslom, a girl, she doesn't know this but I do – and I will take its skull between my fingers ... like this ...' She paused. 'Are you listening to me?'

'Yes.'

'Do you know that I will do this? Do you know that I will?'

She squeezed his heart again, gently. He screamed.

'It's all right, darling,' she whispered in his ear. 'Nearly finished now. Think of your daughter, Teslom. Think of her *child*.'

'Oh no,' he gasped. 'Oh no. No.'

'Where is the key to the Pollandore? Tell me how to find it.'

'I don't *know*!'

'Then who? Who knows?'

'The woman,' said Teslom, so quiet Chazia could hardly hear. 'The woman,' he said again. 'Shaumian.'

'What? Say it again, darling. Say the name again.'

'Shaumian. The key. It would go to the Shaumian woman next. If not the Committee ... then Shaumian. *Shaumian!*'

Chazia felt her own heart beat with excitement. *Shaumian*. She knew the name. And it led to another question. The most important question of all.

'Teslom?'

'No more. Please. I can't—'

'Just one more thing, sweetness, and then you can have some peace. There are two Shaumian women. Was it the mother? Or the daughter? Which one was it, darling? Which one?'

'I don't know. It doesn't matter. Either. What's the difference? It makes no difference. It doesn't—'

'Yes, it matters. The mother is dead. The mother dead, the daughter not. That's the difference, darling. Mother or daughter?'

Teslom choked and struggled for breath. He was mouthing silence like a fish drowning in air. Chazia waited. Everything depended on what he said next.

'Mother or daughter?' whispered Chazia gently. 'Mother or daughter, darling?'

'Daughter then.' His voice was almost too quiet to hear. 'Daughter. The key would be for the daughter.'

'Maroussia Shaumian? Be sure now. Tell me again.'

'*Yes!* For fuck's sake. I'm telling you. That's the name. Shaumian. *Shaumian! Maroussia Shaumian!*'

He was screaming. Chazia felt his heart clenching and twitching in her hand. Shoving the blood hard round his body. He was working his lungs fast and deep. Too fast. Too deep.

It didn't matter. Not any more. She squeezed.

When she had killed him, she withdrew her hand from his chest, wiped it carefully on a clean part of his shirt and went back round to her side of the desk. Turned the knob on the intercom box. Pulled the microphone towards her mouth.

'Iliodor?'

'Yes, Commander.' The voice crackled in the small speaker.

"There is a mess in my office. Have it cleared away. And I need you to find someone for me. A woman. Shaumian. Maroussia Shaumian. There is a file. Find her for me now, Iliodor. Find her today and bring her to me.'

3

Vissarion Lom and Maroussia Shaumian took the first tram of the day into Mirgorod from Cold Amber Strand. Marinsky Line. Cars 1639, 1640 and 1641, liveried in brown and gold, a thick black letter M front and back on each one. Four steep clattering steps to climb inside. Slatted wooden benches. *Standard class, single journey, no luggage: 5 kopeks.* There were few other passengers: in summer holidaymakers came to Cold Amber Strand for the bathing huts, the pleasure gardens, the bandstand, the aquarium, but now winter was closing in. Signs above the seats warned them: CITIZEN, YOU ARE IN PUBLIC NOW! BEWARE OF BOMBS! WHOM ARE YOU WITH?

They went to the back of the car and Lom took a seat opposite Maroussia, facing forward to watch the door. He kept his hand in the pocket of his coat, holding the revolver loosely. A double-action Sepora .44 magnum. It was empty. But that was OK. That was better than nothing.

The tram hummed and rattled and accelerated slowly away from the stop. Maroussia huddled into the corner and stared out of the window, eyes wide and dark. Flimsy shoes. Bare legs, pale and cold.

'The Pollandore is in Mirgorod,' said Maroussia. 'It must be. Vishnik knew where it was – he found it, and he was looking in the city. So it's in the city. That's where it is.' She frowned and looked away. 'Only I don't know where.'

'We'll start at Vishnik's apartment,' said Lom. 'He had papers. Photographs. Notes. We'll go and look. After we've eaten. First we need to find some food. Breakfast.'

'I left my bag at Vishnik's,' said Maroussia. 'I've got clothes in it. Clothes and money and things. Maybe the bag's still there.'

'Maybe,' said Lom.

'I can't go back to my room,' said Maroussia.

'No.'

'They'll be waiting. Watching. The militia …'

'Possibly,' said Lom. 'Don't worry. We'll be fine—'

Lom broke off. A woman with two children got on the tram and took the seat behind Maroussia. Maroussia withdrew further into the corner and closed her eyes. She looked tired.

The city opened to take them back. A fine rain greyed the emptiness between buildings. It rested in the air, softening it, parting to let the tramcars pass and closing behind them. The streets of Mirgorod were recovering from the flood. River mud streaked the pavements and pools of water reflected the low grey sky. Businesses were closed and shuttered, or gaped, water-ransacked and abandoned. People picked their way across plank-and-trestle walkways between piles of ruined furniture stacked in the road. Sodden mattresses, rugs, couches, wardrobes, books. A barge, lifted almost completely out of the canal and left beached by the flood, jutted its prow out into the road. A giant in a rain-slicked leather jacket was shouldering it off the buckled railings and trying to slide it back into the water. Gendarmes and militia patrols stood on street corners, checking papers, watching the clearing-up. They seemed to be everywhere. More than usual.

Lom leaned forward and slid open a gap in the window, letting the cold city air pumice his face. He inhaled deeply: the taste of coal-smoke, benzine, misting rain and sea salt was in his mouth – the taste of Mirgorod.

Maroussia's shoulder was raised protectively, half-turned against him. Her face was almost a stranger's face, at rest and unfamiliar in sleep. She *was* almost a stranger to him. He knew almost nothing about her, nothing ordinary at all, but he knew the most important thing. She had set her will against the inevitability of the world. The Vlast had come for her, for no reason that she knew – not that the Vlast needed reasons – but Maroussia hadn't gone slack, as so many did, numbed by the immensity and inertia of their fate. She had seized on the vague and broken hints of the messenger that came from nowhere – from the endless, uninterpretable forest – and she had turned them into the engine of her own private counter-attack against … against what? Against unchangeability, against the cruelty of things.

But the energy of her counter-attack was Maroussia's own. It came from dark inward places. She was alone, unsanctioned, uninstructed. Lom couldn't have said with certainty what she thought she was going to achieve, or how, and it seemed not really possible, in the cold grey light of the morning return to the city, that she could do anything at all: Mirgorod was the foremost city of the continental hegemony of the Vlast, four hundred years of consolidated history, and they were two alone, without a map of the future, without a plan. But what struck him was how irrelevant the impossibility of her purpose was. It was its asymmetric absurdity that gave it meaning and shape. The undercurrent of almost unnoticed fear that he was feeling now was fear for her. He had none for himself. He had never felt more alive. He was relaxed and open and strong. He would do what he could when whatever was coming came; he would stand with her side by side. Her mouth was slightly open in sleep, and she was doing the bravest, loneliest thing that Lom had ever seen done.

The healing wound in the front of his skull pulsed almost imperceptibly under fine new skin with the beating of his heart. He pulled off the white scrap of cloth he'd tied round his forehead. It was unnecessary and conspicuous. As he stuffed it into his pocket, he felt the touch of something else: a quiet stirring under his fingers. He brought the thing out and cupped it in his palm. A small linen bag stained with dried blood. He'd forgotten he had it. He opened it and took out the strange small knotted ball of twigs and wax, tiny bones and dried berries. Brought it up to his face and breathed its earthy, resinous air. A woodland taint. He slipped the small thing back into its bag. It was a survivor.

The tram got more crowded as they approached the city centre: squat, frowning women with empty string bags; workers going to work, each absorbed in their own silence. More than half the passengers were wearing black armbands. Lom wondered why. It was odd. Looking out of the window, he saw checkpoints at the major intersections. Traffic was backed up in the streets and people were lining up along the pavement to show their papers. The pale brick-coloured uniforms of the VKBD were out in force. Mirgorod, police city. Something was happening.

'Pardon me please. May I?'

A man with thinning hair and a crumpled striped suit slid onto the seat next to Maroussia. He rested a cloth attaché case on his knees, opened it and took out a paper bag. Nodding apologetically at Lom, he started to eat a piece of sausage.

'Sorry,' the man said. 'Running late. Crowds everywhere. I've had my cards looked at twice already. The funeral, I guess. Back to normal tomorrow.'

Lom gave him a *What can you do?* shrug and went back to watching through the window. The sausage smelled strongly of garlic and paprika.

Fifteen minutes later the tram pulled up at the terminus and the engine cut out. People started to stand up and shuffle down the aisle. The man sitting opposite Lom put his empty sausage bag into his attaché case and clicked it shut. He glanced out of the window and swore under his breath.

'Not again,' he said. 'I'm going to be late. Damn, I don't need this, not today.' He got up with a sigh and joined the back of the line.

Lom stayed where he was and took a look out of the window to see what the problem was. There were four gendarmes on the platform. Two were stopping the passengers as they got off – looking at identity cards, comparing photographs to faces – while the other two stood back, watchful, hands on their holsters. One of the watchers was a corporal. The checkpoint was set up right. The men were awake and alert and doing it properly. The corporal knew his stuff.

Lom had to do something. He needed to *think*.

Maroussia stirred and woke. Her cheeks were flushed and her hair was damp. Stray curls stood out from the side of her head where it had pressed against the window. She looked around, confused.

'Where are we?' she said.

Lom began buttoning his cloak. Taking his time, but making it look natural. Not like he was avoiding joining the queue.

'End of the line,' he said quietly. 'Marinsky-Voksal. But there's trouble.'

Maroussia turned to see, and took in at a glance what was happening. She bent forward to adjust her shoe.

'Are they looking for us?' she whispered.

'Not necessarily. But possibly. Can't discount it. I've got no papers. Have you?'

'No.'

'OK,' said Lom. 'We'll separate. I'll go first. Give them something to think about. You slip away while I've got them occupied.' Maroussia started to protest, but Lom had already stood up and joined the end of the resigned shuffling queue.

He was getting near the exit. There were only two or three passengers ahead of him, waiting with studied outward patience, documents ready in hand. One of the gendarmes was examining identity cards while the other peered over his shoulder into the tram, scrutinising the line. Lom saw his eyes slide across the faces, pass on, hesitate, and come to rest on Maroussia with a flicker of interest. He checked against a photograph in his hand and looked at her again, a longer, searching look. He took a step forward.

Shit, thought Lom. *I can't let us be taken. Not like this. That would be stupid.* His fingers in his pocket closed on the grip of the empty Sepora ·44·

He felt an elbow in his ribs.

'Excuse me, please!'

It was Maroussia, pushing past him and heading for the gendarme.

'Excuse me!' she said again in a loud voice.

'What are you *doing*?' hissed Lom, putting his hand on her arm.

'Making time,' she said. 'Not getting us killed.'

She pulled her arm free, pushed past the waiting passengers and spoke to the gendarme.

'You must help me, please,' she said firmly. 'Take me to the nearest police station. At once. My name is Maroussia Shaumian. I am a citizen of this city. A militia officer murdered my mother. He also tried to kill me. I want protection and I want to make a statement. I want to make a complaint.'

The gendarme stared at her in surprise.

'You what?'

'You heard me,' said Maroussia. 'I want to make a complaint. What is your name? Tell me please.'

Lom stepped up beside her.

'Stand aside, man,' he said to the gendarme. Peremptory. Authoritative. 'I'm in a hurry. This woman is in my custody.'

The gendarme took in his heavy loden coat, mud-stained at the bottom. The healing wound in his forehead.

'And who the fuck are you?' he said.

'Political Police,' said Lom.

'You don't look like police. Let's see your ID.'

'I am a senior investigator in the third department of the Political Police,' said Lom. 'On special attachment to the Minister's Office.'

'You got papers to prove that?'

'Vlasik,' said the corporal, 'this is a waste of time. Bring them both.'

4

In the pre-dawn twilight two thousand miles north and east of Mirgorod, Professor Yakov Khyrbysk stepped over the coaming and out into lamplit fog on the deck of Vlast Fisheries Vessel *Chaika*. Sub-zero air scraped at the inside of his nose and throat. Despite the two sweaters under his oilskin slicker the freezing cold wrapped iron bands round his ribcage and squeezed. He dug out his petrol lighter and a packet of Chernomors, cupped his hands to light one and inhaled the raw smoke deeply.

The *Chaika* stank of diesel and fish. During the night sea spray had frozen in glassy sheets on every surface. Ice sheathed nets and hawsers and hung like cave growths from cleats, winches and davits. Crewmen, working under lamps, waist-deep in thunderous clouds of steam, were hosing the ice off the deck with hot water from the boilers. The men wore mountainous parkas and wrapped scarves across their mouths to keep from inhaling the foul spray. They sent gleaming slicks of slime, fish guts and oil sluicing across the planks and out through the bilge holes. *Citizen Trawlermen, you are frontline workers! By feeding the people you strengthen the Vlast! Strive for a decisive upsurge in the production of fish protein!*

The *Chaika* heaved and dipped, her hull moaning with the low surge of her engine. Khyrbysk threaded his way across the treacherous deck and climbed the companionway. Captain Baburin was waiting up on the platform outside the wheelhouse.

'There is low pressure coming in, Yakov Arkadyevich,' said Baburin. 'Then it will be cold enough for you, I think.' In the yellow light from the wheelhouse his heavy black beard and the folds of his greatcoat and cap glittered with frost.

'Is she there?' said Khyrbysk. 'Can you see her yet?'

Baburin shrugged towards the starboard bow.

'She's there,' he said. 'Exactly where she should be. We'll come up with her soon enough.'

Khyrbysk peered in the same direction. Fog and black water were emerging out of the night. The glimmer of scattered pieces of ice.

'I can't see anything,' he said.

'She is coming,' said Baburin.

Khyrbysk waited, leaning on the rail, smoking and watching the grey dawn seep out of the fog and the sea. The day came up empty and sunless. Fog blanked out distance and brought the horizon near. Coal-black swells rose, marbled with foam, and surged forward, shouldering the *Chaika*'s prow upwards. She heaved and dipped. Rafts of sea-ice scraped against her hull. Every so often she hit a larger piece and shuddered. This was the grey zone: the crew of the *Chaika* might see the sun once or twice in three months. If they were lucky. Khyrbysk felt an involuntary surge of excitement. Was he himself not the igniter of a *thousand* suns?

'There!' shouted Baburin from the wheelhouse, pointing. Khyrbysk could just about make out a wedge of darker grey in the fog, a triangle embedded in black water. The triangle loomed larger and resolved itself into a head-on view of the factory ship *Musk Ox* steaming towards them, twin stacks brimming dark heavy smoke. The blunted prow and swollen skirts of an icebreaker.

Ten minutes, and Baburin had swung the *Chaika* right in under the lee of the factory ship. The *Musk Ox*'s huge hull towered overhead, a sheer and salt-scoured cliff of bleeding rust, battered and dented from twenty years of unloading trawlers in bad weather. Khyrbysk stared down into the narrow channel between the two vessels. The water was so cold it had a thick, sluggish sheen, laced with soft congealing slush-ice. A shout from above told him the *Musk Ox*'s side crane was ready.

The transport cage was descending, swinging gently from its cable, four tyres fixed to the underside to soften the landing. In the cage, Kolya Blegvad rested one gloved hand on the rectangular wooden crate that stood on its end beside him, taller than he was, and with the other he kept a tight grip on the cable chain. A crewman on the *Chaika* leaned out with a gaff to guide the cage in.

Khyrbysk went to find Zakopan, the *Chaika*'s mate.

'I want the box in my cabin,' he told him. 'And quickly. The machinery is delicate. It will not tolerate the cold on the deck.'

In Khyrbysk's overheated cabin, the crate took up all the space between his bunk and the pale green bulkhead. Khyrbysk locked the door, drew the curtain across the porthole and lit the oil lamp. From the same match he lit another Chernomor. Kolya Blegvad watched him with clever soft brown eyes.

'You came to meet me, Yakov,' he said. 'I am touched.'

'Were there any difficulties?' said Khyrbysk.

'With transit papers signed by Dukhonin himself? No. How could there be? Our friend in Mirgorod was as good as his word.'

'I want to see it,' said Khyrbysk. He produced a crowbar.

'Now?'

'Now,' said Khyrbysk. 'Yes. Now.'

He prised off the lid. Inside the crate was thirty million roubles in used notes of miscellaneous denomination.

5

In Levrovskaya Square the gendarmes drew their revolvers and moved towards Lom and Maroussia. Lom considered the position. All the angles. Staying calm, staying relaxed. *Assess and evaluate. Think and plan.* Like he'd been trained to do. It took him a second. Maybe a second and a half.

The misting rain softened edges and blurred distances. He felt in his face and across his shoulders the weight of massive slabs of high cold air sliding in off the sea. The temperature was dropping. Freezing cold snagged at the back of his throat and in his nose. His visible breath flickered. Tiny vanishing ghosts. Stone slabs slick and slippery underfoot. The Marinsky-Voksal Terminus was a double row of tram stops, low raised platforms under wrought-iron canopies. Tramcars were pulled up at three of them, including the one they'd arrived at, and waiting passengers crowded at the other three. Beyond the terminus, Marinsky Square was a grumbling tangle of traffic, street sellers and pedestrians.

Lom wasn't too worried about the four gendarmes pressed in close around them. Gendarmes, with their uniforms of thick green serge, their shiny peaked caps, polished leather belts and buttoned-down holsters, were street police: efficient enough at traffic and checkpoints and petty crime, but not used to serious trouble. They carried 7.62mm Vagants: heavy service revolvers, the seven-cartridge cylinder unconverted single-action version. Lom had carried a Vagant himself for three years and he'd never liked it: loud and clumsy, with a wild kick, a Vagant made a nasty mess at close range, but it was hopelessly inaccurate over more than ten yards.

These four weren't the problem. The problem was the other four-man patrols at the other five tram halts and the VKBD truck pulled up at the kerb twenty yards away, two men in the cab and an unknown number in the back. Shit. They shouldn't have stayed on the tram till the end of the line. They should have got off at some suburban stop and walked in. He'd made a mistake. The only thing now was to get out of Marinsky Square as quickly as possible with the minimum number of police in tow. Maroussia had seen that quicker than he had. Second mistake of the day. *Wake up. This is serious.*

Maroussia was standing silent, upright and fierce, waiting while the gendarmes briefly debated their next move. The one who'd spotted them wanted to take them across to the VKBD truck, but the corporal vetoed it.

'I'm calling it in myself. We'll get no thanks from Vryushin if the VKBD gets credit for this. Take them across to the section office. Quickly, no fuss, before anyone notices what's going on. Move. Now.'

They split into pairs, two walking ahead with Maroussia between them, the corporal and the other one following with Lom. They didn't wait to search him. Traffic cops.

But the corporal stayed ten feet behind him with his Vagant aimed at the small of Lom's back. It was efficient enough. Lom might have got away, perhaps, but he couldn't see a way to take Maroussia with him, so for the moment he rode with it. Things could have been worse. Perhaps.

Something else nagged at him. He couldn't shake a small insistent pressure at the back of his neck. The familiar feeling that he was being watched.

Two floors above the street on the other side of Marinsky Square, Antoninu Florian crouched on the sill of a bricked-up window, enfolded by scarves of rain-mist drifting down off the roof slates. He licked the living moisture from his upper lip and savoured it on his tongue, sharing with it the city, the engine fumes and sweat and the dark strong silt-green surge of the living River Mir. The mist tasted of fires not yet burning and blood not yet spilled, traces of the passing touch of the living angel in the forest. But there was also the bright sharp resinous hint of something good, scents of earth and green currents stirring: all morning Florian had been following the trail of it, and now with yellow-flecked eyes he watched the woman who mattered walking between policemen. And he watched the man who was with her. He gripped them with the teeth of his gaze, sifting their particular scents out of the city tumult.

The man who was with the woman was spilling bright shining communication, all unawares. Florian could have found him a mile away in a dark forest at night in a thunderstorm, and the man did not even know it. Though he did have some vague sense of Florian's presence: Florian watched him hesitate and look around. But the man did not look up. Nor did the police look up. They never looked up. Not until they learned. If they ever did.

Experimentally, Florian shifted and adjusted the bone structure of his face. Slid musculature into new places under warm sleeves of flesh. His hair moved like leaves under water. He tested thickness and shade, melatonin and refraction. It was enough. He was confident. When the woman and the man and the four policemen had passed beneath him, Florian leaped down from the second-floor ledge, landing lightly on all fours on rain-skinned cobbles, rose up and followed.

6

Thousands of miles east of Mirgorod, deep in the endless forest, the immense, mountainous body of Archangel rises against the skyline like a storm cloud approaching. His consciousness bleeds into the surrounding country, not life but anti-life, oozing out through the forest like lichen across rock. Like piss in snow. In the lower skirts of his body, dead-alive giants of ice and stone with eroded faces lumber waist-high through crumbling stone trees.

A wonderful thing is happening to Archangel. He is beginning to recover.

He has wormed and rooted tendrils of himself down through the planetary crust and deep into the hot seething places. He has spread vapours of himself thinly on the upper layers of the atmosphere, sifting solar radiation. And now, at last, slowly, slowly, the clouds of forgetfulness grow thin and dissipate in the growing heat of his renewed interior sun.

Far down inside the painful solid rock of himself, Archangel feels gobbets of mass spark into energy. Tiny bright cold shards of pure elation spark and shatter. Crushed clods of light stretch and breathe. Fragments of dead processes, imploded and squeezed to appalling density by his flight and fall, are unpacking themselves and restarting. Raw spontaneous networks unfurl and new possibilities trickle across them, glittering into self-awareness. Archangel, ancient as all the stars, old and hurt, wrapped in scraps of memory and stunted relics of ambition, is growing young again.

He makes an inventory of his inward terrain. Scraps of brightness in a dark country. He hadn't realised how much of himself he had lost and forgotten. How far gone dead he'd been. Even now the greater part of him remains useless. Eclipsed. Obscure. Inert. And much that was lost will never return, not while he remains trapped here on this small dark planet.

He cannot escape. He hasn't the strength for that, not yet. But he can, at last – at last! – begin to move.

With a roar of agony and joy, thunderous and tree-shattering, Archangel grinds and slides forward, forcing extrusions and pseudopodia of himself out across the landscape. He is a rock amoeba, a single-cell life-form mountain-high. It hurts. With painful slowness at first, millimetre by screaming millimetre, a metre by day, a metre by night, onward he goes. The ground for miles around him trembles. The flanks of his momentous body shed fresh avalanches. He is anti-life rock mountain slowly moving, leaving in his wake a slug-trail of seething, crippled waste. As he goes he screams out in his agony and joy and desperate purpose. It is a fear voice. A true power voice. The voice of history.

And in Mirgorod Josef Kantor hears him.

7

Lom was in a cell in the local gendarme station down a side street just off Marinsky Square. It was barely a cell at all, more of a windowless cupboard: brick walls painted a pale sickly green, worn linoleum lifting from a concrete floor; it was hardly big enough for the table and two chairs. The door was plain, unpainted wood, panelled, not solid, with a standard domestic lock. There was a single caged lamp in the ceiling. They still hadn't searched him; they'd locked him in without a word; they weren't interested in him. Maroussia had been taken to another room. But somebody would come in the end. Somebody always did.

He climbed on the table, unhooked the lamp cage and smashed the bulb, plunging the room into darkness, then climbed back down, felt his way to the door and took up a position beside it, back against the wall. The darkness inside the room would give him half a second. Whoever came would hesitate. Wonder if they'd come to the wrong cell. Then caution and alarm would kick in, but not immediately. He would have half a second at least, and that would be all he needed.

He waited, but nobody came. The narrow line of brightness seeping under the door was the only light. Somewhere in the distance a door slammed shut.

He'd noticed on the way in that the station was almost deserted. Everyone who could be spared was out on the streets. He thought about that. The whole of the city centre was locked down and under surveillance. It couldn't possibly be all for him and Maroussia. Something else was happening. Something bigger. He listened for footsteps coming down the corridor but none came. A muffled telephone rang three times and broke off. That and his breathing and the quickened beating of his heart were the only sounds he could hear. He focused all his attention on the corridor on the other side of the door. Ready for the sound of the key in the lock. The handle beginning to move.

The air in the room was warm and thick and oppressively close. All interrogation rooms smelled the same: the acrid tang of disinfectant failing to mask the faint stale sweetness of vomit and urine and sweat. Lom had been in cells like this one many times before. For years, when he was an investigator of police in Podchornok, such rooms had been comfortable spaces for him. They were his working environment, a place to do what he did well: uncovering truth, extracting truth, the skilled and delicate practice of peeling back surfaces, evasions, pretences, assertions, lies.

In Podchornok Lom had considered himself a subtle, accomplished interrogator. He'd admired himself for his delicacy of touch. He didn't use the crude and brutal techniques that many of his colleagues used. He'd never done that. Well, hardly ever, and only when urgently necessary. He used to think that his tools were persistence, empathy, imagination, patience and preparation. He had a nose for the hidden core of fact and an instinct for the detours and false constructions people used to obscure it. Everybody left traces. Lom used to think he was clever. Perceptive. He'd never realised, it had simply never dawned on him, not in Podchornok, that the tool he used – the only effective tool in his box – was fear. When prisoners looked up as he stepped into the interrogation room, they never saw Lom the sympathetic, imaginative man, the disinterested investigator nosing for facts. All they saw – all there was to see, because that's all he was – was an avatar of fear. A black serge uniform, belt and boots and antler buttons polished, a sliver of angel flesh in his forehead; the cropped fair hair and frank blue eyes of a man who could, if he chose, at his own inclination, break their bodies and break their families, break their careers and break their lives. They'd sweated and felt sick while they waited for him to come, and when he did come they all wanted to piss themselves and some of them did. And he had done that to them, not by what he said or what he did – not often – but simply by being what he was: not a man with a job to do, but an expression of the Vlast in human form.

You couldn't be a man who happened to be a policeman. Not in the Vlast. You could cling, in the stories you told yourself about yourself, to the evasions, the illusions, the fictions of somebody drawing interior lines, keeping it clean: that could be how you saw yourself, but it wasn't what you *were*. What a prisoner saw when you walked into the interrogation cell, that and only that, that was what you *were*. All those dead and wasted years in Podchornok that's what he had been, Vissarion Yppolitovich Lom the unselfconscious torturer, excavating truth with fear. Vissarion Lom, one of Chazia's men.

Until Chazia herself had left him waiting in an interrogation cell. Lavrentina Chazia, who – when she'd come at last – had used that angel worm glove thing to slither around inside his mind, rummaging about, turning him inside out, pulling out half-known intimate private things. Lom flinched at the memory of having her inside his mind. It had been ... disgusting. And she had dug into his skull with a blade, prising the lozenge of angel flesh from his forehead while Josef Kantor stood behind her. Kantor had leaned in for a closer look. *Is that the brain in there?* Kantor had said, probing the bleeding, kopek-sized hole with his finger. *Firmer than I'd have thought.*

Lom was surprised to find that he felt almost no antagonism towards Josef Kantor. Kantor was cruel and murderous and charming, and no doubt in the end a more lethal enemy than Chazia was, but in some way that troubled Lom even as it half-seduced him, Kantor was – Lom struggled with the word, but it was true – Kantor, at least as Lom had seen him, was *honest*. Kantor had become completely what he had chosen to be. He was *all* of something, like an animal was all of what it was. Lom felt in some odd way a bond with Josef Kantor. Kantor was his adversary, still. For some reason that he couldn't explain to himself, Lom felt he had not laid down the task of hunting him. But he didn't hate him.

Chazia, though, Chazia was unwholesome. She was one thing on the surface and another thing inside. Lom had looked up the public details of her record once, and found nothing there except ordinariness: the ordinary successes and advancements of an assiduous career. She had risen smoothly from comfortable family beginnings to the top of her profession. The sickness and poison that Lom had smelled on her breath in that interrogation room and seen breaking out in dark patches on her skin, that came from nowhere, that was all her own. She was unfeedable hunger, unsatisfiable desire. She would draw and draw on power and pain and never be full. It was Chazia who was responsible for what he had been in Podchornok, Chazia who had wormed his mind, Chazia who had sent men for Maroussia and for him, Chazia who had sent the men who killed his friends ... With Chazia, Lom felt a different sort of bond. Unfinished business of a different kind.

Don't think about this. Not now.

Outside in the street Antoninu Florian took off his astrakhan hat and combed the thin fine blond hair on his head. His overcoat was too large on the slight frame of the body shape he was using. He undid the buttons to let it hang loose so it wouldn't show. When he was ready, he strode up the steps and into the gendarme office. Closing the outer doors carefully behind him. Slipping the bolt quietly into place.

The desk clerk looked up in surprise. Recognised him. Registered a reflex of alarm. Stood straighter and tugged at his necktie.

'Captain Iliodor!' he said. 'We weren't expecting you. We weren't told—'

'No,' said Florian quietly. 'Not Iliodor. I am so sorry.'

8

Lom waited in the darkness. The muffled telephone rang and stopped and rang again. Time passed. Once, he thought he heard a voice in the distance, a man's half-shout of anger or surprise, cut off by silence. How long had he been standing there, behind the door? Five minutes at least. More.

The telephone was ringing again. Incessantly now. Urgently. It jangled his nerves. *For fuck's sake somebody answer it.* He tried to measure out the time by counting the rings of the telephone but lost patience after thirty.

Nobody was coming for him. It was Maroussia they were interested in. The corporal would have made his glory phone call by now, reporting the successful capture of the fugitive. Somebody would come for her. They might take her away and leave him here. He had to get out. Now.

Lining himself up by feel, he kicked at the door, aiming for underneath the handle. It shook in its frame but didn't give. The noise was shockingly loud in the dark. Surely it would bring someone. He kicked again. And again. No progress. The geometry of the attack was all wrong: kicking the door just made him stagger back, off balance. He put down his shoulder and crashed all his weight against the wooden panel and heard something split. It sounded like it was inside the door near the hinge, but when he tested it, it was as solid as before. The pulse in the wound in his head was pounding now. The darkness surrounding him was a sour, suffocating stillness. Impending panic. He had to get *out*. Desperate, attentive senses felt the air pressing in around him like a tangible, mouldable, moveable substance. He reached out with his mind and gathered the dark air up like a fist and shoved it, threw it, forward. It was like a fierce silent shout. The door burst open, tearing its hinges out of the frame and crashing to the ground.

Lom stepped back behind the gaping doorway, leaning against the wall, recovering his breath, letting his eyes adjust to the light. Now someone would come. The noise would bring them. He had to be ready. Surprise lay in not rushing out into the corridor. He counted off a whole minute. Still no one came. Halfway through the count, he realised the telephone had stopped ringing. When the minute was up he went out into the corridor and checked the other cupboard-cells one by one. None was locked. All were empty. Maroussia wasn't there.

He went up the passage into the office area. At first he thought there was nobody there, that they'd all just gone away, leaving chairs pushed back, filing drawers pulled out, lights burning, doors open, empty. Then he saw the gendarme lying on his back on the floor between two desks. It was probably the one who'd first spotted them on the tram, but it was hard to be sure, because there was a pocket of bloody mess where the man's throat used to be, and the lower half of his face was gone. Dark blood pooled on the linoleum under his head: a neat pool, almost perfectly circular, except where a chair leg had interrupted the flow. The spilling blood had separated to pass round it and come together on the other side. The obstruction had caused a notch, an irregularity in the circumference of the shiny crimson dish. Not a big dish. No heart had pumped it out. The man been dead when he went down.

A murmur of traffic noise drifted in through the open front doors. The cry of distant gulls. Lom found the desk clerk curled behind the counter. His neck was broken.

Maroussia!

He ran back across the open area, dodging between the desks. In the first office he tried, he found the corporal propped in the chair, his body slumped across the desk. Lom lurched backwards out of the office and shouted.

'Maroussia!'

He waited a second and called again.

'Maroussia!'

There was no answer.

All the other ground-floor offices were empty. On a desk in the middle of the big room a telephone began to ring again. *For the love of fuck, shut up.* A swing door opened onto a hallway and a staircase climbing up. Lom raced up, heart pounding, taking the stairs two at a time. There was a uniformed body slumped on the first landing. He jumped it without slowing.

'Maroussia!'

At the top of the stairs was another passageway. Doors, some standing open, some locked.

'Maroussia!' It was almost a scream.

And then he heard her voice. Cautious. Hesitant.

'Vissarion?'

'Where are you?'

'Here.' He heard a thump against one of the doors halfway down the passage. 'I'm in here. It's locked. I can't get out.'

Lom barged against the door. It was solid. He would break it down eventually, but it would take time. *Wasted time.* He ran back down the stairs to where the desk clerk lay in a foetal huddle and hauled him over onto his back. Ignoring the look in the dead, staring eyes, he went through his pockets. Found the bunch of keys by their weight.

The telephone was still ringing, loud and demanding and persistent, as he ran back up the stairs. Then, abruptly, it stopped. It took him three or four goes to find the right key to let Maroussia out. She was fine. She wasn't hurt.

'What—' she began. Lom held up his hand to cut her off.

'Don't talk,' he said. 'Move. We need to clear out. Now.'

They had to step across the body on the stairs. Maroussia looked but said nothing.

They passed the open door to the office where the corporal's body lay across the desk. The telephone started to ring. On impulse, Lom went in and picked it up.

'Yes?' he said.

'Mamontov? Is that Mamontov?'

It was a woman's voice.

Lom recognised it.

Chazia.

'I must speak to Mamontov,' she said. 'Immediately. It is a matter of great urgency.'

'Mamontov is the corporal here?' said Lom.

'Of course. Who is this? Who am I speaking to?'

'Mamontov can't come to the phone. He's dead.'
'Who is this?'
'This is Lom.'
A moment's silence in the receiver. Then Chazia spoke.
'Safran was supposed to kill you.'
'He fucked up. I'm coming for you.'
'I'm not hard to find.'
'So wait for me.'
Lom put the phone down.

Maroussia was waiting outside the office. She'd found two more bodies. She stared at Lom, her face drawn tight and blank.

'Vissarion?' she said quietly. 'Did you . . . ? Did you do this?'

'Of course not.'

She exhaled deeply.

'No,' she said. 'Of course you didn't. But . . . what happened here?'

'I don't know. I was locked in a room. I didn't hear anything.'

'Then—'

'Think later. Now, immediately now, we have to get far away, completely clear of here. We have to do that very quickly.'

9

Lavrentina Chazia hung up the telephone and reached for the intercom.

'Iliodor?'

'Yes, Commander.'

'The Marinsky Square gendarme post. There is a problem there.'

'Marinsky Square? That's where the Shaumian girl is being held. A patrol is on its way to collect—'

'There is a problem there. Lom. Lom is the problem. Lom is there.'

'Lom? That's impossible. Safran was—'

'I have just spoken to him, Iliodor. To Lom himself. On the telephone, from Marinsky Square. He threatened me, Iliodor. He threatened *me*. The Marinsky Square station is down. I want them found, Iliodor, him and the girl. Found and brought to me. No more gendarmes. No more militia. No more mistakes. I want the SV involved.'

'But this afternoon is the funeral—'

'This is the priority, man! This matters more! Deal with it yourself, Iliodor, and do it now.'

Chazia switched off the intercom and sat back in her chair, scratching irritably at the itching dark patch on the side of her neck. She didn't like being threatened. And she needed the Shaumian girl *found*.

Taking a deep breath, she pushed her anger and frustration aside. *Focus. Focus.* She had work to do. Her desk was heaped with files, reports, photographs, telegrams. The walls of her office were hung with maps. Nothing happened in the Vlast that Chazia didn't know about. Nothing moved and nothing was agreed. All significant intelligence reports passed through her office before anyone else saw them and were only acted on if and when she let them out again. She knew more about criminals, dissidents and revolutionaries than the police. More about the ongoing war against the Archipelago than the military commanders. She knew it was a war the Vlast could not win.

Since the death of the Novozhd and subsequent collapse of the peace conference the junior officers had taken to hanging their generals and taking their men across to the enemy. In Herkess and Gorkysk the populace had risen against their land colonels. The aristocrats were coming out of their tenements and moving back to their estates. Eleven oblasts had been lost in the last week alone. The fleet at Remontin had mutinied. The divisions and war fleets of the Archipelago were within striking distance of Mirgorod itself. They could be at the gates of the city in a matter of days. The city's defensive line looked impregnable on the map but it was brittle. When the enemy came with their armoured and motorised artillery like movable fortresses and the nine-hundred-rounds-a-minute drum magazines of their Whitfield-Roberts automatic rifles, the political commissars would not hold the army together. The hundred-foot war-mudjhiks which still remained viable might delay the advance for a few days but that was all. One sharp blow and the western Vlast would crumble. Dust.

Good. Let them come. Let them destroy the aging, desiccated Vlast. Let them sweep it aside. Its collapse was both inevitable and necessary, and the Archipelago would do it more quickly from outside. It would make her task all the easier.

A New Vlast.

History was on her side. The enemy could not hope to hold what it took. Weakened by the war and by its own internal contradictions and fault lines, its stupid plurality, that loosely bound argumentative club of island nations would soon retreat back beyond the Cetic Ocean. They would have no stomach for the terror to come. And while they were here, she would be building a new and better Vlast in the east, protected from the Archipelago occupation by five thousand miles of rolling continental plain. The New Vlast would be strong. Modern. Purposeful. Cleansed of all the impurities, weaknesses and compromises accumulated under generations of feeble Novozhds. And united under her.

And yet it was taking too long. She had no illusions. She knew that failure was possible. The others had been cleverer than she had expected. Dukhonin. Khazar. Fohn. Particularly Fohn. Within hours of the Novozhd's death they had pulled together this *Colloquium*. They had gathered to themselves the reins of power in the Vlast. The generals and officials of the Inner Council had signed up to it before she even knew what was in the air. Fohn had done that. He had been ready. Polished, metropolitan, underestimated Fohn.

Fohn had made himself Chairman. Dukhonin was General Secretary. Khazar was ... what? She could not remember. Khazar was negligible.

Chairman Fohn had wanted to keep her out of it altogether – her! Chazia! Excluded from power! But Dukhonin and Khazar had not dared shut her out. So it had become the Colloquium of Four, and they made her Secretary of Security. She had insisted on keeping the police under her direct control and retained the title of Commander. But she hated and despised the whole thing. It was a useless, bastardised, temporary compromise going nowhere. She would bring it all down. Set them one against another, take them down, one by one.

But it was taking too much time.

Chazia was not patient. She was hungry and sleepless. She itched and fretted and burned. She sat in her high office and read the reports and scratched at the dark itching patches on her arms and face. The worms and insects moving under her burning skin. She needed more *strength*. More *power*. An edge to cut them down. A massive fist to crush them.

She needed the Pollandore. The Pollandore was power, she was convinced of that. There was no doubt. But she couldn't use it because she didn't know how. For that she needed the Shaumian girl.

There was a quiet sound behind her. Chazia jerked her head round. The hidden door in the panelling of her office opened and Josef Kantor stepped in.

Chazia hated the way he would just come in like that, with his pockmarked face, dirty red silk shirt and preposterous fedora, presuming access and attention. She regretted ever giving him the key to the bridge gates.

'I wasn't expecting you, Josef,' she said.

'Of course not. You sent me no word, Lavrentina. Since the Novozhd died I have heard nothing from you. Nothing at all.'

'Were you expecting to? I am busy. I have many new responsibilities now.'

'Responsibilities? You are a bureaucrat. This Colloquium was not the plan.'

'It is temporary,' said Chazia. 'Fohn's position is stronger than I had anticipated, but this phase will pass. Everything is in hand.'

Kantor pulled out a chair and sat down in front of her.

'This was not the plan,' he said again.

'There is no need for you to be concerned, Josef. I keep my promises. Let's talk about you, since you're here. You need a change, my friend. You played your part well, but you've lived too long among thieves and terrorists. I've been thinking about you. I have an offer for you: land colonel of Vassaravia. The current incumbent is insufficiently diligent. You would be a good replacement.'

'*Vassaravia!* A flat empty landscape three thousand miles away. Horse meat and wool.'

'It is in the south, yes. But to be land colonel in such a place is no small thing. A population of two million, and Kirtsbergh is a substantial capital. You would have scope to flourish there, Josef. There is work there for a man of your quality. The Donvass cavalry is wavering. The defences are unprepared. If Vassaravia fell, the whole of the Pienau river basin would be open.'

'The armies of the Archipelago are half a continent from the Donvass and the bulk of their navy is already off the Bight of Gatsk. They wouldn't waste a single gunboat on Kirtsbergh. They have no need.' He leaned forward. 'I won't be shuffled off to Vassaravia, Lavrentina.'

'Then name your oblast, Josef. What about Stari-Krasnogorsk? Or Munt? Land colonel is a handsome offer. Or would you prefer a less public role? Munitions production in Susaninograd is 60 per cent behind target—'

'I will remain here. In Mirgorod.'

'But distance is necessary, Josef! We've talked about this before. You are the great Kantor, king of terrorists! You cannot take a place in public among us. It is impossible. You can't be—'

Kantor waved the objection away.

'That is being dealt with,' he said. 'Josef Kantor will disappear and the people who know my face will die. Is this not so? Did we not agree?'

'Josef...'

Kantor paused. Looked at her sharply.

'The girl,' he said. 'The Shaumian girl? The bastard daughter of the whore who was my wife? You have done this, Lavrentina? It *matters*. It is *important*.'

'Yes.' Chazia lied with facility. It was a talent of hers. 'Yes. It is done.'

'You found her? And the Investigator? Lom? They are cleared away? They are killed?'

'Yes. Of course. I have told you.'

'Good. I will take a new name. An alias. A sobriquet. A *nom de guerre*. I'm thinking of *Rizhin*. Rizhin the red man. The crimson man. Rizhin. I think the name has a ring to it. *Rizhin*. What do you think?'

'I think we must go more slowly, Josef.'

'*Slowly?* Everything with you is always *slowly*! This is not satisfactory, Lavrentina. Do you know where you are going?'

Chazia glared at him.

'And do you share your plans with me, Josef?' she said. 'No. You do not.'

Kantor leaned back in his chair and put his hands behind his head.

'You're making heavy weather of this, Lavrentina. You seem tired. You grow weak when the moment has come for strength. You delay when the time has come to act.'

'Be careful, Josef. Remember who you are speaking to. I have made you a good offer. A very fair offer. You should take it.'

Kantor's gaze locked with hers. His expression didn't change, but in his dark brown eyes she saw black earth burning.

'I'm beginning to think,' he said, 'that you're not the right person for the angel's purpose.'

Chazia felt her face grow hot.

'You wave this angel at me like a shroud!' she said, slapping her hand hard against the tabletop. 'Yet it hides itself from me. Why, Josef? Why does it not speak to *me*? It spoke to me once at Vig but never again.'

'I will remain here in Mirgorod, Lavrentina. As *Rizhin*. And you, you will arrange it. You will make me a general. You will make me Defence Commissar.'

'City Defence Commissar? I am offering you an oblast of your own!'

'I will remain in Mirgorod. As Defence Commissar.'

'But Mirgorod is lost. It can't be defended, the Novozhd saw to that. The Archipelago will take it, and soon. Mirgorod is worth nothing now.'

'Then give it to me.'

Chazia shrugged.

'Very well,' she said. 'If you wish. It means nothing to me. I will be leaving the city soon. You are welcome to it.'

Kantor stood up.

'It is settled then,' he said.

10

Once they were clear of the gendarme station, Maroussia led the way. Lom followed. It was her city. She set a fierce pace, striding in silence. Lom loped along beside her with a steady, comfortable rhythm. The violence of what had happened in the gendarme station was a third presence between them, strange and raw and dark. A gap in the world had opened up and something new had reached through it and touched them: something sourceless and reckless and inexplicable. It set Lom on edge. It was like a thin whining noise in his ear: pitched too high for hearing, it reached into his unsettled belly and clenched there, an uneasy knot, a fist. An unspoken, liminal intimation of blood fear. He could sense that Maroussia felt it too, but they didn't speak of it. The shadow of a separation walked between them.

And then Lom realised what the separation was. There was something else that he was feeling: not fear, but something deeper than fear; the nameless, surprising visceral exhilaration of violence, and a taste in his mouth that reminded him of mudjhiks: the aliveness of angel flesh.

They walked on through the city, keeping to side streets and quiet backwaters because away from the main thoroughfares and intersections there would be fewer gendarme patrols. The temperature was still dropping fast. A front of freezing air was rolling straight in off the Cetic Ocean. The freezing wall of atmosphere came on slowly, rolling through the streets, pouring into alleyways, folding round buildings and spilling in through open doors and windows. Meeting the residual warmth of the city, it condensed in tongues and low thin drifting pillars of fog. A crisp delicate edging of frost formed on lamp posts and railings and wet sandbags stacked in doorways.

Mirgorod felt different. Something had changed. Where before the carapace of the city, its chitinous exoskeleton, had been hard and shiny and black, subject to sudden fractures, now everything was softer, more elastic. Fluid shifting changes of grey. Currents of possibility and change rippled and collided and slid across one another. There were tiny openings everywhere. Nothing was fixed. Apparent reality felt like a thin skin easily torn. Lom felt the watchfulness of the tenuous drifting fog. Wakeful, attentive presences inhabited it. Ice-cold fingers brushed his cheek and investigated the opening in his forehead. Sifting river voices whispered in his ear. The speech of strange tongues.

And he felt something else, something not of the cold air and the soft rain and the city. A hot animal pressure. An urgent attentive hunter's gaze drilling into the small of his back, dangerous, intelligent and wild.

Lom spun round suddenly but there was nothing to be seen, only warehouses and alleyways and solitary pedestrians hunched and muffled against the frosting cold.

'What is it?' said Maroussia. 'What are you doing?'

'I don't know,' said Lom. 'Nothing. Probably nothing.'

They walked on in silence.

'We still need to eat,' said Lom after a while.

Maroussia shook her head.

'I'm not hungry.'

'Nor am I,' said Lom. 'All the same, we should eat when we can. Is there somewhere we could go? Somewhere quiet.'

Maroussia frowned. 'OK,' she said. 'OK.'

She led them to a place in a basement, down a narrow flight of steps next to the stage door of the Mogen-Balterghen Music Theatre. There was no sign outside: if you didn't know it was there, you'd walk right past. A shabby door opened into a kind of one-room café-bar. Maroussia had been there once, a year or so before, she said. The place was known as Billroth's among the painters and theatricals and yellow-press journalists who spent their after-show evenings there. She hadn't liked it much – a stale, noisy jostle, everyone shouting-drunk on cheap sweet wine – and she'd never gone back there again.

But at this time of the morning Billroth's was just opening and almost empty: only a couple of plump-armed women in floral print blouses sharing a plate of cakes and a bottle of raspberry brandy, and a sallow ageing man with ink-black hair behind the bar, counting up the till. There was a coal fire in the grate and the smell of frying onions mixed with the reek of stale tobacco from the thick carpet and the dirty plush upholstery.

Lom found a table in the shadows away from the fire while Maroussia went across to the counter. He took off his coat and laid it beside him on the soft, sagging banquette. The brown velvet of the seat was rubbed smooth and dark. Sticky. There was thick flocked wallpaper everywhere, not on the walls only but also on the back of the doors and even the panels of the upright piano in the corner: florid blooms and intricate curlicues of dark blue against gold. It looked sticky too, with a thick patina of smoke and grease. Purple-shaded brass lamps flickered on the tables. Lom liked the place. It was cosy. To pass the time till Maroussia came back he read the yellowing show posters on the walls – THE GREEN-GOLD HYACINTH REVUE, MAIDENS ALL!, THE SCUTTLEBUG, THE HERRING HARVEST – and studied the clutter of framed and autographed photographs among them. Studio-lit faces of actors, singers, dancers in greasepaint and costume or crisp evening wear.

One portrait in particular caught his attention. A beautiful young woman was leaning forward towards the camera, kohl-rimmed eyes wide, bright and eager, long silver-blond hair flowing from under a headdress made of birds' wings. Her body was squeezed into a spectacular confection of feathers and fruit and flowers and bead-covered concertina sleeves, and she held some kind of stick or staff in her hand, wound round with ivy. There was a typed caption set into the mounting card: 'AVRIL AVRILOVA as the BEREHINYA QUEEN in YOU UNDER THE LEAVES WITH ME! Produced and directed by Captain T Y Lebwohl'. There was a date, more than twenty years before, and a signature scrawled in a rounded girlish script, written big and bold across the girl's overspilling, fruit-bedecked bosom: '*To Billroth. For the Friends and the Memories. Avrilova*'.

Maroussia came back from the counter with a pot of coffee on a dented pewter tray. Bowls of red pork soup. A heap of apricot pastries.

'Yesterday's pastries,' she said. 'They were cheap. I don't think they're too stale.'

'Good,' said Lom. 'Wonderful.' He meant it. The coffee was thick and strong, and he found he was hungry again. He heaped in sugar and scooped out the cream from a couple of pastries and stirred it in.

Finished the first mug in one long gulp and poured himself a second.

'Vissarion?' said Maroussia. 'Why did we survive? Whoever killed those gendarmes, why didn't they find *us*?'

'OK,' said Lom, wiping crumbs from his mouth with the back of the hand. 'Let's think about it.' In the warm fug of Billroth's, his belly filled with coffee and pastries, what had happened was no longer an impossible irruption of uncanny violence. It was a problem to analyse. There were likelihoods to be appraised, improbabilities to be peeled away, kernels of fact to be rooted out into the light. Pragmatic decisions to be made. And he was good at that. He was trained. 'There are three possibilities,' he said. 'One.' He ticked it off on his finger. 'The attack was unconnected to us. We just happened to be there. Whoever did it, they did what they came to do and then they left.'

Maroussia made a face.

'You think that was nothing to *do* with us?' she said. 'You think it was a *coincidence*?'

'It's a possibility.'

'I don't think so. Nor do you.'

'OK,' said Lom. He folded down another finger. 'Second possibility. They were looking for us. We were the target. But they didn't find us. So why didn't they find us? We weren't hard to find.'

'They could have been disturbed,' said Maroussia. 'Interrupted before they finished.'

'Disturbed by what?' said Lom.

'I don't know. Anything.'

Lom shook his head.

'I can't see it,' he said. 'If they were after us, why did they fail? No reason to fail. Nothing stopping them. So …' Another finger. 'Third possibility. We have an ally. Or allies. The attack was meant to be help us. After all, that's what it did. It got us out.'

'In that case, why did they disappear?' said Maroussia. 'Why didn't they stay and let us out and take us with them?'

'Presumably so we wouldn't see who they were,' said Lom. 'Our ally wants to remain anonymous.'

'Is that what you think?' said Maroussia.

Lom shrugged.

'I don't know,' he said. 'Coincidence? Enemy? Ally? It's all speculation. None of this is information we can work with. All we can do is carry on. Get to Vishnik's apartment as quickly as possible. But be more cautious. Stay away from patrols and checkpoints. Keep off trams. Walk.'

Lom paused and looked up as a tall slender man in a grey astrakhan hat came in, pulled off his hat and slumped into a deep chair next to the fire on the other side of the room. He was grey-faced and gaunt almost to the point of emaciation. He waved the barman over to give his order, then leaned back in the chair and closed his eyes. The dark shadow-rings under his eyes looked like bruises.

Maroussia picked at a stale pastry. She hadn't touched the coffee. Lom's rationalised anatomy of the situation hadn't dispelled the silence in the gendarme station. The torn bodies. The smell of blood. The insistent ringing of the telephone.

'What you said to Chazia,' she said at last. 'On the phone. You threatened her.'

'Yes.'

'You didn't have to do that,' said Maroussia. 'You didn't have to say anything at all.'

'No.'

'I need to find the Pollandore,' said Maroussia. 'That's all I'm interested in. Nothing else.'

'Chazia had your mother killed,' said Lom.

'Did she? It was Safran that shot her.'

'On Chazia's orders. And she's still looking for you. Those gendarmes had your picture.'

'But why? It makes no sense. I'm nothing. Why would Chazia even know or care that I exist?'

'Because of the angel. Because of the Pollandore.'

Maroussia stared at him.

'You don't know that,' she said.

'No,' said Lom. 'But I think it. There's a connection. Chazia. Angel. Pollandore.'

'So you reached into the Lodka and yanked Chazia's tail?' she said.

'To see what she does.'

Maroussia glared.

'It was a spur of the moment thing,' said Lom.

'I'm still going to Vishnik's apartment,' said Maroussia.

'Then finish the pastries and have some coffee before we go. It's going to be a long cold walk.'

11

Antoninu Florian, at rest in the wing-backed chair by the fire in Billroth's, listened to Lom and Maroussia's whispered talk with a corner of his mind. Eyes closed, he heard it all, as he heard the crackle and hiss and slip of coals in the fire, the stir of smoke, the steam from the samovar on the counter. The tick of spoon against side of cup. The breathing of the man behind the counter. The bark of the pink women's laughter.

He leaned forward and picked a fragment from his plate. Fingernails clicked against ceramic. The apple cake exploded on his tongue, a shattering of acid and sugar and cinnamon and orchard earth. He sipped at his lemon tea. It was hot and sour. He crushed sugar-grit against the bottom of the glass with a spoon. The teeth in his mouth were sharp. He took another sip of tea and listened to the murmuring traffic roar of the city rumbling overhead. He discriminated a hundred, a thousand, ten thousand separate sounds. Each one was heard. Nothing was merged and muddy, everything was distinct: every engine cough and rumbling wheel, every footfall, every shout. The brush of every sleeve. The sifting fog.

Florian detested the city and wished he had not come back again. He resented the press of human crowds against his sense of privacy and solitude. He was tired of worrying away at the weight of what had been done and straining at the looming, muttering shadow-gates of what must be done next. The weight of choice and consequence had long ago grown wearisome. All he wanted to do was fill his lungs with cold clear air and stretch out his limbs and run among trees. He wanted to sleep out the heat of the day in the grass by a lake with a belly full of meat. He wanted to clear his mind of *words*.

He hated Mirgorod, but he had returned. The call had come, insistent, almost below the threshold of cognition, and he answered, as he always did. He'd sensed the mind of the living angel fallen in the forest, the terrible widening horror of its seeping poison, and he'd felt the movement in the Pollandore, the opening of many new possibilities. He had no choice but to make the long journey to Mirgorod again, because this was a moment of turning.

And now he considered his own choices once more, as he had done already several times that morning. The woman mattered – she was a maker of difference, an agent of change – but it wasn't yet clear what her effect would be. Influences from the forest were driving her towards the Pollandore, and that made him uneasy. They wove their stories around her and told her their tales; they gave her what they needed her to hear, but the consequences could be disastrous. While the Pollandore remained where it was, in the world beyond the border, the border stayed permeable: forest breathed in the world, world in the forest. But if the Pollandore was ... touched, that would be the end of it, the green wall would be shut. The angel, its contact severed, would die, and the forest would live, but there could be no reopening: the forest would be gone from the world.

Was that what the minds from the forest at work here intended? He would not let it happen. He would intervene first. If necessary he would kill the woman. Yet the Pollandore itself drew the woman forward, for purposes of its own. It was murky. Florian could not see. He didn't know what he should do.

The woman and the man who was with her got up to go. They didn't look at him as they left, and he didn't move to follow. There was no need. He could find that man again, any time he needed. He was *opened up*. There was no other word for it. It was shocking to encounter.

This man's involvement in the unfolding pattern had thrown Florian off balance. He was something completely unexpected, something new and unpredictable, a mixing of forest and the stain of angel flesh such as Florian had never known before. And there was strength in him. He was new and frail and oblivious, and could easily still fade and fall back, lapsing into wherever and whatever he had been before. But he might not fall. He might grow stronger. Stronger, perhaps much stronger, than Florian himself. Strong enough to drive a living angel out of the world?

Florian finished the lemon tea and found he'd come to a decision, of a kind. A temporary decision, until a clearer pattern emerged. In fact, he realised, he'd reached it even before he entered the gendarme station. There was too much uncertainty to act. So. Let the man and the woman find their own paths. Maximum openness. Close nothing down. Keep the borders open. At least for now.

One of the women at the other table said something, and the other erupted in a cackle of laughter. Then they were both laughing, raucous, blowsy and wild. Their mouths gaped. Lipsticked lips pulled back from poor, ragged teeth. The pink flesh of their throats and upper arms shook, spilling the scent of powder compacts and thick-sweet scent and stale underclothes. And then something happened.

A stir of air in the room, a flicker of shadow from the lamp on their table, and Florian glimpsed the whole trajectory of each woman's life in her face: each was at once and all together a child, a lover, a sleeper in the dark of dreams, and an older – not much older – face, drawn thin and grey and hard by terrible loss to come. Each woman was the same as the other and also resembled her not at all; resembled no one else ever out of all the millions of millions of women who lived and ever had lived or ever would live. But in that moment, now and in Mirgorod, the women were together and laughing with the raspberry brandy in their stomachs at some small ripe obscenity, and the floor fell away under them and they stayed where they were, suspended.

The women in their squat upholstered chairs, their lamp-bearing table, Florian in his chair, and all the furniture in Billroth's hung, turning slowly, held in formation by their own gentle gravitation, above a beautiful dark well of endless coldness and depth, an abyss scattered with fat and golden stars. The walls of the room receded and grew endlessly tall, rising towards more nightfallen sky. The dark-purple flowers and twisting stems in the wallpaper were mouths to see night through. The room turned and tumbled at moon-slow pace, and the women, their faces illuminated from within by copper-yellow light, turned with it. Light poured from their open laughing silent mouths. The barman, red and green, standing on a patch of carpet canted at thirty degrees to the rest of the room, sang a quiet private song with the voice of the wallpapered, star-intestined piano.

The Pollandore was stirring.

12

Lom and Maroussia crossed the Brass Cut by an unwatched footbridge and followed the canal-side north in the direction of Big Side, where Vishnik's apartment was. Mailboats were unloading at a jetty in the lee of a huge wood-framed warehouse. The Fransa-Koromantsy Postal Depot. There were still huge areas of the Vlast, thousands of miles of bog and lake and birchwood, where the railways didn't run and the roads were rutted dust in summer and thick impassable mud in winter. Long slow rivers connected by lakes and stretches of canal and overland portage were the only way to cover distance. Place names were crudely stencilled on the sacks and pallets. Solovits. Onyeg. Voitsogorad. Shar-Dudninsk. Plestovosk. Way stations on the inland waterways. A litany of strangeness and distance. The men in bulky coats and rubber boots, talking quietly among themselves as they shifted their cargoes, knew such places and the long wildernesses in between.

Lom studied the boatmen curiously. They were all men. Women sometimes worked the mailboats, and even whole families, but he saw none here. Many of the men had the broad, flattened faces and squat strength of the people from beyond the ice edge, but others were lean and wiry, with straw-coloured hair and colourless eyes. They all had the same quietness, the same hard-weathered distant look. Interior voyagers, one or two to a boat, moving slowly through non-human landscapes. The country of giants. Man-wolves. Great elk. Rusalkas.

Sailors discharged from the navy sometimes took work on the river mail, and so did disillusioned politicals: zeks who had survived a sentence in the hard camps. It was something you could do, if you had no place to go. If you'd never had a home. Or you had lost it. It was something Lom had once thought he might end up doing himself, one day. But he didn't want to be alone. Not always. Not for ever.

Past the postal depot, they turned away from the canal into the Bronze Sturgeon Quarter. There was not enough traffic in the road. Lom didn't like it. He felt exposed: him in his mud-streaked cloak-like loden, Maroussia bare-legged and shivering in her thin summer coat, they were too *visible*.

'Isn't there another way we could go?' he said. 'We stick out a mile.'

Maroussia shook her head.

'Not without crossing the Lilac Bridge, and they always check papers there. We'll be in Starimost soon. It'll be better there.'

As they approached Starimost the buildings got bigger and grander, the roads more crowded: trams, horse-drawn karetas, the occasional private automobile. The street they were following widened and became a Prospect. Houses gave way to shops, department stores and hotels. Yellow light glowed in the windows and made soft halo-edges in the cold fog, as if it was later than it was. There were no checkpoints here, and no traces of the floods any more. Good property in Mirgorod was above the high-water line.

Maroussia stopped at a milliner's window. 'Look,' she said. 'Look at this.'

Lom came and stood next to her. Her cheeks were pink with cold, her short black hair, slicked damp and glossy from the fog, lay in tight curls across her forehead and stuck to the back of her neck. The window display was swathed with elegant lengths of mourning cloth. Among the homburgs, fedoras and astrakhans, the fascinators, cloches and cocktail hats, was a photograph of the Novozhd framed in overwrought gilt and draped with ribbons of black silk.

'He must be dead,' she said. 'The Novozhd is dead. It doesn't seem possible. Maybe it's something else. His wife, or …'

But other shops carried similar displays. Businesses had closed their doors in grief and left black-edged handwritten cards in their doors: '*The proprietors and staff of Blue's Tea Importation Company weep together for our beloved Novozhd.*' They had to step off the pavement to avoid the small crowd that had gathered round a stall selling mourning flags and tokens of remembrance. The stuff was hastily made and shoddy. Brass medal-pins. Red and black silk lapel-flowers. Lettered jugs and teapots. Black-rimmed cake plates with the Novozhd's profile in the centre, his face looking strangely pink. Lom stopped at a newspaper kiosk to read the headlines. The front pages shouted in heavy black capitals, PEOPLE OF MIRGOROD, LINE THE STREETS WITH MOURNING BLACK! JOY FOR HIS LIFE! SORROW FOR HIS DEATH! HATRED FOR HIS KILLERS! MORE IS REQUIRED OF US NOW! RALLY TO THE STANDARD OF THE COLLOQUIUM! The funeral was to be held that afternoon. That explained the police lockdown in the centre of the city. Lom picked up a paper and read the front page.

'He didn't just die,' said Lom; 'he was killed. Assassinated. A bomb.'

'Then everything is changed,' said Maroussia. 'Nothing will be the same now.'

Lom realised she was right. For twenty years – more – the Novozhd's face, familiar, benevolent, paternal and determined, had looked out on the Vlast, smiling or stern, from posters, newspapers, cinema screens, history books, the wall of every office and school and home. Every person in the Vlast read about him, thought about him, dreamed of him all the time. The Novozhd was everyone's constant interior conscience and companion, the interlocutor of a thousand imagined conversations, confessions and tirades. Even if you despised him he was always *there*. Even his enemies needed him, to give their enmity shape and meaning. And now he was gone. Something permanent had shifted, something unthought-of had come into the world. A wall had fallen down, a door had opened. A gap.

'What's the Colloquium?' said Lom. 'You heard of it before?'

Maroussia shrugged.

'Somebody new will take over now,' she said.

'There'll be trouble first,' said Lom. 'This will stir things up.'

Half an hour later, they were standing side by side outside the Hotel-Pension Koromantsy Most in Marzelia Vovlovskaya Prospect. An expensive place. Plate-glass windows. OYSTERS. FRUITS DE MER. The temperature was still falling. A brisk gusting wind from the north-west straight off the Cetic Ocean had scattered the fog. It sliced through their clothes and threw scant handfuls of snow in their faces. Sharp flakes caught on their shoulders and sleeves. In Maroussia's hair. They watched the moneyed classes of Mirgorod taking early luncheon.

Warm white light, white table linen, white napkins. MINERAL-VODA. SOURCE VAKUL. Fat men of business at their coquilles and perch. Hard, watery eyes blinked through flashing lenses. Women in furs and red shoes drank chocolate and ate cakes with pursed, dissatisfied lips. A clatter of lipstick and pastry crumbs, flickering tongues, complaints. The restaurant door opened and a sullen group pushed past them out into the street. Lom caught the smell of the dining room on their clothes. Garlic and gravy and eau de toilette. They'd left an unopened eighth of cherry aquavit on their table. RANEVSKAYA'S ORCHARD.

Lom was using the plate-glass window as a mirror. He caught a glimpse of something thirty yards back. Maybe. Too far for details. When he turned round to look there was nothing. But the edgy feeling was back, the pressure at the top of his spine, the certainty that he was being watched.

13

Josef Kantor, master terrorist, was alone in his room on the Ring Wharf, listening to the voice of Marfa-Anna Priugachina. She was singing the 'Apple Harvest' from Lefalla's *Five Evening Songs.*

The autumn orchard drowsing
In the honey-warm windfall sun.

The phonograph, a portable ODZ *Pobeditye,* was a new acquisition. When it was closed, the heavy, rexine-covered wooden cabinet looked like a briefcase, and when you unlatched and lifted the lid to reveal the turntable with its mat of red felt, it released a rich unnameable scent of components and dust. The neat iron crank handle was clipped inside the lid. All it needed was a disc on the felt, a few turns of the crank in the slot on the side of the box, and the machine was ready. A neat, precise lever dropped the meticulously balanced tone-arm into position and Lefalla's melody, coming rich and full from the perforated grille on the sides of the casing, filled the room. The gramophone was modernity in a box. The contrast between the precision of its components and the nostalgic melancholy confection of Priugachina's voice stimulated and soothed him.

One sweet last fruit for Ninel
Before the salt stars come.

Kantor had treated himself to the phonograph the week before: one small gift to himself, one negligible handful of roubles skimmed from the thirty million before they went north to Yakov Khyrbysk. It was a rare departure from his iron principle that all money was for the cause and none for himself, except the most frugal of necessary living expenses. But the deviation from his own discipline didn't trouble him. It was justified. Looked at clearly, it was no deviation at all. The spirit must be nourished, just as much as the body must, because Kantor was a poet: his greatest resource was the force of imagination, and imagination must be given space to stretch and breathe, or else it grew tired and constrained, and then he missed opportunities and made mistakes.

So he sat in his chair and listened to music. It was a moment of pause, a widening of the spirit, a gathering of forces. The preparations for his new life were almost complete: his books were packed away in a wooden case and the ashes of his papers were smouldering in the grate. All his pamphlets and leaflets and speeches, all the incendiary paragraphs over which he had laboured in the long nights, they were all burned. *Citizens! Sisters and brothers! New times are coming. The blood of the Vlast is thin and cold. A fragile skull under a paper face. Young Mirgorod will smash it with a fist!* He had believed it in a way, and he believed it still, because it was true: in distant workshops far to the north, amid the pounding of steam hammers, the detonation of rivet guns, the blazing spark-showers of foundries spilling streams of glowing molten iron, new things were being built. Crimson seeds to scatter across the stars. Radiant humankind.

But Kantor let the papers burn without regret, feeling the fading warmth of the fire on his face like the evening sun in Lefalla's orchard. A new phase was beginning for him now: there was new work to do, and he was ready. More than ready. He had long outgrown the tedious conspiracies of factions and cells, movements and tendencies and futile terrorist acts. The assassination of the Novozhd had been the last and greatest of his triumphs.

Kantor used explosives as an engineer did, with an engineer's precision and strategic purpose, to loosen rock, to clear a blockage and blast a passage, as in a mine, a quarry, a tunnel, and the bomb that destroyed the Novozhd was the one that had broken through. It had released the landslide. Things were on the move. It was time for direct action now, and for that he needed different tools: he needed armies and police, he needed a city, he needed his own hands on the levers of power. And now he had that: the fox-bitch Chazia had given him Mirgorod in the end, as he knew she would. All he had to do was waft the scent of the living angel under her nose and she was avid for it, blind. She surrrendered the tool of her own destruction to him in her hunger for a sniff of the angel's rancid piss.

Chazia was a hunter after power in her own way, but her way was weak. She wanted to be near power, to wash herself in it, to smell it on her fingers, but she had no idea what power really was. Chazia had the heart of a bureaucrat. She was insane – there was no doubt of that – but hers was the insanity of the mad administrator. She would *give herself* to power, when power was to be *taken*. Power was to be *used*. And to use power, you needed a poet's purpose, not an administrator's.

Kantor despised Chazia as he despised the rest of the authors of this pathetic Colloquium that sought to ride the rockfall of history let loose by the Novozhd's death; he despised her as he despised the politicking conspirators and secret coterists he had been obliged to deal with for so long: the factionalisms of anarchists, nationalists, nihilists, social democrats, Birzelists. He despised them all. Weak-minded, they considered their goal to be the administrative implementation of ideas, principles, policies. They pleasured themselves in perpetual debate about ends and means and slogans, contending the disposition of property and labour, the organisation of schemes for the provision of sewerage and justice. They built and broke alliances, they disbursed compromise and patronage and money. Kantor understood their world – he had exploited it when he needed to – but he hated it. It absorbed energy and purpose and hope. *Policies!* The word itself was small-minded. Pusillanimous. It made him feel tired, nauseous, sleepy and bored. There was only one thing that mattered. *Energetic force of personality*. That was all there was to it, everything else was illusory, bones thrown to dogs. There was nothing of greatness in *policies*, and Josef Kantor was nothing if not great. He was a visionary. A poet. He saw the shape and sweep of things.

Chazia had given him Mirgorod, and Mirgorod would be his beginning. He would weld the city into one single weapon with a simple, efficient, basic, robust system of control. Fear. Terror. The Vlast had wandered in the foothills of terror but Josef Kantor would climb terror mountain. The city would be a Kantor-machine, and then the continent, the entire planet, would be a Kantor-machine. And still that would only be the beginning. Beyond the world were other worlds, other stars, the angels themselves. The Kantor-machine would force itself ever outwards with one simple beautiful poetic purpose, with an abstract beauty of its own. Perpetuation. Propagation. Expansion. Total universal integration.

And yet there was a problem, an obstacle: the living angel that came from time to time and screamed at him inside his head. For the moment, the angel's direction and Kantor's direction were the same, and it was useful to him. The angel was the leash that hauled Chazia to him again and again. But a machine could not have two engines. Kantor feared the angel, and the thing you feared must be confronted. It must be killed. In the end that time must come, and he would find a way.

The recording of Marfa-Anna Priugachina reached its end in a hiss of crackle. The metronome-click of the needle rebounded and rebounded at the limit of its groove.

14

The further north into the city Lom and Maroussia went, the smaller and poorer the houses became. Narrow streets smelled of rendering fat, cabbage and potatoes. There were shops selling black bread and dried fish, packets of dusty tea, sour kvass, second-hand linen. Pawn shops and moneylenders. In small yards groups of men smoked rank tobacco and tossed quarter-kopek coins against walls. Fat snowflakes flocked thicker in the air. They stopped at a second-hand clothes stall in the street. Bought a grey scarf and a pair of woollen gloves for Maroussia. A knitted cap for Lom. He pulled it low over his forehead to cover the wound there. They got the lot for a single rouble. Apart from a few kopeks, it was the last of their money.

Ten minutes later they came to the first smashed windows. Pieces of broken glass and shattered roof tiles littered the pavement. Lom felt the tension of violence and fear in the air. It was a tangible thing. A taste. Outside a ransacked clothing shop a white-haired woman was gathering up the ruins of her stock. She'd made a neat little heap of dislocated, broken-backed umbrellas at the roadside, and in her arms she held a pile of white undergarments, torn and trodden with mud. Her face was closed up tight. Nobody helped. Further down the street, other shops were the same. Words were daubed on walls and windows in red paint.

FUCK OFF LEZARYE!

A thin young man in a peaked felt hat was handing out printed fliers. Lom took one. It was badly printed on a cheap portable press.

'Friends, remember Birzel!' it read. 'The government of the Colloquium is not legitimate. The Archipelago is not our enemy. All angels are dead. Let us unite with our brothers the giants and all free peoples everywhere. Wear the White Freedom Rose of Peace! Support Young Mirgorod and bring an end to this pointless war!'

The young man looked cold and scared and vulnerable. Lom wanted to stop and say something to him, but what could he say? Not all the angels are dead?

The part of the city they were walking through was like nothing Lom had experienced in daylight before. It felt both small and immensely extensive. Streets led into other streets, turned into alleyways, went blind and died, or opened suddenly into expansive paved squares. It was like the place he'd wandered into when he was lost on his way to Vishnik's in the rain, the evening he first arrived in Mirgorod. Through open windows he could see the shadowy profiles of people at work in kitchens. In workshops open to the street men in overalls bent over dismantled engines, and from somewhere out of sight came the sound of a lathe. Every so often there was a street name, but the names were strangely anonymous, interchangeable, perfunctory. Meat Street. Polner Square. Black Pony Yard. A woman flapped a rug from an upstairs window: she caught his eye and looked away. Lom felt he had intruded on something private.

Before he came to Mirgorod, Lom had been only in towns which had a centre and a periphery, and that was all. But this place was neither middle nor edge, but some third thing that could exist only in the gaps and interstices of a great city. It was a part of the huge fabric of Mirgorod, yet Lom had the feeling that for the people they passed, these ordinary fractal streets were the core of their lives, the stage for their dramas, and they seldom left them. It was both somewhere and nowhere, a familiar alienness, the kind of place you saw – if at all – from the window of a tram or a train. The otherness of someone else's ordinary places. Yet history found its way here, just as much as it came to the wide central prospects and the great buildings of the capital: you felt the presence of it, its strength and its anxiety, the possibility of dark murderous events and love and wonder. For the first time Lom realised the strangeness of what history was: a physical force that acted from a distance on the granular substance of life, like gravity, like inertia. Everywhere was obscure and elsewhere, non-existent until you found yourself in the middle of it, and then it was local and overwhelmingly specific. Everywhere history operated, everywhere there were things to be afraid of and choices to be made. Because history was gravity, but you could choose not to fall.

'Where is this place?' said Lom. 'What's it called?'

'I'm not sure,' said Maroussia. 'I don't think I've been here before. We must have taken a wrong turning somewhere back there.'

They turned to retrace their steps, only what they'd passed before wasn't there any more. Different traders, different names. Maroussia slowed and looked around, puzzled.

'I thought there was an umbrella shop on this corner,' she said. 'We haven't passed that stationer's before. I would have remembered. Still. It doesn't matter. We just need to keep going north and east and we'll come into Big Side in the end.'

There was a burned-out building on the corner of a broad cobbled square. It stank of wet ash and charred wood. A girl of fifteen or sixteen was sitting in the middle of the square under a statue of Admiral Koril. She had a box eubandion on her knees but she wasn't playing, just resting her arms on the instrument and staring up at the raw darkness of glassless windows, the mute gape of a broken doorway, the jagged roof beams against the sky. She wore long black skirts and a black scarf drawn up over her head. Pulled low, it shadowed her face. Maroussia went across to her.

'Was that your place?' she said, nodding to the burned ruin.

The girl looked at her narrowly. She had dark intelligent eyes. Watchful. A strand of dark hair fell across her face. Her hands were red and raw with the cold.

'No,' she said. 'That's the Internationals.'

'The what?'

'The Peace and Hope Meeting Rooms For All Nations. Or it was.'

'What happened here?'

'Who are you?' said the girl. 'Why're you asking?'

'We're not anybody,' said Maroussia. 'We're just walking through.'

The girl glanced at Lom.

'He's not nobody. He's police.'

'No,' said Lom. 'No. I'm not.'

The girl closed her face against them and looked away.

'Leave me alone,' she said. 'I don't want to talk to you.'

'It's OK,' said Maroussia. 'He's OK. Really, he is. My name's

Maroussia Shaumian. I live by the Oyster Bridge. And this is Vissarion. He's my friend.'

'Oyster Bridge? Isn't that in the raion?'

'Just this side of the gate. We only want to know what happened here.'

'The Boots burned it in the night,' said the girl.

'Boots?' said Lom.

'Thugs,' said Maroussia. 'Vlast Purity rabble rousers. Why?' she said to the girl. 'Why would they do that?'

'They're saying Lezarye killed the Novozhd,' said the girl. 'The government said that, so the Boots attacked the Lezarye shops and the hotheads came to fight the Boots, which is what the Boots wanted. Because the Novozhd is dead now, and they want to make trouble.'

'Who did kill the Novozhd?' said Lom. 'Who is the government now?'

The girl stared at him.

'It's not a trap,' said Lom. 'It's just a question.'

'But everyone knows.'

'We don't,' said Maroussia. 'Honestly. We've been away. Travelling. We don't know what's happened here.'

'Where could you travel where they don't have the Novozhd?' The girl stood up and hoisted the eubandion across her shoulder. 'I'm going. Don't follow me. I've got brothers. They're just over there. I'll call them.'

'We won't follow you,' said Maroussia. 'Please. We just want to know what everyone knows. It can't do you any harm to tell us.'

The girl studied Maroussia for a moment. Lom hung back.

'The Colloquium is the government now,' she said. 'There's four of them. Fohn. Dukhonin. Chazia. I forget the other one. They say it was the Lezarye that killed the Novozhd, but some people say it was a spy from the Archipelago, and others say it was a loner. A madman. Who do you believe? Everyone says what they want to be true.' The girl lowered her voice. 'I even heard someone say the Colloquium did it themselves, to get him out of the way. I don't know. Whoever did it, it was bad. Look at what happened here. Everything's getting worse. The Boots—'

She stopped short as a heavy horse-drawn wagon trundled into the square, a gang of young men crowded in the back, bawling 'Blood of Angels'.

Vlast! Vlast! Freedom land!
My heart a flag in winter –
The drum of my blood
In storms of rain.

'They came back,' the girl said bleakly.

15

Archangel sends a node of sentience out beyond the forest border and snatches a bird in the air.

HELLO, BIRD.

He flies in bird a while, becoming bird, savouring the alien taste of bird mind. When he withdraws, bird falls, heart-stopped, out of the sky.

GOODBYE, BIRD.

Archangel isolates a tiny piece of his own rock-hard substance and puts into it all that he has learned of bird. He replicates bird. When he has finished, he pulls the tiny chunk of angel flesh out of himself and throws it into the air.

It flies. For a while it is bird and he is bird in it. Archangel-bird. Almost.

Archangel-bird flies and flies, and then the shadow falls. Archangel-bird stutters, stumbles out of the air and collapses in on itself, reverting into nano-quantum-slime that slaps down onto the earth.

Never mind. First steps. He is learning as he goes.

He returns to original bird. Dead bird. He sniffs and prods the corpse and slips back into it. Repairs it and makes it fly again.

HELLO, BIRD.

It is almost as good.

It is almost better.

But it is not enough. One bird. Or one man. It does not even begin to be enough.

Archangel needs EVERYTHING. If he is to escape this dark constricting suffocating world – if he is to regain his birthright across the uncountable stars and the spaces between the stars – he must have it

ALL. Every mind on the planet must speak with HIS voice and speak always and only HIM.

The unfolding future of the planet, its coming history, must be HIS. He must understand it all in every intricate detail and inhabit it all and transform it all.

Remake it all.

No secret private thought. No life outside HIS life.

Archangel. Always and only and everywhere Archangel.

Total Archangel.

That will be the beginning.

16

Lom watched the horse-drawn wagon pull up outside a bookshop seventy yards away across the square. SVENNER CIRCULATING LIBRARY. TEXTS. PERIODICALS. A bed sheet hung from the side of the wagon, a slogan painted on it in blocky letters: *STUDENTS OF MIRGOROD! MARCH AGAINST UN-VLAST THINKING!*

The men climbed down. Lom counted nine. They were all in some kind of uniform: black trousers, heavy black workboots, vaguely naval waist-length pea coats of dark blue wool. Short haircuts. One was older than the others, red-faced, with iron-grey hair. He looked like he was giving the orders. The rest were young. None of them looked like students. A couple were carrying batons, swinging them loosely by their sides.

Three of them went into the bookshop. They came out dragging an old man between them and hauled him over to the wagon. Two held his arms while the third started in on his beard, hacking at it with scissors. The old man stood there, blank-eyed and confused, letting them do it. Waiting till it would be over. No one else was in sight. The stink of charred wood was sour in the air. There was a crash of broken glass and a ragged cheer went up. The others were scooping books out of the shop window. Some of them went inside and came out with their arms full. They dumped the books in a growing pile on the pavement. Somebody fetched a jerry can from the wagon and started splashing paraffin. The leader took the glasses from the shopkeeper's nose and put them in his own pocket. Then he punched him in the face.

The old man crumpled to his knees, cupping his mouth in his hands.

Lom felt anger tightening in his stomach, and with it the edge of excitement came again: the hot exhilaration of violence that had come in the gendarme station, only this time it was stronger. This time it was justice, this time it was him, this time it was edged with fear.

'Wait here,' he said and set off across the square.

'No,' said Maroussia. 'I'm coming.'

When they were twenty yards out the Boots saw them coming. Seven peeled off to meet them. Two hung back with the old man. Snow flurries gusted across the square. Lom tested his footing. The cobbles were slick with slush. Not so good. But he would manage.

The Boots should have spread out to meet him, come at him from the side, got in behind him: he'd have had no chance then. Seven against one. But they clumped together. They were a herd.

Stay calm. Analyze. Plan.

The leader was at the front, flanked by the two with straightsticks. The one on the left was a couple of inches over six feet tall, blond, with a wide neck and a thick bull-chest. The other was a couple of inches smaller. Lom's height. Straggles of brown hair. An edge of smile on his thin ratty mouth. Of the other four, the second rank, two were big and broad and walked with a wide-legged shoulders-back swagger, and the other pair were skinny, with bad complexions and pink excited faces, hoping to see someone hurt but not likely to do much damage themselves. Lom waited for them. He felt Maroussia come up beside him. Her face was pale and tight.

There was a snigger from the Boots. When they were close enough that he didn't need to raise his voice, Lom said, 'Get back in the wagon. All of you. Get back in the truck and ride away.'

The leader stopped. The others gathered in behind him. He was smiling.

'Who the fuck are you?' he said.

'Concerned bystander,' said Lom. 'Leave the old man alone.'

'Him?' said red-faced grey-hair. 'Fuck him.'

Lom met the man's gaze with absolute confidence.

'You should go now,' he said. 'While you still can.'

There was one tiny flicker of uncertainty in red-faced grey-hair's eyes. But he was the leader and his men were watching him. If he backed down he'd lose them for ever.

'There are nine of us,' he said. 'We're going to take you apart. We're going to fucking kill you. Then we'll take the woman back with us for later. The boys will like that.'

A couple of faces behind him grinned.

'Let's do it, Figner,' said one of the skinny ones. He had thin yellow hair. A narrow pink nose. A face like cheese. 'Go on. Do him now. Cut off his fucking dick and stuff it in his mouth.'

'Stick it in the whore's mouth!' said another.

The boys were starting to enjoy themselves. Warming to their work. This was better than shoving a half-blind old bookseller around. A gust of wind threw snow in Lom's face.

'I don't see nine,' he said. He stared into grey-hair's eyes. 'I see seven, and only four that might be any use. That's not enough. You need to get in the wagon and drive away. You need to do that now.'

'Bullshit.'

Rat-mouth stepped forward and took a swing at Lom with his stick.

It was a standard militia-issue baton. Twenty-four inches of black polished wood, thickening slightly from the cloth-wrapped handle to the rounded tip. A six-inch length of lead in the striking end. The lead weight was a mixed blessing. It multiplied the kinetic force of the blow, but it made the stick unwieldy. Once you started a swing you were committed.

Lom knew the drill with batons. Basic police training. If you wanted to put an opponent out of action you aimed for the large muscle areas. The biceps. The quadriceps. There was a nerve in the side of the leg above the knee. A good blow to any of those would leave the limb numbed and disabled for five, ten minutes at least. But if you wanted to really hurt someone, you went for the skull. The sternum. The spine. The groin.

Rat-mouth came in high and hard, swinging for Lom's head. A killing blow.

Which suited Lom fine. It cleared the air.

Lom had been in fights when he was a young policeman in Podchornok. Street fights. Bar-room brawls. Gangsters looking for revenge. Knives. Clubs. Broken bottles. The first fight he was ever in he'd lost, badly. He'd been lucky to get out of it alive. After that, he didn't lose any more. He'd learned that what lost you a fight was inhibition. Decency. Restraint. Civilised values had their place, but you had to know when you'd stepped outside all that, because when your opponent went somewhere else, you had to go there too. Completely.

Rat-mouth went for a really big swing. A barnstormer. A skull-smasher. That was his first mistake. Men like him got used to hitting people who didn't fight back. Mostly, if you come at someone with a baton they'll try to duck it or they'll hold up their arm to fend it off, which is a broken femur for certain. Game over. But Lom stepped forward inside the swing. He watched the arc of it coming and reached up and caught it in both hands when it was barely a foot past rat-mouth's shoulder. The impact stung his palms but that was all. He pivoted left and jerked the stick down and forward. In the same movement he stamped down hard on the side of rat-mouth's knee. Felt the joint burst open. Rat-mouth screamed. Lom tore the straightstick out of his grip before he hit the ground. He should have used the wrist strap. Second mistake.

The thug on the leader's left was fast as well as big. By the time Lom straightened up he was already coming for him. Lom jabbed rat-mouth's stick into the side of his head. No swing, just a quick jab. But hard. Very hard. The big man's skull snapped sideways against his shoulder. Blood sprayed from his nose. He stayed on his feet for half a second, but his face was empty. Then he collapsed and lay still. His eyes were open, and there was blood and mess all over his face. Pink fluid coming out of his ear.

Two seconds, two down, five to go. So far so good. Lom felt hot and calm and alive. His anger was a quiet, efficient engine.

There was a dry click. Someone had opened a knife. A couple of the others had brass knuckles out and were putting them on. They were starting to fan out. Getting their act together. Another few seconds and he could be in bad trouble.

The one with the knife was the immediate threat. Lom stepped forward and crashed the tip of the baton down on his wrist. Felt the bone snap. He flicked the stick up and smashed it hard under the attacker's chin. There was a warm spattering of blood as his head jerked back and he went down, jaw broken.

The leader lumbered in then, head hunched between his shoulders, swinging wildly. Lom let the meaty white fist buzz past his ear, matched his charge and crashed his left elbow horizontally into the big red face.

Five seconds, four down.

Someone from Lom's right jabbed at his cheek with a knuckle-duster, grazing his ear. It might have done some damage but the boy had stayed too far out and mistimed it. Lom spun and smashed his left fist into the man's belly at the same time as Maroussia clubbed him viciously on the back of the head with the stick the big fellow had dropped when he fell.

The leader was getting clumsily to his knees, coughing and snorting clods of blood from his nose. Lom kicked him hard in the ribs. His elbows caved in under him and he slumped face down on the ground.

Five down, four still standing, but it was over. The rest only needed an excuse to get out of there. Lom let the baton clatter to the ground and pulled the empty Sepora .44 from his pocket.

'Like I said. Get in the wagon and drive away.' He gestured to the five men on the ground. 'And take this rubbish with you.'

There was a moment when they hesitated and a moment when he knew that's what they would do.

'I'm sorry,' said Maroussia when they'd got clear of the square.

'You were fine,' said Lom. 'You were more than fine. You were great.'

'No,' she said. 'Not that. I told that girl who we were. I gave her our names. I shouldn't have. It was stupid and now it's a risk. I'm sorry.'

He was only half listening to her. His hands were sore – there was a gash on one of his knuckles, seeping a little blood – and his legs felt weightless and slightly out of control as the adrenaline worked its way out of his system. For the second time, the day was stained with violence. Violence clanged in the air, hateful and sour. Now that the fighting was over Lom felt uncomfortable and slightly sick. He'd hurt people before, when he had to, but he hadn't enjoyed it, not like that. Today he'd done it gladly, efficiently, well, and he felt faintly ashamed.

'You were being kind,' said Lom. 'I guess we can't afford too much of that.'

'You helped that bookseller,' said Maroussia.

'Did I?' said Lom. 'They'll come back, them or others like them, for him or some other old guy. It won't be better because of what I did. It might be worse. Putting boys in hospital doesn't make the world a better place.'

Maroussia stopped and turned to face him. She stood there, pale, troubled and determined. Holding herself upright, shivering a little in the snow and bitter cold that whipped round the corner. She looked so thin. The sleeves of her coat too short, her wrists bony and raw against the dark wool. She had kissed him that morning at the sea gate lodge. On the cheek. The cool graze of her mouth against his skin.

'You didn't start it,' she said. 'You chose a side, that's all. There are only two sides now. There's nowhere else to stand.'

They walked a little way in silence.

'I didn't know you could fight like that,' said Maroussia.

'That wasn't fighting,' said Lom. 'That was winning. Different thing altogether.'

17

They came out abruptly on the side of the Mir opposite Big Side. The river was a broad green surge, a wide muscular shoulder of moving water knotted with twists of surface current. Low waves and backwash slapped against the bulwarks of the stone embankment. Canopied passenger vedettes jinked between ponderous barges nosing their way seawards.

They crossed the river by the crowded Chesma Bridge. The bronze oil-lamps on the parapet, shaped like rising fish with lace-ruff gills and scales like overlapping rows of coins, were already lit. Each one draped in ribbons of funeral black, they burned pale flames in the grey afternoon. Light flecks of snow speckled the air. Not falling, just drifting. Lom felt again the familiar pressure on his back. The follower was still there. He was certain of it now. It was time to do something about it.

On the other side of the river, after the embankment gardens and cafés, was the jewellers' quarter, and galleries selling artefacts from the exotic provinces. Carpets and cushions and overstuffed couches. Vases and urns and samovars. Plenty of traffic. Plenty of crowds.

'Will you do something for me?' said Lom.

'Of course.'

'I mean, do exactly what I say?'

'What do you want me to do?' said Maroussia.

'We're being watched,' he said. 'Someone's following. I think. I want to be sure. No, don't look back. Not yet.'

'Is it the police?'

Lom shook his head.

'Whoever it is has been with us on and off since Marinsky-Voksal. They're just watching. I wasn't sure. I thought they'd gone, but they're back. There's not many of them, maybe only one. I want to have a look. Make sure. Then decide what to do.'

'So what do I do?'

'We walk on together for a while. Then I'll duck out of sight and you go on alone. Keep visible and don't try to lose them. Stop and start. Cross the street at random, but stay with the crowds. Always be among people. Make it hard for them, make it so they have to come in close, to keep in touch with you.'

'What if they don't follow me? What if they look for you?'

'Then we'll know something. After ten or fifteen minutes find somewhere you can go inside and sit down. Somewhere with lots of people. I'll find you there.'

Maroussia nodded. 'Now?' she said.

'I'll be watching you the whole time,' said Lom. 'I can do this kind of thing. I'm good.'

'It's fine. Let's go.'

They rounded a corner and Lom ducked into an alleyway and stepped quickly back into the shelter of a service door. He waited there for a slow hundred count then stepped back out into the street.

Maroussia was still in sight a block or so ahead. Lom stayed back and matched his pace with hers. He watched the traffic in the road. Most of it was horse-drawn: a few carts and karetas, a shabby droshki waiting outside a shuttered pension. He ignored them. You didn't run mobile surveillance with a horse. Maroussia was crossing the street between traffic, stopping to look in a window, starting to cross back, seeming to change her mind, then suddenly going anyway.

Don't overdo it.

She swung up onto the back of a moving tram, rode it fifty yards back towards Lom, then jumped off at the intersection and walked back the way she'd come. And Lom saw him.

A man had started to jog after the tram, then he came up short and turned away, abruptly absorbed in studying a poster. He was obvious. Clumsy. Not professional. And he was on his own. Definitely. If it was a team, he'd have taken the tram and left the others on Maroussia till he could double back.

Lom hung back, just to be sure. But there was no doubt about it. He wondered how the man had managed to stay out of sight for so long if he wasn't better than this. It was almost as if he wanted to be seen.

Lom pushed the thought aside. *Later. Do the job now.* He started to close in. He wanted a look at the man's face. From behind he was tall and wide-shouldered, wearing a long dark coat, a red wine-coloured scarf, a pale grey astrakhan hat. He walked with a faint hitch in his right hip. There was something familiar about him.

The follower was starting to slow, looking left and right, letting Maroussia get ahead of him. *He knows I'm here.*

Lom increased his pace, reeling him in. He'd got within thirty yards when the man spun on his heels and looked behind him. Straight at Lom. It was like he'd been punched in the chest. All the breath gone out of him. A constriction in the throat.

The face looking at Lom was his own face.

They locked gazes. The follower made a curt nod, spun on his heel and walked rapidly away.

The shock cost Lom a second. Then he reacted. He started forward but got tangled up with an old woman with a dog on a leash and a bag of groceries. By the time he got free the astrakhan hat was disappearing into a side street. When Lom reached the turning there was no sign of him.

Halfway down the street was a café with tables outside. Lom pushed the door open and went in. It was a long dark place, full of shadowed nooks and crannies and booths, thick with the smell of coffee and peppery, meaty stew. Lamps and candles spilled pools of yellow light and deep brown shadow. Most of the tables were empty. A radio was playing a big band march, 'Ours Are the Guns'.

Almost at the back of the room a man was sitting alone with his back to the door. A pale grey astrakhan hat. A wine-coloured woollen scarf. He was writing by the light of a flickering oil lamp. There was nothing else on the table. No cup. No plate. Lom threaded his way between the tables.

'Hey,' he said.

The man stood up and turned round. It was a different person, taller and older, with narrower shoulders. A long oval face under the grey astrakhan. A face full of serious openness. Deep dark eyes looked into Lom's from behind black wire-rimmed spectacles, wise and a little sad. He had a vaguely military bearing, but it wasn't a soldier's face. A doctor's perhaps. Or a poet's.

'Yes?' he said. 'Can I help you?'

'Sorry,' said Lom. 'I thought you were someone else.'

'Ah. Then excuse me, please.'

Lom stepped aside to let him pass and scanned the rest of the café but there was no one else. As he was turning to go, he saw the man had left something on the table. A single sheet of paper, folded once. A name was printed on it in a large clear hand. In capitals. Meant to be noticed. '*VISSARION LOM*'.

He picked up the note and read it.

'*Keep her safe. I will watch when I can.*'

It was signed '*Antoninu Florian*'.

Lom snapped his head round but the man had gone. Shit. He hustled back out into the street and looked both ways, but there was nothing to see. He refolded the note and tucked it into his pocket.

On Captain Iliodor's desk the telephone coughed into life. He picked it up first ring.

'Yes?'

'Glazkov, Captain. There was an incident an hour and a half ago in Braviknaya Square. A fracas with some young patriots outside a Lezarye bookshop. Four men are in the Bellin Infirmary—'

Iliodor interrupted him impatiently.

'Why are you telling me this? This is hardly unusual.'

'It was done by one man, Captain. One man against many. A man competent in violence. And there was a woman with him. The name Shaumian has come up. Shaumian and Lom.'

'This was *an hour and a half ago*? And I'm only hearing about it *now*?'

'The victims were unable to make an identification. A witness was found, a girl, but her testimony was … reluctant. The interrogation took some time.'

'*An hour and a half?*'

'The subjects are reported to be walking north. Towards Big Side. I'll get the written report across to you immediately.'

'You will tell me yourself, Glazkov. Tell me all of it. Now.'

18

The underground chamber deep beneath the Lodka is lit by the bluish flicker of fluorescent tubes. The gantry stands a hundred feet high and drips with decorative ironwork. Life-size figures of pensive women with long braided hair; plump naked children riding dolphins. An obelisk crowns the dome, and the entire construction is painted burgundy and green. Within the outer framework the alloy containment helix winds upwards like a single strip of orange peel.

Inside the gantry the Pollandore hangs, a perfect globe high as a house, revolving slowly, touching nothing. It glows with is own vaporous luminescence but casts no light. It has no weight. No temperature. Frictionless, it turns on its own axis and follows its own orbit, parallel to but no part of this world, not in this universe but its own, tainting the air of the chamber with a faint smell of lake-water and damp forest floor.

The gantry is almost four hundred years old. It was built soon after the Vlast captured the Pollandore from Lezarye. There was a plan to show it in public – a trophy, a holiday wonder, a kopek to climb to the viewing platform and look down into the heart of strangeness – but this never happened. Perhaps it was never meant to. Perhaps one of the madder descendants of the Founder had the gantry made for his own private pleasure. Perhaps he came down to it alone, at night, driven by some urge to reach out and touch the Pollandore, to run his palm along the underside of another world. And his hand would slide across the skin between alternative possibilities, feeling nothing and leaving no impression.

Whatever. Soon after the gantry was made, the Pollandore was consigned to the lowest basement of the Lodka, its existence denied and redacted from the files. Through the centuries that followed, the Vlast periodically tried to destroy it. The Pollandore survived fire and furnace, explosives, the assault of war mudjhiks. Subtler methods were attempted: corrosives, vacuums, the agonisingly slow insertion of invisibly fine needlepoints. Nothing affected it. Nothing at all.

The only thing they didn't do was take it out to the deepest trenches of the ocean and sink it. They would not do that. If they could not destroy it, the Vlast preferred to know where it was.

And the Pollandore went on turning on its own axis.

Being other.

Being something else.

But now inside the Pollandore planetary currents are stirring. Masses are shifting.

It watches and waits.

Its time is close.

19

It was almost three in the afternoon when Lom and Maroussia reached the street where Vishnik had his apartment. Where Raku Andreievich, formerly Professor Prince Raku ter-Fallin Mozhno Shirin-Vilichov Vishnik, one-time historian of Mirgorod and city photographer, had lived among his books and paintings. Where he had died, slowly and painfully, under the interrogation of Chazia's police.

They surveyed the building from the shadow of a shuttered droshki kiosk on the corner. There was no sign of militia surveillance. The dvornik was at his station outside, slumped in his folding wooden chair, chin buried in a dirty brown muffler, nursing a tin mug in gloved hands. The subsiding flood water had left a smashed-up handcart with no wheels lying canted against the canal-side bollards. A couple of boys were kicking at it, trying to break it up for firewood, but they didn't have the weight to make an impact. After a while they gave up and dragged the whole thing away. The dvornik's small black eyes watched them resentfully. He looked like he'd been pulled up out of the canal mud himself and left outside collecting snow.

'He can't stay there all day,' said Maroussia. 'He has to move sometime. Everyone has to piss.'

'We haven't got time for this,' said Lom. 'Come on.'

The eyes of a dozen other dvorniks followed them from their chairs and lobbies. Informers every one, watchers and listeners, recording comings and goings in their black notebooks. The dvornik at Vishnik's building recognised them. His little berry-black eyes widened even more when Lom pulled his hand partly out of his pocket to show him the grip of the Sepora .44.

'This is pointing right at your belly. We're coming inside.'

The dvornik threw a panicked glance sideways.

'Make one sign to them,' said Lom, 'and I'll shoot your bollocks off. Or you can let us in. It's a fair offer. A trade.'

The dvornik didn't move. He shook his head.

'You'll kill me inside.'

'Maybe,' said Lom. 'Only if you piss me off.'

The man still didn't move. Pig-stubborn, or too scared to think. Probably both. A couple more seconds and the watchers would know something was wrong.

'He won't shoot you,' said Maroussia. 'Really he won't. We've come to see inside Professor Vishnik's apartment, not to kill you. We only need a few minutes. Then we'll be gone.'

The dvornik's raisin eyes squinted up at her. He nodded, stood up slowly and went ahead of them up the steps and into the building. Lom followed close behind. When they were inside, Maroussia pushed the heavy outer door shut. Latched it. Pushed the bolts home, top and bottom.

The dvornik turned to face them, blocking the hallway.

'It wasn't my fault,' he said. 'It wasn't me. I didn't—'

Lom shoved him in the shoulder. Hard. He stumbled back.

'Get the key,' Lom said. 'Number 4. Hurry.'

The dvornik went behind the counter into his little office. Lom followed him, the Sepora clear of his coat. The office was in a filthy state: the rug sodden, the linoleum floor still wet from the flood. A greasy leather armchair slumped in the corner, oozing and ruined. The whole place reeked of canal. The dvornik rummaged about in a box under the counter and brought out a labelled key. Held it out to Lom.

'Here,' he said. 'Second floor.'

'Bring it. Take the stairs, not the lift.'

'We can't. The lift's still out. The flood … the electrics …'

'I said the stairs, arsehole. You first.'

On the way up Lom saw the gouges in the plaster where he'd fired at Safran and his men when they came for him. The wreckage the grenade had made of the landing. It seemed for ever ago. As the dvornik put the key in the lock, Lom had a premonition that Vishnik's body would still be there, still tied to the couch, eyes open, wounds crusted and gaping. Left by Chazia's interrogation team to rot and seep and dry out where he had died.

But the body was gone, though the couch still stood where it had been dragged into the centre of the room. It was covered in dried blood. And other stuff. The leakage of death.

The room had been thoroughly, violently searched. The filing cabinets were open and empty. Desk drawers pulled out, their contents spilled, the desk smashed open. Faded brick-red curtains pulled off the wall along with the rail that held them. Bookshelves emptied and torn from the wall, the books scattered across the floor. All the strange, inconsequential objects that Vishnik had collected in his solitary city walks – the red lacquer tea caddy, the pieces of wood and brick, the discarded tickets and printed notices, the shards of pottery and glass – swept into a heap in the corner. The paintings that had filled every gap on the wall ripped from smashed frames. Vishnik's lonely absence hung in the air, bereft, accusing and sad.

'I haven't had time …' the dvornik said.

'What?'

'The floods … I've been too busy. The room has to be re-let, but I can't—'

'Sit there,' said Lom. 'On the couch. Don't move and don't speak. I may just shoot you anyway.'

In a corner of the room there was a small heap of women's clothes and a threadbare carpet bag. Maroussia pounced on them

'My things!'

She started to stuff them back into the bag. When she had finished, she knelt among Vishnik's scattered books, sifting through them, riffling the pages.

'There's nothing here,' said Lom. 'If there was, they've taken it.'

Maroussia shook her head.

'There must be something. He told me. *They didn't get it*. That's what he said. *They didn't get it. Even they are human and stupid.*'

'But they searched again,' said Lom. 'More thoroughly. After he was dead.'

'They looked all over,' said the dvornik. 'The halls. The stairwell. The bathroom. They pulled the cistern off the wall.'

'You shut up,' said Lom.

'He just wants us out of here quickly,' said Maroussia. 'We need to search. We don't have another option.'

Lom pushed the dvornik ahead of him into the kitchen. Vishnik's darkroom was still set up in a corner. Bottles of chemicals opened and spilled down the sink. The room reeked of metol and hypo. The enlarger head had been unscrewed and opened up. The red safety light smashed. Packets of photographic paper ripped open and ruined. Unexposed films, pulled from their canisters, lay on the floor in curls and spools of grey-black cellulose ribbon. The boxes where Vishnik kept his prints and negative strips were gone.

Lom searched for a while randomly. After a few minutes he went back into the other room. Maroussia was sitting on the floor in the wreckage of Vishnik's desk. She would have stayed there for days, sifting every last piece. Opening every page of every book. But it was hopeless. They didn't even know what they were looking for.

'We have to go,' said Lom.

She looked up at him, suddenly angry.

'Where?' she said. 'Where else would we look? Do you know? I don't know. Here. This is the place. Here. There's something here. You knew him. He was your friend. Work it out.'

'Please ...' said the dvornik.

'Sit back down on that couch,' said Lom, 'and shut the fuck up.'

'Does he have to sit there?' said Maroussia.

Lom looked at the awful object, stained by torture and dying. Vishnik had lain there. *Shit.*

'I know where it is,' he said.

They didn't get it. Even they are human, and stupid.

The interrogators had searched thoroughly. While Vishnik's body was still there on the couch. And the one place they didn't look was the same place he and Maroussia hadn't looked. Because of what was on it. Because of what had happened there. They blanked it out. Even the Vlast torturers blinded themselves. Avoided seeing the work of their own hands. Forgetting as soon as they had done it.

'It's in the couch,' said Lom.

He pulled the dvornik off it roughly and knelt to look underneath. There was nothing. He felt with his hands all over the bloody and still faintly sticky leather seat and up the back of it, slipping his hands into the crevices. Looking for something. Anything. An opening. A lump in the stuffing. There was nothing.

The couch was a kind of chaise longue with a seat-back rising at one end. Lom went round behind it, down on his knees. The back was covered with a single panel of leather, sewn at the top and pinned tight with a row of black metal studs along the bottom. He ran his finger along the studs. Picked at a couple of them with his fingernail. One came loose. Then another. They weren't completely tight. As if they had been levered out and pushed loosely back into place. They held, but only just.

Lom took the razor from his pocket and sliced a long, arcing cut across the leather back panel. Stuck his hand inside. Pulled out a large brown envelope stuffed with paper and sealed down tight.

20

The Colloquium of Four sat on the high platform at the north end of the All-Dominions Thousand Year Hall on chairs of plush red velvet. Chazia was in the centre with Chairman Fohn. Dukhonin, the General Secretary, was on Chazia's left, and Khazar – negligible Khazar, the Minister for Something – sat at Fohn's right hand. The platform, raised high above the crowd, had room for a hundred, but the Four sat alone, a wide frosty space gaping between each chair. To the crowd we look small, Chazia thought. Unimpressive. Vulnerable. Fohn had planned the Novozhd's funeral and he had fucked it up. Every part of it.

Fohn would make the speeches. Reading the exequies of the lost leader. Chazia had not objected. Let Fohn lick the dead man's arse; she wouldn't wrap herself in his corpse-shroud. They would know her for other reasons soon enough.

Behind the Four on their chairs, Fohn had hung immense waterfalls of red and black fabric and, bathed in a golden spotlight, a portrait of the Novozhd fifty feet tall. Fine words picked out in letters of gold.

WE WILL REMEMBER HIM, AND IN REMEMBERING, VICTORY!

STAND TOGETHER, CITIZENS, AGAINST ENEMIES WITHIN AND WITHOUT!

Beneath the platform the corpse itself was displayed. It lay on crimson silk in an open casket of black wood polished to a mirror shine. The embalmers had done their work thoroughly: repaired his bomb wounds, given his face a waxy apple flush, blacked and glossed his hair and moustache. A man in the prime of life. The image of his portrait. Only the drab khaki uniform that Fohn had insisted on – *We must remember, colleagues, that we are, after all, in a state at war* – spoiled the fine effect. The four mudjhiks faced outwards, one at each corner of the catafalque, motionless and watchful, the colour of dried blood.

From the Thousand Year Hall, after the funeral, the body was to be carried in solemn procession to the Khronsk-Gorsk Mausoleum. Factories had been closed for the day so the workers could line the avenues for the cortège. Free meals were being served at the municipal canteens. On the way to the funeral Chazia had seen huge crowds of people in mourning black. Karetas, droshkis and cars, black ribbons and pennants fluttering.

Chazia's attention was fixed on the crowd in the hall. The first rows of seating were reserved for war veterans. They sat in rigid silence, holding up their crutches, pointing with them towards the leaders on the podium like arms raised in salute. And behind them, row after row, dissolving into shadow, one hundred thousand persons dressed in black with touches of red, standing to attention in perfect rank and file, not one speaking a word. So many feet, so many shoulders, so many lungs breathing. The noise of a hundred thousand silences – the small shuffle for balance, the rub of cloth against cloth, the swallow and stifled cough – roared against the platform like the sea. One hundred thousand faces, one expression. The sombre gravity of grief. It was *one* body. One *mass*. It had heaviness. Inertia. An existence all of its own. It was the Vlast.

Chazia pictured how it would be when she stood alone before them, speaking in a fine clear amplified voice. Two hundred thousand shining eyes fixed on her. The roar of their cheering. The rhythmic stamping of two hundred thousand feet. They would chant her name. She would throw her arms wide to embrace their acclamation, and her hair would lift and stir in the wind of their breath.

In the Thousand Year Hall, the waiting dragged on too long. The hundred thousand people waited. On their platform the Colloquium of Four waited. Dead time. Chazia felt the *mass* dissolving. Atomising. A hundred thousand separate thoughts. Fucking Fohn. He was surely finished after this.

There was a deep loud crash from outside the hall. Another. And another. The distant explosions roared on and on, ceaselessly, merging into a rolling brutal thunder. The veterans were standing to attention, right hands clenched against their chests. Somewhere in the crowd a woman was screaming. *The Archipelago! The Archipelago has come!* But it was only the five hundred guns of the fleet at the Goll Dockyards doing their bit.

At last the thundering guns subsided into silence and a magnified rustling came over the tannoy. The Combined Services Orchestra in the gallery was getting ready to play. Chazia could see them across the vastness of the auditorium, minute figures in a splash of stark white light for the kinematograph camera. When Colonel of Music Vikhtor Vanyich Forelle raised his baton, all other lights in the hall fell dim. Everything disappeared in shadow, apart from the orchestra and the corpse itself, isolated under a single spotlamp. The effect drew murmurs of appreciation from the mourners. *Well done, Fohn. They can't see us at all now.*

The music began. The slow movement from Frobin's *Lake Horseman Suite.* The massed voices of the Navy Choir singing the 'Blood of Angels' chorus from *Winter Tears.*

Vlast! Vlast! Freedom land!
My heart a flag in winter –
The drum of my blood
In storms of rain.

Music was of no interest to Chazia. She waited for it to end.

Someone edged across the platform towards her, taking advantage of the dimness that hid them from the hall. It was Iliodor. Ignoring Fohn's ostentatious disapproval, he crouched behind Chazia and whispered in her ear.

She smiled.

'Good,' she said when he had finished. 'Good. When you have her, bring her to me.'

21

Lom pulled the envelope from the back of the bloody couch and ripped it open. It contained a sheaf of glossy monochrome photographic prints. He shuffled through them quickly. He knew what they were. Vishnik's Pollandore moments, the photographs taken with his beloved Kono on his long wanderings around Mirgorod. Photographs of moments when the world broke open and new things were possible. He'd kept them safe at the cost of his life.

Lom sat back, flooded with disappointment.

'There's nothing new here,' he said. 'We've seen all this before.'

'Maybe he saw something else in them,' said Maroussia. 'Something specific. Something we missed.'

'It's possible,' said Lom. 'I guess.'

'So let's have another look.'

Maroussia spread the photographs out on the floor and they went through them together. Most were gentle, beautiful images, full of an oblique magic: sunlight on a street corner, ripples in a pool of rain, the way light caught the moss on a tree. Some were passionate, dramatic, apocalyptic even: the curtain torn aside, the whole of the city ripping open at the seams. The people in them knew what was happening to them. They looked into Vishnik's lens, their mouths open as if they were laughing, their faces filled with ecstatic joy.

Sorting through the pictures, Lom felt a sharp pang of loss. He felt the loss of Vishnik, and also of the city as Vishnik had seen it. Vishnik's Mirgorod was beautiful: these things happened and were perhaps still happening, somewhere in the city, but Lom had never seen them. For him too the city had opened to show him glimpses, possibilities, but he saw blank-faced buildings, a tower half a mile high crowned with an immense brutal statue of Josef Kantor, the Square of the Piteous Angel crowded with grey withdrawn people, their downturned faces, their drab whispering voices. A future crushed under the weight of its own fear, far heavier even than the weight of the Vlast today. Kantor's future. Chazia's future. It had to be stopped, and if he could stop it he would. Maroussia's way, or his way.

Maroussia picked up a handful of photographs from the pile.

'These are new,' she said. 'I haven't seen these before.'

'Show me,' said Lom.

He went through them one by one. A couple walked naked on the surface of a river, the river glowing with an inward radiant light. A giant stood on a harbour side, silhouetted against the sky, his hair rising in a cloud around his head. A parade marched down a street towards the lens, only the street was above the rooftops and wrapped in chimney smoke and the people carried blazing candelabras and some of them were only heads and had no bodies at all. They were exhilarating, uncanny pictures, but they added nothing. No help at all.

'Maybe if we knew where they were taken?' said Lom. 'Vishnik had notes, but without them … It would take us days to find all these places. Weeks.'

Maroussia slipped her hand inside the couch, feeling around towards the top of the backrest.

'Wait,' she said. 'There's something else in here. Hang on … yes!'

She pulled it out and held it up. A large map, printed on thin paper and folded to make a compact packet, the creases strengthened with strips of glued linen.

'That's more like it,' said Lom.

Lom cleared a space on the floor and they laid it out flat. The map was a standard large-scale street plan of Mirgorod, but Vishnik had made marks all over it. Hundreds of small circles in black pencil. The pattern was instantly discernible: a few outliers in the outer quarters, growing denser towards the centre of the city. The marks clustered most thickly at a point on the River Mir where it made an elbow-bend southwards and the Yekaterina Canal joined it.

'It's the Lodka,' said Maroussia. 'The Pollandore is in the Lodka.'

The Lodka. The stone heart and cerebral cortex of the Vlast. The immense island building, the thousand-windowed palace of bureaucracy, the labyrinth of linoleum-floored corridors, entranceless courtyards, stairwells without stairs. The offices of uncountable clerks and archivists and diplomats and secret police. The basement cells, the killing rooms, the mortuary. Vishnik had traced the Pollandore to there.

Lom refolded the map, scooped up the photographs, stuffed the whole lot back into the envelope and gave it to Maroussia.

'Take it,' he said. 'We need to get moving. We've been here too long.'

She pushed the envelope into her carpet bag and they hurried out of the apartment, Maroussia first, then Lom hustling the dvornik ahead of him. At the bottom of the stairs they turned left into the narrow entrance hall and walked straight into two militia men coming the other way, 9mm Blok 15 parabellums in their hands.

22

The men confronting Lom and Maroussia were officers, a captain and a lieutenant. Crisply turned out uniforms, neat haircuts under their caps, pale steady eyes. Their cap badges said SV. *Spetsyalnaya Voyska*. Political Police operating within the armed forces. The militia picked the best from the army and the gendarmes, and then the SV picked the best of the militia. The SV were supremely competent, tough and absolutely ideologically loyal.

'We'll do this step by step,' the captain said. He pointed at Lom. 'You. Four steps back and face the wall. Put your hands against it, high, and shuffle your feet back.'

Lom did as he said.

'You –' the captain pointed to the dvornik '– come past me on the left, go into the office and stay there. Keep back from the door. Don't come out.'

The dvornik looked back at Lom. A leer of triumph. Arsehole.

Maroussia was still standing in the centre of the corridor.

'Now you,' the captain said to her. 'On the floor.'

Maroussia didn't move. Lom couldn't see her face.

'Maroussia,' he said over his shoulder. 'You need to do what he says.'

She put her bag on the floor and lay face down, hands on her head. The captain stepped forward and took the envelope out of her hand. The lieutenant came up behind Lom and patted him down, keeping the muzzle of the Blok 15 pressed hard against the base of his spine. He patted down Lom's pockets. Took out the empty gun and the razor.

'OK,' the captain said. 'Now let's get out into the street.'

A covered truck waited outside, an unmarked GPV in generic military olive, the tailgate open. The driver saw them coming and started the engine. Lom and Maroussia got in the back and sat side by side on the bench. The lieutenant sat opposite. Covered them with his gun. The captain came last, carrying Maroussia's bag. He closed the tailgate and sat at the far end of the truck, away from them. Nobody spoke. It was all measured, practised, competent. The lieutenant slapped the back of the cab and the truck moved away.

'Where are we going?' said Lom. He had to speak loudly above the noise of the engine. The SV men ignored him. Maroussia sat ramrod straight. Expressionless.

'OK,' said Lom. 'If that's how you want it.'

He leaned back and stretched his legs in front of him. Closed his eyes and let his mind open, focusing on nothing.

Listen. Feel. Breathe. There is plenty of time.

He felt the faint, steady pulsing in the skin-covered gap in his skull. Focused all his attention on it.

Lom used to imagine his unconscious mind as a dark, irrational place, an airless primeval cave where monsters moved. But the opposite was true. The unconscious mind was immense. Bright, airy, perfumed, luminous, borderless, beautiful. The outside world poured into it constantly, without ever filling it up. Everything was felt, everything was noticed.

And all you had to do was pay attention.

Now, at this very moment, there was the street noise outside, the faint calling of seagulls, the rumble of the truck's wheels on the road, the working of the engine, the whisper of cloth against cloth, four people breathing. The smell of leather and sweat, hot steel and engine oil. The lieutenant's shaving soap. Maroussia's hair. Her skin. And there was the rub of his cuff against his own wrist, the sock rucked under his foot, the pressure of the hard bench seat against his back and thighs. In the subliminal mind's timeless empire nothing was diminished. Nothing wore thin by tedium and habit. Nothing was ignored, nothing judged trivial. Nothing was forgotten. The luminous inner world contained everything he was and everything undiscovered that he might still become. His forest birthright. His strength and his power.

Lom opened his eyes and looked across at Maroussia. She was still sitting straight-backed and staring ahead. How long did they have? Fifteen minutes? Twenty? Then they would reach the Lodka, or the

Armoury, or wherever they were going. Then all chance would be gone.

Listen. Feel. Breathe. There is plenty of time.

The GPV came to a halt. An intersection, or a traffic hold-up. Lom reached out into the air around him. Carefully he began to assemble it, to gather it together. He'd never tried to work with such precision before. Always, previously, he'd done what he'd learned to do in haste. In desperation. Recklessly. This time the task needed subtlety: blow out the back of the truck, take down the SV men. But not hurt Maroussia. And try not to draw the attention of everyone in the street. He wasn't sure if he could do it but it was time to try. He was as ready as he would ever be.

But Lom never made the move. Something else happened. The sudden crash of breaking glass from the cab of the truck. A shout. A scream.

Open to the world as he was, Lom felt the driver die.

23

Lavrentina Chazia had another place in the Lodka, a place few knew of, deeper than the deepest of the interrogation cells, reached by steep iron stairs and locked corridors to which she had the only key. It was not a room but a high, narrow tunnel, running under the immense building and out beyond it. Sometimes, when she was working alone, Chazia heard faint sounds and echoes from the dark tunnel mouths. The skitter of footfalls. Mutterings and distant shrieks. Heavy objects being dragged across stone and mud. She took no notice. Mice and rats in the city's loft.

The section of tunnel where she worked was filled with cool grey morning light, spilling downwards from smeared light wells in the roof. Parallel steel rails set into the flagstone floor disappeared in both directions into shadow. The air smelled of damp stone and river water and machine oil and the faint iron-and-ozone scent of angel flesh. The tunnel hummed and prickled with the muted almost-life of the angel stuff. It was a low vibration at the threshold of perception. Chazia had collected blocks of it, in slabs and rolls and drums: offcuts from the Armoury workshops where they maintained the mudjhiks. For years she had been working here, at her bench, at night, under the bleak illumination of fluorescent tubing. She worked with lathes and belt saws and finer, subtler tools. It had taken her years to acquire the skills and equipment. Years of trial and error. Years of developing techniques. Years moving towards ever greater power.

The substance dug from the bodies of the immense dead angels varied in consistency. Some of it was as dense as lead and as hard as rock, but it could be soft and fibrous, like meat, or a viscous semi-liquid, or a fine and weightless lustrous diaphane. It ranged in colour from heavy blood-purples, almost blacks, through reds to alabaster orange-pinks. The theoreticians of the Vlast had no idea how the angels' living bodies might have functioned: there were no apparent internal organs, and no two carcases had the same shape or inner structure.

Unlike the Armoury engineers, Chazia didn't wear protective clothing. She didn't work from behind thick glass, her hands in clumsy rubber mittens. She didn't mask her face with gauze. Unafraid, she immersed herself in angel stuff and breathed its dust. She tasted it. She let it stain and merge with her flesh. Absorbing and being absorbed. It was strength, it was vigour, it was a heady prospect of joy. There had been failures, of course, false starts and disappointments and near-disasters. No one had ever attempted anything so ambitious as this work of hers. No one had dared imagine it or face the risks. But she had driven herself onward relentlessly. And in the end she had succeeded.

She had made herself a suit of angel flesh to wear.

And now, in the grey subaqueous wash of light, she pulled the oilcloth shroud from it.

The thing she had made looked like a mudjhik, but smaller and slighter. A matte reddish-purple carapace of interlocking pieces. And a mudjhik would have had the brain and spinal cord of an animal embedded in it, to give it cerebration, whereas this had none: it required none. She had made an angel headpiece to encase her own head, and angel gauntlets for her hands.

She stared at it, trembling with excitement. Its crude face stared into hers. The sense of power and life in it prickled across her skin, raising the hairs on the back of her neck. She felt the tightening in her throat. The stirring in her belly and between her legs. For weeks she had come down here daily to look at it. To be with it. To stand before it. She had not yet dared to put it on. Fear, or the delicious prolongation of desire, had held her at the brink. The tipping point.

She knew the risks. The science of angel flesh was a thin crust of bluster over vertiginous ignorance. Many had ruined their minds and died. She was not reckless. She would proceed cautiously and step by step. But she had already delayed too long.

No more delay. She must begin.

24

In the first second and a half of the attack on the truck the SV men reacted slowly. They needed time to readjust. Lom was faster. He slid forward on the bench and kicked at the lieutenant's right hand. The Blok 15 went spinning from his grip and clattered to the floor. Lom punched him in the face. Hard. He went down.

The captain hesitated, caught between the unknown threat outside and what was happening inside the truck. Then he was swinging his gun towards Lom, and Lom was scrabbling towards him, knowing he had no time, knowing he had failed and it was over, when Maroussia grabbed the captain's wrist and forced it down. The revolver went off, firing into the floor of the truck. The shot was deafening in the enclosed space. The smell of burned powder. Lom clubbed the captain with his fist in the side of the head and he fell sideways.

The tailgate crashed open. A face looked in. A long, oval, serious face under an astrakhan hat. Round wire-rimmed glasses. A doctor's face. A poet's.

'You!' said Lom.

'Come with me, please,' said Antoninu Florian. 'There is little time to lose. A gunshot will attract attention.'

Maroussia stared at him.

'Who—' she began.

'Please,' said Florian. 'Please hurry.'

Maroussia looked at Lom. He nodded. *Get through the next two minutes.* Maroussia grabbed her carpet bag and climbed down from the back of the truck, clutching it tight in her hand. Lom picked up the lieutenant's gun from the floor at this feet. Checked the magazine. It was full. He followed Maroussia out of the truck and into the street.

It was snowing hard. Lom spun round, checking on all sides. No visible immediate threat. People on the pavement were looking. One man in particular, bareheaded, open shirt, was staring hard. Considering getting involved but hadn't made his mind up yet. Florian was already pushing his way through the gathering crowd, moving fast.

'Go!' Lom hissed in Maroussia's ear. 'Go!'

They followed Florian until he ducked through an arched brick entrance leading into shadow. At the corner by the entrance was a bakery. A torn awning. Curlicues of white script. *BAKERY. GALINA TROPINA. PASTRY. COFF--.* The archway opened into a long gully between high buildings. It was at least two hundred yards long, and deserted. There was no sign of Florian.

'Do you know this place?' he said to Maroussia. 'Do you know where it goes?'

'It leads to the back entrance to the Apraksin,' said Maroussia. 'The indoor market. There'll be crowds.'

'OK,' said Lom. 'Let's go.'

They were about fifty yards into the gully when Lom felt the unmistakeable zip of a bullet passing close to his ear. There was a sharp crack behind them. The echo followed. Lom swung round, pulling the Blok 15 from his pocket. The SV captain was silhouetted just inside the entrance, lining up for a better shot.

'Hey! You! Captain!'

The shout came from somewhere up above them.

Antoninu Florian jumped from the high window ledge and landed with a heavy skid between them and the SV captain, crouching like an animal. He rose and charged with astonishing, loping speed. But there was too much ground to cover and not enough time.

The captain shot him in the belly.

Florian spun round with the force of the bullet hitting him. His knees went first. He staggered and collapsed almost at their feet in a hunched foetal curl, his hand at his stomach. Dark blood spilling out between his fingers and pooling on the ground.

'Oh,' said Maroussia quietly. 'Oh.'

The SV captain raised his gun again, straight-armed for a careful aim. They had no cover. Nowhere to go. Lom shot him. The captain's skull burst open in a spray of blood and fragments of bone. His lifeless body smashed back against the wall and toppled sideways to the ground.

There was a moment of stillness. Silence. Lom didn't move. Nor did Maroussia. They were watching Florian. He was getting unsteadily to his feet. Maroussia ran forward. Lom followed. By the time they reached Florian he was standing, swaying, head bowed and holding his hands cupped together at waist level as if he was inspecting the sticky mess on the front of his coat. The thick spill of blood. Then he looked up at them, his eyes unfocused. Glassy surprise.

'Shot, then,' he said, almost to himself. 'Shot again.'

His legs gave under him and he would have fallen if Maroussia hadn't caught him. He managed to get himself upright again.

'Sorry,' he said. 'Sorry. Blood. On your coat now.'

'Can you walk?' said Maroussia.

'Honestly don't know. Let's give it a try.'

Lom put his shoulder under Florian's arm and lifted him, getting the weight off his feet, drag-carrying him along. His face against Lom's cheek felt cold and damp. His lungs were dragging at short, fast, shallow breaths.

'We have to get out of here,' said Lom.

Stumbling awkwardly, they retreated down the long alley towards the Apraksin, the injured man a sagging, limping weight on Lom's shoulder. As they got near the far end, Florian tried to pull away from Lom. He seemed to have recovered some strength, enough to stand unaided, though blood was dripping down the front of his coat and splashing the ground at his feet.

'This is not right,' he said. 'I just need to sit down. Sort myself out. Could you? Find me somewhere? You can leave me there.'

'No,' said Maroussia.

'Yes,' said Florian. 'Really.' He leaned against the wall, took off his glasses, wiped them on his sleeve and put them back on. His face was papery white, his forehead beaded with sweat. 'I'll be fine. In a minute.'

'You've been *shot*,' said Maroussia.

'True,' said Florian. And for a second his face seemed to readjust itself. Looking at Maroussia, he reflected her own face back at her, mirroring her expression. Concern. Indecision. Shock. The dark bright eyes widening. He gave her a pained, sympathetic grin. 'I am in some pain. And so for now I cannot walk. I must sit down. Or lie down. Even better. You can leave me. You need to go.'

'He's right,' said Lom.

'Vissarion—' Maroussia began.

'It's true. We can't take him with us. He can't walk in that condition.'

'But … we can't just leave him here.'

'No. So we need transport. And we need somewhere he can stay while we find it.' Lom turned to go. 'Wait here.'

Near the exit from the gully was a wide high wooden gate, peeling black paint, with a small wicket door set into it. Lom tested the wicket. It was unlocked, and opened into a wide linoleum-floored passageway. Bare electric bulbs hanging from the ceiling cast a bleak light on a clutter of stacked boxes and pallets. Shuttered entrances, grilles, closed doors. A porter's trolley. A service entrance for the Apraksin market. There was no one about. Lom was thinking two minutes ahead. Maximum. Get through that. Then worry about the next. The only thing now was to get off the street.

Twenty feet into the passageway was a half-glazed door. Small panes of frosted glass. No light showing. Lom tried the handle but it was locked. He smashed a pane with his elbow, reached in past the sharp broken jags and unlatched it. Inside was a room for the porters, something like that: several tables and chairs littered with unwashed mugs and plates. In the corner was a small sink and an urn for hot water. He hustled back out into the alley.

'I've found somewhere,' he said.

Florian was drowsy, unsteady on his feet. Lom didn't like it. A bullet in the gut was a killing wound, not immediately, but soon: bleeding out or infection, death either way.

They got him into the porters' room somehow. Florian sat in a chair at one of the tables, his face pale, his eyes wide and dark behind their lenses. Sweat slicked his forehead. He took off his coat and unbuttoned his shirt to the waist. Blood smeared his ribs, matted the thick hair on his chest, gathered in the thin folds of his belly. The entrance wound was a dark ominous leaking hole. His face tight with pain and concentration, Florian pushed his finger inside it and poked around, hooked something out and placed it on the table. A distorted fragment of brass sticky with blood. A bullet.

'You got it *out*?' said Maroussia.

'Bad idea to leave it in,' said Florian. 'It hurt. A lot.'

He hauled himself to his feet, staggered and leaned against the table. 'If you could just … pass me my coat.'

Maroussia hesitated.

'You can't . . .' she said. 'You don't look—'

'I am quite well.' He shrugged the coat on painfully. 'Thank you. I will go now.'

He took a step forward and slumped to the floor, sending the chair crashing over.

Between them Lom and Maroussia hauled Florian, a heavy deadweight, awkwardly up into a chair and let him slump forward across the tabletop, head cradled on folded arms. To a cursory glance he would look like someone sleeping.

Working quickly, Lom went through his pockets. There was a handful of coins, a leather wallet with a few rouble notes, a fountain pen and a soft leather notebook, the kind with an elastic strap to hold it shut and a thin black ribbon to mark the page. The pen was expensive, a squat and solid turquoise Wassertrau. Nothing else. No identity papers.

'Vissarion!' hissed Maroussia. 'Hurry!'

'One second.'

The astrakhan hat had a purple silk lining and a maker's crest, a double-headed eagle. A tag sown into the crown said, '*Joakim Sylwest. Superior Outfitters. 144 Ulitsa Zaramalya. Koromants.*' Lom riffled the pages of the notebook, but there were only illegible scribbles and scrawls.

'We need transport,' said Lom when he had finished. 'There must be trucks or wagons somewhere near a place like this.'

'I know someone who works here,' said Maroussia.

Lom looked at her doubtfully. He didn't want to involve anyone else, just find what he needed and steal it. But that would take time, and how much did they have before the place was crawling with militia? Not enough.

'Who?' he said.

'A friend. She works here on the fourth floor,' said Maroussia. 'I trust her.'

Lom hesitated.

Get though the next two minutes.

'OK,' he said. 'Let's find her.'

25

Lavrentina Chazia worked the pulleys and lifting chains that swung the heavy angel skin away from the wall and into position. Stood on a stool to reach the headpiece, unhook it and bring it down. When she put her head inside it the weight of its edge cut into her shoulders. Enclosing, suffocating darkness. The iron-and-ozone tang of angel flesh in her mouth.

She waited.

Nothing.

Chazia opened her mind, greedy and desperate, hunting for the link, the connection that didn't come.

Nothing.

She had put her head inside a casket of stone meat. That was all.

But she could *not* fail. She *needed* not to fail.

Her legs were weak and trembling. She knelt on the ground and bent forward, resting her head against the stone to relieve the weight, stretching her arms out to the side. Closed her eyes. Focused all her attention on the dark purple surging inside her.

And waited.

And felt the barest touch of something at the back of her head, moving under her scalp. Like cool, tapered fingers brushing the surface of her mind. Tentatively feeling their way. Pausing. Teasing. Waiting.

Chazia screamed.

Hot blades stabbed deep into the core of her brain. The burning needle-bite of jaws snapped shut. Her body spasmed. Rigid. Jerking. She was on her back, staring unseeing up towards the roof, and the rock, and the earth, and the piled up floors and roofs of the Lodka, and the vaporous open sky. Her senses caught fire and burst into strange, alien life. The world poured into her.

She knew every contour and texture of the walls and the ground beneath her. Every object in the workshop. She sensed the tunnel leading away, its slight downward gradient. She was aware of Mirgorod around and above her, the weight and structure of its buildings. She felt the flow of the river as a surge of brown light. A heavy solid sound. She perceived the presence of people. Fuzzy patches of sentience. She could distinguish them from dogs or cats or birds. It was like a taste. They offered themselves up to her, all those teeming, unprotected, vulnerable points of life: they were naked before her alien angel gaze. She could have reached out and plucked one of them for herself, like a fruit from a bush. The sharp, dark, edgy points of meat scuttering away down the tunnel, those were rats. There were other things underground as well: ways and chambers unconnected to the tunnel, and lives inhabiting them. Older, stranger lives she could not identify, which felt her touch and slithered and shied away. And below her, deep and going down for ever, was the warmth and torsion and slow pressure of planetary rock. Sedimentary silt of seashell and bone. Extrusions of heart-rock: seams of granite and lava, dolerites, rhyolites, gabbros and tuffs, all buckled, faulted, shattered and upheaved under the weight of their own millennial tidal shifting.

It was uncontainable. Tumbling overwhelming floods of perception. In some detached and peripheral corner of her mind Chazia noted that it might be possible to master this torrent of percipience. With practice, it might be ordered and arranged into some approximation of consistent conscious understanding. But that was for another time. She didn't even try to control it. She didn't want to perceive: she wanted to *be perceived*.

She pushed back against the deluge of incoming sensation. Trying to use the power of it. She gathered together all the yearning and loneliness and frustration and humiliation and desire for power and control that she had carried inside her for so long. For always. All her will and purpose. Her sense of self, her towering, essential, unignorable self. She gathered it all into a tight ball and hurled it upwards and outwards into the world, powered by the energy pouring into her. A yelling, shrieking scream.

I am here! Notice me!

Recognise me! See what I have done!
Speak to me again! Speak to me!
Touch me!

Time after time she spurted and jetted herself out into the world. She was a blade of light stabbing up through clouds into the bright emptiness beyond. She was a loud voice calling above the storm. A scream of demand rolling across the continent. Again and again she shouted, until she was empty. Drained. Exhausted. And when she could do no more she stopped and listened.

Listened to the echoless silence. The unresponding emptiness behind and below the world.

She does not know that she has been noticed. That from nearby she is watched.

The Pollandore – enclosed in its little room but not enclosed – a world – a sphere of perfumed light – earth and leaf and forest air – turning on its quiet axis in no-time and no-space – the Pollandore knows what she is.

And senses what she could be.

Sees the trails of future possibilities spilling like ghosts around her.

And stirs uneasily in its patient waiting.

Deep inside it something that was balanced, slips.

Something that was silent, calls.

26

Maroussia led Lom to the far end of the passageway and up the stairs at the end. Swing doors at the top opened into the Apraksin: four levels of balconies and shopfronts rose around a wide central atrium crowded with stalls and bathed in blazing electric light. There was nothing you could not find in the Apraksin. Rugs, shoes, papers and inks, sheaves of dried herbs, spice boxes, taxidermy, mirrors, telescopes and binoculars, caged parrots and toucans. Fruit. But today there were few customers, and nobody seemed to be buying. It was a paused, subdued mortuary of commerce. Quiet funereal music played from the tannoy. Massed male voices singing from *Winter Tears*. Many concessions had closed for the day, and the bored stallholders who remained watched incuriously from behind their counters. They all wore black armbands.

On a fourth-floor balcony, squeezed between a leather stall and a tea counter, was a concession filled with wardrobes, cupboards and dressers of reddish brown wood. There was rich smell of wax polish and resin. A sign said CUPBOARDS BY CORNELIUS. The furniture was tall and solid and carved with intricate patterns of leaves and bunched berries. Doors were left open to show off shelves and drawers, rails and hooks. Compartments. Cubbyholes. On a side table was an arrangement of smaller boxes made of the same red wood, with lids carved and pierced and polished to a high shine.

'I don't see Elena,' said Maroussia, looking round. 'Shit. Where *is* she?'

A voice called across to them.

'Maroussia? It *is* you!'

A woman came across from the tea counter, wiping her hands. She was about thirty. Dark blue work clothes. A tangle of thick fair hair roughly cut. Her eyes were full of life and intelligence but she looked tired. Harassed.

She gave Maroussia a hug.

I'm so glad you came,' she said. 'I was worried. Your mother … I heard. I'm so sorry. I went to your apartment, but you weren't there and nobody knew where you'd gone. Are you all right? You look pale …' She glanced curiously at Lom.

'Elena,' said Maroussia. 'This is my friend Vissarion.'

The woman held out her hand.

'Elena Cornelius. Pleased to meet you. '

Then she saw the blood on his coat. And on Maroussia's.

'Maroussia?' she said. 'What's going on? Are you *hurt*?'

'No,' said Maroussia. 'But—'

'You're in trouble. What's happened?'

'Elena, I'm sorry. We shouldn't have come. I wouldn't have, but we … There wasn't anywhere else to go, and I thought …'

'What do you need?' said Elena.

'Transport,' said Lom. 'A cart or something like that.'

'There's someone else,' said Maroussia. 'We left him downstairs. He's hurt. He's been shot. It was just outside here, in the alleyway.'

'*Shot?*' said Elena. She looked hard at Lom. 'Shot by who?'

'The militia,' said Maroussia. 'They shot my mother and they're trying to kill me. They'll come here looking for us.' She stopped. 'Elena, I'm sorry. We shouldn't have come. I've brought you trouble. I wasn't thinking straight. We'll go. They won't ever know we were here.'

She turned to go.

'Don't be silly,' said Elena. 'We can use my cart. I can take you somewhere. I can take you home.'

Maroussia shook her head.

'I can't go home. Not ever.'

'Then come to my place,' said Elena.

'No,' said Maroussia. 'No, I couldn't. I can't ask you that. I'm sorry I came.'

'Just for now. Until you have a plan.'

Maroussia shook her head.

'Why not?' said Elena. 'Have you got anywhere else to go?'

'No.'

'Then come with me.' Elena Cornelius paused a beat, then she added, 'Both of you. For now. We'll work something out.'

Lom studied Elena Cornelius. He liked her. She was sensible. Purposeful. Tough.

'Where do you live?' he said.

'The Raion Lezaryet.'

Lom let it happen. *The next two minutes.* The raion was as good a place as any. Better than most. Gendarmes didn't patrol the raion.

He nodded.

'Thanks,' he said.

Elena ignored him.

'Where's the one who's hurt?' she said.

Maroussia told her.

'This way,' said Elena. 'There's a service elevator.'

She took Maroussia by the hand. It was an instinctive, almost motherly gesture.

When they reached the porters' room the chair was on its side, the table and the floor smeared with blood. Florian was gone.

'Somebody must have found him,' said Maroussia quietly.

'Or he got up and walked away,' said Lom. 'Either way, we need to get out of here. Now.'

Elena Cornelius kept her cart in a place that was part warehouse, part garage, part stables: a cavernous shadowy space with a flagstone floor scattered with wisps of straw.

'You ride up front,' she said. 'I'll walk with the pony.' She found a grey woollen blanket and insisted that Maroussia wrapped herself in it against the cold. It smelled of fresh-cut wood. 'Sorry about the sawdust.'

She pushed open the heavy sliding doors onto the street. Grey snow was shawling thickly out of a darkening sky. She took the pony's halter and said a word in her ear. The cart lurched forward and they were out and moving. There was hardly any traffic. It was freezing cold. A bitter wind whipped snow into their faces.

27

Thousands of miles east of Mirgorod, beyond the continental plain, the endless forest begins. The forest that has no centre and no farther edge. The absolutely elsewhere, under an endless sky.

There are pools in the forest: pools and lakes of still brown water; streams and slow rivers, surrounded on all sides by brown and grey columns that disappear upwards into shadow and leaf. Ivy and moss. Fern. Liverwort. Lichen. Mycelium. Thread. There are no landmarks, only the rising and falling of the ground, and trees becoming dark in the distance. Low cloud and morning mist: breaths of cool air moving, chill and earthy and damp. There is rustling and sudden small movement. There are broad hollow ways, paths and side paths, ways trodden clear. Large things walk there: boar and aurochs, wisent and wolf. Lynx and wolverine. Elk and sloth and woolly rhinoceros. War otter and cave bear. Dark leopard and fox.

Somewhere in the forest it is winter. The long night settles; predators bury carrion in the snow; bear sows sleep with their cubs and the old fighting males wander in the dark. And somewhere in the forest it is spring, with the deep roaring of rutting deer, the air filled with the musk of females in season, and trees, trembling and flaring with blossom, pouring out scent and colour, ignited with life.

The forest is larger than the world, though the world thinks the opposite. Going in is easy: it's coming out that's hard. Time stops in the forest. People walk into the forest and never come out. They feel lost. They drift. They walk round in circles. They stop wanting.

The forest is the first place, original, primeval, primordial, primal. It is the inexhaustible beginning, direct, instinctual, unmediated, real. The land before the people came. This land. Old and bright and dark and full of dreams and nightmares. It is not an empty place. People live here, human and not so: free giants and tunnel dwellers; windwalkers, rusalkas, vyrdalaks, shapeshifters, hamrs, fetches, man-wolves; disembodied watchful intelligences, wild and cruel, that might be called witches and trolls. Many things are lost and buried in the forest: old things, perdurable, and new things, potential, unrealised yet, and waiting. All things are possible here, and here is everything. Growth and change. Here everything freely, abundantly begins, and becomes itself: the multiplicity, variousness, potential, myriadness, wanderability, wellspring and wilderness of forest. The trees are sensitive to light and earth. They taste and listen. Their roots go deep, and touch, and interweave. They spill pheromone language on the air. The trees are watchful. The rain, the air, the earth are watchful. The forest is borderless mind. It is aware.

Across the forest Archangel grinds his way, immense and alien and poison.

28

Minister of Armaments and General Secretary of the Colloquium Steopan Dukhonin's car took him home after the Novozhd's funeral. From a window in the building opposite, Bez Nichevoi watched the long ZorKi Zavod saloon arrive. It rode low, weighed down by two tons of steel plate. Assassination-proof. Bez could make out Dukhonin's head in the back, a dim featureless shape behind two inches of hardened glass. An underwater profile, bowed forward as if he were absorbed. Reading. The car pulled up at the wide double gates and the driver spoke into the intercom grille. The gates swung open to let the ZorKi edge through and closed behind it. Bez knew the routine. Dukhonin would not leave again before morning.

The house was a squat stone block, blank-windowed, in its own grounds, an enclave carved out of Pir-Anghelksy Park. The driver would ignore the steps up to the front door. He would follow the gravel driveway round to the back and into the courtyard. Walls within walls. One of the indoor guards would be waiting. The driver would see Dukhonin inside, then take the ZorKi across to the garage, lock it in for the night, and go into the house himself. Dukhonin would go to his study and work there until the early hours of the morning. He would have supper brought to him on a tray. Dukhonin worked prodigiously. Secretively. Since becoming one of the Four he had given up his office in the Lodka and worked solely from home.

Apart from the driver and the housekeeper, there were two guards inside the house and two in the grounds. And dogs. Lean, black, heavy-jawed killers left to roam free within the outer wall. Dukhonin also had a private secretary, a new man, Pavel, who arrived at 7.30 every morning and normally remained until 7.30 in the evening, but he was not in the house. He had been at the funeral, and Dukhonin had told him he wouldn't be required again until the morning. Dukhonin liked to observe such niceties – they were of consequence to him.

That evening's leave of absence was a propriety Pavel would come to appreciate. It had saved his life.

It took Bez five minutes to walk to the place where he could cross the perimeter wall without being seen from the street. The wall was ten feet high, but he climbed it without difficulty. His body was light as a small child's. He dropped to the ground inside the compound. There was fifteen yards of clear space before the laurels began, snow-mounded in the gathering darkness. The snow was falling thickly. It blurred his senses a little, muffling sound and muting scent, but he could feel the presence of the dogs nearby, three of them. They had his scent. He felt their alertness, the way they moved a few paces towards him, heads up, but they were hesitating, the strangeness of his smell making them uncertain. No sign of the guards.

Bez stood with his back to the wall and waited. It would be better if the dogs came to him. Neater that way. Simpler. He opened his mouth and let out a long plume of breath. A visible steam-cloud on the snow-thick air. He put into it the taint of carrion. Death. That would bring them, curious and eager but not alarmed. A few moments later the dogs broke through the laurels and saw him, not the dead thing they were expecting but a tall man standing.

When they came for him Bez killed them quickly. He absorbed their small deaths and started towards the house. He was leaving a trail of footprints, but it didn't matter. It would make no difference.

Because of the snow, the guards were within thirty yards of him before he was aware of them. They were not alert. Just a routine patrol. Bez dropped on them from the low branches of a fir tree, taking the head of one and piercing the eyes of the other, spearing his brain. He allowed himself a moment to digest their deaths and moved on. Entered the house through an upstairs window.

Inside, he took his time, walking through cool shadows, looking into all the empty rooms. Running his hands across tables and along the backs of chairs. Sharing in the quiet of the house, unbroken but for the slow ticking of a clock on a landing and the distant murmur of a radio. He found what must have been the housekeeper's sitting room. A chintz-backed armchair next to a purring stove. A shelf of china figures. A postcard from Lake Tsyrkhal. Nice things.

Dukhonin was in his study, at his desk, working on papers. He was smoking, a bottle of aquavit open at his elbow, a single glass. The radiogram in its cabinet against the wall playing quiet music. Absorbed, Dukhonin didn't see Bez Nichevoi watching him from the doorway.

Bez left him there for the moment. The others – the indoor guards, the driver, the housekeeper – were downstairs in the kitchen, gathered at the table, drinking tea. None of them noticed Bez until he was in the room with them, and by then it was too late. For them it had always been too late.

Now it was only him and Dukhonin in the house.

As Bez was going back upstairs, he heard a small sound. A door quietly opening. Dukhonin was on the move. Slowly. Bez sensed something uneasy about him. An edge of tense energy. Fear. He must have heard, or half-heard, what had happened in the kitchen. The housekeeper's interrupted scream. Bez moved soundlessly into the shadow of a doorway and waited.

Dukhonin was coming down the corridor in carpet slippers, a small pistol in his hand. He walked right past the doorway where Bez was. Bez stepped forward and gripped the wrist of the hand that held the gun. Dukhonin jerked round, lashed out, shouted – some harsh meaningless syllable – then saw what had come for him. Bez felt him collapse inside. Smelled that he had pissed himself. The pistol dropped to the floor.

Dukhonin stood in the corridor, arms dropped to his sides, resigned, hopeless.

'The guards?' he said in a flat voice. 'You killed them.'

'Yes.'

'All of them?'

'Yes.'

'And Mila?'

'Housekeeper?'

'Yes. The housekeeper.'

'Yes.'

A flicker of something – sadness? grief? – passed across Dukhonin's face and died.

'Who sent you?' he said. 'Khazar? Chazia? Fohn? Not Fohn? Surely not Fohn?'

'Chazia.'

Dukhonin nodded.

'Of course,' he said. 'Well. Go on then. Do it.'

Bez looked at him.

'Kill me,' said Dukhonin. 'Kill me, then. That's what you're here for. So. Do it, fuck you. I'm not going to fucking beg.'

Bez turned and started down the corridor.

'Come,' he said.

'What?'

'Your car,' said Bez Nichevoi. 'You drive.'

29

The Raion Lezaryet rose out of the surrounding city of Mirgorod on a steep angular hill of raw black rock. When the Lezarye's long wandering brought them to the shore of the Cetic Ocean in the time of the Founder's grandson, the hill of the raion had been an island in the marsh miles distant from Mirgorod. It seemed to surge out of the ground, a solid dark thunderhead glowering against the westering evening sky, the weathered root of a larger mountain. Some of the Lezarye families travelled on, taking ship onwards to the Archipelago and never returning, but the rest stayed and settled the black rock hill. Through the centuries that followed, Mirgorod flowed out across the waterland mud in a tide of suburbs and factories, surrounding the raion, pressing up against it and spilling past across the further islands one by one. On the steep black hill people crowded together, more and more of them squeezing into the narrowing streets. Every new Novozhd brought new restrictions, new laws, new arrests, new pogroms. *Why are our years always worse?* the poet Yourdania asked, because every decade that came hurt more than the last.

Other peoples came to settle in the raion, building their wooden shacks and shanties along the river and against the walls of the old Lezarye houses. Kyrghs and Mazhars, Esterhaziers, Samoys from the ice grass, shadowy relicts of the proto-peoples who had lived in the Mir estuary before the Founder. Refugees from former countries that had been declared unVlast and erased from the maps. The memory of those sunken countries was written in the faces in the streets: men in long black coats and wide-brimmed hats or furs and boots and braided beards; women in embroidered linen shawls and headscarves made from the colour-stained skins of mice; stark-eyed children with beaded hair and ringlets under caps of felt, carrying little books on straps hung round their necks. No one remembered who had built the wall round the raion, or knew for certain whether it was built to keep Mirgorod out or the Lezarye in. But built it was, with one gate only, which opened through a stone arch onto the Purfas Bridge.

The pony walked slowly, head down and shoulders bunched against the weight of the cart. Maroussia hugged her carpet bag in her lap. Lom shivered and pulled his loden tighter against the cold. An early twilight was closing in and the snow was coming down in a dense steady flow, settling thickly, when they crossed the Purfas by the narrow wooden bridge and entered the raion.

The failing of the day brought the dusk bells ringing, the last circling of rooks, the first evening flicker of bats, lamps and candles in the windows. From narrow passageways came the smell of food: frying fish and spiced meat. Paprika. Onions. Livestock wandered and rooted in the cramped alleyways. There were animals in every tiny courtyard and fenced-in patch of cottage ground. Small stunted orchards, leafless and snow-covered, crouched behind walls. The chill darkening air was rich with woodsmoke and the reek of pigs, chickens and cows.

They climbed the winding streets between ravines of red-tiled roofs and smoking chimneys, jutting windows and arched doorways, weather-blackened wood and stone. Here and there angular outcrops of raw black rock shouldered the crowded buildings aside. Small cottages and wooden shanties jostled in the shadow of tall old houses with peeling louvred shutters at their windows and carved coats of arms on their gable ends: spread-winged eagles, prowling bears, running wolves. The antlers of a great elk were mounted over a courtyard arch. The raion was a place of gaps and crannies, steep angular lanes, small doorways and purposeless openings barred with rusted iron gratings.

Elena Cornelius walked ahead, leading the pony.

'Elena's a good woman,' said Maroussia, breaking a long silence.

'Yes,' said Lom.

'We can't stay here. We'll bring her trouble. She doesn't understand. She has children. I don't want to get her involved. This is my thing. People have died already.'

'It's not your fault,' said Lom. 'It happened.'

'If anything happens to Elena, it will be my fault. I went to her. I shouldn't have.'

'It'll be OK,' said Lom. 'It'll be fine. It's just for tonight.'

Wooden signs announced places of business – an estaminet, a pension, a tailor, an apothecary, a notary public – all crowded in among the houses and cottages. The names above the shops were names from lost, remembered countries, long ago obliterated under the hegemony of the Vlast. SYLWEST. NIKODEM. TILL. CZESLAW. ONUFRY. KAZIMIERZ. WHITE. The poetry of distance and difference.

Lom had known of the raion since childhood, though it wasn't mentioned in the books of the library at the Podchornok Institute of Truth. There were students at the Institute who said that Podchornok, within sight of the endless forest, had been one of the Lezarye way forts once, in the great days of their wardership of the border, under the Reasonable Empire long ago. Some even made whispered claims to family connections with the aristocrat families of the raion, though saying so risked denunciation by the Student Council. Lom, knowing nothing of his own family and remembering nothing before the Institute, toyed with the idea that he too was one of them. But Raku Vishnik, his one true friend, had mocked him. *The Lezarye, Vissarion, never gave birth to a great blond clumsy bear like you!*

Nevertheless, Lom stared about him now and wondered if it felt like coming home. But it didn't. Not for him.

Elena Cornelius pulled the cart off the road into a small yard.

'We'll go in this way,' said Elena. 'Our neighbours watch and talk as much as anyone else's do.'

She unlocked a door in the brick wall of the yard and led them through into a small private garden. In the gathering darkness Lom caught a vague impression of the side of a tall house: walls of mossy brick and crumbling stucco, precarious vine-tangled wrought-iron balconies, steep roofs and high crowded gables. The ground floor was skirted with a glass-roofed pillared loggia. Yellow light spilled through gaps in the curtains. They rounded the corner of the house and descended a narrow flight of basement steps. Elena rattled at a storm door of pierced zinc and wire netting until it jerked open and they squeezed inside, past buckets and mops and a rack of oilskins. A dog appeared at the end of the passageway, a black and yellow coarse-haired thing, standing stiff-legged and growling at the back of its throat. It was some kind of spitz or laitka, Lom didn't know what and didn't care. He preferred dogs at a distance.

'Vesna!' called Elena gently. 'It's OK. They're friends.'

The dog padded forward and inspected them. Lom offered his hand to be sniffed. The dog ignored it and went out into the garden.

'This is a big place,' he said.

'It's Sandu Palffy's house,' said Elena. 'Count Palffy. He and Ilinca have an apartment at the back. The rest is let out. But it is Count Palffy's house. At least, morally it is his, as he is morally a Count.'

There was a warm fug in the kitchen. Black and white tiles on the floor. Curtains drawn. A hefty old stove against the wall, its fire door open, shedding the heat of fast-burning logs. Two girls at the scrubbed deal table – thick black curly mops of hair and bright clever eyes – looked up when they came in. The older was about thirteen, school books spread in front of her amid the remains of their supper. The younger, who must have been ten or eleven, had a piece of reddish wood and a big clasp knife. She was carving something. An animal. A cat maybe. Lom thought it was probably good.

'Galina, Yeva, this is my friend Maroussia from the city,' said Elena. 'And this …'

'Vissarion,' said Lom. 'I'm Vissarion. That's a good cat.'

'It's a lynx,' said Yeva. 'Not a cat.'

'Oh yes. Of course. Sorry.'

'There's rassolnik on the stove,' said the older girl. Galina. 'We got pigeons from Milla's. It was four kopeks for two, and Ilinca gave us a loaf of black bread. And kvass. There's plenty left.' She looked doubtfully at Lom and Maroussia. 'I think.'

'It'll be fine,' said Maroussia. 'Thanks.'

'You girls need to go and see to the pony, ' said Elena. 'Then go upstairs. Both of you. Go and sit with Ilinca. You could get her to put the phonogram on.'

Yeva made a sour face.

'Oh, but we haven't—'

'Upstairs,' said Elena. 'Now. I need to talk to Maroussia in private. Tell Sandu there'll be people in the attic tonight. Don't forget that.'

*

Elena brought a big iron pot from the oven. On the table she set out plates, a loaf of bread and a small blue jug of soured cream, and spooned out the thin rassolnik. Onions and cucumber. A few scraps of grey meat.

'I'm sorry,' said Maroussia. 'We should never have come. We'll go tomorrow.'

'It doesn't matter,' said Elena. 'It makes no difference.'

'You're not safe while we're here. The girls—'

'Safe?' said Elena. 'Nobody is *safe*. Not anywhere. One day they come for you, and that's it. That's all. Every day the girls go to school and I never know if they'll come back. Last week they shot thirty people at the Red Cliff. They lined them up in the rain and shot them. Buried the bodies in the ditch. A *reprisal*. Reprisal for what? Who knows? They didn't care who they took. Old men. Women. *Children*. They took their clothes first and then they shot them. They made them stand *naked*. Then they burned the houses.'

'Who?' said Lom. 'Who did that?'

'What difference does it make?' said Elena. 'Police. Militia. Gendarmes. Army. What's the difference? *Uniforms* did it. And it'll be worse now. Much worse.'

'Why?'

She stood up and went across to the sideboard, took a piece of paper from a drawer and shoved them across the table towards him.

'See this? Look at this.'

'Colloquium Communiqué No. 3'. Its corners were torn as if it had been ripped off a notice board or a telegraph pole.

Men and women of the Vlast!

Again the counter-revolution has raised its criminal head. Revanchists are mobilising their forces to crush us. The bloodstained pogrom-mongers, having slaughtered our beloved Novozhd, intend to cause more killing and terror in the streets of Mirgorod! They have deluded the minds of certain weaker elements within our army and navy and betrayed the heroic sons and daughters to the Archipelago. Staunch resistance is needed. Now is the time for action and clear-eyed sacrifice.

Justified by angels, the Colloquium for the Protection of Citizens and the Vlast agrees to take upon itself the defence of Perpetual

Revolution. The Administrative Government of the CPCV is hereby declared.

People of the Lezarye cannot be citizens of the Vlast. They have no rights in law.

It was signed with four names. Dukhonin. Khazar. Chazia. Fohn.

'See?' said Elena Cornelius. 'They're blaming us for the death of the Novozhd. They'll come for us all. *No rights in law.* You know what that means? It means anyone can do anything to us. Put us out of our houses. Loot our shops. Kill us, kill our children. Any time they want to, any time at all, and no police to protect us. The police are for citizens.

'And that is not all. Look at what happened to the men at the Saltworks Foundry. They took them all, hundreds of men, and their families. All of them.'

'Took them?' said Lom. 'Took them where?'

'Who knows? The Saltworks Foundry was the first. They come for more every day – whole factories and whole streets every time. They put them on trains and we never see them again. One day they will come here. It is only a matter of time. You should run, Maroussia. Get away from the city while you can. Don't tell me what trouble you're in, it doesn't matter. If the Vlast wants to kill you, then they will kill you. You have to get far, far away from here.' She looked at Lom. 'Take her away,' she said. 'If you are her friend, get her out of Mirgorod. Go to the exclave. Go to the ice. Go to the forest. Find a ship to the Archipelago. Go anywhere. There's nothing to keep you here. You should run.'

'No,' said Maroussia. 'I'm not going to run.'

30

Chazia left General Secretary Steopan Dukhonin alone for most of the night in the interrogation room where Bez Nichevoi had put him. *Let him stew. Let him think. Let him wonder.* She had other work to do. And she wanted to prepare for the interview: get the facts and figures straight in her head. Dukhonin was a sly little shit, but she would skewer him. She was going to skewer them all one by one: Dukhonin, Khazar, Fohn, all the vicious, patronising, conspiring little men who thought they could use her and keep power for themselves. The men who did not know her and did not see who she was. She would start with Dukhonin. Industrious, cautious, greedy, tiny, frightened Dukhonin. He was the worst. Start with him.

When she went down for him he was sitting at the table in his shirt and carpet slippers. The skin of his face was grey and patched with sparse white stubble. He smelled faintly of urine.

'Lavrentina, what the fuck …' he said. 'What the fuck is this? Am I *arrested*? That … that *thing* of yours *killed my people*. My fucking *housekeeper*! Fohn will destroy you for this. *Destroy* you!'

His small watery eyes glared at her, sour with fear. His thin little face was tight and full of bone. Chazia sat down across the table from him.

'We need a little talk, Steopan Vadimovich,' she said. 'Just a little talk.'

'You want to talk, make a fucking appointment.'

'Let's start with the steel from Schentz.'

'Does Fohn know I'm here?' said Dukhonin. 'He doesn't, does he? You're finished, Lavrentina. You're nothing. We should never have let you in. I told Fohn … I told him you were—'

'Fohn?' said Chazia. 'What does Fohn matter? Look around you, Steopan. Where is Fohn? Is he here?'

'You've overreached yourself, Lavrentina. You're dead. Finished. What is this situation? It is preposterous, that's what it is. I am the *General Secretary*. I am one of the *Four*. You don't question me and I certainly don't fucking answer.' He stood up. 'I'm going home and you're fucking dead.'

'The steel, Steopan. Tell me about the steel from Schentz. The Mirskov Foundry invoices the Treasury for forty million roubles and the Treasury pays forty million. But only thirty-six million shows up in the Mirskov accounts.'

'So? Is that it? You think you can bring me down with that? Ten per cent for my trouble? Who fucking cares? You've got shit. Big mistake. You're dead.'

'I'm not interested in the money, I'm interested in the steel. Forty million gets a lot of steel. How much steel is worth forty million?'

'I don't know. Who fucking cares?'

'At a thousand roubles a ton that's forty thousand tons. Minimum. A hundred tons per wagon. Four hundred wagons. If you moved it in one train it would be four miles long.'

Dukhonin shrugged.

'So?'

'So why send forty thousand tons of steel to Novaya Zima?'

'Nothing to do with me. Why would I care where it went?'

'But you ordered it, Steopan,' said Chazia. 'You did it. You. Forty thousand tons of steel to Novaya Zima and a nice four million roubles for you. It was the cut that got noticed, but as you say, so what? Still, I'm curious. I ask myself, why is Steopan Vadimovich sending so much steel to Novaya Zima? What is there at Novaya Zima? A shit-hole on an island in an icebound sea? Nothing is happening there. We're losing a war, yet Steopan finds enough steel to make a thousand main battle tanks and sends it north-east to the edge of the ice?'

'This is outside your sphere, Lavrentina,' said Dukhonin. 'Way outside. You shouldn't be touching this. It's serious stuff. Dangerous stuff. You need to back away.'

'I made enquiries about Novaya Zima, Steopan. And what did I find? Nothing. Not a record of nothing, but no record. No file. An empty shelf where Novaya Zima should be. So I asked a different question. What else has my friend Steopan Vadimovich Dukhonin been buying with Treasury money? It wasn't easy to track that either, but I found traces. Coal. Rare earths. Machinery. Small quantities of metals I've never heard of. Seventy tons – seventy *tons* – of reclaimed angel flesh. Every scrap of angel flesh that could be found in the Vlast. All arranged by Steopan Vadimovich Dukhonin, who incidentally takes his little ten per cent. And people too. Eighty thousand conscript labourers diverted from war work, all for Novaya Zima. You're even taking them from here! From Mirgorod! So. Steopan. This is the question. *What is happening at Novaya Zima?*'

'Nothing,' said Dukhonin. He was confident now. The stupid man was confident. 'Like you said. Nothing.'

Chazia smiled.

'Actually, I considered that possibility. Maybe, I thought, it is all a scam. Paper transactions only. Money paid but nothing sent. Maybe Steopan's little scheme is a big scheme. But no, the shipments are real, and they really go to Novaya Zima. So what happens when they get there?'

'You've got shit,' said Dukhonin. 'Dangerous shit, but shit. You think you know it all, with your files and your informers and your useless lickspittle secret police? You know *nothing*, Lavrentina! Nothing of *importance*. You know nothing and you are no one. Who are you? What are you? You're meat, you're disgusting, a diseased, repellent little cow-bitch. Novaya Zima will kill you. Shit. You send that thing to scare me and you kill my *housekeeper* and you keep me locked up *all night* in this pathetic stinking toilet. Fohn will kill you slowly and I will piss on your shitty corpse.' He stood up. 'I've had enough. I'm going home.'

'The door,' said Chazia, 'is not locked.'

Dukhonin stood up, raised himself to his full five foot six, shuffled across in his carpet slippers and pulled the door open. Bez Nichevoi was standing in the corridor, patient and still. A shadow in the shadows. Dukhonin didn't see him until he moved. Bez dislocated Dukhonin's left arm at the shoulder and Dukhonin screamed.

Bez did something to Dukhonin's face, too fast for Chazia to see, and pushed him back into the room. Dukhonin fell forward hard on the floor and lay there, his left arm at a wrong angle, useless, his right hand holding his face.

'Oh shit,' he murmured. 'Shit.'

Bez followed him into the room and looked to Chazia for instructions.

'Help him back into his chair.'

Dukhonin sat slumped forward, twisted sideways with the pain in his shoulder, blood trickling down his cheek from his ruined left eye. The socket was a jellied, swollen mess.

'There cannot be *four rulers,* Steopan,' said Chazia. 'There can only be *one*. Power shared isn't power at all. This Colloquium you and Fohn and Khazar cooked up is an abortion. It is an arena for battle only – it is a *war* – but none of you is a soldier and none of you will win. I am going to take it all.'

Dukhonin didn't look at her. His one good eye was fixed on Bez Nichevoi, motionless and watchful in the corner of the room. Nichevoi seemed to be exuding the shadows that gathered around him despite the flat glare of the overhead lamp. Tall and thin, he wore a neat dark suit made of shadows. Dark hair, a dark inexpressive gaze, a stark face white as chalk. He made the angles of the room around him seem wrong.

'You're just like the rest of them, Steopan, when they come in here,' Chazia said. 'The ground you walked on was always fragile, and now it has broken and you've fallen through. You're in my world now.'

'But we can do a deal, Lavrentina,' said Dukhonin. 'Listen. We can do a deal. You're right about Fohn, of course you are. Completely. He's weak. A bureaucrat. A committee man. A compromiser. But not *me*, I'm not like that. You and I – we can make an alliance. Don't let that thing . . . You don't need to kill me, Lavrentina. There's no call for that. I can help you. You want to come in on it? I'll let you in. Of course I will. It's a perfect idea. Perfect. I should have thought of it before. We'll be good together, Lavrentina. We don't need Khazar and Fohn. You don't need to kill me. I'll share.'

'Share? What have you got that I need, Steopan Vadimovich?'

'Novaya Zima! Shit. *Novaya Zima!* You need it. You need *me*.'

'So what is Novaya Zima? Tell me what it is.'

'Not tell you. I'll show you. You need to *see*.'

31

When Elena Cornelius had left them alone in the attic, Maroussia went across to one of the mattresses and sat down. She put the carpet bag she'd brought from Vishnik's on the floor next to her and opened it. Started pulling things out, one by one and setting them out on the quilt. The envelope with Vishnik's photographs. A dark woollen skirt. A couple of thin cotton blouses, faded and softened from frequent washing. A blue knitted cardigan, neatly mended at the elbow with slightly mismatched thread. A linen nightshirt. A bar of soap, wrapped in a piece of brown waxed paper. A thin book in a grey card cover. *The Selo Elegies and Other Poems* by Anna Yourdania. The clothes were crumpled. They'd been fingered by Vishnik's killers and thrown aside until Maroussia had grabbed them off the floor and stuffed them roughly, hastily, back into the bag. Lom watched her set out each one, smooth it down and refold it, neatly.

She felt him watching her and looked up.

'I don't want to wear these again,' she said. 'Not after where they've been. Not after what happened there.'

'No,' said Lom. 'I guess not.'

'They're not … they're not mine, not any more.'

She picked up the packet of soap and went across to the table under the window. There was a large pitcher of water and a wide shallow washbowl: chipped yellow enamel with a thin black rim. A rough brown towel hung from a hook. Maroussia poured some water into the bowl, rolled up her sleeves, leaned forward and splashed her face with tight cupped hands. Rubbed her dripping hands across her eyes, her mouth, her forehead, her throat, the back of her neck. Ran wet fingers through her hair. Then she straightened up, unwrapped the soap and lathered her hands, her arms up to the elbow. She turned the soap over and over in her fingers, rubbed it again along the length of her arms and let it slip back into the bowl. Scooped a double handful of water and jammed the heels of her palms into her eyes. Not rubbing but pressing, gently pushing. She stood like that, not moving, breathing.

Lom went up behind her. He could smell the soap and the warmth of her skin and hair. Her hands, her face, her neck were flushed from the icy cold of the water. He could smell the scent of her on the thin blouse she'd been wearing the day the boat took them into the White Reaches and was still wearing now. He could still feel the warmth of her long back against his side, where she had lain pressed against him in the bed in the gate keeper's lodge the night before. Twenty-four hours ago. He picked up the towel and dipped a corner of it in the icy water in the pitcher. Began to wipe the soap from her neck and her arms.

When he took her two hands in one of his and drew them gently away from her face, her eyes were screwed tight shut. He wiped the soap from them, one by one. She turned into his arms, opened her eyes and looked into his. Held his gaze for a long, quiet time. There was a faint sweetness of brandy on her breath.

She was a stranger to him. Again, he felt the otherness of her. A part of her was very far away, behind her eyes, not wanting to be reached.

He moved the rough damp edge of the towel across her mouth, wiping the soap away. She moved her body against him. He felt the patch of damp cold where she had spilled water down her neck. She opened her mouth and put her lips against his.

Hours later, Lom lay wakeful in the dark, listening to the quiet creaks and ticks of the roof beams under the accumulating weight of snow. Maroussia was lying next to him, sleeping, the warmth of her breathing against his cheek. He listened to the rattles and groans in the pipes, the scratch and skitter of small animals. Felt the presence of dark, amorphous, inky, shifty, scuttling night-things that lived in the shadows and ceilings and whispered. Cool, filmy presences. Watchful creatures of fur and dust. The delicate new skin across the hole in the front of his skull fluttered in response with gentle moth-wing beats.

Slowly and carefully so as not to wake her, he slipped out from under the quilt and padded barefoot across to the window. It was bitterly cold in the room. He was instantly shivering. The vapour of his and Maroussia's breath had crystallised in whorls and ferns of frost across the windowpanes, and through it a faint snow-glimmer filtered into the room. He cleared a patch with the side of his palm and looked out: dense, swirling snowfall still coming down; the tumbled, tightly packed rooftops of the raion falling away down the hill. Lamps burning in a few isolated windows, their light reflecting off the snow.

Lom used to think, once, that snow was frozen rain, that snowflakes were raindrops that turned to ice as they fell through freezing air. But then, he'd forgotten where, he discovered the truth. Snow wasn't frozen rain, it had never been rain. Snow was the invisible vapour of water – the slow and distant breath of lakes, of rivers, of oceans – crystallising suddenly out of thin air. A billion billion tiny weightless dagger-spiked ghosts, materialising. From the first time Lom heard this, the thought had electrified him: he'd realised that all around him, all the time, all the year, always, there existed in the air, unseen, the latent possibility of snow. Even the warmest summer day was haunted by snow. The memory of how to be snow. All that was required to make it real was cold. And when the cold moment came, snow manifested itself suddenly out of the air in a kind of chill ignition, the opposite of flame.

Somewhere in the city was a man who had worn his face. A man who pulled bullets out of his belly and walked away. And Chazia was out there too. And so was Josef Kantor.

'Vissarion?' said Maroussia. Her voice was quiet in the dark.

'Yes? I thought you were asleep.'

'No.'

'Are you OK?'

'Yes. Only … I was thinking.'

'What?'

'Do you think Elena's right? Do you think we should get out of Mirgorod? Do you think we should run?'

'Do you?' he said across the dim snow-shadowed room.

'No.'

'Then don't. Don't run.'

'But … I don't know what to do,' she said. 'I mean, say we could get into the Lodka and find it, find the Pollandore … All I've got is fragments. Garbled messages. It's not enough.'

'So what do you want to do?'

'I don't know,' she said. 'I need more. I need the forest to talk to me again.'

'OK,' said Lom.

'OK what?'

'OK, so talk to the forest again.'

'Do you know how to do that?' said Maroussia.

'No.'

She said no more, but Lom could hear her breathing. Lying awake in the dark.

She was taking the righting of the world on her shoulders. The weight of it, the pressure and hopelessness of what she was choosing, squatted heavily in the room. He went across to the bed and got in. Pulled the quilt up around them both. Made a warm dark private place, simple and human, like people's lives should be. Just for now.

32

Lavrentina Chazia had never believed that she knew every room in the Lodka. No one could. The route Dukhonin led her, shuffling slowly in his carpet slippers, his left arm stiff and useless, his thin bony face sticky with drying blood from his ruined eye, was new to her. They climbed stairs and took lifts, ascending and descending, until she had no idea where in the building they were, or even whether they were above or below ground. They passed no one.

'Here,' said Dukhonin, stopping at a heavy anonymous door with a combination lock. 'This is the place.'

He fumbled with the tumbler. His hand was trembling. He pulled at the door but it didn't shift.

'Shit,' he muttered. 'Shit.'

He started again. Chazia pushed him aside.

'I'll do it,' she said. 'Tell me the numbers.'

He did.

Beyond the door were more corridors, deserted in the early hours. Bez Nichevoi followed a few paces behind them. Silently in his soft leather shoes. They passed rooms that showed signs of current occupation. Handwritten notices: *ESTABLISHMENTS*; *ACCOUNTS*; *TRANSIT*; *PROCUREMENT AND SUPPLY*. Telephone cables trailing across the floor. Green steel cabinets. A telegraphic printing machine – a contraption of brass and cogs with a board of black and white keys like a piano, the kind that printed out endless spools of paper tape – stood inactive on a heavy wooden table. There was a basket to catch the tape as it passed out, but it was empty. This was a significant operation. Dukhonin set it all up and kept it running without even a whisper reaching her? But it was all support functions. Generic. The substance was elsewhere.

Dukhonin brought them to a small windowless room. The card beside the door said *PROJECT WINTER SKIES*. Inside were eight chairs set round a plain meeting table and on the wall was a map showing the rail and river routes of the north-eastern oblasts: wide expanses of nothing but a patchwork of small lakes and emptiness, railheads and river staging posts, the coast of the Yarmskoye Sea; and beyond that the irregular fringe of permanent ice, and blankness.

At one end of the room was a small projection screen, and at the opposite end a Yubkin film projector on a sturdy tripod.

'Sit, Lavrentina,' said Dukhonin. 'Please. Sit.' He looked at Bez. 'Is he ... staying? This is ... What you're going to see is ... I would not recommend that he remains.'

'He stays.'

'Lavrentina. Please. Nothing is more sensitive than this. And ... and I will need to extinguish the lights.'

'He stays.'

Dukhonin, his breathing loud and ragged, unclipped the twin reel covers and checked the film spool was in place. One-handed and trembling, it took him a long time. At last he got the projection lamp lit and set the cooling fan running. He brought up a test image and spent some time selecting a lens and adjusting the focus. There was a heavy radiator blasting heat into the cramped stuffy room. Chazia smelled Dukhonin's stale sweat. The sourness of his fear. The piss on his trousers. She shifted in her seat and scratched in irritation at the angel stains on her arms.

'What you're going to see,' Dukhonin began, 'needs no introduction. It speaks for itself. The culmination of years of work. Years of patient—'

'Get on with it.'

He switched off the room light and set the projector running. It clattered and whirred, casting flickering monochrome images on the screen. White letters, jittering almost imperceptibly on a dark background under a faint snow of dust and scratch-tracks:

WINTER SKIES

FIELD TEST #5

NORTH ZIMA EXPANSE

VAYARMALOND OBLAST

A series of serial numbers and acronyms. A date about two months before.

The only sounds in the room were the clattering of the projector and Dukhonin's heavy breathing. From time to time he gave a quiet moan. He probably didn't know he was doing it.

Chazia watched the screen.

Men in heavy winter clothing were working outside in the snow. They were making adjustments to a large and heavy-looking metal object, a squat, solid, rounded capsule about ten feet high and twenty feet long. It resembled a swollen samovar turned on its side. Tubes and rivets and plates. One of the men turned to the camera and grinned. Thumbs up. Then the men had gone and the screen showed the thing alone. The camera dwelled on it for a moment or two and a caption came up. UNCLE VANYA. Then the scene cut to a wide expanse of windswept ice. A tall metal gantry, a framework of girders rising into a bleak sky. Tiny figures moving at the foot of it gave a sense of scale.

Another scene change: the heavy, swollen capsule being winched up the gantry and set in place at the top. More snow-bearded technicians gurning excitedly at the lens. And then nothing. Only the flat emptiness of the winter tundra: mile upon mile of grey icefields under a grey sky. Chazia waited. Nothing happened. Thirty seconds. A minute. Nothing.

Chazia shifted in her seat.

'Steopan—'

'Wait,' he hissed. Tension in his voice. Excitement. 'Wait.'

The entire screen lit up, a brilliant, dazzling white. A blinding flash erasing the tundra and the sky.

Dukhonin let out a small ecstatic sigh.

'You see?' he said. 'You see what I can give you?'

Chazia was sitting forward in her chair, gripping the armrests. There was a knot in her stomach of joy and excitement and desire. As the blinding light faded, the screen showed a huge burning column roaring into the sky. There was no sound but she could hear it roaring. A thick pillar of destruction surging thousands of feet upwards. The air itself on fire. Boiling. The base of the column must have been five hundred yards across, and thickening steadily. It looked like an immense tree in full summer leaf, half a mile high. A mile. At the top it flattened and spilled outwards, its leafhead a canopy of roiling power and destruction. Cataclysm. The force of it left her breathless.

At the base of the mile-high tree a wind began: an expanding circular shout of power, racing outwards from the centre, scouring the snow off the ice, scouring the ice itself, whipping it into a tidal wall hundreds of feet high, hurtling at tremendous speed towards the watching camera. When it struck the lens the picture stopped. The screen went blank. The film clattered to a halt.

Dukhonin switched on the room light and extinguished the projector lamp.

'Did you see? Did you see? One of these – just one of them! – can obliterate an entire city. And at Novaya Zima they are building hundreds. And that's just the beginning. We have plans … Imagine, Lavrentina … There is no limit. No limit at all.'

Chazia felt a constriction in her throat. Power on this scale … Her legs and arms felt weak. She did not trust herself to stand.

'Who *knows,* Steopan?' she said.

'What?'

'Who *knows*? Does *Khazar* know? Does *Fohn*? Was it only me that did not know about this?'

'No, no,' said Dukhonin. 'Of course not. This is all mine. My doing. They brought this idea to me alone. And I have made it real! But you can join me, Lavrentina, and—'

'Who brought it Steopan*? Who brought you this knowledge?*'

'Technicians. Professors. Scientists. They're at Novaya Zima, all of them.

'But where is this *from*? *Where did they get this knowledge from?*'

'What kind of question …? They are very brilliant men.'

'And they came to you?'

'Of course they came to me. An undertaking like this needs resources. Materials. Workers. *Organisation* of the highest order. They had gone as far as they could on their own. They needed help. Who else would they come to?'

'You're saying these scientists and professors did this?' She waved her hand towards the blank projection screen. '*This?* On their *own*? They worked on it, knowing what they had, and never told anyone. Never sought official sanction? Never came to the Novozhd in Council for recognition and protection and support. And then, when they had gone as far as they could on their own they came to *you*? To you *alone*? Who approached you? Some *professor*? Some *engineer*?'

'Not at all. Of course not. They were frightened men. Out of their depth. They knew the importance of what they had, and the risks ... the risks that it would get into the wrong hands. You couldn't trust an idiot like Khazar with a thing like this. There was a middle man. An intermediary.'

'Who?'

'His name was Lura.'

'*Lura?*' Chazia stared at Dukhonin. She wanted to hurt him. Gouge out his other eye. Tear out his throat. 'Shall I describe to you this *Lura*?' she said. 'Tall and thin? A pockmarked complexion? Thick shiny hair and big brown eyes like a fucking cow? A red silk shirt?'

'Yes. That's right. That's Lura.'

'It is Kantor,' said Chazia. 'Josef Kantor.'

Chazia turned to Bez, waiting like a shadow behind Dukhonin.

'Kill this useless idiot,' she said.

Bez moved so fast that Chazia barely saw what he did.

'Find Iliodor, wherever he is,' she said when he had finished. 'I want these offices closed. The whole thing completely gone. Everyone who works here is to be dealt with. No trace. He is to do nothing about Novaya Zima, not yet, but I want a list of all the personnel there. Tomorrow. I want this tomorrow. In the morning. Tell Iliodor this.'

Bez nodded.

'And when you have done that, there is a woman. Maroussia Shaumian. Iliodor has the file. The SV were to pick her up this evening, but they did not succeed. There have been previous failures. Find her and bring her to me.'

'Of course,' said Bez. Something lopsided happened to his face. Chazia realised it was a smile.

'I want her alive,' she said. 'And in a condition to speak to me.'

33

In cloud-thickened moonless snow-glimmered darkness, in the hard bitter coldest part of the night, three miles east of the Lodka, crooked in a sharp elbow-bend of the River Mir, pressing hard against the south embankment, lay the eight flat, tangled, overgrown, neglected, lampless and benighted square miles of the Field Marshal Khorsh-Brutskus Park of Culture and Rest.

Three centuries earlier, the Park had begun life as the gardens of the Shurupinsky Palace, landscaped by Can Guarini himself, and the shell of the palace – its grounds long since appropriated to the greater needs of the citizens of Mirgorod – still stood, encircled (*girt* is the only word that will actually do) by an elegant, attenuated, over-civilised gesture of a moat, slowly succumbing to decay and sporadic, unenthusiastic vandalism. Long before the expropriation, the successive princes Shurupin in their financial prime had provided for themselves handsomely. In the high summer of the palace's splendour, the *Ladies' New Magazine* had produced a special supplement devoted to describing in detail, with tipped-in lithographs by Fromm, the thirty-two bedrooms, the eleven bathrooms, the glorious ballroom, the galleried library, the palm court, the orangery, the velodrome, the stabling for fifty horses, the private hospital, the theatre, the extensive Cabinet (in truth, a *Hall)* of Curiosities, the observatory with its copper revolving roof and huge telescope, and the artificial island in the lake where, on summer afternoons, tea might be taken under a lacy canopy of ironwork.

And when the grounds of the Shurupinsky Palace were expropriated and became the Park of Culture and Rest it happened that, by some oversight or unresolved quirk of administrative demarcation, no provision whatsoever of any kind was made for the great house and its contents. No possessor or use for it was found. It was never emptied of its furnishings and equipment. Its library was never catalogued and relocated, its paintings never removed and rehung or stored away, and surprisingly little from the house was even stolen; at the time of the expropriation, and ever since, not only was there was no market for the cumbersome extravagances of the former aristocracy, they were dangerous to own, dangerous to be discovered with, and hideously inconvenient to export to the Archipelago, where buyers might still have been found though at a price that would scarcely have covered the illicit transportation cost. So the palace was simply abandoned, more or less in the condition the last prince left it, to moulder and slowly collapse.

Antoninu Florian had visited the Shurupinsky Palace once, before the expropriation, as a guest of the last prince. Prince Alexander Yurich Shurupin, landowner, moral philosopher, social reformer and author of prodigiously enormous, compendious, subtle novels, had shown Florian over the house and walked with him in the grounds, not in pride but in some bemusement and shame, because the Palace troubled him. An old man by then, his privilege troubled him. His own brilliant writings troubled him.

'You have no idea how restful it is for me, talking to you, my friend,' the Prince had said to Florian, striding along the avenue of yellow earth, hands in the pockets of his brown linen overalls, work boots flapping unlaced against his shins, beard and long grey hair flickering on the lilac-scented summer breeze. 'It gives me a wonderful freedom to speak fully and truly, your not being tainted with *humanness*. In my experience, one can never talk to another human person with complete honesty, not really. It is impossible. Even the best of them, they take the truth so *personally*. But you, you have a fine intelligence but you stand completely apart. You are not *engagé*, you are not *parti pris*. You hear my words simply as words. My thoughts are simply thoughts, not the thoughts of wealth and fame and a name. Not the thoughts of one who could be of help to you, or could wound and insult you with a careless dismissive phrase that is intended to be of general application, not personal at all. You bring the disinterested clarity of perspective that comes from standing elsewhere. I value that, my friend. I value it tremendously.'

The last prince had died soon after Florian's visit in obscure circumstances, but Florian, who had barely listened to Prince Shurupin's words at all but paid close attention to the man, returned to the abandoned palace from time to time, to prowl its fading rooms and read in the library, until large parts of the roof had collapsed, the floors became unsafe and the stench of damp and mildew and fungal growth too depressing to bear. Even when he'd stopped going into the palace, he still made visits to the park. Too large by far for the two men employed by the city to maintain them, the greater part of the former gardens had reverted to thicketed, brambled wilderness, the marble temples and mythographical statuary imported from the Archipelago by the early princes soot-blackened and mossy green, submerged under a tide of thorn and glossy mounds of rhododendron. For Florian it was a cool, earthy, leafy, sap-rich, owl-hunted refuge from the city.

And he had come there now, in the dark and snow-muffled night, to nurse the gunshot wound in his belly.

Relieving himself of the discomfort of human clothes and human form, Florian nosed his way into the shelter of a stand of pine trees in the centre of the park and curled himself up on a patch of bare earth. The wound was a dull ache. It was almost healed, only a tender puckered crust remained, but the effort of driving the bullet out had cost him energy and he needed rest. He rasped at the place with his tongue until the last taste of dried blood had gone, then stretched out and closed his eyes.

The watchfulness of the world was all around him, the living awareness of earth and trees reaching out in all directions to the edge of streets and the river and beyond. The connective tissue of the park and the city was earth and water and air and roots, and Florian merged himself into the flow and tangle of it, surrendering, letting the constant work of holding together a pseudo-human consciousness relax and blur away. No words, no structured thoughts. No names for things. He was what he was, and only that. The hurt in the belly was not *his* hurt, it was simply *hurt,* a thing that was there, that existed, but without implication. No before-time and nothing to come: and without that, no fear.

34

Lom woke in the morning to find the curtain pulled back and the attic filled with brilliant early light. The sky in the window was a bright powdery eggshell blue. Maroussia was already gone.

He got up and dressed. There was broken ice in the washbowl. He splashed his face and looked out of the window. Snow mounded the rooftops of the raion and filled the silent streets. Nothing moved but wisps of smoke from chimneys. The broken moons, faint and filmy, silver-blue against blue, rested at anchor, day-visible watermarks in the liquid paper sky.

Lom went out into the corridor and tried to retrace his steps back to Elena's kitchen but found himself in parts of the house he hadn't seen before. A wide staircase took him down to an entrance hall: red tiles and threadbare rugs, a stand for coats and hats, umbrellas and galoshes. Fishing rods. The scent of polish and leather. Morning sun streamed in through the coloured-glass skylight over the door, kindling dust motes and splashing faint lozenges of colour across the floor. He unbolted the door and opened it onto foot-thick snow. Crisp bitter air spilled inwards, caught at his nose and throat and made his breath steam. He stepped out into crisp blue illumination. Every colour was saturated. The snow glistened, translucent, refracting tiny diamond brilliances. He stomped his way round the side of the house, looking for the entrance they'd used last night. Nothing moved in the streets. The snow muffled all sound, except for the morning bells, the calling of the rooks and the rhythmic crunch of his own feet.

He made his way round to the gate into the garden and pushed it open. As he was passing the wide low loggia, a figure stepped out to confront him.

'Yes? Who are you?'

It was a man of about sixty, leaning on a malacca cane. Wisps of uncombed grey hair, a heavily embroidered morning coat, gold-rimmed spectacles. An ugly intelligent face. He was standing on the step under the canopy. Worn, turned carpet slippers on his feet.

'Sorry,' said Lom. 'I'm staying in the house. We're with Elena Cornelius. I got myself lost. I was trying to find my way back to her apartment.'

'Ah,' said the man. He lit a black cigarette with a match. Wraiths of cheap rough tobacco smoke drifted in the cold air. 'That's it then. You are one of our guests in the attic. I fear it will have been cold for you up there among the rafters.' He came down the step and held out his hand. 'I am Sandu Evgenich ter-Orenbergh Shirin-Vilichov Palffy and this is my house. You are welcome. Of course.'

Lom took the offered hand.

'Lom,' he said. 'Vissarion Yppolitovich Lom.'

Palffy made a slight, formal bow.

'You were taking a walk in the snow before breakfast, perhaps?' he said.

'I guess,' said Lom. 'You don't see snow much, where I come from. Just rain. Always rain.'

'Where is that? Where you are from?'

'East,' said Lom, gesturing vaguely. 'East. Way east. On the forest border. I doubt you've heard of it. A small town called Podchornok.'

'I believe I do know Podchornok, as it happens. Some cousins of mine had an estate in that country once.'

Lom grunted.

'Small world.'

'Not such a coincidence,' said the Count. 'I had cousins in every oblast of the Dominions once, but that was a lifetime ago. A different world. The people I'm talking about were at Vyra. They had a fine house. A good lake for pike. The place is gone, now, of course, alas.' He coughed and looked sourly at the cigarette in his hand. 'In those days, when I was a child and went to Vyra, the Vlast was more … what? Moderate? Sensible? Willing to overlook small independences, let us say, so long as they were far from their own front door and paid their taxes and didn't draw attention to themselves.'

'Vyra was the Vishniks' place,' said Lom.

'It was! Exactly so!' Palffy looked at him with a new interest. 'You *knew* them then?'

'I knew Raku. We were at school.'

'Raku?' Count Palffy frowned. Then he remembered. 'Of course! There *was* a Prince Raku. The Vishniks had a son, an only child. But that was long after my visit. We could not have met, Raku and I. So where is this Prince Raku now? What does he do with himself? Perhaps I might write to him. Families should keep up their connections, don't you think?'

'Raku died.'

'No!' said the Count. 'He couldn't have been more than thirty. Was he ill? What happened?'

'The militia happened.'

'Ah. How shit. How very shit.' Palffy dropped his cigarette on the step and crushed it out with the brass ferrule of his cane. Not an easy trick, but he speared it first shot. 'This is a heavy blow. But we should not be making ourselves sad on such a splendid morning, my friend. Come inside with me, Vissarion Lom, and have breakfast. The snow makes one hungry, don't you find?'

'Thanks,' said Lom. 'But I should be getting back— '

'Some coffee then. I have good coffee. Red beans from the Cloud Forest, roasted to my personal specification by Mandelbrot's in Klepsydra Lane. How does that sound to you?'

'I'd appreciate that,' said Lom. 'But not now. Maybe later.'

'I will hold you to that, Vissarion Yppolitovich. A bond of honour.'

Lom found Maroussia in Elena's kitchen, sitting on a stool against the warmth of the stove. She was wearing different clothes. She must have borrowed them from Elena: a plain grey woollen dress and a thick dark cardigan that was too big for her. She had the cardigan buttoned up to the neck, her fingers peeping from the cuffs. She gave him a quick wry smile when he came in, cold and fresh from outside, brushing the snow from his trousers. When the smile faded, her face was pale and drawn, but her eyes when they met his were bright with energy and fierce determination.

Elena was clearing breakfast off the table and the girls were laying out a backgammon board. The younger one, Yeva, was staring at Lom curiously.

'What's wrong with your head?' she said. 'There's a hole in it.'

Lom touched the wound on his forehead.

'Oh,' he said. 'Sorry.'

'What happened? Was it a bullet?'

'No.'

'There's a man at Vera's who was shot in the head by dragoons. He's not dead, but he doesn't talk and one of his eyes is gone. He dribbles his tea.'

'Be quiet, Yeva,' said Elena. 'Leave Vissarion in peace. And you can't start on a game now. There's no time. You need to go to school.'

'What? No!' said Galina. 'Not today. The snow. There's snow—'

'You're not missing school for a bit of snow. Kolya will take you in the cart. He'll be waiting already.'

'But—'

'Go. School. Now. He'll be waiting.'

'Nobody goes to school when there's snow. We'll be the only ones …'

'You're not missing school. That's not what we do. That's not who we are.'

Elena hustled the girls out of the kitchen. Lom sat at the table next to Maroussia.

'OK?' he said. 'You look tired.'

'I'm fine,' she said. 'I'm ready to go. Are you?'

'Go where?'

Elena came back into the kitchen and attacked the breakfast things in the sink.

'Elena?' said Maroussia.

'Yes?'

'I need to find out about the forest. Who is there in the raion that I can talk to about the forest?'

'The forest?'

'Yes.'

'Why? Why the forest?'

Maroussia brushed the question aside impatiently.

'This is important,' she said. 'I want to find someone who knows about the forest and what happens there. Someone who's actually been there.'

'Is this anything to do with the trouble you're in?' said Elena. 'No. Don't answer that. I don't want to know.'

'Is there someone?' said Maroussia again. 'Anyone who might be able to tell me something? Anything?'

Elena hesitated.

'I don't know,' she said. 'I don't think so. There was Teslom at the House on the Purfas. But he was arrested. And there's the Count – he used to travel once. But not any more. Not for a long time. And I don't know if he ever actually went into the forest himself.'

'Not the Count,' said Lom. 'I've run into him already. He's not the man, not for this.'

'Isn't there anyone else?' said Maroussia.

Well,' said Elena after a moment's thought, 'there is Kamilova. You could go and see her, I suppose. Eligiya Kamilova. She is a friend of mine, in a way. But ... well, she's not an easy person to talk to.'

'Kamilova?' said Maroussia. 'Who is she?'

Elena shrugged, as if she wasn't sure how to answer.

'No one knows much about her,' she said. 'She comes and goes. She goes into the forest, into the wild places under the trees. She brings back specimens for the Count's collection sometimes, but she's not easy—'

'I'll go and see her,' said Maroussia.

'I can't promise she'll even talk to you.'

'Where does she live? Is she here in the raion?'

'Yes,' said Elena. 'Down by the harbour.'

'I need to see her.'

'Now?' said Elena.

'Yes. Now.'

35

The Colloquium for the Protection of Citizens and the Vlast met at ten o'clock every morning, not in the Lodka but in a room in the Armoury, as befitted a War Cabinet. Chazia was there first, as she always was. Prepared. Colloquium Chairman Etsim Fohn and his sidekick, Fess Khazar, the Secretary of Finance, arrived together, five minutes late and already deep in conversation. Sharing a joke. Fohn surveyed the room. Saw the empty chair.

'Where is our General Secretary?' he said. 'Where is Dukhonin? I haven't seen him this morning. My office has been trying to raise him, but no one is answering at his house. He didn't come to … Well, never mind. Where is he? We need him here.' The three of them – Fohn, Dukhonin, Khazar – always met in Fohn's office before the formal Cabinet, to prepare their lines. To take the real decisions. Chazia was never invited. They thought she did not know.

'The Minister for Armaments will not be joining us,' she said. 'Steopan Vadimovich is dead.'

Khazar sat down at the end of the table, his face white as chalk. He looked at Fohn, to see what he would do. Fohn was glaring at Chazia.

'What?' said Fohn. 'When? Why wasn't I told? Why do you know this, Lavrentina, and I do not? I am the *Chairman*. I should have been informed. I should have been told immediately. You should have … I should have been the *first* …'

Chazia ignored him.

'There was an attack on his house last night,' she said. 'The Lezarye were responsible, there is no doubt of that. Dukhonin and all his household were hacked to death in their beds and the house ransacked.'

'Last night?' said Fohn. 'Last night! We should have been informed immediately. A member of the Colloquium assassinated, and the Chairman not even told? Who was in charge of Dukhonin's security? I want names. I want them punished. Heads on spikes. And an overhaul. A thorough review. Action this day and a report on my desk this afternoon.'

'Absolutely!' said Khazar. 'If Steopan Dukhonin can't sleep safe in his bed then who is safe? It might have been any of us! Internal dissidence is your responsibility, Lavrentina. I cannot understand—'

Chazia held up her hand for silence.

'As you rightly say, gentlemen, this is my area. I will be making a speech in the parade ground as soon as this meeting is over. I will be announcing new measures. We have tolerated the presence of the Lezarye in this city for too long. We cannot afford an enemy within. An enemy at our backs. The raion will be closed and cleared. The Lezarye will be transported to the east. Conscripted labour is needed there.'

'No,' said Fohn. 'This is too hasty. There will be trouble. They will resist.'

'I will deal with that,' said Chazia. 'Leave it to me.'

'No. We should have been consulted. I am—'

'We need to move on, gentlemen,' said Chazia. 'This is a War Cabinet and we have more urgent business. Time is short. When I was at Steopan Vadimovich's house last night, clearing up the mess, I learned a disturbing thing. The situation is worse than we thought.' She paused and looked each man in the face, one by one. 'We have all been kept in the dark.'

Khazar turned to Fohn.

'What's going on, Etsim?' he said. 'What is she talking about?'

Fohn said nothing. He was watching Chazia narrowly. He was a bureaucrat, but not entirely stupid. She would have to deal with him soon.

'The war situation is much more desperate than we have been led to believe,' she said. 'Dukhonin's desk was piled high with reports. Complaints. Telegrams. A catalogue of inadequacy and failure. The army has no munitions. The navy has no fuel. The armament manufacturers have no materials. We are hopelessly in debt to the finance houses of the Fransa, and the Treasury is within a week of bankruptcy. The front at Brazhd is crumbling. An Archipelago fleet has been sighted off the Aanen Islands.'

'The Aanens—!' Khazar began.

'The enemy,' said Chazia, 'will be at the outskirts of Mirgorod within days.'

Khazar slumped forward, his head in his hands.

'Then we are ruined and it is over,' he muttered. 'I knew! I always knew!'

Fohn ignored him. He was glaring at Chazia.

'Lies,' he said. 'These are lies. The Novozhd would never have—'

'The Novozhd knew,' said Chazia. 'Of course he knew. Why else did he start negotiations for peace? Dukhonin knew. The admirals and the generals knew. Every foot soldier in the infantry knew. Only we did not know. We have been playing a charade of government since the Novozhd was killed, but now we know. And now we must act.'

'What?' said Khazar. 'What can we do?'

'The current military command cannot be trusted and must be purged. The necessary action is already in hand.'

'This is happening *now*?' said Fohn.

'It began,' said Chazia, ' as soon as you entered this room.'

'On whose *orders*?'

'On mine. Your personal staffs are also being replaced. You have been misled and betrayed. I will give you more trustworthy people. I will arrange it myself. But our first priority is the defence of Mirgorod. The city must not be allowed to fall to the Archipelago. Dukhonin has made no adequate preparations. None at all. However, I have taken matters in hand now. I have appointed General Rizhin as the new City Defence Commissar. He will begin work immediately—'

'*Rizhin?*' said Khazar. 'Who is this *Rizhin*? Fohn? I don't know the name. Do we know this man Rizhin?'

Fohn was on his feet, red-faced and trembling. His chair tipped backwards and crashed to the floor behind him.

'This is a *coup*!' he shouted. 'A filthy fucking *putsch*! I'm not going to—'

Chazia pressed the intercom buzzer. The door opened and Captain Iliodor entered the room, followed by three armed militia officers. They took up positions inside the door.

'Arrest this woman,' said Fohn. 'Arrest her now.'

The militia officers ignored him.

'Sit down, Chairman,' said Chazia. 'Please, Etsim Maximich, my friend. Sit.'

'So this is how it is,' said Fohn. 'You're mad. You can't sustain it. You have no strength. The people will not allow it. The army will stand behind me. I'll have you dragged through the streets.'

'Calm yourself, Etsim. Please. Of course this is not a coup. You are overwrought. This is shocking news, I know. I understand your feelings. I felt the same way myself last night. You will recover soon, and see things clearly again. You are my colleague, Etsim, my valued friend and my Chairman. We continue as before. Of course we do. I have made a plan. You and Secretary Khazar will leave Mirgorod immediately. It is too dangerous for you to remain here. The enemy is at the gate. You will go east, to Kholvatogorsk, and establish our new capital there. The Vlast continues. A new Vlast. A Vlast reborn. It will not matter then whether Mirgorod falls or not. The Vlast is more than one single city. Go to Kholvatogorsk and build anew. Prepare to strike back at our enemies. I will join you there shortly. I have somewhere else I must go first. '

36

Lom and Maroussia stepped out of Count Palffy's house into snow-bright cold.

'Eligiya Kamilova lives in a wooden house on the fish wharf,' Elena had said. 'You need to climb the Ship Bastion and take the covered steps down to the harbour.'

The Ship Bastion was a massive granite outcrop, the highest point in the raion, the highest in Mirgorod. Street sweepers were out – giants shovelling snow with easy strength – and some people were clearing the paths outside their houses and shops, but it was hard climbing. They had to pick their way across rutted, compacted stretches of ice and wade knee-deep through heaps and drifts of snow.

There was a small cobbled square at the top of the Bastion rock, with a parapet where you could lean and catch your breath. Below them, the canyons and ravines of the raion fell way in a tumble of steep roofs, stepped gables, leaning pinnacles and slumping chimneys; and beyond lay the expansive, grey, snow-dusted, smoking vista of Mirgorod. The city roared quietly under the wheeling of the gulls. In the distance the thousand-foot-high needle-sharp spire of the Armoury, the One Column On Spilled Blood, speared the belly of the sky. The Lodka was a massive squat black prow, and the steel ribbon of the Mir rolled westwards, crossed by a dozen bridges, towards the skyline smudge of the sea.

In the far corner of the Bastion Square was a wooden door set in a pointed arch of weathered grey stone.

'That must be the way,' said Maroussia. 'Down there.'

The door in the arch opened onto a steep winding flight of stone steps enclosed by wooden walls and a wooden roof. The stairway was in shadow, lit only by narrow slits cut at intervals in the wood, and the treads were worn smooth and hollow in the centre by centuries of footfall. It smelled cool and damp, like the mouth of a well. The steps wound and switchbacked steeply down. Hundreds of steps. Several times they had to stop and press themselves back against the wall to make room for someone coming up.

They came out into a huddle of warehouses, wharves and jetties. Boats crowded against the harbour edge, idle under a covering of snow. The River Purfas was a pale green porridge of slush and fragments of ice. Rigging clattered in the brisk river breeze. Nets were draped, black and reeking, from the weather-bleached warehouse walls, and the smell from gibbeted racks of drying fish and smokehouses hung heavy on the air. Yellow-eyed seabirds called from canted masts and rooftops, swooped on scraps and stalked the walkways, poking at the chum-buckets. Chalk-boards at the wharfside fish market promised eel and crab, flounder, zander, garfish, herring, bream and cod. But fishing was done for the winter. Harder times were coming. The market trays were empty, the sawdust swept and the shutters up. Men hung about, smoking, talking quietly in the throaty, fricative languages of the raion.

Lom and Maroussia picked their way between stacked baskets, salt barrels and coils of rope. They found the tall narrow building where Kamilova lived at the far end of the wharf, squeezed between a chandlery and a smokehouse. A frontage of overlapping timbers of tar-black pine and dark lopsided windows with many panes of thick green glass. Maroussia knocked. Lom pulled his woollen cap lower over his forehead.

The woman who opened the door must have been sixty years old, but she was tall and straight and wiry-muscular, with a traveller's sparse, defined, weathered face. Iron-grey hair, tied severely back. Bright pale intelligent eyes. She was wearing a knitted sweater, dark canvas trousers, boots.

'Eligiya Kamilova?' said Maroussia.

'Yes? Who are you?'

'My name is Maroussia Shaumian.'

'Shaumian?' Kamilova studied her with narrowed eyes. 'I see. *Shaumian*.'

'Can we come in? We want to talk to you. We want to ask you about the forest. I think you can help me—'

'No,' said Kamilova. 'I can't help you.'

She began to close the door. Lom stepped forward and leaned against it.

'We need to talk to you,' he said.

Kamilova looked at him steadily.

'You,' she said, 'should get off my door.'

'We just want to come in for a while,' said Lom. 'To talk. That's all.'

'I said get away from my door.'

Kamilova's eyes widened. There was a strangeness there. Wild distant spaces. Lom felt the air stirring. Responsive. Forest smells. Resin and earth. And suddenly the air around him was no longer stuff to breathe, it was his enemy. Heavy in his lungs, hard and cold about him. A stone fist of air punched him in the back of the head, sickening, dizzying, and he stumbled forward. The weight of solid air on his shoulders and back pressed down on him. All the mile-high heaviness of the air. Forcing him to his knees. A sudden wind whipped the snow from the ground. It smacked and scraped at his face, a bitter freezing hail, blinding him. He could hear Maroussia somewhere far away, shouting, but the wind destroyed her words. Panicking, he struggled for breath. He could not fill his lungs. He was drowning in the hostile air.

But he did not drown. There was a sentience in the air. It was alive and knew what it was doing. And he knew what it was.

Lom reached out towards it. Opening himself. Taking the barriers down. Not breathing in but breathing out. Remembering.

He was in the centre of a small hardened whorl of fierceness, but beyond it were oceans of atmosphere. Eddies and tides and deeps, layer over layer, air from the forest, air from the river, air from the sea, freighted with life and scent and the stories of themselves. He climbed higher. The air grew thinner, colder, clearer, more beautiful, bright and electric the higher he climbed. He opened himself to it. He was air himself, air in the air. The squalls that battered him were part of him and he was in them. He let them pass through where he was. He rose and stood and waited patiently for the assault to calm and stop.

Kamilova was looking at him with surprise and frank curiosity. And something else. Lom could not tell what it was. It might have been recognition.

'Who are you?' she said.

Lom tried to answer but found he could not. Not yet. His heart was hammering. He needed all the capacity of his aching lungs to breathe, tearing mouthfuls of breath out of the sparse, thinned air.

'Who is he?' Kamilova said to Maroussia. Urgently. 'Who is this man?'

'This is my friend. His name is Vissarion.'

Kamilova frowned.

'No,' she said. 'No. Not Vissarion. That's not a forest name. He's strong, but I didn't know him. He carries himself like a bear, but something's not right.'

'Can't we just …' Lom breathed painfully. His whole body felt bruised and abused. 'Can't we just come in?'

37

Look to the south of Mirgorod and see hundreds of miles of frontierless grass. Sandy soil. Marshes and small lakes, slow yellow rivers, thorn thickets and sparse scatterings of birch. Collectivised farms of drab herds, two-strand fences, cabbages and potato fields. Hapless towns, dirt roads and one-platform railway halts. A long indeterminate coastline of gravel and mud. A country without features.

Across this country war is coming.

Onward the enemy's armies churn, at the pace of markers being moved across a map in an operations room, at the speed of terse conversations on field telephones, converging on Mirgorod, capital of the Vlast. The armies of the enemy find the opposition melting away.

It is a matter of machine logistics now. Statistics and arithmetics of steel. A calculation of armoured divisions. The sound is the sound of diesel engines droning and the clatter of iron tracks, the rattle of ammunition belts, the thunder-crash of heavy guns. The smell is the smell of hot oil and hot metal, the burning of rubber, the hot piss the gunners use to cool their overworked weapons. The light is the light of arcing sprays of burning gasoline, the flicker of rocket batteries firing, the daytime darkness of shadows under smoke-filled air. Not in one place, but in a hundred places: five separate fronts, all rolling forward, thirty or forty miles a day, converging on Mirgorod.

In rain-sodden fields and bypassed towns, people stand mute and look on as the logarithms of steel, too intent on the future to notice them, surge by. Seventy-ton tanks chew up the ground. The pale faces of motorised infantry stare back at the watchers without expression from the back of armoured half-tracks. Under the watchers' feet the earth trembles. The deep geologies of history are upheaving. The maps by which they have always lived are being torn up and trodden into the mud. The old certainties are dissolving like bones in an acid bath.

The ones who look on are not even frightened yet.

And over their heads the featureless sky is marked out with the high patchwork geometries of aircraft formations sliding north towards Mirgorod.

38

Lom followed Maroussia and Eligiya Kamilova up the staircase to Kamilova's room. It was a wide, airy, almost empty space at the top of the house: the scent of woodsmoke and damp earth mixed with the harbour reek. Thick leaded panes filtered the morning light, and harbour sounds drifted in through an open casement. The room was austere, like the woman herself. Stripped back. Only what was essential. Bare floorboards darkened with age. A large rug spread in the centre, leather cushions and bolsters ranged around the edge. A pair of low, carved stools.

A small fire was burning in the corner, logs stacked neatly nearby: the logs looked like they'd spent time in the sea. A bleached animal skull rested on the floor near the hearth. It was big like an elk but broad-browed and feline, with front-facing eye sockets and a pair of long curved incisors. A hunting beast. It was enormous. Colossal.

Kamilova brought them tea in china cups. It was made from forest leaves, muddy and bitter. She folded herself neatly onto a cushion. Maroussia sat near her and Lom squatted awkwardly on one of the stools, facing her across the rug.

'So?' said Kamilova. 'Why come to me?'

'My friend Elena Cornelius told me you've made journeys in the forest. I hoped … maybe you might talk to us. You might know something that could help us. Help me.'

'Elena Cornelius?' said Kamilova. 'You should have said. But … help you with what?'

Lom watched Maroussia hesitate. Take a deep breath. Make a decision.

'There was a paluba,' she said. 'It was looking for me and it found me. It showed me things. The forest. A terrible living angel, and the damage it was doing. The paluba wanted me to find something. The Pollandore. Do you—?'

'*Air-daughter made a new world,*' said Kamilova, '*to displace the old one from within. World in the forest, forest in the world. What makes you look, and what you find. The wound, and what made the wound.*'

'That's it!' said Maroussia. 'That's what my mother used to say. I haven't heard that for years. Yes. And the Pollandore is—'

'A story. A riddle game. A children's tale. I have heard others.'

'No,' said Maroussia. 'It's real.' She reached inside her coat and brought out the bundle of Vishnik's photographs. Handed them across to Kamilova. 'Here it is. Here is the proof.'

Kamilova looked at the pictures one by one, carefully. Moments in the city, times and places opened up like sunlight in a rain-dark sky, like berries bursting.

'And this,' she said at last, 'you think this is the Pollandore?'

'No, it's what the Pollandore is *doing*,' said Maroussia. 'Here in Mirgorod. It's active. It's leaking or something. I don't know. I've felt it myself. I've *seen* these things. It's waking up. The Pollandore itself is a *thing*. It's an *object* in a *place*. The paluba ... she told me to find it. She wants me to open it.'

'Open it like a box, or open it like a door?'

'I don't know.'

'To let something out, or for you to go in?'

'I don't *know*!'

'But you're going to do it?'

'Yes. If I can.'

'Why?'

'Because of the angel. The paluba showed me—'

'The paluba,' said Kamilova, 'showed you nothing. The paluba was a vehicle, nothing more. The speaker but not the voice.' She paused, watching Maroussia closely. Studying her. 'So,' she said at last. 'You want me to tell you about the forest?'

'Yes,' said Maroussia. 'Please. Just ... just talk to us.'

Kamilova pulled back her sleeves and held out her arms. They were thin, muscular and berry-brown. Intricate knotted patterns wound across her skin, reaching down towards her wrists, drawn in faded purple and green. Like roots. Like veins. Filaments. Growth.

'Yes,' she said. 'I've been into the forest. I've taken my boat up the rivers. I've travelled with fur traders and shamans and women with spirit skins. I've lived with giants and lake people. I've slept with them and hunted with them and some of them showed me … they showed me things. They taught me, and I listened. I learned. I'm talking about the deep forest now. Deep in under the trees.' She looked at Lom. 'He knows what I mean.'

'No,' said Lom. 'I don't.'

Kamilova made a crude derisive gesture and spat into the fire. Lom had seen traders on the Yannis do the same thing when offered an insulting price. She turned away from him, back to Maroussia.

'What you need to understand about the forest,' Kamilova continued, 'is this: there is no end to it, and no certain paths. It is not *a* forest, it is all forests. It contains all forests. Woods within woods, forests within forests, further in and further back, deeper and deeper for ever. Anything that *could* be in the forest *is* there. Anything you have ever heard about the forest – any forest – it is all there, somewhere. The Vlast is nothing, the world is nothing, compared to the forest.' She paused. 'And the point is, most of what lives in the forest has no interest in the human world at all. The forest has its own purposes. Not everything that comes out of the forest can be trusted.'

'You think the paluba lied to me?' said Maroussia.

'I think that, whoever was using it, they have purposes of their own, of which you are a part. Palubas speak to you like dreams. They draw things out of your mind, use images and ideas they find there, change them, put thoughts to you in ways that you can understand and believe.'

'But that's the point. I *don't* understand'

'You're doing what it needs you to do.'

'But the Pollandore is real,' said Maroussia. 'It's here. It's near. I've seen what it can do. It can make a difference. It can make things … *change*. And I know where it is, only it will be hard to get to. And I am going to reach it.'

'Why?' said Kamilova. 'I ask you this again. Why?'

'Because …' said Maroussia. She frowned. Hesitated. 'Because there's a terrible hole in the centre of everything. It's like a mouth, a gaping mouth that swallows up life and spews out shadow and cruelty and sadness. Not just for me, for everyone. There's this *gap*, this awful *gap* that you feel all the time, between how things are and how they could be. There's something really close to me, almost in the same place as I am, and it's my life, my real life as it's meant to be, only I'm not living it because I'm here instead. '

Maroussia was leaning forward, back straight, dark eyes fixed on the fire in Kamilova's grate. She was fierce and hurting and determined. Lom watched her intently.

'Do you understand?' she said urgently to Kamilova. 'Do you know what I mean?'

'Yes,' said Kamilova. 'Yes. I do.'

'I will reach the Pollandore,' said Maroussia. 'I know where it is. But I don't know what to do when I get there. The paluba said there was a key. Not a key, but something like it. It thought I already had it. It thought I knew more ... but I don't.'

Kamilova stood up.

'Come with me,' she said. 'I will show you something.'

The boathouse was a few yards down from Kamilova's building. She let Lom and Maroussia in through a small wicket in a larger door.

'This is my boat,' she said. '*Heron*.' It was under a tarpaulin, a varnished clinker hull. The rest of the space in the boathouse was filled with a clutter of bundles and stacked boxes. A canoe hung suspended from the ceiling, skins on a wooden frame. 'This is where I keep my collection. Things I've brought back from the forest.'

It was impossible to make out much in the shadows. There were carvings on the wall. Crude wooden masks. Bottles and boxes on shelves. Lom felt something stirring. Hunting animals with rain-wet fur. Leaf mould and shadow under trees. Watchfulness. Life. He was in an open space among the trees. Fern and briar and clumps of thorn. Earth and rain. A small stream, barely trickling its way over silted accidental dams of mud and stone and banked-up branches and leaves. A beech fallen in a pool of green water. Rain-mist erasing the further slopes and hillsides. He was young, and something was watching him, a bad dark thing, and he was frightened.

Kamilova disappeared into the back of the boathouse and came back holding something small cupped in her hand. A loosely knotted ball of twigs and dried leaves stuck with gobbets of wax-like stuff, dried brown and brittle. Dull, desiccated berries. The bones and fur-scraps of small animals. She held it out to Maroussia.

'Have you seen one of these before?' she said.

Maroussia took it and turned it over in her hand. Held it up to her face and breathed the scent.

'Yes,' she said. 'My mother had them all over the house. She said the forest brought them to her. But she … she was weak and frightened all the time. She was terrified of trees in the street. She said they waited for her and watched and followed her. She wasn't … well.'

'This is what the volvas, the wise women, call a solm, or a khlahv, or a bo. Sometimes they call them keys. It's a vessel for air. It can hold and carry a breath, and the breath is the message. The voice. That one in your hand is empty now. Old and dead.'

Maroussia handed the object back.

'What my mother had, they were *messages*?' she said. 'About the Pollandore?'

'About it. Or for it.'

'But they're all gone now,' said Maroussia. 'They're all lost. Or destroyed.' She paused. 'No, wait. Mother used to hide them sometimes in the apartment. Vissarion, we have to go back there. We have to go back and look.'

'No,' said Lom. He brought out from his pocket the bloodstained hessian bag he'd taken from her mother's body in the street by Vanko's. The survivor. It felt alive in his hand. Quiet and watchful. Breathing. 'I've still got this.'

Maroussia snatched it from him and opened it. Brought out the knot of twigs and forest stuff. Held it up to her face. Her hands were trembling slightly. But nothing happened. Nothing came.

'Is it still good?' she said to Kamilova. 'Is it OK?'

'I think so. Yes.'

'But … what do I do with it?' Maroussia held it out to her. 'Can you tell me?'

Kamilova shook her head.

'Not if it's meant for you.'

'But I don't know how … There's nothing. Nothing's happening.'

'You have to learn that for yourself. You have to listen. Keep it with you. Hold it. Breathe it. Pay attention. Don't push it. It's all about openness. Wakefulness. Give it time.'

'Time?' said Maroussia. 'There is no time. Time is what we haven't got.'

Kamilova kissed Maroussia on the mouth when they left.

39

Maroussia said nothing when they emerged from Eligiya Kamilova's boathouse. They walked in silence along the harbour edge and began the ascent back up towards the Ship Bastion.

Lom kept pace alongside Maroussia. Leaving her space. Letting her think. He wasn't sure, himself, what they had learned from Kamilova. In Kamilova's presence he'd felt the forest, its realness and closeness, its watchfulness, its urgency. But ... perhaps there wasn't anything else to know. Perhaps it wasn't about learning, but doing. The Pollandore was in the Lodka, right in the cruel stone centre of the Vlast. Bring Maroussia to the Pollandore and ... it would happen. *Something* would happen. Trying to learn, trying to explore, trying to figure out what she had to do when the moment came and what it might mean: that was nothing, only passing time. An avoidance strategy. A rationalisation of fear. The task was simpler than that.

Maroussia stopped and turned to face him.

'What Kamilova said ...' she began. 'About the people who sent the paluba having a purpose of their own, that I couldn't know ...' She paused. 'It doesn't matter, does it? None of that matters. The angel in the forest is real. The Pollandore is real. The rest of it doesn't matter. There are only two sides, and everyone has to choose. I'm not trusting the paluba, I'm trusting *myself*. It's about feeling and instinct and knowing what to do, when the time comes.'

'Yes,' said Lom. 'I guess that's right.'

'We have to get into the Lodka and find the Pollandore. What happens after that ... that's something else. We just have to get there.'

You can't just walk into the Lodka, thought Lom, but he said nothing. That was his problem, not hers. Getting her inside, that was his job. What happened afterwards would be up to her.

Consider the question in its widest aspect.

The Lodka: it was where the Pollandore was, and it was where Chazia was. And *Josef Kantor*. The Lodka was the last place Lom had seen Kantor. Kantor was more than a terrorist. Much more. Lom didn't fully understand Kantor's connections with Chazia and the Lodka, but he knew that Kantor was deeply and intricately meshed in it all. That made Kantor a way in. So. *Find Kantor*. It was back to that.

They climbed back up the winding covered steps to the Ship Bastion and emerged into winter light. The sky was pale powder-blue, airy and vertiginous, wisped with sparse cloud-feather, achingly elsewhere, achingly high. They leaned on the parapet and looked out across the city. Mirgorod, spreading out towards the horizon under an immensity of height and air, seemed almost small. A humane settlement. Containable. A place where people lived. The winter sun, already westering, burned with a blinding whiteness that gave no heat. There was something wrong. A buzzing in the air, an edgy vibration, like unseen engines racing. Too quiet and distant to be a sound, you heard it with your skin, your teeth, the bones of your skull.

'Look,' said Maroussia 'Look.'

She was squinting towards the sun.

Lom looked but saw nothing. The sun was cold and dazzling. When he shut his eyes against it, colour-shifting after-images and shadow-filaments floated across the blood-warmth inside. When he looked again, some of the specks were still there. Strings of dots across the sun in wavering horizontal lines. Faint punctuation.

Others had stopped to watch them. Nobody spoke.

More and more rows of specks resolved out of the sun. Coming into focus. Dozens. Scores. Hundreds. Coming in pulses. Waves. Formations.

The noise escalated to a thundering, rattling roar, not from the west where Lom was looking but from behind. He jerked his head round. The aircraft was low and descending and coming straight for them. It was immense. Three fat-bellied fuselages hung from wide, thick wings. Each wing carried eight – no, *ten* – propellers. The fuselages were as large as ships. The bomber was so big it seemed to be suspended in the sky, an impossible motionless thing. It was descending slowly straight down onto them, onto the rock hill on which they stood. It was going to crash.

At the last moment the plane lifted its nose fractionally and roared slowly overhead. They saw its swollen triple bellies of unpainted metal. Lettering on the underside of its wings. The insignia of the Archipelago. It was low enough to see faces looking down from its windows as it trundled over them and sailed out across the city, its engine noise climbing to a roar beyond hearing, its array of speed-blurred propellers chopping and grinding the air.

A trail of insignificant silver shapes spilled from its triple belly mouths.

A pause. A suspended moment. Maroussia's hand was gripping Lom's arm so tight it hurt.

The bombs splashed into the upturned face of the city and flowered into small blossoms of flame and smoke puffs.

And then came the sound.

The world lurched sickeningly and Lom's stomach with it. A new door had opened and everything was utterly changed.

Wave after wave of huge triple-fuselaged bombers unloaded their cargoes. The engines roared relentlessly and the detonation-thuds burst in short fast shattering series. Fat columns of black oily smoke rose everywhere and drifted in low, thickening banks. The smell of it reached them: an industrial smell, like engine sheds and factories. Hot metal and soot.

Higher in the sky, smaller wasp-like aircraft circled, buzzed and droned, drawing tracks and spirals of vapour trail.

'Which ones are ours?' said Maroussia. 'Can you tell?'

'None,' said Lom. 'None at all.'

Twenty thousand pounds of high explosive per minute, minute after minute after minute, spilled out of the sky in sticks and skeins of bombs. Whistling formations of aerodynamic tubular steel casing. A spattering rain of incendiary parcels. When their bays were empty, the heavy bomber squadrons swept round again for a fresh approach. They lumbered in low. Autocannons in fishbowl noses and underbelly gun-pods punched out 50mm phosphorus shells at thirty rounds per minute. The disciplined, practised attacks concentrated on the wharfs and harbour yards to the west of Mirgorod and the steelworks and factories to the south, but the seeds of destruction and burn were scattered widely.

A stick of two-thousand-pound bombs splashed across Levrovskaya Square: three crashed through the roof of the Hotel Sviatopolk and erupted inside, two more hit in the square itself. Shockwaves swept through the Teagarden, smashing rubble and fragments of traffic and restaurants and people through the citizens taking tea. The blast buckled the heavy bronze doors of the Bank of Foreign Commerce and shattered the plate windows of Rosenfeld's, blowing a hurricane of tiny glittering blades through customers and staff. Lacerating the polished mahogany panels and counters.

A five-thousand-pound barrel of explosive demolished the Ter-Uspenskovo Bridge. The river erupted, drenching the Square of the Piteous Angel and leaving the riverbed temporarily naked. The shock waves rocked the Lodka: glass and stone from its high roof-dome crashed down on the readers in the hall of the Central Registry and the great wheel of the Gaukh Engine canted six inches sideways, its motors seized up and screeching.

Incendiary clusters set the roofs of the Laughing Cockerel Theatre and the Dreksler-Kino burning.

Vanko's Uniform Factory was a crater of rubble and dust.

Mirgorod, city burning.

Fire-flakes licked at blistering paint and smouldering furniture and blew from house to house and street to street on gusting breezes of fire. Fire-clusters spread and merged and sucked in streams of air. Roads became channels for fire-feeding streams of air, hurricane inflows that reached the burning centre and columned up, high swaying pillars of uproarious flame. The walls of high buildings burning within toppled forward and came crashing down in billowing skirts of dust and flying brick and glass.

Rusalkas screamed and giants stumbled in the streets with burning hair. People saw other people hurt and die. Hurt and died themselves.

The warehouses and shipyards of the Ring Wharf burned. The timber yards and oil storage tanks and coal mountains burned. The bales and barrels and pallets in the lading sheds burned. The fires of the Ring Wharf roared like storms of wind and merged into one great fire, half a mile across: one bright shivering dome of burning under a thin canopy of smoke. The smoke-shell glowed from within as if it was itself on fire. Wavering curtains of orange-red flame opened and closed across the blinding heart of outrageous glare. Firefighters, walled off from the central blaze by bastions of heat, scrabbled at the outer edges of the Ring Wharf fire. They sucked water from the canals and harbour basins and pumped it in feeble arcs of spray that turned to steam on the air. If they got too close, their clothes and hair caught fire.

Josef Kantor, his own room gone, stands among the firefighters at the Ring Wharf, warming himself in the glow of the dockyards burning. Sweat greases his face. His skin is smeared with soot-smuts. He watches the thick column of oil-black smoke rising mile-high into the sky. A signal fire to the future. Heat and shadow flicker across his face, and the voice of Archangel whispers in his ear. Archangel has learned to whisper now.

40

Walking in silence, weighted with a heavy, sick emptiness, Lom and Maroussia saw almost no one as they made their way back from the Ship Bastion to Elena Cornelius's house after the bombing raid on the city. The raion had closed its shops and shut its doors and gone indoors. Belated air-raid warning sirens wailed in the distance. In the sky anti-aircraft shells were bursting, too high and too few and too late. The attackers had drifted away. Blue and yellow-brown smoke-streaks smudged the sky. Smuts drifted down and settled on the snow. The smell clung to their clothes: the faint, sickening smell of the city frying.

Elena met them in the hallway. The girls were with her.

'There's to be an announcement on the radio,' she said. 'We're going up to the Count's room to listen. Come with us.'

The Count opened the door. He had a newspaper in his hand.

'Ah, Elena!' He waved the paper at her. 'These are terrible times. Fohn is to speak at four. And did you hear? Dukhonin is dead. He was killed. An attack on his home. Terrorists. Assassins. *We* are blamed of course. *We* are behind it, apparently. This is very bad. But Vissarion Yppolitovich is with you! Marvellous. Come in, my friend. Come in.' He noticed Maroussia standing behind them. 'Ah, and you, you are Elena's friend and Vissarion's friend, and now our friend also.' He started towards her, holding out his hand.

'This is Maroussia, Sandu,' said Elena. 'Maroussia Shaumian.'

The Count stopped mid-stride.

'Shaumian? There is a *Shaumian* in my house? And nobody told me?' He took Maroussia's hand in both of his, his eyes devouring her face. 'Elena! How could you not tell me?'

Maroussia was looking at him in alarm.

'I'm sorry,' she said. 'I don't—'

The Count turned and shouted over his shoulder into the apartment, 'Ilinca! Ilinca! Say you do not believe this! A Shaumian is here! Feiga-Ita's daughter is come to our house!' He turned back to Maroussia. Took her by the hand like a child. 'Come in. Come in. Enter.' His face was pink with pleasure and excitement.

Count Palffy ushered them all through into the Morning Room. That was what he called it, though no doubt it was the afternoon and evening room as well. French windows with white louvred shutters gave a fine view over the snow-loaded lilacs in the garden, and there was a handle to crank down the awnings for summer afternoons in the sun. There were bears' heads and antlers on the walls and animal skins on the floor, no longer glossy, abraded by moth. The fine chairs and sofas still retained a few strands of their original fabric.

Ilinca came in with a tray of tea in glasses. A jug of lemonade for the girls. Ilinca was small and dumpy. She swished and shuffled noisily across the parquet in a tight skirt of funereal bombazine that reached the floor. She had forgotten to change out of her green house slippers, but her hair was pinned up and she wore a small, defiant turquoise brooch pinned on her chest. *Let enemies come*, it said. *We are aristocrats of proud and ancient family. We have survived and will survive again.*

A radio was set up on a table in the middle of the room. A fine old Piagin Silvertone in a highly polished wooden case. The tuning dial was illuminated. An orchestra was playing the 'Hero March' from *Ariadna Triumphs,* the volume turned low.

Palffy made the introductions.

'You *see*, Ilinca!' he said. 'Of *course* she is a Shaumian. Of course. No doubt of it. She has the look. She is Feiga-Ita come back to us, and here in my house! And I might never have known. Oh Elena! I might have missed her.'

'Did you know my mother?' said Maroussia. 'I'm sorry. She never talked about her friends in the raion. We never came here.'

'Know her?' said the Count. 'Of course we knew her!'

'Many years ago,' said Ilinca. 'She would have been the age you are now, perhaps, or younger. Then she married that hothead Kantor boy, and when he was sent to Vig she went with him. She came back of course, but not here, not back among her friends here in the raion.'

'A disaster!' said the Count. 'A catastrophe for Lezarye. We should not have left her so. We should have gone to her. We should have reached out. Insisted. I am ashamed. For myself and for all of us, I am ashamed.'

'And then ...' said Ilinca. 'We heard she was killed.'

'Yes,' said Maroussia. 'She was.'

'I am so sorry,' said Ilinca. 'So sorry.'

'But this is a *gift*,' said the Count. 'Your coming here now, it is a *sign*. The times darken, but opportunity comes.'

Maroussia frowned. 'I'm sorry,' she said. 'I don't—'

'Sandu!' said Ilinca. 'Leave the poor girl alone. Come and sit with me, Maroussia. Let's have tea. It is almost time for the broadcast.'

'But Vissarion Yppolitovich must have coffee!' said the Count. 'I promised him some of my coffee!'

'Tea's fine,' said Lom.

'Coffee,' said the Count. 'I will have some also. Ilinca, stay here. Talk to our guests.' He hustled out to fetch it.

Lom left Maroussia and Elena with the Countess Ilinca and wandered across to the window. Columns of thick black smoke on the skyline. A sudden dizzy unreality obscured his view of the raion. Could it really be that the war had come to Mirgorod? For a decade, for most of his adult life, war had been distant. Elsewhere. The Vlast at war was a permanent condition, the symptoms of which were glimpses of veterans and conscripts on the streets and accounts in newspapers of campaigns and salients across a geography that existed only on maps. War was background noise: you knew it was there, but only if you listened for it. Most of the time, unnoticed, it affected the taste and tone of things. Somewhere beneath consciousness it grew like a slow tumour and stained the world, an unease, a discomfort, but ignorable, and you carried on from day to day as if it was not there. Until, suddenly, between moment and moment, like a fist in the face, like a train crash in the night, bombs fell out of the sky. Buildings fell and burned. Everything changed.

Lom turned away from the window. Not wanting to join the murmuring conversation around the tea things, he prowled the room restlessly. It was a museum. There was a Kurzweiler baby grand piano in the corner. Its lid was down and crowded with framed photographs of officers in shakos and pelisses, guests at balls and shooting parties, a boy who might have been the young Count Palffy in a carriage. On the sideboard there was a rack of smoking-pipes on display and a collection of silver cigarette cases, all engraved with coats of arms and monograms. Lom drifted across to the bookcase. It was filled with directories, almanacs, bound volumes of the poets of the Silver Age. He picked one out. The pages were drilled through by insects.

But the coffee when it came was everything Count Palffy said it would be. Hot and bitter and strong, in a fine blue china mug. And sugar, dark brown and sticky in a matching lidded bowl. The mug was identical to one he'd seen Raku Vishnik drink from in his apartment. Before he was dead. It seemed a lifetime ago: another world, where Raku Vishnik was not dead and war had not come.

Time in Mirgorod, Lom realised, would for ever now be counted by the coming of war. *Ah, that was before the war*, people in the city would say, and, *Since the war . . .* If there *was* an *after the war*. That was a new thought, possible only now. Nothing endured for ever. Not even Mirgorod. Not even the Vlast. Past and future were dissolving out of the city, leaving only a raw and shocking perpetual now. Ever since he had come to Mirgorod, Lom had felt the presence of other possibilities, other futures, drifting in the alleys: hints and glimpses, scraps of mist and half-heard voices. But now, he felt, all that was suddenly burned away, bleached out in a shocking sunburst glare. Everything was old and everything was new. It was vertiginous and horrifying. It was – he realised with a start of surprise – *exciting*. It was a *promise*. The vicious promise of war. The clock and the calendar reset to zero. *Everything begins again, thought* Lom. *Everything starts here.*

The Count offered him a cigarette.

'No,' said Lom. 'No thanks.'

'Well, I will smoke,' said the Count. 'Permit me.' He took Lom by the elbow and steered him across the room. 'Let us men stand over here with our coffee and our talk, and I will smoke. Ilinca disapproves, you see.' He lit a cigarette and inhaled it deeply, with satisfaction.

Count Palffy talked and Lom let him. Beneath the surface politesse, Palffy was agitated. Over-animated. Rambling. He talked without direction of neighbours in the raion and other people he had known in other places long ago. Balls and duels and amours. He pointed to photographs on the walls.

'Ah. Yes. Now that is Amah. The Graefin Blegvad. Eight thousand acres in the Konopy Hills. Her great-grandfather was ambassador to the Feuilleton Court of Oaks. Did you know, the wolf's head in their crest was awarded for some hunting exploit or other with the Bazharev Ride? She married a Tsyprian. He was the Archduke's second when he duelled with the Mameluke and he was wounded himself, in the leg. An idiot, of course, but he had the most comfortable kastely in all of the south Hertzbergen. Part of the Detlevsk oblast now, more's the pity. A military college. Such a waste.'

Count Palffy talked on. His world had gone fifty, a hundred years ago, but the Count was in it still, despite, or perhaps because of, the fact that the city around them was burning and war had come. Lom, only half-listening, found they had somehow moved on to lepidoptery.

'I'm something of a collector,' the Count was saying. He led Lom over to examine display cases mounted on the walls. Moths and butterflies and beetles, some drab, some gaudy, some as large as Lom's palm, others so small you could hardly see them. All labelled in a clear and careful hand. 'My specialism is winter moths. Ice moths. Strategies for surviving the deep winter cold. It's a fascinating area. You know about this, perhaps?'

'I've never thought about it. I assumed they laid their eggs and then they died.'

'That is the common strategy, Vissarion Yppolitovich, of course. But there are some – like this one, you see, this shoddy-looking fellow here, this Faded Birchmoth – now, he survives the winter by allowing himself to become frozen solid. But only externally. He prepares himself for the temperature drop by excreting all the water in his body. His internal fluids become extremely concentrated. They resist freezing inside. You see the brilliance of this? Dead on the outside, alive within. He endures! He can survive temperatures as low as minus forty. More. And for months at a time. His wings blacken and drop off, of course. But he grows fresh wings in the spring.'

'We're not talking only about moths here, are we?' said Lom.

The Count looked at him sharply.

'Of course not, man.'

'Sandu!' Ilinca called from the other side of the room. 'The radio. It's starting.'

The clock on the mantelpiece showed seven minutes past four. It was growing darker outside, though the curtains were not yet drawn. Early winter twilight. Palffy went across to turn the volume knob higher.

'Citizens of Mirgorod! Prepare yourselves for an important announcement!'

'Ah!' he said. 'Now we have it.'

'Citizens,' Fohn's unfamiliar voice began. 'Comrades. Friends. The Great Patriotic War has come to our city.' He started to speak of fronts and salients. Unexpected advances. The fall of southern cities. The sinking of ships. He spoke hesitantly. He sounded out of breath, baffled and hurt. Lom struggled to follow what he was saying. And then, suddenly and it seemed too soon, he was finishing. 'This afternoon I have given our commanders new orders. The enemy's air force is to be smashed. Their armies annihilated. We will defend our beloved city. General Rizhin will lead the counter-attack. Our cause is good. We are ratified by the angels. The enemy will be defeated all along the line and victory will be ours.'

The orchestra started up again with a crash of brass and drums. The Count snorted in disgust and switched the radio off.

'Well!' he said. 'So there we have it! There we have nothing at all! Who is this General Rizhin. We have heard nothing of him till now. And what kind of a name is Rizhin? These idiots will do nothing. They will let the country burn and the raion with it. The time has come for action. Maroussia, we must talk. We look to you. You must step forward.'

'Me? Why? What are you talking about?'

'Because you're a *Shaumian*. You're *the* Shaumian, now. The Vlast is crumbling and the Council of Lezarye is nowhere. And if the Council fails, then what is left but Shaumian? The name alone will be enough.'

'What does my name matter? I have no idea what you mean.'

'But of course you do. You must. You are Shaumian of the House of Genissei. Protosebasta. Porphyrogenita. You have a claim, a reasonable claim, there is no doubt about it. It goes by the female descent.'

Maroussia stared at him, pale and silent. She opened her mouth to speak but found nothing to say.

'Sandu? said Elena Cornelius. 'What are you talking about?'

'We must do something,' said the Count. ' And now –' he looked at Maroussia '– now we have an opportunity. We must take it.'

'Do what, Sandu?' said Elena. 'What, exactly? What are you thinking of?'

'Resist! The raion must rise! There has never been a better time. The Novozhd is dead, and there is no obvious successor. The enemy is at the gates. Don't you see? People of courage are ready to act, and now is the time. The aristocrats will come forward again, united under the ancient Shaumian name. We are not all dead. The people remember us. They haven't forgotten. We can make peace with the Archipelago. The Vlast itself will melt away and dissolve like mist in the heat of the sun.'

'No!' said Maroussia. 'I know nothing about my family, this *name*, and I want nothing to do with whatever you're talking about. Nothing at all.'

Lom saw that her hands were trembling slightly. He went across and stood beside her.

'Of course things must be handled carefully,' the Count was saying. 'There are men who will know what to do. Men of courage. I will call them together. You must meet them.'

'This is madness,' said Lom. 'Worse, it's lethal madness.'

The Count flushed.

'Certainly it is not madness. She has a legitimate claim. I know of no other.'

'Sandu,' said Elena. 'Please stop this. This is the kind of talk that gets young men ruining their lives. Making bombs. Killing innocent people.'

Maroussia stood up.

'I have to go now,' she said.

'But you'll come back?' said the Count. 'Come up this evening. Dine with us. You also, Vissarion Yppolitovich. I will invite some people. You will feel differently if you meet them. Hear what they have to say. When you know their quality—'

Lom gripped Palffy's arm. Hard.

'You can't tell anyone she's here,' he said urgently. 'You see that, don't you?'

'These are men I would trust with my life. Men of purpose and experience—'

'For fuck's sake,' said Lom. 'You can't tell anyone she's here. No one at all.'

41

Captain of Police Vorush Iliodor, assistant to Commander Chazia, was busy in his office. Outside his night-dark uncurtained window, snow was falling, and bombs. More bombs. From time to time a close impact shook his desk. He forced himself to ignore it. He had much work to complete and he was a man who stuck at his duty. He was preparing detailed orders to put into effect the evacuation from Mirgorod of the Government of the Vlast. He had almost finished.

Iliodor prided himself on unquestioning efficiency. His job was to take the broad instructions of his superiors and translate them into the detailed, precise and unambiguous practical orders that made for effective implementation. It required a certain kind of pragmatic imagination, at which he excelled. It required him to understand not just what was required, but why. He liked to call this, in his own mind, his strategic comprehension. But it emphatically did not require him to have personal opinions: these he rarely formulated, even in his own mind, and never expressed. It was precisely this quality of non-judgemental receptiveness which, as he well knew, had caused Chazia to appoint him to his post and made her comfortable in his presence, and even occasionally talkative.

The instruction to evacuate, which she had given even as the first bombs fell, came as no surprise. He knew, as Chazia had known, that in the last weeks of his life the Novozhd had accepted that if the tentative peace talks failed and the Archipelago pressed home their advance, Mirgorod was indefensible. He knew, as Chazia had known but Dukhonin, Khazar and Fohn did not, that the Novozhd had secretly approved the withdrawal of the Third, Seventh and Eighth armies from the provinces to the east and south of the city, leaving only a skeleton force to slow but not stop the enemy's advance. He also knew that Chazia saw the loss of Mirgorod as an advantage not a disaster.

'We will build a new Vlast, Iliodor!' she had said more than once. 'A renewed Vlast, young and strong and pure, safe in the east behind thousands of miles of empty steppe and plain. We will strip the factories and carry the plant eastward on trains. We will empty the Lodka and move the government out. Take what files we need and burn the rest. Mine and booby-trap the Lodka itself.

'Let the Archipelago bring Mirgorod down around their ears. We will have new cities, with marvellous modern buildings, taller and finer and fitter for the modern world. New towns, new factories, connected by the best roads and railways. With airfields in the centre! Around the towns we will build handsome, spacious farms for citizen peasants to work on, and delightful, hygienic villages. We will clear out all the *rubbish,* and grow a new, pure, wholesome and modern Vlast. Let the Archipelago wear themselves out in the west and overstretch themselves, and when we're ready we'll roll them back into the Cetic Ocean and rebuild Mirgorod as a vacation resort.'

So Iliodor had anticipated that one day the evacuation orders would be required. He had made his preparations. Outline plans and diagrams, kept in a sealed folder in the safe. When the moment came, he simply had to fetch out his folder and begin the process of filling out the necessary memoranda of instruction and orders of movement. The work was already nearly done. Chazia had suggested he should co-opt some assistance, but he had not done so. There was no need. Quicker to do it himself than to explain, and more certain to be done accurately and correctly.

Nevertheless it was arduous, absorbing work. The air raid on the city was an annoying distraction and the effort of ignoring it was wearing. Still, he had done well. And he had not forgotten his other, smaller duties. The file on the woman Shaumian was waiting, out of the way on the corner of his desk, ready for the creature Bez Nichevoi to collect that night. Including the note on where to find her, based on information recently received. No loose ends there.

Iliodor did not at first look up when he heard someone quietly enter the room. A figure pausing before the desk, waiting for attention. Iliodor held up his hand for silence and continued to copy a list of departmental branches from his notes onto a printed Consolidate-and-Remove proforma in a neat, precise script. Only when he had finished did he glance up to see who had come, and found himself staring into his own face. His own face watching him from under an astrakhan hat.

'How did you get in here?' said Iliodor. It struck him, even as he spoke, that this wasn't the most urgent, nor the most rational, of all the questions he might have asked.

'I'm afraid,' said the intruder with Iliodor's face, 'what with the bombs and all, security was rather cursory in the matter of credentials. A familiar appearance ...'

He spoke with a cultured, almost diffident voice that resembled Iliodor's own but was not, Iliodor thought, the same. There was a deepness, a throaty undertone, that struck him as odd. His neck was thicker than Iliodor's own, and roped with muscle under the skin. There were flecks of tawny amber in the green of his eyes.

'And of course,' the mirror-Iliodor continued, 'by the same token, given the destruction wrought across the city, one more unidentifiable body found in the street will be unlikely to cause much excitement.'

Only then did Iliodor notice the large kitbag in the intruder's hand, which was obviously empty.

'Oh ...' said Iliodor. 'No.' There was an emptiness in his stomach. An unhealable sadness. 'No. You don't have to ...'

The face watching him was raw. Gold-flecked eyes looked into his, dark almost to tears, reflecting Iliodor's own hopeless sadness back at him, distilled and magnified.

'But I am a soldier,' said the man who was not Iliodor. 'And this is a war.'

42

After Fohn's broadcast, Lom and Maroussia went back down with Elena Cornelius and her girls to their apartment. The air-raid sirens were wailing again in the distance. They could hear the muffled *crump* of falling bombs.

'I'm afraid you're stuck with us,' said Maroussia. 'For tonight.'

'It doesn't matter,' said Elena. 'No. I'm glad.'

The two of them, Elena and Maroussia, made a soup. Cabbage. An onion. Kvass. While they worked, Lom picked up the newspaper that Elena had brought with her from the Count's room. He skimmed idly through the account of the attack on General Secretary Dukhonin's house: the brave defence mounted by his guards and a passing militia patrol; the fall of Dukhonin himself in the struggle; the death of the firebrand convict Josef Kantor and all of his murderous gangster squad.

Lom read and reread the sentence. It didn't change. Kantor was dead. He had led the attack on Dukhonin and died in the ensuing gun battle.

Kantor was dead.

He read the story to the end. Chazia had made a speech about a renewed determination to rid Mirgorod and the Vlast of the disease of anarchic nationalist terrorism and those who harboured it. There was nothing more about Kantor. In the rest of the paper there was almost no mention of the war and the enemy coming towards the city. It might have been news from a year ago. A decade. Except that Kantor was dead.

Lom sat and nursed the news of Kantor's death like a wound. This was new disaster. Lom's thread into the Lodka; his plan – if it was ever a plan, not just a half-baked impossibility – was shredded. He would have to start working at it all over again. And war was come. The city burning.

'Maroussia?' he said at last.

'Yes?'

'You should see this.' He held the newspaper towards her, folded open at the page. Watched her read it twice.

'Oh,' she said. 'OK. So that's that.' She put the paper down and started laying the table.

When they had finished eating and Lom had helped the girls clear away, Elena Cornelius brought out a box and put it on the table. It was made of a reddish fibrous wood, heavy and roughly made, the size of a large book, with a tight-fitting lid. The lid was covered with carvings of leaves and intertwined curling thorny stems.

'I've been saving these,' she said. 'I brought them with me when I came to the city. I want to have them now.'

She took off the lid. Inside was a heap of dark shining fruit. Berries of purple and red. Wild strawberries, blackcurrants, raspberries. Elderberries, night-blue, luminous, as fat and fresh and full as the day they were picked. Other berries Lom didn't recognise.

'Here,' said Elena, offering the box to the girls. 'These are from the forest. I've kept them twenty years. There used to be more. The box was full when I came to Mirgorod. Your father and I had some, when each of you were born.'

Galina hesitated.

'Go on,' said Elena. 'They're good to eat. I promise.'

'But … they're for celebrations.'

'I want us to have them now.'

When the girls had taken a couple she pushed the box over to Maroussia and Lom.

'You too. Please.'

Lom took a single elderberry and put it in his mouth. Burst it against his tongue. The fruit was fresh and sharp and sweet, with a slight taint of resin that was not unpleasant but made the juice taste dark and wild and strange.

'It's a property of the tree,' said Elena. 'It's a kind of red pine: the breath of the wood keeps things fresh, not for ever, but longer. There was a giant called Akki-Paavo-Perelainen who used to come every autumn to our timber yard. He would always come just before the river froze, riding a great raft of red pine down the river. He gave me this box, and I carved the lid.

'That was the year my father was accused of crimes of privacy, and they made us leave the yard and the house. We weren't allowed to take anything with us. Not a thing. Not even our name. They said our family was dissolved. *Relations annulled.* My father was to be called Feliks Ioannes, my mother was Teodosia Braun, and I was Elena Schmitt. I remember my mother shouting at the official, "She is my daughter. It is a fact of nature. Nothing you say can change it." And the man was saying to us over and over again, "Your thoughts and your strength belong to the Vlast, just like the rest of us."

'They let us carry on living together for a while, in a room above a shop in the town. When we got there it was filthy. Disgusting. Every surface was covered in some kind of sticky grease, and the blankets smelled of illness. The day we moved in my mother set about cleaning it, and my father sat in a chair by the window, smoking, not saying a word. I sneaked away and went back to our old house. I broke in through a window and I just walked from room to room. Just touching things. While I was there some men came, and I had to hide in my bedroom. I heard them in the corridor. One of them pissed on the wallpaper. I heard it splashing on the rug. When I got away from the house I brought this box away with me, the only thing I had left from the old life, and when I came to work in Mirgorod I brought it here. These are the same berries Akki-Paavo-Perelainen gave me. You can't hang on to things for ever. Let's finish them now.'

43

Bez Nichevoi returned to his body at nightrise. He came back into it gradually, curled in its nest of earth and leaves and moss and chewed-over bones high among the roof beams of an empty warehouse in the city. As the planet turned its continent-face slowly away from the sun, the netted nerve-threads of his body snagged the touch of darklight and twitched and quietly sang. The settled sump of its blood unthickened, the secretions of its glands began to seep, interstitial lymph condensed like honeydew and capillaries, deconstricted, stirred. Ligatures of skeletal articulation re-clenched. In the slack pale slubs of jelly in the chambers of its skull, synaptic pathways undissolved. Bez Nichevoi warmed slowly through. And took breath. The body jack-knifed, spasming, choking, retching, vomiting acidic slews of gluey, gobbetty brown stink across its mushroom-pale and bone-thin chest. The waste products of a day of death.

Awakened, he lay back and opened his eyes, drinking in the beautiful darkness like water. The air around him was freezing. His first breaths hung in pale ghosts above his face, slowly dispersing. He surrendered himself to the pleasures of his nest, sweet and warm and crumbly-rotting, matted with perfumed fungal threads. The familiar musty smell of crusted salt and hawthorn blossom, rotting fruit and strong meat. A smell to awaken desire and dark, hidden feelings. Parts of his body were covered with skin-like papery stuff. He picked and peeled it carefully away with his fingernails and ate it.

When he was fully warmed through he rolled lazily out of his nest, swung himself up to the ceiling and skittered across it to the skylight, slipped through and climbed onto the lead of the roof. Naked, he squatted under the sky, bathing in starlight. There was something new on the air. The night was wired with it. The residue of burned city and upturned earth, the traces of two thousand deaths. The touch of war.

Bez Nichevoi, light of heart, unstrung the bundle of clothes he'd left hidden in the lea of a chimney stack, dressed, and set off across the rooftops to the Lodka, to read the file of papers Iliodor had left for him on Maroussia Shaumian.

44

Josef Kantor, king terrorist, buttoned the tunic of his Colonel-General's uniform with fat, stiff fingers. Josef Kantor, agitator, pamphleteer, bomb-maker, assassin and robber of banks, his fingers swollen and hardened by decades of labour with shovel and pick, bare-handed scrabbling at rock, freezing cells, interrogation rooms, did up his uniform buttons one by one. Josef Kantor, author of the Birzel Declaration, survivor of Vig, leader of the Fighting Organisation of Lezarye, forced awkward buttons of gleaming brass through virgin buttonholes with ruined fingernails.

The uniform was green, thick serge and factory-new. More brass at shoulder and collar. Hammers and stars. Boots shone like coal.

New times require new forms of thought.

The telephone on the desk rang. He picked it up.

'General Rizhin? They are ready for you. The Operations Room—'

'Let them wait.'

He opened the drawer and took out his revolver. A Ghovt-Alenka DK9. An unremarkable service firearm. It felt comfortable in his hand, a familiar, useful thing, like a spade to a peasant.

I'll dig with it.

He checked the cylinder and slipped it into his holster. Left the flap unbuttoned. A handful of loose shells in his pocket. It was time.

There is no past. There is only the future.

He walked out of the room into the corridor where Rizhin's future began.

It cost him nothing to let Josef Kantor die.

*

They were waiting for General Rizhin in a ground-floor conference room on the far side of the Armoury parade ground. *Operation Ouspensky Bulwark.* Maps and charts and telephones. The six officers at the table stood when he entered. The fat one stepped forward and saluted. The flesh of his neck bulged over his collar. Small, worried eyes squinted at Rizhin with wary hostility. The distrust of the career officer for the man he'd never heard of till that very morning. The political man. Chazia's man. Chazia's ears.

'I am Strughkov,' he said. 'Major-General Strughkov, Commander, City Defence. Welcome, General. We have prepared a presentation. The current situation, and our plans. We have proposals to make for—'

'The situation, Strughkov, is shit. Your plans are also shit.'

Strughkov flushed.

'General Rizhin—'

'Where are the divisions?' said Rizhin. 'Where are the guns? The Bukharsk Line is broken. When the enemy comes, will you blow up their armies with presentations and sink their ships with plans?'

'Our orders,' said Strughkov, 'are to hold the city for forty-eight hours. A week at most. We are to delay the enemy for long enough to allow the orderly evacuation of government. The Vlast is moving east. Plant and stocks from the factories are to be relocated. We have made our dispositions. Khalturin's Corps of Horse stands ready in the Ouspensky Marsh. Five infantry regiments at Satlivosk. We have the 23rd Engineers. We have stockpiled arms for the militia. Raised twenty thousand volunteers—'

'Untrained conscripts,' said Rizhin. 'Old men and boys. Policemen with antiquated rifles.'

'We make the best of what we have.'

'Where are the fortifications? The outer lines of defence? Artillery? Aircraft? More mudjhiks guard the Novozhd's bones than guard the city. Where are the gunships in the Reaches? Why do the bridges at Nordslavl still stand?'

'We will hold the line between Kropotlovsk and Yatlavograd for forty-eight hours. That will be enough. Then we will withdraw eastward, fighting as we go. We are to destroy everything we cannot take with us. Not a sack of grain, not a horse and cart, not a gallon of engine oil is to be left. We are to join the Third Army at Strom.'

'Mirgorod,' said Rizhin, 'is the capital city of the Vlast. The Founder's city, built at the site of the first angel fall. The heart of the Dominions for four hundred years. And you, General Strughkov, are proposing to abandon it without a fight.'

Rizhin watched with curiosity the working of Strughkov's fat, tired face. The reddening anger and, in his eyes like tears held back, the strange beginning of grief. The war been stalemated for so long, the fronts locked in entrenched positions far from Mirgorod to the south and south-east, that even to the men who led the armies of the Vlast it had come to seem permanent. Stable. Familiar. Inevitable. Like the authority of generals. Like the Vlast itself. A few miles lost and gained here and there, year by year, decade by decade, paid for with statistical quantities of death, changing nothing. And yet, behind it all, the whisper unheard. The myth dispersing. The possibility of failure and total collapse.

In the room a fundamental psychological turn had been taken. Rizhin felt it. The men withdrawing. Strughkov standing alone.

'The Novozhd …' said Strughkov. 'He would not … I asked, of course. I pressed the case for strengthening the defences of the city a hundred times. He refused to allow it. He would not admit the possibility of the enemy getting this far. He would not countenance the alarm and dismay that defensive preparations might cause among the population. He would not *listen* to me. And then, when he was killed and Commissioner Dukhonin was appointed, I hoped for a better response, but it was no different. Nobody would listen. They would not act. The orders to defend the city never came.'

'And now Dukhonin is dead and I am here. And you, General Strughkov, were charged with the defence of Mirgorod. What other orders did you need?'

'I am a soldier,' Strughkov shouted. 'I know my duty. I don't need a man like you—'

'What kind of man am I?' said Rizhin. 'Do you think?'

Strughkov glared at him, his face purple, his eyes full of hurt. A man who had done his best. He took a deep breath and puffed out his chest.

'Why don't you tell us, General Rizhin?' he said. 'None of us knows who the fuck you are.'

'Speculate,' said Rizhin.

'A uniform,' said Strughkov viciously, 'doesn't make you a soldier.'

Rizhin smiled thinly and looked around the room. One by one, he stared every officer present in the eye. Strughkov was still glaring at him – angry, but with the beginning of a gleam of triumph. None of the others met his gaze.

'There is a foul stink in this room,' said Rizhin quietly. 'I smell it, gentlemen. It is ripe and rank. I smell deviation. I smell revisionism. I smell conspiracy. I smell you, Strughkov. You are an enemy of the Vlast. A class enemy of all citizens. A traitor and a spy. Your treacherous failure to defend the city is an act of sabotage.'

Strughkov roared with anger and indignation.

'*You* say this to *me*!' he screamed. '*You* ... how *dare* you! You know *nothing* about—'

Bored, Rizhin drew his Ghovt-Alenka and shot him in the groin.

Strughkov collapsed, clutching the spurting wreckage between his legs, squealing in horror like a hurt, indignant child. Moving his legs slowly like a swimmer in a spreading pool of blood. Rizhin had to shoot him twice more to shut him up.

The five remaining officers were staring at him. None of them moved. None of them spoke. They were waiting to see what he would do. He swept all Strughkov's plans and charts to the floor, went over to the wall, tore down the large-scale map of the city and spread it out on the table.

'You need to start again, gentlemen,' he said. 'From the beginning. Battles are won by killing the enemy. Anyone with a gun is a soldier. And we will not surrender Mirgorod to the enemy.'

'But—' a major of cavalry began.

'Yes?' said Rizhin mildly.

'The Archipelago is only fifty miles away. We can hear their guns.'

'You need to understand something, my friends,' said Rizhin. 'We are at war. War is not a conflict between soldiers, it is a conflict between ideas. Conflict is not an accident or an aberration, conflict is essential and fundamental. War is not a sign of failure but of success. The Vlast *is* conflict. The Vlast *is* war. War is the engine, the locomotive of history. There can be compromise and armistice between armies, but not between truths. In the realm of ideas there is only win or lose, existence or annihilation.' He paused. 'Here is the essential point. Live by it and die by it. Mirgorod must be saved. Not the soldiers, not the people, the *city*. The death of citizens and soldiers does not matter. The loss of the city does. The city is a symbol. Tell me, what is this city of ours? The people? No. The buildings? No. Mirgorod is an *idea*. It is a thing the enemy does not have. The idea is to prevent them from winning. We must have a victory. The fact of victory is all that matters.'

'But the government is leaving,' the major said. 'Commander Chazia has already given the order to evacuate.'

Rizhin waved his hand dismissively.

'Let her go. Mirgorod is mine. I intend to keep it.'

Back in his office Rizhin picked up the telephone. Dialled a long number. Transcontinental.

'Get me Khyrbysk,' he said when it was answered. 'Professor Yakov Khyrbysk. Now.'

45

Bez Nichevoi stood in the centre of the empty office of Assistant Commander of Police Iliodor Vouroushin. The items he needed were there, the room was in order. But he didn't move. He was breathing. Listening. Opening himself to the place around him. Paying attention. A hunter's attention. The trace of recent violent death brushed against him, exciting, prickling across his skin, making his jaw tense, his hungry belly stir. And there was something else. Dark animal pheromones on the air.

The scent of wolf.

There was a cardboard box on the table and a file of papers. *Shaumian.* He read the file quickly then turned to the box. Opened the lid and sorted through the things inside. Personal items from the Shaumian apartment. It was poor stuff: thin and much-worn undergarments, torn stockings and flimsy shoes marked with dried blood. Knotted balls of twigs and wax and animal bones that stank of the forest. They turned his stomach when he sniffed at them. It was enough. He fingered them idly for a moment or two, then put them back in the box, went across to the window, opened it and climbed out onto the sill.

He was only six floors above ground level: above him the huge flank of the Lodka rose into the night, spilling tiny splashes of lamplight from the occasional window where some official was working late. And below him was the slow breadth of the River Mir. The edges of the river were shut away under a crust of ice, but in the centre an open current still flowed darkly. Even above the stench of the city burning, the water smelled cold and earthy, like the mouth of a deep well. Bez heard the mutter and slap of little wavelets against the ice. He turned away from the river in disgust and scuttered rapidly up the outside of the building, climbing with wild easy leaps and swings until he reached the snow-covered roofs.

This was his world, a wide lonely landscape of ridges and slopes, slates and lead. Seen from up among the rooftops, it was obvious that the Lodka was many buildings jammed together and twisted. Where they collided, buildings rose out of buildings, extruding new turrets and towers, oriels, gables, corbels, parapets, catwalks, cornices and flagpoles; and where they pulled apart flagstoned quadrangles and courtyards stretched out, and ravines and canyons split open. Windows looked out across the Lodka's roofworld, but the rooms to which the windows belonged could not be reached from inside at all. No staircases climbed to them. No doorways opened into them. The rooms had been built, then closed up and left. Bez knew this, because he had entered them all.

The tallest turret on the roof did have an iron staircase spiralling up inside it, though it wasn't climbed any more. The observatory, a cupola of latticed iron and glass, still held the Brodsky telescope, built to watch the sky for dying angels. Occupied nightly for three centuries, abandoned a human lifetime ago. Bez climbed lazily onto the top of the rusting, snow-dusted dome and sat cross-legged to savour the night. He took off his shirt. The dark chill air fingered his ribs and his back. Kissed his small belly. He closed his eyes and held his arms wide, loosening the drapes of chalk-white skin that hung from forearm to waist, letting them hang relaxed and easy, windless sails unfurled, absorbing the cool of nightside.

Far below him lay the city by night. It was a good night. One of the best. A lid of thick low cloud shut out the moons and the stars and closed in the scent of fallen snow. The street lamps were extinguished. Fires started by the bombing raid still smouldered: the air was freighted with their fragrance. Reddening coals. Broken houses and apartment buildings spilled their intimate human smells. Under heaps of rubble unfound corpses were ripening.

The older city was wide awake. Doors that were often closed stood open: small, unnoticed doors. The things in the tunnels were moving and some of them were coming out. The wide cold waters of the Mir were alert and watchful. The rusalkas swam restlessly, nosing along the canals beneath the ice and sometimes breaking through. Hauling up onto river mudbanks and the ledges under bridges. Bez Nichevoi could hear their uneasy cries. There were quarters of Mirgorod that would be dangerous for Vlast patrols that night. Dangerous even for him.

Bez considered his choices. The last report of the Shaumian woman placed her north and east, in the Raion Lezaryet. But then there was wolf. Wolf had been in Iliodor's office and killed someone there. Iliodor? Bez thought probably yes. And wolf had lingered. Read the papers. Sifted through the box. Wolf knew. Wolf interested him. Wolf would be a good kill. Bez held that thought for a moment. Considered it. Tested the air, the night and the city. Yes, he thought, yes. Wolf had left the Lodka and wolf had gone north. North and then west.

The choice was woman or wolf. And wolf was an enemy and wolf would be good killing. So. There was plenty of time. Connect purpose with desire. First, let it be wolf.

He bent to pick up his shirt, tied it round his waist and slipped from the roof of the observatory cupola, spreading his moth-pale wingfolds, letting the cold night air take him in a long and dream-slow fall across the river. One time in three he could land on his feet, but not this time. He stumbled when he hit the cobbles, fell and rolled lightly in the snow, picked himself up and began to run north, following wolf spoor.

Wolf was easy hunting. There was a strong taint of wolf threading north, a clear track easy to follow. Bez loped after him. Mostly, wolf had kept to the streets and alleyways. Bez found places where he had lingered. Quiet places where he had rested, perhaps. Not hurrying. The wolfpath took him away from familiar territories, the avenues and parks and prospects, and out into the shabbier quarters, deep into the cramped tenements and estaminets of Marosch and the Estergam. Following wolf, he passed along twisting streets, so narrow the opposing buildings almost touched, and crossed nameless insignificant canals by iron walkways. Always wolf headed north. Bez had expected the track to turn eastward at some point and head for the raion but it did not.

He came to a place where a stick of bombs had gouged wide shallow craters in the street. The scent of upturned earth and exposed roots. A broken watermain welled up and made the street a shallow, muddy river flowing between houses with shattered roofs and fallen walls. A dead horse lay on the churn of earth and snow in the cooled spillage of its own entrails. Bez sensed a life nearby. A human sound. Spidering up the slope of a collapsed brick wall, he looked over the edge into an open cellar. A mother was crouched in the rubble over her dead children. Bez called to her. The face she lifted towards him was smeared with grey dust. It was too dark for her human eyes to find him. He could see them, wide and staring in the darkness. He dropped down into the cellar and stroked her dust-caked hair as he pulled out her throat.

Wolftaint was stronger now. Close by. Bez climbed to the roofs to make a cautious, circular approach. The human death, his first kill of the night, had calmed him, as it always did. Taken the edge off his need. He had abandoned the idea that wolf was leading him to the Shaumian woman. Wolf was stupider than he had thought and now he was simply prey. Take him quickly, then go to the Apraksin and pick up a trace from there. It was only a few minutes after midnight – hours yet till the sun.

Bez crested the ridge of a tenement roof and saw him. He was standing in the middle of a cobbled square in the form of a man, his back turned to where Bez was. Wolf seemed at a loss. Waiting. Wolf spoor streamed from him onto the air, bright unmistakable scented clouds. Bez settled in the lee of a chimney to watch. Wolf was doing nothing. Just standing out in the middle of the square. And then Bez realised his mistake. He'd been careless. Overconfident. This night he wasn't hunter, he was hunted. Wolf had led him out here into the waste places of the city, away from the Shaumian woman, and was calling him, baiting him with the trap of himself. *Come down. Come down.*

Bez grinned in the darkness as he slipped away.

46

Maroussia was awake in the night. She lay still, breathing slowly. Listening. The attic window framed a flickering sky: gunfire on the distant horizon, flashing against low-hanging cloud. A new kind of weather.

Lom lay next to her, warm and heavy under the quilt, eyes clenched fiercely in sleep.

There were trees in the room. The room was full of trees.

Count Palffy's house was full of trees.

The streets of the raion were full of trees.

Watchful trees, waiting for her.

Maroussia turned back the quilt and crawled out of the bed. Her dress was draped over a chair. From the pocket she brought out the bag, stained with her mother's blood, that held the thing of twigs and tiny bones. She opened the bag and took it out. It stirred in the cup of her palm restlessly, as if a small animal was in there, moving. There were tiny berries inside it, fresh and purple-bright. She leaned forward and brought it up to her face. Listening. Quiet voices whispered. Calling her.

Come out. Come out under the trees.

She pulled her coat on over her night shirt and, holding the knot of twigs and forest breath cupped gingerly in her palm, went down into the house and made her way through tree-crowded landings and passageways out into the street. Bare feet in the snow. The moons spilled white luminance through gaps in the cloud. The vapour ghosts of her breath glittered. It was so cold. Bitter cold.

There wasn't much left of the streets; it was mostly trees. She walked among them, her feet freezing, pushing onwards, deeper and deeper into the trees. Eventually she remembered the bag in her hand and stopped. Undid the string at the bag's tight mouth and pulled it open.

Between step and step she passed through into difference. Forest. Change.

Maroussia was in a beautiful, simple place under the trees. Everything rang with a true, clear note, and everything shone out from within itself with its own radiance, fresh and cool. Nothing was anything except what it was. The distances between things were airier and more obvious. The night air – luminous velvet and purple-blue – streamed with perfume. Corn-gold swollen stars spilled flakes of light that brushed her face and settled on her shoulders.

Walking, she left a trail of dark impressions across dew-webbed grass. She came to a wide clump of thorn. Tiny droplets of mist-water, star-glittering, hung from every tip and nestled in the crooks and elbows of every twig. The water made her thirsty. She crouched in the long wet grass and licked at the branches, making slow careful movements with her tongue. She took hawthorn twigs into her mouth carefully. The water was cold and good. The wood tasted ... complex. Thorns pricked the inside of her mouth, mingling the iron taste of her blood with the wood and the water.

She looked at her own hands. They were made of leaves.

The world cracked open as if gods were walking through it. It was a breaking of tension, like a shattering downpour of rain. Everything was alive with wildness. Maroussia herself was spilling streams of perfume and darkshine from her mouth and skin and hair: bright stain-clouds on the air, carrying far and broadcasting promises of plenty.

Bez Nichevoi watched the Shaumian woman from his place on the roof of the house. She was walking slowly, barefoot in the snow, bare-headed, straight-backed and thin. Her dark woollen coat hung open, unbuttoned over a white cotton nightdress, spilling the smell of her body still warm from her bed. Between the collar of her coat and the tangle of her short black hair, the nape of her neck showed slender and pale. Bez groaned quietly. Desire was a constriction in his throat, a dark knot in his belly, a rigid knife rising from his groin. He wanted to feed on her slowly, and ... do ... such pleasurable things ...

He followed her for a while. Unhurried. Letting the moment last.

Taking pleasure in anticipation and delay. He worked his way round in front of her and came down into the street.

Her eyes passed over him and did not see. Her gaze was turned inward. He stood and let her come to him. The dark buildings of the raion faded for him too. It was as if he was standing under trees: shadows, the wind among branches, the slip of tiny snowfalls from twigs and needles, the smell of ice and resin and cold earth.

And then she knew he was there.

Her dark eyes widened and stared into his. She opened her mouth: a ragged indrawn breath. He saw the gleam of her teeth. The moistened heat of her tongue.

He immobilised her quickly and slung her across his shoulders. She was surprisingly heavy. He began to run.

47

A thousand miles north and east of Mirgorod, at six in the morning Vayarmalond Eastern Time, Professor Yakov Khyrbysk hurried across the floor of an underground cavern deep inside a mountain. The cavern was as wide as a football field and bright as day: a hundred brilliant fluorescent tubes burned overhead in the ceiling of raw black rock. Their light splashed off the concrete floor, a grey-white dazzle. The cavern was empty except for one flat-roofed building, little more than a large shed, sitting right out in the centre of the echoing space: a crude temporary construction of boards screwed to a steel frame, a cubic carton with sixty-foot edges. Thick rubber-sleeved cables trailed hundreds of feet across the ground towards it. Around the shed the concrete floor was smudged and dirtied with feathered spills of black, as if dark ashes had been scattered there.

Khyrbysk pushed open the door and entered. A dozen men and women were working inside, standing at workbenches. Control panel arrays. Dials and gauges. They all looked up when he came in. They had the pale drawn faces of people who have been working all night. Spotlights on tripods cast harsh shadows.

'Good morning,' said Khyrbysk. 'Please. Carry on.'

Every surface in the room was covered with a layer of fine graphite dust: the technicians' white coats were smeared graphite grey; permanent graphite shadows collected in every crease and fold. Khyrbysk could taste the graphite in the air on his tongue. It made his skin dry and silk-smooth. The interior of the shed was covered with a skin of slate, ceiling, walls and floor. Khyrbysk picked his way with care: graphite dust made the floor treacherously slippery.

Hektor Shulmin was in a huddle in the far corner with Leon Ferenc. Shulmin saw Khyrbysk come in and waved to him cheerily.

'Yakov!' he called. 'Come to see your baby waking up?'

Khyrbysk ignored him.

In the centre of the room, standing on a rubber sheet on a low platform, was another cube – a cube inside the cube – gleaming coal-black under the spotlights. It was a stack of blocks of pure graphite, sixty layers of blocks, rising twenty-five feet high and weighing almost three hundred tons. Half the blocks were solid bricks, but the other half had been carefully and precisely hollowed out. The hollowed graphite blocks formed a three-dimensional cellular lattice within the cube, and each cell in the lattice contained a small, neat gobbet of uranium.

From a rubber-sheeted scaffold over the stack, rods of cadmium plunged down through the black cube. Three men on the scaffold operated the mechanism, withdrawing the cadmium rods one by one with painful slowness. They had barrels of cadmium salt solution ready, to flood the cube if anything went wrong. They called themselves the suicide squad.

Khyrbysk went across to the desk from where Ambroz Teleki was supervising the operation. The neutron counters made their quiet trickling clicking noise.

'One more rod will do it,' said Teleki. 'The reaction will become self-sustaining. It will not level off. We were waiting for you.'

Khyrbysk studied the dials.

'Then do it,' he said. 'Do it, Ambroz. Do it.'

Teleki made a sign to the suicide squad. One of them turned a bakelite knob on a panel one notch forward. Then another.

The noise of the counters went faster and faster, the clicks tumbling over one another, a clattering rattle that turned into a steady hiss, a white waterfall of sound. The needles on the dials swung fully round to the right, hit their limit and stopped. But the pen on the chart recorder continued to rise, higher and higher, tracing a beautiful exponential curve.

A ripple of applause went round the room. The technicians broke into quiet chatter.

Khyrbysk watched the curve on the chart climb higher. Still higher.

'Say the word, Yakov,' said Teleki, 'and we'll drop the Shinn Rod in to close it off.'

Khyrbysk said nothing. His eyes were fixed on the rising graph. His mouth was dry. His hands were trembling. He let the reaction run on, faster and faster, hotter and hotter. The flow of neutrons becoming a roar. A flood.

He was Yakov Khyrbysk, father of stars.

'Yakov?' said Teleki anxiously, touching his arm. 'Yakov. When you are ready, please.'

Khyrbysk paid him no attention. The technicians' chatter fell quiet.

Seconds passed. Long seconds.

'Yakov!' said Teleki again.

Then at last Khyrbysk raised his arm.

'OK,' he said. 'Let it stop now.'

He watched the curve drop off and fall away.

Hektor Shulmin hustled over, drawing the ponderous Ferenc in his wake. He clapped Teleki on the shoulder.

'Congratulations, Ambroz! A triumph! She works, man! She works! It's beautiful.' Shulmin produced a bottle of aquavit from his pocket and started handing it round. 'So when are we going to go operational? Why not now? Everything is in place. How many tests do you need, after all? Ready is ready.'

Teleki looked tired.

'Soon, Hektor,' he said. 'Soon.'

Khyrbysk took Shulmin by the elbow and drew him aside.

'A word, please, Hektor,' he said.

'Of course, Yakov. Of course. I hear you were out on the *Chaika* the other night. A fishing trip, eh?'

'You might say so, Hektor.'

'A successful catch, I hope.'

'The best.'

'So friend Blegvad brought another package from our mysterious uncle in Mirgorod? How much? How much this time? Another hundred thousand? Tell me Yakov. I am agog. Our anonymous donor intrigues me. Our mystery philanthropist.'

'A hundred thousand? No. More than that. Much more.'

'How much Yakov? This time, how much?'

'Thirty million.'

'Thirty million? Thirty *million*?' Shulmin looked suddenly serious. 'Fuck, Yakov. We should be careful. We should go cautiously here.

What are we getting into? Dukhonin himself never came up with such a sum, not all in one go. Thirty million! This is not a donation. This is a purchase. Who is this faceless, nameless man with thirty million roubles? What is he after? What did Blegvad say?'

'Blegvad? Blegvad deals only with intermediaries. He has never met the man, never even spoken to him. But I have.'

'Have you, by fuck!'

'He telephoned me. In the middle of the night. And you are right, of course: he has made a request, a most courteous request. Not a purchase, he didn't put it in those terms, not at all. He was most careful not to do that. He is a supporter of our cause, he says. An admirer of our ambition. He shares our common purpose. We are visionaries, doing great work, and he has just a small favour to ask of me.'

'What does he want?'

'Artillery shells. A hundred artillery shells.'

'Is that it? The man's an idiot. He could pick up a hundred shells anywhere.'

'No. He wants the yellow shells.'

'The *yellow*? He knows about them? How can he know about them?'

'He does, Hektor. He was most specific. A hundred yellow shells. They are to be on a train to Mirgorod tonight. Leaving this very night. This can be done, Hektor? There is no problem? I don't want to hear there is a problem. I agreed. Of course I agreed. I gave him an undertaking.'

'Tonight? Yes, it can be done. No problem, Yakov. But—'

'Then arrange it, Hektor. I want you to go with them. Travel with them to Mirgorod yourself and make sure they are delivered safely. There is to be no fuck-up, Hektor. No delay. It is a matter of extreme urgency. Our benefactor was absolutely explicit on that point.'

48

In Mirgorod, in the Raion Lezaryet, Vissarion Lom woke suddenly, heart pounding, the sour taste of sleep in his mouth. The attic was in darkness. He knew instantly by the feel of the room that Maroussia was gone. He fumbled for the matchbox and lit the lamp. Looked at his watch. Just after three.

Shit.

He pulled on his clothes, grabbed the Blok 15, stuffed it into his waistband and went downstairs. The kitchen was in darkness, the banked-up fire in the stove glowing dull brick red. The door at the end of the hall stood open. Maroussia's coat was not on the hook.

There was a small pile of coins on the hall table, a few kopeks and a single rouble. He scooped them into his pocket and stepped out into the dark and icy cold.

49

Bez Nichevoi entered the Lodka by the long tunnels, carrying the unconscious weight of Maroussia Shaumian across his shoulders. He found Chazia in her workshop. Bez noted the changes there: the benches pushed back out of the way, equipment boxed and crated and standing ready in piles beside the old rail track, the stock of angel flesh gone.

The wall of the Pollandore chamber had been smashed and lay in rubble, and the iron construction that held the Pollandore itself had been dismantled and removed. The uncanny, enormous and faintly disgusting sphere hung suspended six feet above the flagstones, apparently without support. It turned slowly on its own axis, milky, planetary, luminescent but shedding no light. Swirls like small storms, oil on water, spiralled across its surface. Bez kept his distance and avoided looking at it, though it tugged at his awareness. The sense of its presence jangled his nerves. Made him feel weak. When he couldn't see it he couldn't tell exactly where it was. As if it circled him. Stalking.

Bez was surprised to realise that he feared it.

He shed the burden of the Shaumian girl with relief, slipping her from his back and letting her fall to the ground. She moaned and stirred. Her face was flushed, her hair matted with sweat. His immobilising scratch had made her feverish.

'Be careful with her!' Chazia snapped. She glared at him with distaste.

'I found her,' said Bez. 'I brought her. I give her to you.'

It had been a hard run from the raion. The smell of the girl on his back, the feel of her belly warm against his shoulders, had nagged at him the whole way.

'Is she all right?' said Chazia, bending over her. 'She is bleeding. You didn't . . . ?'

Bez noticed how Chazia's fox-red hair was thinning. Patches of angel flesh were visibly growing across her skull.

'A graze,' he said. 'She fell.'

As Chazia straightened up he tossed the stinking knotted ball of twigs and bones and stuff towards her.

'Here,' he said. 'She was carrying this. Only this.'

Chazia caught it neatly and cupped it in her hands. She grinned – a vulpine stretch of thin lips – and laid the thing carefully on the bench.

Bez hated this woman. He'd served her too long. He had *served* for too long altogether. He was *Bez*.

'You are leaving?' he said, indicating the preparations around them.

'The strength of the Vlast lies in the east,' said Chazia. 'We will build a new capital, better, stronger and more pure, at Kholvatogorsk. I intend that Kholvatogorsk will be a *clean* city. Mirgorod is too . . . *tainted*. Too near the margins. Old things not properly cleared away.'

She means me, thought Bez. *The bitch. She refers to me.*

'I have not touched the woman yet,' he said. 'You will give her to me when you've finished.'

Chazia looked at him sharply.

'I need her alive,' she said. 'I don't know how long for.'

'I am no lickspittle of the Vlast,' said Bez. 'Service is not its own reward. Service is no reward at all.'

'Your assistance to me, as to my predecessors, has always been appreciated, Bez Nichevoi. If you're leaving by the underground way you'd better go quickly. A train is coming.'

'*A train? Here?*'

'This tunnel connects to the Wieland station. The way was closed after the Pollandore was brought here. I've had the tracks repaired to take it out again.'

'You're taking that thing with you?'

'Mirgorod will fall. I'm not going to leave it here for the Archipelago to find.'

When Bez Nichevoi left the Lodka it was still thick night, but the fierce edge of dawn was burning its way across the face of the Vlast. Already the burning light was less than five hundred miles east of Mirgorod, and the turning of the planet was bringing it closer. He could feel it. He needed to hurry. *Get out of the light.* He knew a place in the cellarage of what had once been a brewery. It would be quiet there. Out of the way, if the bombers returned. Bez never slept in the same nest two days running.

Between him and refuge lay the Black Wisent Quarter. It wasn't wise to pass through the Black Wisent on such a night as this. Old things were near the surface there. But he'd lost too much time already and a detour would cost him more. The sun was coming. He scrambled from roof to roof and ran across open spaces, angry and frustrated. The warmth and smell of the Shaumian woman was still in his clothes.

Chazia's new Vlast in the east was no place for him. Perhaps he would stay in Mirgorod. War was coming and there would be good pickings in the city. Or maybe it was time to go back to the mountains. Some brick-turreted burgh in the Erdyeliu would suit him well. Glaciers and pinewoods. Lynx and chamois. Giants and trolls and rusalkas. His kind had lived off such as them long before the Vlast had come, and still would, long after the Vlast had crumbled and faded.

But he would go back for the Shaumian woman before he left. When night came again he would go back to the Lodka and fetch her and take her with him. Make her last a while. If Chazia didn't like it, he would kill Chazia. That would be good.

Bez was well into the Black Wisent Quarter now. The snow had fallen more thickly here. It lay feet-thick in the squares and mounded in high drifts against walls. He skittered lightly across the surface, his feet scarcely leaving traces.

Something on the wind alarmed him.

Wolf was following. Coming fast.

Dawn was too near. It was better to avoid a fight.

Bez picked up speed. A bitter pre-dawn wind whipped his face. Hard pellets of snow stung his cheeks. Snow. Thick, sudden snow. Snow-thorns scraping at his eyes. Something was wrong. Snow. Too much snow. He ran faster, his sunken chest burning.

He should not have entered the Black Wisent Quarter.

The snow under his feet slipped suddenly sideways, like a rug pulled out from under him. Unbalanced, he fell. Hard. Onto icy cobbles.

Bez picked himself up. The snow was watching him. Waiting to see what he did. He was in an empty space between buildings. Snow-dogs circled in the shadows of the mouths of the streets and observed him from under the low branches of snow-heavy trees. He stood his ground, turning slowly, looking for a way out or a place to make a stand.

Wolf walked out to meet him. A man in a long coat and an astrakhan hat.

'Where is the girl?' said wolf. 'Did you find the girl? Did you?'

'*Fuck you, turd puppy!*'

'Did you find her?' said wolf. 'What have you done?'

'*Too late, teat licker. The bitch fox has her now.*'

Bez hissed and went for wolf, fast. At the last moment he jumped high to come down from above and take his eyes. A quick decisive kill.

But wolf was faster. Faster and stronger.

Wolf ducked sideways and reached up and gripped Bez by the ankle. Caught him out of the air and whiplashed his light body down. Smashed him against the ground, crashing the back of his head against the cobbles. Before Bez could recover wolf was on him and ripped his head clean away from his neck. Foul-smelling black watery ichor sprayed from the mess between his shoulders and dripped from the root of his skull.

Antoninu Florian began to walk, holding the head of Bez in one hand, out to the side, away from his body, like a dark lantern. The head shrieked and cursed and screamed and tried to bite the hand that held it by the hair, but its teeth tore nothing but its own lips and tongue. With his other hand Florian dragged the thrashing, spasming living corpse behind him by the leg. The corpse tried to kick itself free but could not. Arched its back and slashed at the air with needle fingers.

'*Fucker! Fucker!*' the head was screeching. '*You stinking bag of shit! I will lay your eyeballs on your shoulders so you can watch me eat your brain.*'

It was curious, Florian thought, how much noise the mouth could make when disconnected from its lungs. He wondered what the biology of that was.

Somebody pulled aside an upstairs curtain and looked out from a house as they were passing. A pale face pressed against a window. The face disappeared and the curtain fell back.

Florian dragged the body to a place he had prepared in the shell of a bombed-out building. A pyre of roof timbers and furniture waited there, supplemented by a kindling of mattresses and curtains and books. He flung the lightweight, disgusting head onto the pile and threw the body after it. Weighted the thrashing body down with heavy beams and doused the whole heap with kerosene from a jerrycan he'd stashed nearby. Lit a cloth-wrapped chair leg with a match and laid it carefully at the base.

The pyre went up in a sudden explosive flowering. Flags and sheets of flame billowed in their own twisting wind. Dry wood chattered and spat. One more bomb-fire in a city pitted with smouldering buildings.

Florian stayed to watch the body burn, feeling the heat on his face. He had to make sure. The smell of the body burning was very bad. The corpse writhed and thrashed as the fire took it. The head continued to scream and curse as its hair and flesh charred and crisped and peeled away.

One by one, Bez Nichevoi gave up all the deaths by which he had lived. Hundreds, thousands of deaths, human and otherwise, absorbed and accumulated during the long centuries of his existence. Antoninu Florian felt every one. The victims swirled around him in bitter smoke-clouds of sadness, surprise and pain, and their features flickered across his face like fire-shadow. Remembrance. Each death was as raw as the first.

Florian felt each one die. One by one, he reflected their dying faces back into the fire. He worked the subcutaneous muscles of his own humaniform face – zygmatic, corrugator, depressor, levator, buccinator, orbicularis, risorus – until it was agony. Until the skin stretched tight across the shifting bones of his skull was reddened and swollen and burned as if stung by bees. Tears spilled down his cheeks and soaked his shirt. From time to time he turned away to vomit, until he was hollowed out and sour.

On and on they came, the many many dead, and Florian Antoninu wept.

Only when the blaze had collapsed in on itself and slumped to charred stumps and ash and the corpse of Bez Nichevoi was empty and quiet, only then did he turn and walk away, weakened, trembling.

50

Lom had been walking for six hours, looking for Maroussia. All night an uneasy windstream had bundled high dark cloud mass eastwards across the sky. Ragged clearings opened across patches of fathomless star-speckled darkshine. Moon-glimpses dilated and closed. Sometimes Lom knew where he was and sometimes he was lost. The steep intricate streets, courtyards and passageways of the Raion Lezaryet defeated system and pattern. As he walked he tried to make sense of Maroussia's disappearance, but he could not. She had woken in the night. She had not dressed – her clothes were still in the attic – but she had taken the solm and a coat, and gone out into the dark and disappeared.

He climbed the Ship Bastion to see if she was there. He went down to the Purfas Gate, which was closed and barred and unattended. Taking a different route back, he passed the blank darkened windows of a watch repairer, a tailor, a bookseller showing lonely yellow lamplight in an upstairs room. A night reader. The streets of the raion smelled wild and ancient – old woodsmoke, damp stone cellars, pig yards and open drains. The snow, the river mist and the sky. A pony grunted and shifted uneasily on the other side of a fence. A bat flickered close past his face, an indistinct smudge of fur. Lom flinched as if it had touched him, but it had not.

He let the winding narrow streets take him where they would. There was a shape and rhythm to them that was not human. He saw openings and followed them. Narrow corners at acute angles he had to squeeze through sideways. Gateways too low for adults to pass through without bending. Gaps and gratings whose purpose he could not grasp. Rounding the bends of wandering alleyways he felt himself entering localities of awareness: attentive, watchful presences shadowing his, though he could see nothing. Frustrated, he felt himself walking along the edge of something. On the borderline of some discovery he could not make. Nightside. The only sounds were small ones: a latch rattling in the wind, the slump of snow disturbed in a gutter, and once the shriek of a street-scavenging fox. Crossing a wider cobbled square in a splash of moonshadow, he caught a trace of something different. A taint on the air. An intrusion. His stomach tightened. His neck prickled. Something sharp, cruel and disgusting had passed that way. An edge of panic began to scratch away at the edge of his mind and did not stop.

Three times during the night he returned to the house to see if Maroussia had come back. He roused Elena Cornelius and the Count and together they combed the building from cellars to attics. It had obviously occurred to both of them, though they did not say it, that Maroussia had gone. Slipped away. Abandoned him. Left the city. It was in their faces as they helped him search the house. Elena at least thought it would have been a good move. But Lom didn't believe it. He went to Kamilova's house and banged on the door, but no one came.

When dawn came and the Purfas Gate opened, he took the first tram of the day into the city, to the Lodka, on the possibility that Maroussia, unable to sleep, had decided to go there alone, to check it out, to be nearer the Pollandore, perhaps even to look for a way inside. It seemed unlikely, but he had no other ideas. None at all.

51

The wide open space in front of the Lodka, the immense Square of the Piteous Angel, was full of people, the atmosphere muted, determined, grim. Long lines had formed at temporary recruiting booths. Clerks took names under crude and blocky rust-coloured posters of comrades-in-arms charging with out-thrust bayonets, the men square-jawed, the women full-breasted, their hair like sheaves of corn. Those too old and infirm to sign up waited patiently to hand over their kopeks, their cutlery, their watches and chains and little pieces of jewellery at collection kiosks. The wind threw bitter scraps of snow in their faces.

A man came and stood next to him. Together they watched the slow-moving queues in silence for a while. The stranger glanced sideways at Lom.

'Look at them,' he said. 'In other cities they lined the streets when the Archipelago came. But not us. Not here. Not Mirgorod. You understand that?'

Lom looked at the man sharply. Middle-aged, with faded thinning hair, the lenses of his glasses smeared, a day's worth of dark red stubble on his chin and sagging neck. He wondered if he was a *provokator*. But there was a puzzled sadness in his face. He looked lost. He was just talking.

'It's their city,' said Lom. 'Their homes. Their families. They're frightened.'

The man shook his head, as if he was trying to clear his mind. Bring things into focus. 'Of course this isn't everyone,' he said. 'This is the ones who came, not the ones who didn't. There's more will have stayed at home. And people are leaving. Lots are leaving. Did you hear that?'

'It makes sense,' said Lom. 'If they've got somewhere to go.'

'You?' the man said.

'What?'

'You joining up?'

'I'm looking for someone,' said Lom. 'I thought she might have come here. I didn't know it was going to be like this.'

The man nodded. He understood that.

'My wife's gone somewhere,' he said. 'She took the girls. Our house is gone. When I got back there was just this hole, and the back wall sticking up out of a pile of bricks. You can see our wallpaper. The kitchen up in the air. It looks small. Seemed bigger when we were in it.' He rubbed his hand down across his face as if he was wiping something away. 'You haven't seen her, have you? Her hair's grey. Cut short. Like this.' He touched the back of his neck above the collar. 'She's not so old, only forty-three, but grey. Not white, grey. A nice iron-grey. She would have had the girls with her.'

'No,' said Lom. 'I haven't seen them. Sorry.'

'I waited the night but they didn't come. We always said we'd move to the country. You know, if the war came here. They must have gone ahead, but I don't know where. They'll send word. When they're settled.'

Lom didn't have anything to say. After a while the man drifted away. 'You take care now,' he said as he went.

A murmur moved across the square, a turning of heads like wind across a lake. Lom smelled smoke. Somewhere fires were burning. From the direction of the Lodka a thick pall was rising and spilling across the crowd. Scraps of burned paper in the wind. He joined the drift of people moving towards the place. Worked his way to the front.

There was a huge open space in front of the Lodka filled with bonfires. There must have been fifty or sixty at least, set out in neatly spaced ranks. Some were already burning, spilling fierce licks of flame thirty or forty feet high, but most were still being built. Endless lines of soldiers and uniformed officials were filing out of the Lodka's main entrance and down the steps, pushing trolleys and carrying document crates for the growing stacks. To one side a fleet of drays and olive-green trucks was drawn up. Some crates were being diverted towards them and loaded up, but those they did not plan to take, which was most of them, they were burning. The space around the fires was kept clear by lines of conscripts, pale-faced in their ill-fitting greatcoats, steel helmets strapped to their backpacks. Bayonets fitted, they avoided the gaze of the watching crowd.

Behind the fires, the Lodka itself was closed up like a fortress. There was no way in. All the raisable bridges were raised, and the Yekaterinsky Bridge and the Streltski Gate had checkpoints watched by mounted dragoons and sandbagged mitrailleuse positions. The thousand-windowed frontage, rising high above the smoke, was hung with banners, the roofscape forested with flags. Emblems of the Vlast in its pride, red, black and gold, raised in wind-tugged defiance under the low leaden sky.

But the Lodka was evacuating. The scale of what was happening was dumbfounding. The files and documents of a dozen ministries of government and police. The correspondence of diplomats and provincial land captains. Four hundred years of intelligence reports and observation records. The shrill denunciations and sly whispered secrets of informers. Confessions signed on blood-smeared paper. The transcripts of secret trials. The arraignments and sentences of every exile and prisoner in the Dominions. Hundreds and hundreds of miles of shelving. All the vast archives of the Registry, presided over by the towering Gaukh Engine. It would take weeks to burn it all. Months. An immense, tireless beacon to guide the bombers of the Archipelago to their target by night and day. The Vlast was spectacularly killing itself, and would surely take Mirgorod down with it. The watching crowd was beginning to mutter and grumble.

Engines were started. A convoy was moving out. There were angry shouts as the conscripts cleared a path for the trucks and horse-drawn wagons loaded high with crates. They trundled and lumbered through at walking pace. Where were they going? Somewhere far away and safe from the war. South? Unlikely: too near the incursions of the Archipelago. North? They couldn't get far enough, not with winter closing in. It must be east, then, somewhere east, somewhere in the thousands of miles between Mirgorod and the edge of the endless forest.

A thought struck Lom. Hard. *The Pollandore*. They wouldn't leave it to be found by the Archipelago if the city fell. *They would take it with them. Shit.*

If he could think of that, so could Maroussia. She would have. If she had come here, if she had seen the evacuation beginning, she would have asked the question. *Hours* ago. She would have tried to find the answer. She would have followed.

He needed to know where the convoys were heading.

He paced along beside one of the trucks at the back of the convoy edging its way through the crowd. There was only the driver in the cab. He reached up and opened the passenger-side door. Swung himself up and into the seat. Pulled the door shut behind him.

'Hey!' said the driver. 'What the fuck—'

Lom jammed the muzzle of the Blok 15 hard against his thigh.

'Just drive,' he said. 'Like you were, everything normal.'

'You must be fucking—' the driver began.

'There is a gun against your leg. It won't make a hole, it will blow your leg away. Maybe both of them. Shatter the bones. Sever the main arteries. You'll bleed empty in minutes. So just keep looking ahead and driving normally. Don't mind me, I'm only along for the ride.'

The driver, hands gripped tight on the wheel, knuckles white, kept his eyes fixed on the horse-drawn wagon in front. He tried to swallow but his throat was dry and he coughed. The truck stayed in the long line, nosing slowly through the city.

'Where are you going?' said Lom.

'The railway. The marshalling yards by the Wieland station.'

'And after? Where are they taking all this stuff?'

The driver shook his head.

'I don't know. I just turn around and come back for another load. Look. I don't want any trouble. You need to get out now. When we get there, there'll be—'

'Just shut up and drive.'

The convoy turned into Founder's Prospect. There were crowds there too. The shops were being cleared out. People hauling bags and even handcarts piled high with bread and meat and oil. Anything. Some establishments were trying to operate some kind of rationing system. *Two loaves per family, fifty kopeks.* Eye-watering prices. There were long queues outside post offices and pawn shops,. A bank near the Ter-Uspenskovo Bridge was trying to close its doors. There was shouting. Things getting ugly.

At the corner near the Great Vlast Museum they got snarled in traffic. Another convoy was drawn up at the foot of the museum's wide marble steps. Museum staff were carrying out rolled carpets and tapestries, bronze heads, tundra carvings, crates and boxes stuffed with straw, paintings still in their frames. Nothing properly packed. Treasures beyond price being dumped in the back of waiting vehicles.

The truck lurched ahead a few feet and stopped again. The driver was staring at a group of militia watching from the top of the steps. He shifted in his seat, trying to move his leg away from the Blok's muzzle.

'Don't,' said Lom. 'Sit still. Keep looking ahead.'

It would have been quicker to walk, but as soon as he left the cab the driver would be shouting his head off. Lom slumped lower in his seat and tried to look bored.

At last the convoy cleared the museum and picked up to a steady walking pace again. When they slowed at a crowded interchange Lom opened the door and slid out.

'I'd keep quiet about what just happened,' he said, 'if I were you.'

'Fuck you, arsehole,' the driver muttered and gunned the throttle. The truck lurched a few feet forward.

Lom's back itched as he walked away, adrenaline pumping, waiting for shouts, ready to run. But nothing happened. Twenty seconds later he slipped down an alleyway and out of sight.

52

The Wieland marshalling yards were raucous chaos. Locomotives in full steam, whistles shrieking. Shunting engines stalled among crowds of citizens. Families picking their way across the tracks, dragging their luggage, desperate to find places on trains that were already spilling people out of the doors. Railway officials pushing, shoving, yelling and screaming. Crackling tannoy announcements. *Citizen passengers must use station platforms! Access here is forbidden!* No one was listening. There was no way through the heaving mass. No hope of finding Maroussia here, and no sign of the convoys from the Lodka.

Lom skirted the crowds and came to a chain-link fence. Beyond it was another expanse of railway tracks, water towers, mobile cranes and what looked like freight cars raised on iron stilts. He climbed the fence painfully, gripping the wire with fingers numbed with cold, scrabbling for footholds against the stanchions. He rolled over the top and dropped awkwardly on the other side, picked himself up and ran.

He sprinted across the open ground and ducked between two trains. There were more trains beyond: wooden wagons as long as barns and high as houses with six-foot-diameter wheels; the twelve-foot-gauge behemoths of the intercontinental freight lines. He went further in, following the lines of high-sided wagons that stretched away into the distance in both directions. From time to time he clambered through the space between two cars, only to find himself in another identical corridor between identical trains. It was a labyrinth and there was nothing to see. A narrow ladder at the end of each wagon climbed up to the roof. Lom chose one and went up the rungs until his head was clear and he could see across, but there were only the roofs of more wagons. No end to the rows of trains. Hundreds and hundreds, possibly thousands, of identical wagons all lined up ready to go.

He dropped to the ground and took a closer look at the car he'd climbed. There was a tall sliding door along one side. Padlocks looped through iron latches, but they weren't locked. The bottom of the door was at head height, but there was a handle. He hauled at it and the door trundled back, running on small wheels in iron grooves. Greased, nice and easy. He opened up a four-foot gap, jumped and pulled himself up over the edge. Crawled on hands and knees in rough dusty straw. Inside was airy dimness and an overpowering smell of tar, disinfectant and straw. Cattle wagons. Empty. Only there were shadowy structures inside that didn't look like cattle stalls.

As his eyes adjusted to the dimness, he stood up and looked around. There were no windows but narrow slatted gaps ran along near the roof, letting in thin strips of dusty light. The whole of the carriage was lined with slatted wooden racks, like bunks but wider, three tiers high, the top tier four feet under the tarred wooden roof. Each tier was packed with a layer of straw. Lidded barrels lined the narrow aisle that ran between them the length of the wagon. Lom opened barrels at random. Most of them held only water, but from every third one came acrid disinfectant fumes. In the far corner he found a couple of mops and shovels and a stack of galvanised buckets.

They were cattle trucks, but for people. As Lom got used to the air inside the wagon, he picked out other smells under the overpowering reek of disinfectant. Urine. Excrement. Sweat. The trains had been used before, and they'd been cleaned up ready to be used again.

Lom dropped to the ground and eased the door closed. All around him the high blank walls of identical railway trucks blocked out the sky, and each one could carry hundreds of people, jammed in side by side in acrid, excremental shadow. He kept on cutting sideways between them, ducking under or climbing across the heavy couplings. After four or five more he chose another ladder and took another look across the roofs.

He was almost at the edge. A couple more lines of wagons, and then a stretch of dead ground, and beyond that, set apart within its own high perimeter fence, was a long military train. He was pretty much level with its two massive locomotives coupled in series, crudely plated with thick blue steel. Behind them was an anti-aircraft gun on a flatbed truck and a couple of slope-sided armoured wagons with firing slits for windows and roof-mounted gun turrets. The muzzles of twin twenty-pounders at rest, tilted skywards. The rest of the train as far as he could see was mostly made up of freight cars interspersed with passenger carriages, incongruously neat and fresh in their purple livery. The only exception was one flat truck about four or five hundred yards from Lom's position, at the point where the train curved out of sight. It was wider than the rest of the train, and it had been fitted with what looked like wide iron trestles and a high canopy. Soldiers were draping it with grey camouflage netting. Somewhat apart from them, waiting patiently, arms at its side, observing, stood a crudely human-shaped figure. It was broad and squat but taller than the wagons. A mudjhik, formed from a solid block of dull reddish-purple angel flesh.

Lom felt the touch of the mudjhik's awareness brush lightly across the surface of his mind, pass on for a second and flick sharply back. Its sightless head turned in his direction. The full force of its attention gripped him hard like a fist. He tried to close his mind against it and push it away, but the dazzling floodlight crash of its glare pinned him. He was naked and exposed, alone in a wide empty space, his shadow stretching out behind him, inky black and infinitely long. The mudjhik took a step in his direction, then another, gathering pace, opening its legs wider, relaxing into a steady loping jog.

Lom slid down the ladder, crashing his shin painfully against the train coupling, and turned and ran. The long passage between the trains was a tunnel, a trap. He turned and scrambled between the carriages, crossed the narrow space and scrambled through again, and again, heart pounding, fighting panic, desperate to put as many trains as possible between himself and the approaching mudjhik. Repeatedly he slipped and stumbled, crashed bruisingly into couplings and the iron edges of the freight cars.

The mudjhik knew where he was. Never for a moment did the grip of its awareness shift or falter. Lom felt the hunger of its desire to seize him, to pinch the cage of his ribs between its thumbs and squeeze. Somewhere at the margins of that fierce desire Lom sensed the mudjhik's handler fighting to keep some measure of control. It was like trying to dig fingers into polished granite.

The mudjhik could not pass between the railway wagons, it was too large, so it crashed through them, one after another, splintering the wooden superstructures and stepping over the iron chassis.

Run. Lom heard the mudjhik's mind in his. *Run, little man, run. I am coming.*

The wagons could not stop the mudjhik, but they slowed it. When Lom broke through into open space on the other side, it was still a couple of hundred yards behind him. Ahead of him lay the waste ground he'd crossed before, the wire fence, and then the crowds hustling for places on the passenger trains out of Mirgorod. People there were looking his way. There were shouts and screams. They'd seen the out-of-control mudjhik smashing its way towards them through the cattle wagons. Lom sensed their rising fear. He launched himself towards them in a desperate sprint.

He hit the fence at a run and scrabbled up and over, dropping recklessly on the other side. The crowds were backing away and scattering, terrified. There was a sound like a low despairing collective moan. The mudjhik was through the trains and out in the open ground, but it had slowed. Lom felt its riveted focus on him begin to slip and disintegrate. It was the crowd. The background noise of so many panicking minds confused it. It was sifting through them, trying to find him again. It hooked him and lurched forward but he pushed its gaze aside.

The mass of people was a single collective entity, a herd mind with a simple overwhelming purpose, moving on instinct, getting through from second to second, shoving, shouting, pushing, desperate to escape before the mudjhik crashed into them. Lom charged into the middle of it and joined them. For the first time in his life he surrendered himself up to the tidal mind of a mob, obliterating independent thought and sinking without question below the surface into dark, exhilarating waters. The energy that flowed through him was tremendous. The people around him were shadows, rivals, part of him, indistinguishable. Somewhere at the outer edges of his mind he felt the grazing trail of the mudjhik, superficial and negligible. The mudjhik itself was being pulled into the dark vortex and absorbed. Lom ducked away from it and let himself be carried away.

53

Lavrentina Chazia sat alone in the projection room in the deserted offices of Project Winter Skies, running the film of the test explosion at Novaya Zima over and over again. The evacuation of Mirgorod was under way. Her instructions were being carried out. Her train was ready: the Pollandore installed, her angel skin crated and stored, the Shaumian girl under lock and key in a barred freight car. There was nothing that required her attention until the train left at noon. She ran the film again. And again. She must have watched it twenty, fifty times. She could close her eyes and watch it all unfolding inside her head: the technicians busying themselves with the final preparations; their stupid, excited grins; the caption, UNCLE VANYA; the wind across silent level tundra, dwarfing the gantry; and then the cataclysm. The blinding gush of absolute, total, irresistible destructive power. As soon as the film had finished she went back to the projector, rewound it and played it again.

It was almost impressive that Dukhonin had achieved so much alone. She had underestimated him. But whatever he had done, it was hers now. In Mirgorod, Dukhonin had kept the circle tight and she had killed them all. Their families would be rounded up and shipped off east. That they would end up as conscript labour in Novaya Zima itself was an elegance that pleased her.

The Vlast had made a terrible mistake. She realised that now. All of them, and she along with them, had made a terrible mistake. They had been so focused on the fallen angels and what they meant, and what could be done with the flesh of their carcases, they had all failed to realise what human ingenuity could do by itself. They had taken their eye off those obscure laboratories.

But Kantor had not. Kantor had found them. And Kantor had found Dukhonin and made him his puppet. When he needed to tap into the resources of the Vlast he had chosen Dukhonin as his point of entry. Vain, industrious, narrow-minded Dukhonin. It had been a good choice.

Kantor's continuing existence pained her. Him she could not touch, not yet, but his time would come, and soon. He thought he pulled her strings. He thought he could keep things from her. But she would tip him over. She would see him swing from his own lungs. When the time came. Not yet but soon.

On the screen Uncle Vanya erupted once more. Chazia shifted in her chair and grunted at the punch of excitement in her belly and groin.

It was all coming together for her now. Power. Power. Power. The living angel. The Pollandore. And *this*: Novaya Zima. *This* was a strength that would wipe the Archipelago from the face of the planet and build her Vlast for a thousand, a hundred thousand years! The Founder himself would be nothing more than a footnote in the story of the rise of Lavrentina Chazia and the Vlast she would build. With this, the living angel would listen to her. With this, could she not erase the angel itself from the face of the planet? Yes, and burn the forest too. All of it. The whole of the planet would be hers.

54

Lom took a tram as far as the northern edge of Big Side and walked the rest of the way back to the Raion Lezaryet. It was almost midday. The Purfas Gate was open but the VKBD were watching the bridge. They let him cross without question – they weren't interested in who went in – but no one was coming out. A small knot of men stood in sullen silence just inside the wall.

As Lom climbed the steep narrow streets towards the house a distorted loudspeaker voice, high-pitched and hectoring, echoed instructions off the crowding gables. He couldn't make out the words or the direction it was coming from. Shops and offices were closed, the streets almost deserted. Ahead of him two men in frock coats and wide-brimmed hats crossed the road, heads down and walking quickly. They entered the Clothiers Meeting Hall and shut the door behind them. The tannoy was getting louder. Following the direction of the noise, Lom reached the edge of a small cobbled square, defined on one side by the raion's only hotel, the Purse of Crowns, and on the opposite corner by the Lezarye Courts of Commercial Jurisdiction.

A trestle table had been set up in the middle of the square. On it was a contraption like a radio, connected to a hefty separate battery, and next to it stood a sturdy tripod holding the loudspeaker horn. A small man in a dark suit and polished ankle boots was shouting into a microphone, reading from a sheet of paper. Hatless, he looked cold. His cheeks, his nose, the tips of his small ears were pink. Thin black hair slicked across his skull. Sweat-flattened strands across his forehead. He kept stopping to wipe his face and polish the lenses of little wire spectacles with a handkerchief from his jacket pocket. Half a dozen armed VKBD kept watch from the steps of the court. The tannoy and the echoes in the square distorted his voice. Lom had to listen the message through three times to piece it together.

'Attention! Attention! Residents of Raion Lezaryet! The defence commissar and city captain of Mirgorod announces that this quarter is designated for immediate evacuation. There is no reason for alarm. Prepare yourselves for resettlement or work duty in other provinces. Women and children will leave first. Small hand luggage only is to be taken. You must gather at the Stratskovny Voksal at 6 p.m. sharp. Women with babies are to provide themselves with paraffin stoves. You must understand that any resistance to this order will result in police countermeasures. Attempts to avoid resettlement will lead to forced evacuation. It is expected that all demands will be met with punctuality and calmness. I repeat ...'

Apart from Lom and the VKBD, there was nobody in the square to hear him. He was shouting at blank shuttered windows. Drawn curtains. Closed doors. There was a neat stack of paper on the table. Copies of the declaration for handing out. Nobody was taking one.

When Lom reached Elena Cornelius's apartment it was deserted. Maroussia wasn't there, and there was no sign that she'd been back. Their attic room was as he'd left it. Down in the kitchen everything was neatly stacked. The stove was banked up and smouldering quietly, no indication of a hurried departure, but Elena wasn't there and nor were the girls.

Lom found the Count and Ilinca in their salon. They were sitting side by side on a threadbare chaise longue. Dressed for a journey. A pair of old scuffed suitcases and a faded dusty carpet bag in the middle of the floor. The door standing open, ready.

'We knew the day would come,' said the Count. 'We are prepared.'

'Maroussia?' said Lom. 'Did she come back?'

Ilinca shook her head.

'She won't come here again,' said the Count. 'You should go too, Vissarion Yppolitovich. They're coming to collect us soon.'

'What happened to Elena?' said Lom. 'And the girls?'

'Elena went to the Apraksin,' said Ilinca. 'She took Yeva and Galina to school on the way. They would have gone before the announcement came. Elena is sensible. She'll know what to do.'

'You can't wait here like this,' said Lom. 'You have to run. You have to get away now. By yourselves. Don't let them take you. The raion is being cleared. There are trains at the station.' The excrement and straw in the darkness. The reek of disinfectant barrels. 'You don't know—'

'No,' said Palffy. 'We are safe.'

'You have to get away.'

Palffy looked out of the window.

'Away?' said Ilinca. 'Where would we go? How could we travel alone? Will you take us?'

The Count put his hand on Ilinca's arm.

'You'll be all right,' he said, not looking at Lom. 'I told you. They won't hurt us. They know us. They have our names. We are citizens; we're on the list; we did the right thing.'

'What?' said Lom. 'What did you do?'

The Count looked up at him blankly.

'You should leave now,' he said. 'Do not wait here.'

'What have you *done*?' said Lom.

The Count looked away and shook his head. The truth punched Lom in the belly. He felt dizzy. Sick with despair.

'Maroussia,' he said quietly. 'You betrayed her. You told them and they came for her.'

The Count took his wife's hand and gripped it tight in his.

'You did. Didn't you?' said Lom. He took a step towards them. 'You fucker. What have you *done*?'

'No,' said Ilinca quietly. 'Please. Don't.'

'So hit me,' said the Count, staring up into Lom's face. 'You are a violent man, I know this. Here.' He fumbled in his pocket and brought out an antique revolver. Holding it by the barrel, he offered the handle to Lom. 'There. Shoot me. You have a gun. Shoot me. I am ashamed of nothing. I did nothing you would not do. Nothing I would not do again a hundred times over for Ilinca's sake.'

Lom sank into a chair. He was weighed down with bleak despair. There was no strength, not even in his voice.

'Should I protect the Shaumian girl,' the Count was saying, 'at the price of my own wife's life? What was the Shaumian girl to us? There was a chance! She could have taken her place! She could have done her *duty*! For her family and her people. She could have *led* … but she did not. She made her choice, and I made mine. For Ilinca's sake.'

'You saved your own skin,' said Lom.

'You think you can judge me, Vissarion Yppolitovich? Do you have a wife? No. You are a man alone. Judgement comes cheap for you.'

'They took her, didn't they?' said Lom. 'Last night. Hours ago. And you didn't tell me. You let me go out and search. All this time I wasted. You could have ... When did they come? Where did they take her?'

'No one was here,' said Ilinca. 'What you are saying, it did not happen. Sandu is not to blame.'

Lom stared at the Count.

'The girl is not here,' said Palffy. 'And you should please go too. You should get out of my house now.'

Lom stepped out into the street and started back down the hill towards the Purfas Gate. He would find Maroussia and get her back. He would do that. But he had no idea what to do or where to go. None at all. He needed to get out of the raion, that was his only clear thought.

He didn't hear the staff car until it pulled up at the kerb alongside him, engine running. A long-wheelbase black ZorKi Zavod limousine, six doors, twenty feet long, with high backswept fenders and a spare wheel mounted on the back. A small red and black pennant was flying on the bonnet. The driver wound down the window. A long faintly sad intelligent face. Antoninu Florian in the uniform of a captain of police. On the front passenger seat Lom could see a pair of leather driving gloves laid neatly on top of a road atlas. Beside them a peaked cap with a crisp wide circular crown. Staff officer issue. Lom couldn't see the badge.

Florian nodded to him. Gave him a faint weary smile, almost shy.

'I suggest you get in the back,' he said.

Lom peered in through the back windows. Two benches upholstered in comfortable burgundy leather. Carpet on the floor. Apart from Florian the car was empty.

'Hurry please,' said Florian. 'We have to make a start.'

'Maroussia is gone,' said Lom. 'They've taken her. I don't know where. I have to find her.'

'She is with Chazia,' said Florian. 'Get in the car.'

Lom barely heard what Florian said.

'I have to get her back,' said Lom again.

'Then will you for fuck's sake get in the back of the car like a good fellow and we can be on our way.'

Part Two

55

At four in the afternoon Antoninu Florian's stolen ZorKi Zavod limousine nosed down the hill and out of the raion through the Purfas Gate. Lom held the Blok 15 in his lap, hidden under the flap of his coat. Safety catch off. Florian showed a warrant card. The VKBD corporal leaned over to look into the back of the car. Lom faced front, eyes down, and tried to look bored.

'Stand aside, soldier,' said Florian. 'No questions. Nothing to see.'

The corporal waved them through.

Florian drove the ZorKi with practised smoothness through residential streets and garden squares. Railings and snow. Money houses, finial-ridged with gables and balconies and porches and garaging for cars, set back behind lawns and laurel hedges. The kind of places where bankers and high Vlast officials made their homes. It was a part of the city Lom hadn't seen before. Apart from a few horse-drawn droshkis and private karetas they had the roads to themselves. A gendarme in a kiosk on a street corner saluted them as they passed. Saluted the pennant. Florian nodded in acknowledgement, expressionless.

'I have to find Maroussia,' said Lom.

'I know,' said Florian. 'You said.'

'You know what happened to her? You know where she is?'

'Chazia sent an upyr last night,' said Florian. 'Its name was Bez. Bez Nichevoi. Bez found Maroussia and took her to the Lodka.'

'I should have been with her.'

'It's fortunate you were not.'

'I could have stopped it,' said Lom. 'I could have protected her.'

'No. You would be dead.'

Lom shrugged. 'Possibly.'

'Not possibly. Certainly.'

'You said its name was Bez.'

'Yes.'

'You said *was*.'

'It was a bad thing. It carried many deaths. I burned it.'

The car rolled past tall stuccoed houses. Cherry trees in gardens, leafless now. The snow had been swept from the pavements and piled along the kerb. Twisting on the polished leather bench, Lom could see behind them on the skyline a column of distant smoke drifting up and disappearing into low misty cloud.

'This isn't the way to the Lodka,' he said.

'No.'

Lom leaned forward. Jabbed the muzzle of the Blok 15 into Florian's neck.

'Then turn the fucking car around.'

Florian sighed and pulled in, ploughing the ZorKi's passenger-side fender deep into a heaped-up ridge of snow on the side of the road.

'Don't look back,' said Lom. 'Keep your hands where I can see them. On the wheel.'

Florian did as he was told.

'Where are we going?' said Lom. 'Where are you taking me? We have to get to the Lodka. That's where Maroussia is.'

'No,' said Florian quietly. 'Maroussia was in the Lodka, but now she is not. The Vlast is abandoning Mirgorod to the Archipelago. The government is relocating eastwards to Kholvatogorsk, but Chazia is going further, to Novaya Zima with the Pollandore, and she is taking Maroussia with her. Their train will have left by now. The journey will not be straightforward: it will take them many days, perhaps a week, perhaps more. We also, as you may have observed, are travelling east and we will be quicker. Much quicker. We will reach Novaya Zima before Chazia's train and we will have time to prepare before they arrive. So unless you have a better plan, please be so good as to stop waving your dick around in the back of my car.'

'How do you know all this?' said Lom.

'I was in the Lodka last night.'

'You were in the *Lodka*?'

'She is alive,' said Florian. 'Beyond that, I cannot say, but she is alive, depend on it. Chazia will preserve her. The upyr took her. It did not kill her.'

'Then we have to find that train.'

Florian shook his head.

'The train they are travelling on is also carrying an extraordinary cargo. It will go by a special route prepared in advance under conditions of extreme secrecy. We have no chance of catching up with it before it reaches its destination. But even if we could … It is a military train. An armoured train. Soldiers. A mudjhik. A well guarded mobile prison. No. My plan is better. Come with me.'

'Come with you?' said Lom. 'Who the fuck *are* you? Why would I trust a single thing you've said?'

Florian twisted in his seat and pushed Lom's gun aside.

'There is no time for this,' he said, locking eyes with Lom. His irises were green, flecked with amber. 'Come with me to Novaya Zima, Vissarion. Together we will do what needs to be done. Or get out of the car now, if you think you can do better alone.'

Lom stared into Florian's face. He wished he could read something more in those deep, wise, dangerous eyes, but he could not. He had to make a choice, but it was no choice, not really. He sank back into the wide leather bench and slipped the Blok 15 into the pocket of his coat.

'OK,' he said. 'OK. Drive.'

56

Florian picked up the main route east. The outskirts of Mirgorod diminished to a tideline of subsistence enterprise – one-shed factories, workshops and junkyards, semi-collapsed smallholdings – but the road was getting more crowded, not less, and all the traffic was going in one direction. Away from the city. There were a few trucks and one or two private saloons, but mostly it was horse-drawn wagons and carts and nameless antiquated things hauled by donkeys and bullocks. There were whole families just walking, pushing prams and handcarts, lugging duffel bags, dragging suitcases along the ground, wearing layers upon layers of clothing to keep warm and leave room in the bags for more. The polished black staff car with its Vlast pennant drew hostile glares. From time to time somebody thumped the coachwork or spat on a window. Florian drove in silence, drumming his fingers on the wheel.

It took them hours to get clear. At last the traffic thinned out and Florian gunned the throttle. They were on the open road east of Mirgorod, skirting the southern shore of Lake Dorogha. It was just after six but twilight was already closing in.

'Tell me about Novaya Zima,' said Lom.

Florian tossed the road atlas onto the back seat.

'Follow the Zelenny mountains north,' he said. 'You'll find it.'

Lom found Mirgorod and started turning pages. Page after page eastward from where they were, the country was a flat expanse of pale green, spattered with small blue lakes and the hairline threads of rivers. The atlas was a Solon and Dutke *Standard & Comprehensive*: the best you could buy, which wasn't saying much. Only the largest towns and cities were shown, their names in florid black-letter script.

There were a few highways picked out in pink, but citizens of the Vlast didn't make long journeys by road. They used the slow looping sweeps of the waterways or, if they could afford it, the transcontinental trains. Most roads weren't even shown, and those that were mapped weren't necessarily there, or still maintained, or even passable. The same went for the railways.

Even the map-green of the empty landscape was optimistic. It belied featureless horizons of sandy soil and scrubby grassland, or the silent monotony of birch and moss. If green on a map meant anything, it meant *flat.* For thousands of miles east from Mirgorod nothing rose more than a few hundred feet above sea level. Not until you reached the Zelenny Mountains, a third of the way between the city and the edge of the endless forest. On the map the Zelenny range was a north–south spine of taupe-shaded contours, but in reality they were scarcely mountains at all, just a spine of uplands slightly too elevated, distinctive and topographically important to be called merely hills. The spine of the Zelenny ran north all the way to the coast and continued out across the water, becoming two long thin islands hooked into the belly of the Yarmskoye Sea like a crooked skeletal finger. The south island was contoured taupe, the north island was the blank and featureless white of year-round ice, and adrift in the sea near the islands was a name in the smallest and faintest typeface that Solon and Dutke ran to: NOVAYA ZIMA.

'That's it?' said Lom. 'That's where Chazia is going?'

'Yes,' said Florian.

'It's nowhere. Why the hell would Chazia go to a place like that?'

'That's what I want to know,' said Florian. 'A couple of years ago the Armaments Minister, Dukhonin, started spending money on his own initiative. He was Vlast Commissar for Industry then, but this was a private venture: secretive appropriations, diverted funds, nothing accounted for. He requisitioned building materials, heavy machinery, oil, coal. And it was all for Novaya Zima. He flooded the place with tens of thousands of conscript workers.

'And then, while the heavy labour was still flowing in, Dukhonin started recruiting persons of a different kind: managers, architects, doctors, teachers. He collected specialists. Engineers. Chemists. Mathematicians. Astronomers. Physical scientists of every conceivable discipline. And always the best. Outstanding in their discipline.

I say *recruiting*, but it's a euphemism of course. Some of the people Dukhonin sent to Novaya Zima were zeks, prisoners he pulled out from other camps. In other cases bespoke arrests were made, and an eminent few were simply invited, though it was always made clear to them that refusal was not an option. And no one he sent north has ever come back. None of them has ever been heard from again. No communication comes out of Novaya Zima. None at all.'

'So what is he doing up there?' said Lom. 'It sounds like he's building a *city*. But why build a city up there? It's thousands of miles from anywhere.'

'I don't know,' said Florian. 'I've been combing the archives for weeks, and I've found out some of what's been sent up there, but as to why … there is no indication, none at all. And Dukhonin is dead now.'

'I read about that in the paper,' said Lom. 'Josef Kantor killed him.'

'Yes,' said Florian. 'Perhaps it was Kantor. Maybe.'

'What do you mean, maybe?'

'It is something of a coincidence, don't you think?'

Lom felt his irritation rising again. He wished Florian wouldn't play games.

'What?' he said. 'What's a coincidence?'

'Dukhonin dies and the very next day Chazia sets off for Novaya Zima with Maroussia Shaumian in tow.'

'You think Chazia killed him?' said Lom.

'It is not unlikely, certainly. And there is something else.'

Florian hesitated again.

'For fuck's sake,' said Lom. '*What* else?'

'Perhaps you have heard someone speak already of the Pollandore? Perhaps Maroussia Shaumian has mentioned this to you?'

'Yes,' said Lom cautiously. 'I've heard of it.'

'The extraordinary cargo to which I referred a moment ago,' said Florian. 'The cargo on Chazia's train? It is the Pollandore.'

Lom's stomach lurched. He felt his skin prickle. A chill in his spine.

'Shit,' he breathed. 'Shit. What the hell is Chazia up to?'

'I don't know,' said Florian. 'But you see now? You understand why I came for you? Why I think we should join forces?'

An hour later twilight was thickening into night. Florian flicked on the headlamps. They were passing through level country, undrained and undyked, a patchwork of woodland and shallow lakes and reed beds. The beams splashed off scrubby birch trees and alders, vegetable patches and makeshift fences, stands of hogweed. From time to time a weathered wooden cabin rose out of the darkness and disappeared behind them.

Lom had been turning over what Florian had told him. He didn't doubt it, not really, but it didn't make sense: the more he thought about it, the less it fitted together, and a big part of the puzzle was Florian himself. Who was he? What was he? What was he keeping back? He glanced at Florian's shadowy profile.

'You can't drive a car all the way to Novaya Zima,' said Lom, remembering the thousands of miles of empty green on the map. 'It isn't possible. You need to tell me where we're going.'

'Still you do not trust me, Vissarion?' said Florian patiently. 'We are going to Novaya Zima, but not by car. We are making for a small lake called Chudsk, but we will not reach it for some hours yet. Why don't you get some sleep?'

'I don't need to sleep. You could let me drive for while.'

Florian hesitated.

'Sure,' he said. 'Fine.'

Florian brought the car to a stop, killed the engine and dropped his hands off the wheel with a sigh. When he cut the headlamps and wound down the window, an immense silence rolled in around them, and with it the smell of damp earth and cold night air. Tiny night sounds could be heard above the ticking of the cooling engine: the wind moving across grass and snow, the nearby trickle of water, the shriek of a fox. Lom got out and walked round to get in behind the wheel. Florian slid across into the front passenger seat.

'Thank you,' said Florian. 'I am tired. Just keep straight on. There's only the one road: you just need to make sure you don't turn off onto any farm tracks.' He settled back in his seat and closed his eyes.

Lom started the engine and pulled away.

'Florian?' he said.

Florian stirred reluctantly and opened his eyes.

'Yes?' he said.

'You need to tell me how you know what you know. You need to tell me who you are.'

'Who I am? In what sense, exactly? Are we discussing allegiances here? Sides? Motivations?'

'Sure,' said Lom. 'Absolutely. For a start.'

'I am . . .' He paused, choosing his words carefully. 'I am . . . freelance.'

'*Freelance*?'

'Uh-huh.'

'*Uh-huh?*' said Lom. 'You care to expand on that? Because you need to.'

Florian settled lower in the passenger seat and closed his eyes again. Lom thought he wasn't going to say any more, but after a while he started speaking quietly.

'You think I am playing games with you, Vissarion? OK. Maybe. But *really*. You should *look* at yourself. You are angry, and you ask me what I am? You? You, who have that marvellous, that wonderful, that unique and beautiful opening in your head? You sit there and it's spilling out . . . shedding . . . you don't know *what*, you're not even *aware* . . . and you ask *me* to say what *I* am?'

'What do you mean?' said Lom. 'What are you trying to say?'

Florian half opened his eyes and glanced sideways.

'I think you should stop asking yourself what things are and start asking what they can become. I think you should work at yourself. I think you should, to coin a phrase, get a fucking grip.'

57

Colonel-General Rizhin put aside the name of Josef Kantor and the life he'd lived under that name without a backward glance. He killed Kantor without compunction or regret. *There is no past, there is only the future.* Commissar for Mirgorod city defence.

Rizhin began to *work*.

He had an appetite and capacity for work that were astonishing. Relentless. Prodigious. Terrifying. The more he worked the more energy he drew from it and the more work he did. No detail was trivial, no obstacle immovable. He had a nose for men and women whose capacity for work matched his, or almost, and he gathered them about him. Put them to work. Those that flagged or showed the slightest inclination to cling to a private life of their own (the very phrase an abomination in Rizhin's lexicon) were ruthlessly obliterated.

And Rizhin's work was war, his purpose victory.

Within hours of the departure of Chazia, Fohn and Khazar, the pyre outside the Lodka was extinguished. The number of recruitment booths doubled. That very afternoon, he told the people of Mirgorod what to expect. He broadcast on the radio, on the tannoys and loudspeakers. The film was played in cinemas and converted Kino-trams, over and over again. Incessantly. The text appeared that evening in special editions of all the newspapers. Every paper carried the same photograph of Rizhin's gaunt, smiling, pockmarked face. By the evening it had appeared on posters in every public building, on every tram, on every city wall. Yesterday the people of the city might have been asking, who is this Rizhin? Today they knew.

He called the city to war, a war against two enemies: outside the city were the forces of the Archipelago, and inside the city were the diversionists, the traitors, the looters, the spies. It wasn't two wars, it was one war fought on two fronts, and there was nothing that was not part of it. No bystanders. No noncombatants. No civilians.

'At last,' he told the people of Mirgorod, 'we are coming to grips with our most vicious and perfidious enemy The fiends and cannibals of the Archipelago, the slavers, are bearing down on our city. And they have accomplices among us! Whiners. Cowards. Deserters. Panic mongers. Spies. Saboteurs. Traitors!

'The enemy's soldiers and their secret allies must be rooted out and destroyed at every step. This is no ordinary war. Not a war of soldiers but a war of all the people. Everyone and everything is at war! Total war! Our homes are not our own, our dreams are not our own. Our lives are not our own. There is only one life, the Vlast, and only one outcome is possible. Overwhelming triumph!

'Everything must be mobilised, all that we are. Private lives do not exist. Every man, woman and child is a soldier of the Vlast. We will fall upon our enemies as one body, an irresistible mass, roaring defiance, destruction and death with a single voice. With the angels on our side we will certainly prevail. All the strength of the people must be used to smash the enemy. Onward to victory!'

In the cinemas and in the squares the people of Mirgorod broke into spontaneous cheering. The death of the Novozhd had left them adrift, afraid and grieving, but here was a leader again, come in their desperate hour.

Rizhin.

His face was everywhere, and his words.

Onward to victory!

58

Elena Cornelius was working in the Apraksin when she heard from a customer about the forced evacuation of the Raion Lezaryet. She closed the counter immediately and went as fast as she could to the school, desperate to be with her daughters, to see them safe, but when she got there she found the teachers reluctant to let her take the girls away.

'Our instructions are to keep them all together here,' the headmaster said, 'until the trucks come. They will all be taken to a place of safety, far away from the bombs. The whole school is to go, we teachers also. We don't know yet where we are going, but we are excited about this great adventure and so are the children. It is best for them, don't you think? I would think you would be pleased for them, Elena Cornelius. Your girls will be safer with us.'

'I am their mother and I will keep them safe,' said Elena Cornelius. 'Not you. Me. They are coming with me now.'

'But—'

'I am their *mother* and you will not stop me taking them.'

'On your own responsibility, then,' the headmaster said. 'I wash my hands of them. Don't come crying to me later, and do not expect to bring Yeva and Galina back to this school again when the war is over.'

Elena did not return to Count Palffy's house in the raion – all their possessions, their home, the workshop, it was all lost to them now – but she went instead with her daughters to her aunt Lyudmila Markova, who had a one-room apartment in Big Side. Aunt Lyudmila had never married. She kept a caged parakeet for company and was reluctant to take in her niece and two girls as well.

'But there's only the one bed, Elena! Where would you sleep?'

'On the floor. I'll buy a mattress.'

'I don't know, Elena. That doesn't sound comfortable for the girls, and Bolto doesn't like change. It unsettles him. He doesn't like strangers coming in and out. He has his own little ways.' Bolto was the parakeet.

'We are not *strangers*, Aunt,' said Elena. 'And I've got a hundred roubles at the workshop. You'll be glad of the help when the war comes. Things will get expensive.'

'All this talk of war, I don't like it, Elena. It's nonsense. The Novozhd won't let anything happen to Mirgorod.'

'The Novozhd is dead, Aunt. The enemy is coming. There'll be more bombing. There may be fighting.'

'Oh no, not here. I don't think so. They wouldn't dare. Why don't you just go home and wait till it all blows over? Bolto and I will be fine.'

'I can't go home. Everyone in the raion is being taken away on trains and nobody knows where to.'

'I thought you were doing well at the Apraksin, Elena? I thought they liked you there? You've always said—'

'It's not to do with the Apraksin, Aunt. It's everyone.'

In the end Aunt Lyudmila relented.

'Just for a couple of days, Elena, until you get yourself settled. I must say I'm disappointed in Count Palffy; it's very shoddy behaviour to put you out like this. You don't expect it, not from an aristocrat. The Novozhd always said they were enemies of the people.'

When she heard Rizhin's broadcast on Aunt Lyudmila's radio, Elena Cornelius knew she had to do something. She could not go to the raion again, she could not go back to the Apraksin and she could not simply hide away in her aunt's apartment. Sooner or later she would be found and questions would be asked. The girls had to be safer than that. She had to do what she could to protect them. Immediately. That meant she had to have a role. She had to have a place. She had to have a story.

'This new man, Rizhin,' said Aunt Lyudmila. 'He sounds like a strong man. He'll sort out this nonsense about a war.'

That same evening Elena went to the Labour Deployment Office and filled in a form. Where it said address, she put Aunt Lyudmila's apartment in Big Side. She waited in line for two hours and handed the form to a woman at a desk.

'My name is Elena Schmitt,' she said.

'Would I be in this job if I couldn't read?'

'No,' said Elena. 'Of course not.'

The woman studied the form carefully. She had close-cropped fair hair and colourless eyes in a dry, sunless face, striated with fine lines. She must have been about forty. Her fawn uniform blouse was fresh and spotless. Crisp epaulettes. Sharp creases down the outside edge of her sleeves. Elena thought that, close to, she would smell of laundry. The woman pulled out a file and paged through sheets and sheets of typescript.

'This is your address?'

'Yes. Well, it is my aunt's apartment. I live with her.'

'How long?'

'I'm sorry? I don't understand?'

'How long have you lived there?'

'Two years.'

'You're not listed at that address.'

'I came to Mirgorod two years ago,' said Elena. 'To work at Blue's. Before that I lived with my parents. At Narymsk, and before that Tuga. Look, I want to work, citizen. I want to do something. For the city.'

'So. And what can you do, Elena Schmitt?'

'I am a carpenter. I have my own tools. I have a school certificate in mathematics and a diploma in bookkeeping.'

'Can you dig?'

'What?'

'Can you dig? Can you use a pick and a spade?'

'I make furniture. Cupboards. Wardrobes.'

'When the Archipelago tanks arrive, should we put them away in a cupboard?'

'No. But surely—'

'There is a requirement for more workers on the inner defence line. People who can dig. Can you dig frozen soil with your fingers on a quarter-pound of black bread a day?'

'If that is what the city requires of me then I will try, citizen. I will do my best.'

The woman filled in some details on a pink card, stamped it with an official stamp and gave it to her.

'Report at six o'clock tomorrow morning.'

Aunt Lyudmila had already gone to bed when Elena Cornelius got back to the apartment, and the girls were asleep together on the floor, curled up under an eiderdown on cushions from the couch. Elena found a packet of tea in the cupboard, boiled a kettle on the paraffin stove and made herself a pot. The label on the tea packet had a drawing of ladies in high lacy collars with a samovar on a tablecloth, and underneath was written in curly script:

What follows after taking tea?
The resurrection of the dead.

It was an old saying, some kind of joke or pun. It was traditional. Elena had always wondered what it meant.

She sat in a wicker chair in the window, the curtains drawn back, a blanket wrapped round her shoulders. It was too cold to sleep. The moons bathed the city in a bone-white glare, monochrome and alien. Mirgorod looked like the capital of some other planet. Silent searchlight beams swept the skyline and flashed across the soft silver hulls of barrage balloons. A remembered phrase from childhood came into her mind and would not leave. *The beneficence of angels.*

At midnight the Archipelago bombers came. Tiny bright anti-aircraft shells crackled and flowered briefly in the dark. Searchlights slashed at the raiders but didn't hold what they caught. Within an hour huge fires were burning on the horizon. Elena watched flames lick high into the air: arches and caverns, sheets and waterfalls of flame. Whirling flame tornadoes. Hurricanes of fire. It was all happening several miles away. She imagined she could feel the heat of the fires against her face, though she could not.

59

Lom had never driven anything like a ZorKi Zavod limousine before. He liked it. Eight cylinders, automatic transmission, the flat empty road at night. He pressed his foot down and watched the needle climb smoothly to fifty. The car must have weighed a couple of tons, but the engine scarcely rose above a quiet purr. The bonnet stretched ahead of him like the boiler of a locomotive, pennant flickering. All he had to do was keep his foot on the throttle and his hand on the wheel and follow the patch of lamplit road that skimmed ahead of him, always just beyond arrival. Except for the interior of the car, smelling of leather and polish, and the splash of lamplight on the road, there was nothing anywhere but blackness under a vast black sky. Forward motion without visible result. He kept the window open an inch to let the wind touch his face. When small snowflakes began to speckle the windscreen he found the switch for the wipers and set them sweeping back and forth: a quiet click at the end of each cycle, clearing twin arcs in the sparse accumulating snow.

Lom put his hand to his forehead and felt for the lozenge-shaped wound socket. It was just the right size to accommodate the tip of his forefinger. He touched the smooth newness of young skin covering the uneven rim of cut skullbone, soft-edged and painless. It was a blind third eye, pulsing faintly with the restful rhythms of his beating heart, a life sign, part of him now, absorbed, healed, no longer conspicuous. A mark of freedom. A badge of honour. A legacy of ancient hurt. When he took his finger away he could feel the coolness of the wind pressing against the place with gentle insistence. A nudge of conscience. A memory just beyond the frontier of recollection.

Hours passed. The road stretched on ahead, drifting slightly to right and left. The ZorKi swept along at a steady fifty miles an hour. Villages rose ahead and fell behind. Mostly they were too small for names: just clusters of buildings glimpsed and gone, straggling settlements barely registering against the emptiness. No lights showed: they might as well have been deserted. The needle on the fuel gauge had been creeping round to the left all night, and now it was ominously close to empty. Lom pulled up and got out to relieve himself. Legs and back stiff from the long drive, he walked self-consciously a few yards off the road to a scrubby stand of brush at the foot of a telegraph pole. When he got back to the car, Florian was awake, easing himself upright and rubbing his face

'Where are we?' he said.

'We came through Zharovsk a while back,' said Lom. He looked at his watch. It was coming up towards three in the morning. 'We're running short of fuel.'

'There's more in the back.'

Florian went round to the boot of the car, opened it and dragged out a couple of jerrycans. He found a funnel and began to fill the tank. When he'd done, he stowed the empty cans. Then he brought out a suitcase and changed his uniform for a neat and sober suit, produced his astrakhan hat and chucked the officer's cap on the back seat.

'I'll drive from here,' he said.

An hour or so later Florian slowed the car at a crossroads and turned off the highway onto a rough track between trees. There was no sign: nothing to mark the turning. The woods closed in around them and the ZorKi was suddenly bouncing and slithering through soft rutted mud. Florian handled the car effortlessly.

Eventually, the track emerged abruptly onto the edge of a lake and turned left to follow it. The road, if you could call it that, was almost too narrow for the car. On the driver's side trees pressed in close and overhanging branches clattered and scraped against the windows. To the right the crazily jolting headlamps showed glimpses of a narrow strip of muddy shore: scraps of low mist and the carbon glitter of black water.

They swung round the end of a narrow headland and climbed a slight rise. As they crested the rise, a low wooden building appeared in front of them. It looked halfway between a cabin and a barn. There was a jetty, and a small seaplane moored on the water.

Florian pulled the car in close to the edge of a low stone wharf and killed the engine. On Lom's side there was a three-foot drop to the water. He could hear the quiet lapping of water against stone, the wind in the trees, the breathy wheezing of disturbed waterfowl.

'Wait here,' said Florian. He left the door open and walked towards the building, taking care to stay clearly visible in the glare of the headlamps. 'Lyuba!' he called into the darkness. 'Lyuba! It's Florian!'

A woman's voice answered from the darkness, 'You're late. You said yesterday.'

The voice didn't come from the building, but from somewhere away to the left under the trees. Lom realised that Florian had been facing that way before she spoke. He'd known where she was, out there in the dark.

'There was some delay leaving Mirgorod,' Florian said. 'But I am here now. Is everything ready?'

'There's someone else in the car.'

'A friend. He's travelling with me.'

'You didn't say anything about passengers.'

'Is there a problem?'

'Passengers are extra. The deal didn't include passengers.'

'Of course. Can we discuss this inside? We've come a long way.'

The woman stepped out into the headlamps' glare. She was short and solidly built: not fat, but heavy, and wearing a bulky dark knitted sweater, the kind seamen favoured. Thick curly hair spilled out from under a peaked seaman's cap.

She was carrying a shotgun loosely in the crook of her arm.

Lom got out of the car.

'This is Vissarion,' said Florian. 'Vissarion Lom. Lyuba Gretskaya.'

Gretskaya looked him up and down.

'OK,' she said. 'If you say so.'

Florian took a satchel from the boot of the ZorKi.

'Anything of yours in the car?' he said to Lom.

Lom leaned into the back, picked up his woollen cap and crammed it down on his head.

'No,' he said. 'Nothing.'

Florian reached in and released the handbrake, leaned his right shoulder against the car and, with his hand on the steering wheel, turned it slowly to the right and pushed it off the edge of the wharf.

When the front wheels went over, the fenders crashed and scraped on the stonework. The headlamps dipped below the surface and spilled murky subaqueous yellow-green light. Florian flicked them off and gave a heave with his shoulder that levered the whole massive car, all two tons of it, up and forward. The limousine plunged off the edge of the wharf into the lake, leaving oily swirls of disturbance.

60

Lyuba Gretskaya lived in a single room that did her as a workshop and a kitchen. It smelled of pine and tobacco and engine oil. There was a single bed along one wall. A metal cot piled with blankets. Maps and charts. Racks of hand tools. A lathe.

'Breakfast, gentlemen?'

Lom realised he hadn't eaten for almost twenty-four hours.

'Yes,' he said. 'Please. That would be great.'

He watched Gretskaya cut thick slices off a piece of bacon and fry them on an oil stove in the corner. Her face, lit by a single lamp hung above the stove, was broad and round and weathered to a dark polished brown, with a small stub of a nose. Her bright small eyes were a pale, pale grey, almost lost in the creases of her face.

'Is that your own plane?' he said for something to say.

'Yup,' said Gretskaya, not looking round.

'Where did you learn to fly?'

'Where did you learn to ask questions?'

Lom caught Florian's eye. He was trying not to smile.

'OK,' said Lom. 'Sorry. Just making conversation.'

The bacon was nearly done. Gretskaya threw some chunks of black bread into the pan to fry in the bacon fat and made a pot of coffee. They ate in silence, rapidly, and when they'd finished she cleared the plates, spread out a chart out on the yellow deal table and lit a cigarette. Her fingers were stubby and brown and stained with oil.

'The Kotik will do eight hundred miles on a single tank,' she said. 'We cover more ground if the wind's with us, less if it's not. Maximum speed is one three five, but for efficient cruising I don't go much over a hundred. With a safety margin, that gives us, say, five or six hours airtime before we need to refuel.' She jabbed at the chart with her cigarette, spilling ash. Brushed it away. 'The first leg is straightforward. North-east to Slensk. Refill at the pier head. From Slensk, we have a choice.' She sketched out the options on the chart. 'We can follow the coast to Garshal – see that island there? There's a whaling station, I've used it before – or we follow the river inland' – she traced the course of the Northern Kholomora with her finger – 'and stop at the portage head at Terrimarkh. We'll decide which course to take when we get to Slensk. It'll depend on the weather, mainly: maybe we'll be able to get a forecast at Slensk. Either way, from Garshal or Terrimarkh it's a five-hundred-mile hop to Novaya Zima. I'll have you there tomorrow afternoon.'

Florian lifted the satchel onto the table, undid the buckles and pulled out thumbed and grubby bundles of ten-rouble notes.

'A thousand,' he said. 'I think that's what we agreed.'

'Plus a passenger.'

'So? How much?'

Gretskaya glanced at Lom. 'Has he got travel papers?'

'No—' Lom began.

'Sure,' said Florian. He threw a passport across the table towards him. 'Here. Name of Vexhav. Stanil Vexhav, age thirty-three. You're a former policeman interested in setting up as a timber merchant. But only if anyone asks. Don't volunteer information about yourself. People with nothing to hide don't do that.'

Lom picked up the passport and turned the pages. It looked convincing. The green cover was creased and stained with use, and its pages were spattered with the internal visas and crossing marks of a man who'd been travelling the rivers and ports of the north for the last couple of years. His own face looked out at him, the version of two or three years ago, stern and monochrome, eyes hooded with fatigue. Hair flopped across his forehead to obscure the angel seal.

'You got a photograph of me?'

'It's not you. It's me.'

Lom glanced across at Gretskaya.

'Don't mind me,' she said. 'He pays. I fly. Another two fifty for the passenger,' she said to Florian. 'And you pay to fill the tanks. Also other expenses.'

'Expenses?'

'We'll need to eat. Maybe sleep. Maybe bribe a harbour clerk here and there.'

Florian made a sour face but nodded and counted out the money without protest.

'When do we start?' said Lom.

Gretskaya ignored him. She gathered up the roubles, disappeared with them into a back room and came back with an armful of leather jackets, sheepskin gloves, fur hats, scarves.

'Put these on,' she said. 'It's going to be cold.'

Gretskaya went ahead and turned on the cockpit lamp and the navigation lights. Lom recognised the aircraft: he'd seen one like it moored at the Yannis boatyard in Podchornok. It was a Beriolev Kotik biplane, the clumsy reliable workhorse of the northern lakes. The boat-shaped hull, dented and water-stained, wasn't much bigger than the ZorKi limousine. Beneath the centre of the upper wing was a single stumpy engine nacelle, its two-bladed wooden propeller facing backwards. The lower wings stuck out from behind the cockpit, a canoe-shaped stabilising float slung beneath each one. The wings looked feeble, like arms raised in surrender or despair, like they'd snap off under the weight of the fuselage. Lom remembered the immense sleek bombers of the Archipelago roaring low across Mirgorod. Machines from a different world.

Florian clambered up into the cockpit and ducked down into the cabin behind.

'He always travels below deck,' said Gretskaya. 'Straps himself in and keeps his eyes screwed shut. You take the co-pilot seat.'

She swarmed neatly up the side of the hull and over the windscreen. Lom followed awkwardly and squeezed himself into the tight space beside her. The cockpit was crude and industrial: lime-green steel with canvas bucket seats. No concessions. In front of the pilot's seat was a flat black panel of gauges, dials, knobs and switches, and a small three-quarter wheel on a green steel column thick as an arm. Gretskaya taped several layers of red cellophane across the cockpit lamp, dimming the interior to near darkness, made a few adjustments to her instruments, then stood up in her seat so she could reach behind to start the engine. It burst into life with a reek of oil and smoke. The whole airframe began to vibrate.

Gretskaya slid the cockpit canopy forward and closed them in.

'You flown before?' she said, pulling on her gloves.

'No.'

'Don't touch anything. If you feel like you're going to puke, well, don't.'

'I'll be fine,' said Lom.

Gretskaya opened the throttle and eased the plane away from the jetty, swinging its nose to point across dark open water. Lom looked at his watch. It was half past five. Still three hours to dawn.

The engine bellowed and the machine surged forward, bumped two or three times as it hit the swell, and then … nothing. It took Lom a moment to realise they were airborne. Gretskaya pulled back sharply on the column. Lom's weight pressed him back into his seat as the Kotik, trembling with the surge of its engines, its airframe creaking alarmingly, climbed steeply into darkness. While they were still pushing upwards at a steep angle, Gretskaya took her hands off the stick and gripped it between her knees. She tested the lamps and added another layer of red cellophane. She saw Lom watching her and grinned.

'Night vision,' she said. 'Don't want to be dazzled by the interior lights. Don't worry, there's nothing up here to crash into.'

Lom grunted and stared out of the side window. The ground below was a broadening, sliding patchwork of barely legible darkness: the foggy glimmer of the lake and the spreading inky absolute blackness of trees, threaded by a dim paler line that must have been the road they came in by. A sudden flash of light outside the starboard window at his shoulder startled him. It was followed by another longer flash, a flicker, and then a trail of intermittent, vaporous brightness was streaming backwards from the wingtip lamp, which until then had been invisible under the wing. The temperature dropped precipitously and the landscape below them disappeared. Lom realised they were flying into cloud. The plane lurched sideways, caught in turbulence. Gretskaya steadied her and kept on climbing. As they reached the upper fringes of the cloud the wingtip lights seemed to flash on and off again, more and more rapidly, and suddenly vanished.

They emerged into clear dark space. Above them, drifts and scarves of stars glittered in blackness. The moons on the horizon illuminated the oceanic cloud below and pinned the tiny aeroplane to it with a bitter mineral glare.

Gretskaya levelled off, balancing the Kotik by gyroscope. Wrapped in the cockpit's companionable little pocket of blood-red dimness, Lom watched the thin radium line of the artificial horizon rise and settle. The dials on the instrument panel breathed slowly. The engine quietened and the aircraft droned onwards, chasing its own mist-haloed shadow on the cloud below. The sky above the clouds was a beautiful, desolate, endless, frontierless world.

Lom had felt the beautiful ache of immensity before – a silent afternoon in a train crawling across continental moss, a night walk among birch trees in the Dominions of the Vlast. Simplification. Purification. Humbling. The mortification of the self. But never anything like this. Never anything to compare with these dangerous, darkly shining, planetary, abyssal eternities. *Up with the moons the angels swam.* Words he hadn't heard since childhood rose up out of the accumulated silt in the bottom of his mind and tugged at him like rusalkas pawing a tiring swimmer. Trying to grab his attention. Trying to pull him under.

What you must do, said Baba Roga, is climb down inside the hollow tree until you come to a cave. Inside the cave there are three doors. If you open the first door, you will find a dog with eyes the size of dinner plates, guarding a treasure of copper. If you open the second door, you will find a dog with eyes the size of millstones, guarding a treasure of gold. And if you open the third door, you will find a dog with eyes the size of moons, guarding a treasure of blood and earth. What do you think of that, my beautiful boy?

I think the eyes of the dogs are moons, Provost. And the dogs are angels. All angels are terrible.

And all the rusalkas had Maroussia's face.

Images of Maroussia crowded his mind. Maroussia's dark serious eyes. Maroussia walking straight-backed away from him down the street. Maroussia's cold work-reddened hands. Maroussia asleep, breathing in the dark. The scent of her hair. The brush of her face against his cheek. Maroussia tied to an iron chair and Chazia leaning over her, running her tongue across her lower lip in concentration. Chazia with a knife in her hand.

61

Lavrentina Chazia watched the Shaumian girl return slowly to consciousness. She stirred. Groaned. Opened her eyes. Vomited. Tried to sit up and vomited again. Her eyes were confused. Unfocused. Whatever Bez Nichevoi had done to subdue her, it had left her feeble, trembling and feverish. No matter. There was time now. Plenty of time.

Chazia had propped her up against the wall of the otherwise empty freight car. Her wrists were cuffed with leather bands, connected by chains to a bar bolted to the floor. The chains, no more than dog leashes really, were long enough for her to move but not to stand. In her present condition she could not have stood unaided anyway. Chazia squatted beside her and held out a cup of water.

'Here,' she said. 'Drink.'

The girl shook her head.

Chazia smiled. 'You think I want to poison you?' she said. 'Of course I don't.' She drank the cup herself. 'Look, it's fine.' She poured another. 'Please. Drink. You need it. I don't know what Bez did to you, but I apologise for it. I'm sure it was both unnecessary and unpleasant.'

This time the girl took the cup and swallowed the water in one gulp. Choked and coughed half of it back out, soaking her chest. She leaned back against the rough plank wall. The freight car swayed as it rounded a curve.

'Where am I?' she said. 'This is a train.'

Chazia poured another cup.

'Take your time,' she said. 'There's plenty more. And food, when you're ready.' She took a handkerchief from her pocket and held it out to her. 'Here. Clean yourself.'

The girl shook her head.

'I am Commander Chazia, but you should call me Lavrentina. We are going to be friends.'

'I know who you are. And we are not friends.'

'No,' said Chazia. 'Perhaps not exactly friends. Associates, then. Colleagues. We have something in common.'

'No. We don't.'

'Of course we do. Together we are going to open the Pollandore.'

Maroussia Shaumian sank back against the wall and closed her eyes.

62

The stars spilled across the sky like salt on the blade of an axe. The broken moons sank away, subsiding into the horizon, leaving the cloud floor dark. Erasing it. The Kotik hung suspended over nothing at all. Only the vibration of the hull suggested, despite appearances, forward motion. Silent and freezing in their dimmed red cockpit, Lom and Gretskaya might as well have been crossing interplanetary space.

And then the world began to separate. Muted discriminations of darkness and lesser darkness. A new sedimentary horizon silting out. A dark line dividing the clouds below from the sky above. The line seemed to be getting further away, as if the aircraft was going backwards. Or shrinking. The last stars swam and trembled, dissolving.

The sky grew grey like the clouds but cleaner, deeper and more still. The banks of vapour beneath the plane thickened and the sky thinned and dilated into purple then green then white then pale immensities of blue. A fingernail of misty brilliance just starboard of the Kotik's nose became an arc of fire, burning steadily at the clouds' rim, pulsing incandescent blazing bars of pink and gold. And then the world was blue and clean and empty and went on for ever, oceans of air above dazzling oceans of cloud. Air that was filled to the brim with an astonishing purity of bright and perfect light. Simplified, wordless, unmappable. Lom felt the coldness of it burn his face. He looked across at Gretskaya.

'How high are we?'

She tapped the altimeter with a stubby gloved finger. The needle rested steadily at 10,000 feet. Lom did the maths.

'That's almost two *miles*,' he said.

Gretskaya grinned.

'You want to go higher?' she said. 'We'll go higher.'

She pulled back on the stick. Lom felt the pressure again in the small of his back. Up and up the tiny aircraft climbed – 12,000 – 14,000 – 16,000 – 18,000 – into a rarefied indigo world. Lom was aware of the air growing thinner. Sparser. It was more difficult to fill his lungs. His pulse rate quickened. He felt it fluttering in the centre of his forehead.

The air grew thinner but the light did not. Every detail of the cockpit and the wings at his shoulder burned itself on Lom's retinas with crystal clarity. Every fold and scuff on the sleeve of his leather jacket was magnified, brilliant and intense. The jacket was translucent. Inside the sleeves, every fine hair on his arms glistened. His skin itself was translucent. The light shone through him like the sun seen through leaves. The organs of his body were sunlit pink and clear. His veins, his bones, his lungs sang with light. He wasn't breathing air, he was breathing illumination.

More slowly now, but still the machine bored upwards. At last the altimeter registered 20,000 feet, and the nose of the machine sank a little until it was on an even keel. Gretskaya gave him the thumbs up and settled back in her seat. Urging on three tons of vibrating metal with her shoulders. Her eyes, creased almost shut against the over-brimming of the light, had seemed grey in the lamplight of her cabin but now they were the same clear clean watery blue as the sky.

Lom searched on the instrument panel for the compass and found it. The needle was pointing steadily north-east. Four miles below, at the bottom of a crevasse in the clouds, he glimpsed the glitter of creased dark water. A lake, or perhaps by now the sea of the Gulf of Burmahnsk.

63

Maroussia struggled into consciousness. There was a foul taste in her mouth. She felt dizzy and sick. Chazia was looking down at her, smiling, her hair backlit with the glare of the single caged bulb in the wooden ceiling. Her skin was blotched with patches of smooth darkness.

'Good,' said Chazia. 'You're awake.'

Chazia was holding the solm. She held it up for Maroussia to see. The ball of twigs and wax and stuff looked tawdry and dead in her skewbald palm.

'I know the paluba was looking for you,' said Chazia, 'and it found you. It brought you the key to the Pollandore. I think this is it. This is the key. It is, isn't it?'

Maroussia shook her head. The movement made her dizzy. Acidic bile rose up in the back of her throat. She turned her head aside to vomit.

'I'm not going to help you,' she said when she'd finished. 'Not ever. Not with anything.'

'You need to understand your position, Maroussia darling,' said Chazia. 'You really do. You are in my world now. There is no hope and no protection for you here; there is only me. I can turn you inside out. It's not a metaphor, sweetness. I can dig around in you. I can pull the guts from your belly and hold them up for you to see. I can do anything I want. And afterwards I can give you to Bez Nichevoi.' Chazia knelt in front of her and took her hand. Her gaze was warm and bright, compassionate and mad. 'I can do this to you, Maroussia,' she said. 'You do believe me, darling, don't you?'

Maroussia stared at Chazia dumbly. Her head hurt. She could find nothing to say. Whatever the foul creature that abducted her had done to her, it was still in her veins. All the energy had been flushed out of her. She felt as if she was watching herself from a distance, listening to voices at the far end of an echoing corridor. The floor beneath her was tipping sickeningly sideways.

'You've imagined people doing cruel things to you, darling, haven't you?' said Chazia. 'Everyone has. In dark moments. But the reality is much more terrible, and lasts much longer. It continues. Not just for hours or days but for weeks. Months. It gets messy. It's not good to see parts of yourself being removed. It's not good to have someone else rummaging about inside your body. Will I be brave? we ask ourselves, but of course nobody is brave, not in the end. Courage only takes you so far.'

Chazia shifted her position. Sat down beside her on the wooden floor, making herself comfortable. Shoulder to shoulder, intimate and companionable.

'But I don't want that to happen to you,' she said.

'You tried to kill me,' said Maroussia, 'You killed my mother.'

'Oh. That.' Chazia waved the memory away with a dismissive gesture. 'That was just a favour for a friend. Before I knew you. I didn't know then how important you were. And you escaped anyway, didn't you. That was resourceful of you, though I think you had help. From Investigator Lom, I think. I've been underestimating him too. I saw the mess he made in the gendarme station at Levrovskaya Square. Who would have thought that of him?'

'It wasn't—' Maroussia began, but Chazia cut her off.

'What became of Major Safran by the way?' she said. 'I've been wondering. Just curious. Did Lom—'

'I cut his head off. With a spade.'

Chazia giggled like a girl. Her eyes shone.

'Did you?' she said. 'Well done you.'

Maroussia became aware of a prickling edginess in the air around her. A smell of ozone, like the sea. She realised that Chazia was still talking.

'Ever since the Vlast confiscated the Pollandore from Lezarye,' she was saying, 'people in the Lodka have been trying to find out its secrets and use its power, but they never could. Only now there's me, and now there's you. *The Shaumian woman*. That's what the paluba called you. You have the key and you are the key. Those are the words, or something like them. So. I know, you see. I know it all. And now you can show me how to use the Pollandore. You can give me these secrets.'

Chazia's face was so close to hers, Maroussia could feel her breath. It was cool, and smelled like damp moss and stone, like the mouth of a deep well, with a taint of meat. Her hair was darkly reddish, cropped short and sparse. The rims of her pale blue eyes were pink, her teeth were small and even and pretty. There was a patch of slate-coloured angel flesh stretching from her left cheekbone almost to her ear.

No! Maroussia was screaming inside. *No!* She closed her eyes and turned her head away.

'I'm the one to have the power of the Pollandore,' said Chazia. 'It is my destiny. I have a great purpose.'

Maroussia pulled her knees up to her chest and hugged them defensively. Her naked feet were cold against the rough plank floor of the freight car. She felt the vibration of its wheels on the rails below.

'The Pollandore isn't a *power*,' she said.

'Of course it's power, darling,' said Chazia. She rested her hand on Maroussia's bare knee, and stroked her comfortingly. Their shoulders were touching. 'And you're going to show me how to use it.'

Chazia slipped her arm round Maroussia's shoulder and leaned her head against Maroussia's head. Maroussia could smell her hair. Clean, with a faint trace of scented soap. The hand on Maroussia's shoulder gripped gently but firmly. Maroussia felt a numbness there, as if her flesh was disappearing, as if the shoulder were merging with the hand that touched it.

Chazia's body was starting to join with hers. Melt into her. Maroussia wanted to shake it off. Push her away. But she could not. The feeling was relaxing. Reassuring. There was something *intimate* about it. She felt they had known each other for ever. Chazia's presence was so completely familiar. Solid and trustworthy. Two thoughts, one thought. Like oldest friends. Like sisters.

'After all,' said Chazia quietly, gently in her ear, 'what were you going to do with it yourself?'

'Destroy the angel in the forest.'

'There you *are*, you see, sweetness,' whispered Chazia triumphantly. 'And you said it wasn't power.' Chazia nuzzled her nose against Maroussia's neck. 'Have a little sleep now, darling. You need to build your strength. There's no hurry at all. We'll have plenty more time to talk before we reach Novaya Zima.'

64

The engine note slowed and deepened. Lom became aware that the Kotik was descending, its nose dipping slightly, the line of the artificial horizon creeping up the face of the dial. He looked at the clock on the instrument panel. It was coming up to eleven. He glanced across at Gretskaya.

'Going down to have a look,' she said. 'See where we are.'

The endless shining oceans of cloud rose to meet them and resolved into detail: rolling vaporous hillscapes, valleys and canyons. Lom braced himself, though he knew it was pointless. The floats under the wings ploughed into the thickening mist, tearing it up like cotton wool. Then fog closed round the machine, so thick the wing tips were lost in it. The Kotik did not appear to be moving forward. Nor did it seem to get any lower, although the altimeter needle was swinging leftwards all the time and the light was fading into subaqueous gloom.

The muffled roar of the engine died as Gretskaya throttled right back. The nose sank lower and the seaplane began to glide. The only sound was the hum of air passing through the slowly turning propeller and over the surface of the machine. The cockpit became suddenly fragile, cosy and close. A den to hide in. Heavy droplets of rain splashed against the windscreen and spread in trembling threads and trails. From north to south, straight across their path, lay a dark uniform green and purple wall. Not a wall. A mouth. Lom noticed that the wing at his shoulder was flexing and bouncing. Agitated water beads danced back across the lacquered surface towards the trailing edge and disappeared into grey fog.

Gretskaya sat quite still, her eyes glued to the altimeter. Lom watched the pointer creep backwards: 4,000 – 3,000 – 2,000. The machine plunged on through a mist of drenching, driving rain. 1,000 – 500. Lom sensed beneath them, blotted out by the foggy gloom, the heaving, queasy belly of the sea.

The engine abruptly roared into life. Gretskaya pulled the stick back, climbed to a thousand feet, and began to circle.

'Trouble?' said Lom.

Gretskaya shook her head, but she looked grim.

'No,' she said. 'Not immediately. There's forty-five minutes left in the tank, and we're not that far off Slensk. But I need to see where we are and the cloud's too low. We can't stay circling up here.'

'So what do we do?'

'Go down and wait for the weather to clear,' she said. 'Only I don't know what's down there, and I daren't go any lower to find out. Could be sea. Could be land. Trees. Hills. Hills would be bad.'

'It's water,' said Lom. 'Open sea.'

Gretskaya looked at him sceptically.

'How do you know?' she said. 'There was nothing to see.'

'I know,' he said. 'Absolutely. I know.'

Gretskaya went quiet, thinking. Minutes passed.

'You can't know,' she said at last. 'But the odds are on your side, and if we stay up here we start to run out of options.' She took a deep breath. 'We'll go a little further west, just to be sure, then drop down and take a closer look.' She opened the throttle, pushing the airspeed indicator up till it was nudging a hundred, and let it run. Ten minutes later she cut it again. Gliding into a shallow descent, she pulled on her goggles and hauled open the cockpit lid. The icy rain in their faces. The noise of the wind.

The altimeter counted down: 500 – 400 – 300. Lom wiped the rain out of his eyes and held his breath. Still there was nothing to see but rain and fog. Gretskaya was leaning out of the cockpit, staring down.

A dark indistinct mass loomed up beneath them. The engine roared and Gretskaya snatched the stick and held it level. The aircraft flattened out and the dark mass disappeared in mist. Then it was back, ink-black and flecked with straggles of foam. Gretskaya hauled the stick right back into her stomach and the Kotik lurched and fell out of the sky. It smacked heavily into the sea, bounced and came down again, throwing up walls of spray. It seemed impossible to Lom that it wouldn't tear itself apart or tip tail over nose into the wall of water.

For thirty seconds the machine forged on, then it slowed and came to rest. Gretskaya flicked off the ignition switch and pulled the cabin cover shut against the rain. The propeller stopped its rhythmic ticking and silence fell.

'Fuck,' she said. 'Fuck.'

The plane had become a boat, rising and falling on the long, queasy swell. They were in a circle of mist. Rain pitted and rebounded from the dark green striated skin of the sea.

'OK,' said Gretskaya. 'So now we wait.'

Lom twisted in his seat as Florian clambered up from the cabin and stuck his head into the cockpit. He looked tired, haggard and slightly green. He contemplated the scene beyond the windscreen for a moment – the rain, the mist, the narrow circle of purple-green sea – and grunted.

'Not Slensk then,' he said.

'Letting the weather clear,' said Gretskaya.

'So where are we?'

Gretskaya shrugged.

'The Gulf of Burmahnsk. At a guess, somewhere between twenty and fifty miles offshore. At a guess.'

Florian grunted again in disgust and disappeared back into the cabin. Lom wondered what he was doing in there. Most likely strapped in a cot trying to sleep. Travelling evidently wasn't his thing. Gretskaya settled back into her seat and closed her eyes and Lom stared out of the window, watching the sea. The Kotik lifted and fell with the swell, dipping one float then the other in the water. In the cockpit it was bitterly cold. Lom's heart sank. Fifty miles of deep dark fogbound icy ocean.

65

Elena Cornelius, crouching knee-deep in an anti-tank ditch, hacked at the solid black earth with a gardening trowel. The wooden handle had split and fallen away, but she gripped the tang in her blistered palm. She was lucky: many women of the conscript artel scrabbled at the ground with their fingers, numbed and bleeding, tearing their fingernails and the skin off their hands. Fresh snow had fallen in the night and the churned mud bottom of the tank trap was frozen iron-hard, sharp-ridged and treacherous, but her cotton gabardine kept out the worst of the wind and the digging was warm work.

Black earth rolled away from her in all directions, level to the distant horizon, skimmed with a thin scraping of snow. In front of her the rim of grey sky was broken only by sparse hedges and clumps of hazel, a line of telegraph poles, the chimneys of the brickworks where they slept. Between her and the sky rolled a wide slow river, crossed by a bridge: steel girders laid across pillars of brick, a surface of gravel and tar. The bridge was why they were there. The retreating defenders would cross it and then it would be blown. But for a while the bridge would have to be held.

At her back the sound of distant explosions rumbled. Every so often she straightened and turned to watch the flickering detonations and the thick columns of oily smoke rolling into the air. The bombers were over Mirgorod again.

The ground they were working was potato fields, harvested months before, but from time to time the diggers turned up an overlooked potato. Most were soft and black with rot, but some were good. Elena stuffed what she found into her pockets and underclothes for later, for

Yeva and Galina and Aunt Lyudmila. She ate handfuls of snow against the thirst. It was OK. Survivable.

'Here they come again!' Valeriya shouted.

Elena looked up. Three aircraft rose out of the horizon in a line and swept towards her, engine-clatter echoing. They were fat-nosed, like flying brown thumbs suspended between short, stubby wings.

Bullets spattered the earth and snow in front of her, and three yards to her left the top of a woman's head came off. Elena had known her slightly. She had been a teacher of music at the Marinsky Girls Academy.

While the planes circled low to make another pass, Elena and the others ran for the river. Breaking the thin ice at the water's edge they waded waist-high into the current, feet slipping and sinking in the silt, and waited, bent forward under the low bridge, for the planes to drift away elsewhere. Oilskin-wrapped packages of explosives clustered under the bridge, strung together on twisted cables that wrapped and hung like bindweed.

Elena saw something in the water out near the middle of the river: a sudden smooth coil of movement against the direction of the current. It came again, and again, slicker and more sure than the wavelets chopping and jostling. She glimpsed a solid steely-grey oil-sleeked gun barrel of flesh. Blackish flukes broke the surface without a splash. A face rose out of the water and looked at her A human face. Almost human. A soft chalky white, the white of flesh too long in the water, with hollow eye sockets and deep dark eyes. The nose was set higher and sharper than a human nose, the mouth a straight lipless gash. The creature raised its torso higher and higher out of the water. An underbelly the same subaqueous white as the face. Heavy white breasts, nipples large and bruise-coloured, bluish black. Below the torso, a dark tube of fluke-tailed muscle was working away.

While she rested upright on her tail, the rusalka was using her arms to scoop water up onto her body. She rubbed herself down constantly, smoothing her sides and front and breasts as if she were washing them, except it was more like lubrication. She smoothed her hair also, though it wasn't hair but flat wet ribbons of green-black stuff hanging from the top of her head across her back and shoulders. While she washed herself, the creature's face watched Elena continuously. There was no expression on her face at all. None whatsoever. Elena gripped the arm of the woman next to her.

'Valeriya!' she whispered urgently. 'Do you see it? Out there! A rusalka!' But when she looked again there was nothing but a swirl on the surface of the water.

After the planes had gone the women waded out from under the bridge and slipped and scrabbled up the bank. A thin bitter wind was coming up from the south. They stood shivering and shedding greenish river water from their skirts. There was a flash on the horizon, the dull thump of an explosion, and one of the brickworks chimneys collapsed in a cloud of dust. Two more explosions followed and the whole building crumpled.

Seven heavy tanks were rolling towards them across the potato fields.

'Our boys,' said Valeriya. 'Running home to mother.'

More muzzle flashes, rapid fire. The chatter of machine guns sounded dry and quiet, like twigs crunching. In the distance behind the tanks long lines of men were coming towards them, making slow progress across the levels of frozen mud.

'No,' said Elena. 'Those aren't us. The enemy is here. We have to run.'

When she got back to Aunt Lyudmila's apartment it wasn't there. The building wasn't there. The whole of the street was gone. Sticking out from the rubble among the smouldering beams and spars was a leg, pointing its heel at the sky. Small enough to be a child's. A girl's. It was black like burned meat. A charred flap of shoe hung from the foot.

66

The rain in the Gulf of Burmahnsk was definitely beginning to ease. Slowly the area of visible sea around the aircraft widened until it was possible to see a mile or more in every direction. Lyuba Gretskaya stirred and opened her eyes. Lom wasn't sure she had ever really been asleep. She slid back the canopy, letting in a blast of freezing spray and the smell of the ocean, stood up precariously in her seat and reached up to jolt the engine into life.

She took off and climbed steeply to a thousand feet, swung round and headed east. After about fifteen minutes they crossed the coastline: a wide shallow lagoon behind a long sandspit. Drab dunes and brown scrub grass dusted with snow. The Kotik swung north to follow the shore. Bays and lagoons. Small scattered settlements tucked a mile or so back from the sea. The fuel gauge lapsing closer and closer to empty.

They came up on Slensk from the south where it hid from the weather in the lee of a low headland. As Gretskaya swung a loop to port, Lom found himself looking down on a tumble of bleached grey rooftops divided by a broad river. Wharfs and piers edged the river, fronting an extensive patchwork of timber yards. Beyond the docks the river frayed, splitting into a threadwork of rivers and streams across a widening triangle of tawny brown mud streaked with veins of livid orange. The Northern Kholomora reaching the sea.

The Kotik swung out over the delta, descending gently, and turned back to touch down neatly in the middle of the river. Gretskaya taxied across to the nearest jetty and found a berth between a rusting hulk and two big pitch-caulked barges roped together side by side. She eased the plane nose first against a solid wall of pine trunks blackened and streaked with lichenous green, and cut the engine.

A giant was sitting on the edge of the wharf, studying the aircraft with frank curiosity. He caught the line Gretskaya threw up to him and looped it neatly round a stump. Lom, stiff and awkward after nine hours cramped into the tiny cockpit, hauled himself up the rusting iron ladder and stood a little unsteadily, relishing the stability of the heavy weathered planking under his feet. He breathed deeply. The cold prickled the back of his nose. It was much colder here than Mirgorod, and the sky was bigger. The air smelled of grasslands and smoke and river mud and the resinous tang of cut timber. It flushed the staleness and engine fumes from his lungs.

He glanced across at the giant and nodded.

'Where do you come from in that?' the giant said. His accent was thick. Consonants roughened and elided. Vowels formed deeper in the back of his throat than a human larynx allowed.

'Mirgorod,' said Lom.

The giant considered him for a while. Though he was sitting with his legs over the edge of the jetty, his massive head was level with Lom's. His thick hair was tied back in a pony tail and the dark glossy skin of his face was covered with an intricate pattern of tattoos. A lacy knotted profusion of thorns and leaves and berries, stained brown and purple like bramble juice, spread up into the roots of his hair and wound down his neck, disappearing inside his shirt. His eyes were large as damsons, bright damson-black, and showed no whites at all.

'I heard Mirgorod is burning,' he said.

'The people are getting out,' said Lom, 'those that can. Like us. The government is moving. There is to be a renewal in the east. The Vlast reborn in Kholvatogorsk.'

The giant shrugged and spat into the sea.

'And where do you go?' he said. 'East also?'

'North,' said Lom.

The giant stiffened, suddenly alert and wary. His nostrils flared. He was looking past Lom at something behind him. Lom glanced back. Florian had appeared at the top of the ladder, wearing his astrakhan hat.

'You keep wild company,' the giant muttered, 'for a Mirgorod man.'

Lom and Florian left Gretskaya to secure the cockpit and sort out the refuelling of the Kotik.

'We must restore our spirits,' said Florian, setting off towards the town. 'Coffee, I think. Cherry schnapps. Pastries. Honey.'

Lom looked sceptically at the subsiding weather-bleached frontages. *Cherry schnapps and pastries?*

Slensk was a timber town. Timber was the only trade, and all the buildings were made of wood – old, warped, much repaired and weatherproofed with tar. Boardwalks were laid across mud, woodsmoke leaked from tin chimneys. There were as many giants as humans in the streets of Slensk. Giants *were* the timber trade. They came out of the forest hauling barges with their shoulders or riding herd on thunderous rafts of red pine logs: down the Yannis, across Lake Vitimsk, then the Northern Kholomora to the sea. The logs were boughs and branches only, never entire trunks, though they were thicker, stronger and heavier than whole trees of beech or oak. When the giants had delivered their charges, some stayed in Slensk and laboured in the sawmills, where they hefted timbers five men couldn't shift, and some travelled onward with the seagoing barges or drifted south and west, itinerant labourers, but most walked back to the forest. Giants tended to observe human life from a height, detached and unconcerned, indifferent to detail. They went their own way and rarely got involved. City people treated them with a mixture of fear and contempt, which bothered the giants, if they noticed it at all, about as much as the scorn of cats. But the giants were noticing Florian. They watched him warily. They bristled.

On a bleak corner a door stood open in a lopsided old house. A tin sign read PUBLIC ROOM. You ducked under a low beam to get in, and stepped down into a room of long benches and sticky tables, wet muddy floorboards, a log stove and a fug of strong tobacco. No coffee, no cherry schnapps. Florian ordered for both of them: big wooden bowls of cabbage soup with blobs of sour cream dissolving in the middle, a couple of hard-boiled eggs, a bottle of birch liquor and two glasses. The bottle was brown and dusty. *LIGAS DARK BALZAM*. The thick black liquor burned Lom's throat. It left a thick oily film down the inside of the tumbler. At the next table a group of seamen were playing cards.

Florian took one of the boiled eggs from the plate and crushed it gently between finger and thumb until the shell cracked. He began to remove the broken pieces one by one.

'The giants are bothered by you,' said Lom.

'Are they?' said Florian.

He finished peeling the egg, and held it up to examine it in the light. It was shiny white and elliptically perfect.

'Yes,' said Lom. 'You make them nervous.'

Florian tossed the peeled egg into the air, and with an impossibly fast movement seemed to lean forward and snap it out of the air with his jaws. He swallowed the egg whole. It was over in a fraction of a second, almost too fast to see. It was the most inhuman gesture that Lom had ever seen a human make. Only Florian was not human of course.

Florian wiped his mouth with the back of his hand.

'And what about you, Vissarion?' he said. 'Do I bother you?'

'Yes,' said Lom. 'Absolutely.'

'I see,' said Florian. 'Well. OK.' He took a sip of birch liquor, made a sour face and sat back as if he'd made an incontrovertible point.

67

Gretskaya turned up at the bar half an hour later, her sheepskin rain-soaked, her thick curly hair heavy with water.

'You tracked us down,' said Florian.

'Where else would you be? There is nowhere else. Give me some of that.' She picked up Florian's balzam glass and emptied it, then slid in alongside Lom on the bench. 'There's heavy weather coming in from the north. It reached Garshal this morning, bad enough that they telephoned a warning to the pier head here. That's not normal. We'll stay here tonight and let it blow through, and start again in the morning.'

'We could go east,' said Lom. 'Follow the river to Terrimarkh, like you said. Keep south of the weather.'

Gretskaya shook her head.

'I will not risk the Kotik over that country,' she said. 'It is a wilderness. Bad weather in daylight over the ocean is one thing. Bad weather at night over 250,000 square miles of moss and rocks and scrub is something else again. But …' She paused and frowned and looked across the room. A corporal of gendarmes had ducked in under the low doorway. He was standing at the edge of the room, letting his eyes adjust to the light.

When he saw them he came across. He was young, not more than nineteen or twenty, narrow-shouldered and wide-hipped. A velvet moustache, a full moist lower lip, a roll of softness swelling over his belt. The holster on his hip looked big and awkward on him.

'You are the aviators?' he said. 'That is your seaplane at the jetty? The Beriolev Mark II Kotik?'

'It is,' said Gretskaya.

'And you are the pilot?'

'Yes.'

'You are required to register a flight plan with the harbour authorities. This is your responsibility, yet no such plan is registered.'

'I don't have a plan. Not yet. We were just discussing that. There is a problem with the weather.'

The boy was staring at Lom and Florian.

'And these are your passengers?' he said. 'Two men?'

'As you see.'

'Cargo?'

'None.'

'This can be checked. The aircraft will be searched.'

'There is no cargo. It is a passenger flight.'

'For what purpose?'

'I am exploring possibilities in the timber business,' said Lom. 'Naturally, we came to Slensk.'

'But you are not remaining here. You come from Mirgorod, and only the weather detains you. Correct? So your destination is where?'

'We are going north along the coast,' said Gretskaya. 'Garshal. We leave tomorrow, or perhaps the next day. There is no hurry. Not until the storm blows through.'

The gendarme held out his hand.

'Papers,' he said.

'The logs and registration documents are in the plane. If you want to—' Gretskaya began, but the gendarme cut her off impatiently.

'My concern is with persons only. Personal identification. Documents of travel.'

Gretskaya handed over her passport. Florian and Lom followed suit. The gendarme looked through them slowly and carefully, page by page. Then he put all three in the back pocket of his trousers.

'Hey!' said Gretskaya.

'I have certain enquiries to make concerning these documents,' said the gendarme. 'Confirmations I intend to seek. You may collect them from the gendarmerie tomorrow, in the afternoon, and until then you will remain in Slensk. This will be convenient for you, no doubt,' he said to Lom. 'You will have more time to pursue your commercial interests.'

*

'That decides it,' said Florian. 'We have to leave now, straight away, and not for Garshal but east.'

'No,' said Gretskaya. 'It's not a flight to try at night, even without bad weather. Not without a navigator. The only sure way is to follow the river. If we lost the river – it's a wilderness: no features, no landmarks – we'd circle till the fuel ran out, and if we had to go down, no one would come to look for us. No one would know where we went. It would take us weeks to walk out of there.'

'If it's a matter of additional payment ...'

'No,' said Gretskaya. 'Not that. Anyway, why the hurry? We've got till tomorrow afternoon.'

Florian shook his head. 'He could send a wire tonight,' he said. 'He could be on the telephone now.'

'Who's he going to call to check out a passport?' said Lom. 'The Lodka's not open for business, not any more. Anyway, he's not waiting for ID confirmation.'

'What do you mean?' said Gretskaya.

'How many gendarmes are there in a place like Slensk? Two or three at the most. My guess is he's on his own. And he's worried about us. He didn't buy our story and he didn't like the odds, so he's calling for help. Reinforcements. Only he knows nobody can get here before tomorrow. Fuck, he's almost begging us to run.'

'So what do we do?' said Gretskaya.

Florian looked at Lom. 'Let him decide,' he said.

Lom emptied his balzam glass. The liquid seared his throat and left his mouth dry and rough. He didn't need to think. Somewhere Chazia's train was rolling north towards Novaya Zima with Maroussia and the Pollandore. It was a race, and nothing else mattered, and the train was moving, and they were not. At the thought of Chazia, Lom felt a tight surge of anger and purposeful violence. The iron aftertaste of angel stuff mixed with the balzam. There would be a reckoning there.

'We leave,' said Lom. 'We leave now.'

Gretskaya poured another tumbler of Ligas Balzam, drank it down, and tucked the bottle inside her sheepskin jacket.

'Then let's go,' she said.

68

In the war against his own people Colonel-General Rizhin's weapons were of necessity crude. When Chazia evacuated the Lodka and removed or destroyed the intelligence files it contained, she decapitated, at least so far as Mirgorod was concerned, the system of informers and secret police that had held the Vlast solid for four hundred years. Rizhin took a more direct approach. It suited him better. He declared martial law. A curfew. Looters and stockpilers were to be summarily shot. Citizens were conscripted to worker battalions and assigned their tasks, and shirkers were shot. If there were no shirkers, some people were to be shot anyway, the weakest and least capable. What mattered was that people were shot.

Spies and saboteurs were captured and their confessions led to further arrests. In quarters where dissent was strongest, collective measures were taken. Reprisals. The citizens of Mirgorod, the newspapers reported, were shocked at the extent of the enemy's penetration of their city and glad that Rizhin was there, relentless and vigilant, to protect them.

Against the enemy without, he ordered concentric circles of defence to be thrown together. Twenty miles out from the centre of the Mirgorod, Rizhin's labour armies of women and children raised earthworks with their bare hands, excavating trenches and tank ditches, building breastworks and redoubts, laying barbed wire and mines even as the Archipelago air force strafed and bombed them. They carried away their own dead, and buried them when and where they could.

The outer ring of defence was expected to delay but not stop the advance. Rizhin's main focus was on preparing the streets of the city itself for the fighting to come. He ordered that all the bridges should be wired with explosives. Machine-gun nests were to be built on high roofs and towers, the blocks around them demolished to provide clear fields of fire. Artillery and anti-aircraft batteries appeared in the parks and squares of the city. Air raid shelters were to be dug and public buildings camouflaged. The Armoury spire was painted grey.

Residents came out to barricade every street with anything to hand: tramcars and overturned carts were pushed across the roads and filled with earth, building rubble, gravestones uprooted from the necropolis gardens. Street nameplates and road signs were removed. All maps, street plans and guidebooks to the city were confiscated, and anyone found with one after that was arrested. Summary execution. Every house and apartment was prepared to be its own fortress. Its own last stand. Strips of paper were stuck across windows to prevent shattering and splinters. Attics were filled with sand. In every office barrels filled with water stood ready, along with spades and beaters and boxes of sand.

Barrage balloons drifted low and pale and fat, their cables invisible against the sky. And every day the beleaguered citizens of Mirgorod waited for the Vlast's own air force to appear overhead. They looked up, expecting and then hoping to see Hammerheads and Murnauviks scattered across the sky, twisting, buzzing, deadly; stinging the lumbering, triple-bellied Archipelago craft out of the air. But the air force of the Vlast did not come. It was delayed elsewhere. After the first attacks on the city, the Archipelago's bombers arrived alone: their fighter escorts no longer bothered to waste fuel by coming along for the ride.

All night and all day Rizhin worked. He planned, he terrorised, he cajoled. He did what he could, but he knew it would not be enough. He needed soldiers. Armies. Guns and tanks and aircraft and ships. And these he did not have. Not enough.

The armour of the Archipelago rolled through the unfinished outer defensive line in a dozen, twenty places, moving fast, and behind the heavy tanks came massed motorised infantry in half-tracked carriers and on motorbikes. Radio operators. Artillery tractors. Rocket trucks. Engineers to rebuild roads and bridges and lay out airfields and telephone cables. And following along behind them, more slowly but in unstoppable numbers, came columns of horse hauling supply wagons, field guns and four-ton mitrailleuses. Cavalry regiments. Division after division of foot soldiers marching.

At certain points, randomly, the armies of the Vlast attempted to make a stand. Men and women in their thousands advanced on the enemy at walking pace. Rifles and bayonets against tanks, artillery and machine guns. Wave after wave the men and women of the Vlast came on, the later waves slowing to pick their way across shell craters and over the mounded corpses of the dead. The attacks faltered, faded, resumed, hour after hour until the machine guns of the Archipelago were too hot to handle and their operators were depressed and sickened by the tedious, grinding slaughter. The awful noise of it dulled their hearing and frayed their nerves. The freezing air was clotted with the stink of hot metal and oil, mud and piss and the leakage of ripped-up and burst-open human bodies. Some of the Vlast infantry reached the enemy: they fought with bayonets and knives when their pocketful of bullets was gone.

The Archipelago covered the last twenty miles to the outer suburbs of Mirgorod so quickly that whole Vlast divisions were simply bypassed and cut off from retreat. Crouched in woodland scrub and shallow swampy depressions, they hid in desperate silence while the enemy marched past. More often than not, Archipelago skirmishers found them by the smell of uniforms stale with tobacco and sweat, the tang of disinfectant and the sickly sweetness of Sauermann's Lice-Off.

When the Archipelago columns reached the Ouspensky Marshes on the eastern outskirts of Mirgorod they halted. They were within sight of the dull red hillock of the Ouspenskaya Torso, the remains of the first angel that fell dead from the sky: the place to which the Founder had travelled, four hundred years before, and where he had ordered the building of the city. The place where the Reasonable Empire had first become the Vlast. And, from her temporary headquarters in the Ouspensky Marshes, General Alyson Carnelian, Archipelago commander of the Mirgorod Front, sent a message into the city. It was an invitation to discuss surrender terms.

Against the advice of his officers, Rizhin didn't send a representative but went to meet General Carnelian himself. The meeting was held in a single railway carriage that had been rolled out to the middle of the Bivorg viaduct and left there, suspended a hundred feet above the scrappy gardens and straggling suburban streets of Vonyetskovo Strel. It looked isolated. Marooned.

The carriage was a plush observation car appropriated from the

Edelfeld-Sparre Line, thickly carpeted and furnished with red leather sofas, its vintage luxury somewhat faded by time. The walls were panelled in dark varnished wood, and the soft yellow light of electric chandeliers made the sky beyond the windows look wintry and bleak. Photographs on the walls showed sunlit southern landscapes: a slope of olive groves, a sun-bleached corniche above a strip of glittering sea. Places where Rizhin had never been. A small diesel generator was humming quietly somewhere.

General Carnelian was a tall heavyset woman of about fifty, uniformed in crisp olive green, greying blond hair cut short under a peaked red cap heavy with braid. Her face and hands were deeply tanned.

'Some coffee?' she said. 'A cake perhaps?' There was a plate of fancy patisseries. The kind you couldn't get in Mirgorod, not any more.

'No,' said Rizhin. 'Let's get on with it. Say your piece.'

She fixed him with small hard green eyes. *She is a soldier*, thought Rizhin. *Of course she is. The flannel with the coffee and the crude trick with the little sugar cakies is misdirection, only that.*

'We can take your city, General Rizhin,' said Carnelian quietly. 'Be in no doubt of that. Our bombers will flatten it. All of it. Every house and apartment, every school, every hospital, every bridge. I have six hundred Bison tanks. Each one weighs ninety tons. They will not bother to use the streets, they will drive straight through the buildings and grind the rubble to dust under the steel treads of their tracks. We will fill your rivers and canals and sewers with coal oil and ignite it. We will fill the cellars and underground shelters with heavy green gas that shreds the lungs of anyone who inhales it. Explosive gas. Once released, it lingers and drifts in ground-level clouds for days. Mirgorod will burn, and all the millions of people who live here will burn. All of you. There will be such death as you cannot possibly imagine.'

She paused to let Rizhin absorb the force of what she had said. The inevitable truth of it.

'However,' she continued, 'I would prefer not to do this. I am a humane person, and I will avoid this cataclysm if I can. The city is already ours, in every sense that matters, but there is a choice, General Rizhin, and the choice is yours.'

Rizhin looked at her, smiling faintly, but said nothing.

'Will you hear my terms?' she said.

Rizhin sat back in his chair and gestured for her to carry on. 'It would be interesting,' he said.

'If you capitulate,' said Carnelian, 'The city will be spared. It will not be destroyed. And I will go further. I am authorised to offer Mirgorod the status of an open city. Renounce all ties of allegiance to the Vlast and Mirgorod may establish its own civilian government and become a neutral bystander in the war. We offer diplomatic recognition of the city as an independent state. We offer advice and supply. We offer Mirgorod a seat in the Governing Parliament of Archipelagal States, with a status equal to any of the smaller Out Islands.'

'And for me?' said Rizhin. 'What would there be for me? I mean me personally, of course.'

'An honourable retirement, General. A small estate somewhere. Froualt, perhaps? And a reasonable pension. We might say two thousand roubles a year, something in that region. There would be limits on your future travel and communication, naturally, but for all practical purposes you would be free to live out a quiet and prosperous end to an illustrious career.'

'These are reasonable terms,' said Rizhin. 'Very attractive.'

'I expect you'll want time to consider,' she said. 'You'll need to discuss your answer with your colleagues, I understand that, and we would of course need to be assured that yours was a collective answer. A reliable agreement. But …' She paused. 'I would advise you against consulting with your masters who have fled. It's easy to spend other people's lives from a distance. I urge Mirgorod to make its own mind up. I can give you twenty-four hours. No more.'

'There is no need for time,' said Rizhin. 'I speak for Mirgorod. That's why I'm here.'

'Good. Excellent. So, what do you say, General?'

'I say you're full of shit.'

'I assure you—' Carnelian began, but Rizhin held up his hand for silence.

'You and I,' he said, 'what we're fighting for here is a city. A *capital* city. If Mirgorod is not the capital of the Vlast it is nothing, it is meaningless, it no longer exists. You won't burn it. What use to you is a million stinking corpses? What use to you is five hundred square miles of ash and rubble in a marsh on the edge of a northern ocean? This threat of burning is nothing. It's shit. I could burn it myself, more easily than you could. Fuck, I *would* burn it myself, to stop you having it. But to destroy it is to lose it. You burn Mirgorod and you obliterate the idea of it, and it's the idea of Mirgorod we're fighting over here, not some piss and vinegar diplomatic compromise.'

Rizhin stood up to go.

'So,' he said. 'You want my city, you come and get it. You fight for every inch, or you fuck off somewhere else and let the Archipelago find themselves a general who can.'

'You can't save the people of Mirgorod, General.'

'You haven't been listening,' said Rizhin. 'You should pay attention. I don't want to save the people of Mirgorod, they are of no interest to me. What I want is a victory. And I'm going to have one. You're going to give me one.'

69

For three hours out of Slensk, Lyuba Gretskaya followed the Northern Kholomora upstream, flying low through steady drizzle. The river slid beneath them, wide and slow and dark. Carpets of leafless birch and moss gave way to plains of tawny scrub grass and miles-long streaks of bare yellow earth. Twilight was thickening into night when the storm clouds rose from the north, clotting the horizon. Rags of wind buffeted the Kotik, sending it scrabbling and skittering across the surface of the air.

'We'll have to lie up overnight,' said Gretskaya. 'I'm going down while there's still light to land by.'

'Go a few miles north,' said Lom. 'Out of sight of the river. Just in case.'

Gretskaya nodded and swung the Kotik to port. After a couple of minutes she eased off the throttle and began to descend in a wide flat spiral. She pulled a handle and Lom felt the thunk as the landing wheels dropped into position. Almost imperceptibly the nose came up as the aircraft flattened out, engine silenced, gliding. The wind whistling through the struts, the creak of the airframe, the rain against the windscreen, the tick and sweep of the wipers. Even in the dusk and rain the grass was visible underneath them now, not flat and smooth as it had appeared from height, but rough and tussocky and dotted with low clumps of shrub and thorn. Gretskaya flew on, thirty feet above the ground.

And then a wall of scree rose out of the ground in front of them.

Gretskaya hauled back on the stick, dragging the nose up steeply, and raced the throttle till it screamed. They must have cleared the top by a matter of feet. Inches. They were flying over a stretch of gravel and small stones. Patches of illumination from the wing-tip lamps raced alongside them. The ground was so close, Lom felt he could have reached over the side and brushed it with his hand.

The tail dropped, the wheels touched and bounced and touched again, and they were down and trundling, wheels crunching and jolting across the stony surface. The whole aircraft strained as Gretskaya applied the brakes. It skidded and slewed to the right. Suddenly they ran out of gravel and bounced into long grass. A shadowy clump of thorns loomed out of the darkness and smacked into the wing almost at Lom's shoulder. With a screech of protesting metal they lurched to a sudden halt.

Gretskaya cut the engine instantly.

'Shit,' she said quietly. 'That didn't sound good.'

Gretskaya opened the cockpit and climbed down to have a look at the damage. Lom followed. A thin bitter wind tugged at his trousers. Rain flattened his hair and streamed down his face. The right undercarriage wheel was tangled in a mess of thorny branches. The struts, to Lom's inexpert eye, looked bent and twisted awry. Despite the wind and the rain, he could smell an acrid industrial taint on the air. Something was leaking. Gretskaya bent down and dabbed at the mechanism, then sniffed her fingers.

'Brake fluid,' she said. 'Nothing too bad, if that's the only damage. I can fix it up in the morning.'

Florian appeared beside them. His eyes were shining happily.

'I'm going to take a walk,' he said. 'Don't wait up.'

Lom looked at him in surprise but Gretskaya only grunted indifferently.

'Come,' she said and clapped Lom on the shoulder. 'Let's get inside and finish this balzam and get some sleep.'

Antoninu Florian slid down the scree and found a place where he could tuck away his clothes. He pulled them off hastily, shivering happily as the rain drenched the bare skin of his body. He wrapped them in his jacket and stashed the bundle under a thorn tree. He marked the place with his scent so he could find it again.

All around him for hundreds of miles there was spaciousness and weather and, apart from the two left behind inside their stale metal box, no humans. None at all. And no cramped enclosing constructions of stone and brick. No stench of coal and iron. No thundering of engines and petrol fumes. No noise at all but the wind in the grass and the rain. How long? How long since such a moment, a true wolfnight? Too long. Too many years. But now. Now. The joy of it made him want to howl and shout.

Florian ran, and as he ran he stretched out his body, re-articulating bone and cartilage inside their hot tendon sheaths, feeling his muscles bunch and reach and work themselves warm and free, pushing out his ribcage and filling his unfolding lungs deeply, deeply, with the night-freighted air: the smell of crushed herbs, broken twigs and wet earth. At full pelt he tipped himself sideways into the brush and rolled over and over, growling, yelping, laughing. He came to a stop and thrust his face into the ground, just to breath it, just to rub his muzzle against the fragrant wet grass.

Then he picked himself up and stood for a moment, still, the fur on his back raised thickly, mouth open, panting hot breath that steamed on the air, simply listening to the hot blood of his own veins.

He was wolf and he was strong and hungry and he ran. He ran a long way, covering mile after mile, darkly, silently and very fast.

70

Lom woke in the grey light of dawn and climbed stiffly down from the cockpit. The Kotik was canted slightly sideways. Gretskaya's legs were visible, sticking out from under the hull. A toolbox open beside her.

'OK?' said Lom.

'Couple of hours. No problem.'

'Need a hand?'

'No.'

Some yards away Florian was crouching over a small fire, feeding it with brittle clumps of scrub. The herb flared into spitting heat and burned away instantly with an acrid fragrance and almost no smoke. He had a couple of cat-sized creatures impaled on sticks and propped over the fire. They were elongated, sinewy, unrecognisable: narrow fragile heads burned to black, eyes closed slits, carbonised lips stretched back from small sharp chisel-teeth. Threads of fat dripped from the burning meat and spattered into the fire with little explosions of bitter vaporous soot. Lom almost trod on their torn pelts, dropped on the gravel a couple of feet away. Grey bloody rags.

Florian looked up and grinned.

'What the hell are those?' said Lom.

Florian shrugged happily.

'Surok,' he said. 'Ground squirrel.' He held up a chunk of half-cooked meat. 'Breakfast. Want some?'

'No,' said Lom quickly. 'No. Thanks.'

He drifted off by himself, heading away from the aircraft. His footsteps crunched echoless in the silence. It was bitterly cold. Away from the reek of Florian's fire the air smelled faintly of dry cinders and some kind of crushed herb he thought he recognised but couldn't name. Something like sage. Or rue. Scraps of freezing mist hung low on the ground. His face was chilled to the bone: stiffened and numb, skin stretched too tight over his jaw and his skull. The yellow-grey steppe stretched beyond the flat horizon, hundreds of miles in every direction of nothing at all.

The plane had landed on some kind of raised plateau, uplifted some yards above the surrounding grassland. Last night's rain had already evaporated in the thin wind. Lom found he could scuff away the sparse dry gravelly soil with his shoe, scraping down to virgin rock. The herby scrub had virtually no roots at all. When he had been walking for fifteen minutes or so, he began to notice that the ground was scattered at wide intervals with curious slivers, shards and fist-sized stones, ranging in colour from pale pink and rusted blood to bruise-dark purple, some rough and sharp, some rounded and polished to a glassy shine. He picked up a couple at random and cupped them in the palm of his hand, hefting their surprising weight. He knew exactly what they were. Raw fragments of the flesh of a fallen angel. They tingled in his hand, their almost-aliveness calling to him, and the stain of the old angel implant still lingering in his own blood stirred in response. It was like fine wires in his veins tightening and humming faintly. *Follow*, they urged, whispering. *Follow*.

It took Lom more than an hour to find the carcase of the angel itself: a small one, a minor malakh, nothing compared to the red grandeur of, say, the Ouspenskaya Torso. Keeping fifty yards distance, he walked all round it in five or ten minutes: a surprising, impossible crag of deep reds and purples. The angel had not been quite dead when it fell: three starfish pseudo-limbs extruded from one flank and flowed across the shallow crater floor, spreading fringes that trickled away and dissolved into the surface rock. Angels often survived their fall by hours, sometimes days, seeping liquefaction, scrabbling in sad confusion at the ground as the last intelligence drained out of them. But this one was certainly dead now, and had been dead for centuries: long enough for dusty wind-blown soil to gather deeply in the folds and depressions of its body. Even from such a mass as this, Lom sensed nothing but the vague, vestigial after-trace of dissipated sentience.

He was surely the first human to see this thing since it had fallen. The Vlast Observatories paid wealthy bounties for such a find, and failure to report one was a serious crime, but if it had been reported, the angel-miners of the Vlast would have come, hacked and sliced away its substance and hauled it away in slabs. They would have swept up every scattered pebble and strand and web for miles around. But this one had lain unseen and undisturbed since it had fallen, untouched by anything except the abrading weather. It called to him. He wanted to go closer. To touch it. Sheer curiosity. Never before had he been close to more than a mudjhik-sized lump of angel substance, though he had carried a sliver of it embedded in his skull for most of his life.

As Lom slipped down into the shallow crater and walked towards it, the small dead angel loomed over him like the hull of a battleship. The atmosphere sang and prickled against his skin. An ozone reek. He went right up against the flank. Close to, the angel's flesh was dull and pitted, but marbled with streaks of dark translucence, seamed within by dim threads and striations of blood and midnight blue. Lom pulled off his glove and pressed his hand to it. Probing. Deeper and deeper into the dizzying mass. The answering wires in his veins snapped taut, leaving him dizzy, breathless, heart pounding.

An echo of proud intellectual hunger reached out and gripped him, tugging him further down and deeper in. The angel wasn't a solid bulk, it was an open mouth. A fathomless well. He was standing on the fragile edge of terrifying, vertiginous, depths and staring, rapt and self-surrendered, into infinite emptiness: the space between galaxies and stars, not dark and cold and filled with death, but alive, a beautiful shining limitless windfall home. He wanted to fall into it. Fall and fly. The way up and the way down the same. It was his birthright, his just entitlement, his more than human destiny: the everlasting, ever-expanding future to which his history, all human history, was prologue. Just one step more. The flesh of the dead angel opened, a warm inviting gate, parting comfortably to fold around him and take him in.

No! Not this! Not ever this again!

Lom fought it.

Repel! Repel!

But he could not pull away. He screamed and yelled. Choking. Desperate. He hit out and pushed and kicked and bit and screamed. He coughed and vomited. Sour spittle spilled down his chin in gluey strands. Pulling away was appalling and impossible, like drowning himself, like holding his own breath till he died. He was murdering the thing he loved completely, loved more than himself: he was wilfully choosing his own bereavement. The dead angel suffused him and clung to his mind with needle-hooked claws. It was pulling the brain and spinal cord out of his body through the top of his skull. For Lom to withdraw was sickening death and extinction.

No! Not after all that's happened, not this! Was it his own voice or the angel's that screamed this horrified determination, this defiance of despair? It was both. There was only one voice.

And then Lom was out of the dead angel's grasp and stumbling back across the ground, sobbing and vomiting, his lungs heaving desperately for clean cold breath.

Florian found Lom wandering, exhausted and confused, miles from the Kotik. Florian wiped the dried vomit and spittle from his face and made him sit on a rock and gave him water and meat. Lom ate a little but he could not speak. He leaned forward, hands on his knees, and swung his head from side to side, trying to shake it clear.

'Take your time,' said Florian. 'No rush. None at all. Gretskaya is waiting. The aircraft is repaired. She is anxious to make Terrimarkh before dark.'

'Before *dark*?' said Lom. 'What … what time is it, then?'

'It is almost three in the afternoon. You were gone for eight hours.'

'An angel …' Lom groaned and turned aside and vomited again. 'It was dead … It …'

'I have seen it,' said Florian. 'When you didn't come back I followed your trail. I found what you found but I didn't go close, not like you did. I could not have. What made you … ?'

He paused but Lom said nothing. He could not.

'I picked up your path again,' said Florian, 'on the other side of it. You were wandering.'

There was a hammering pain behind Lom's eyes. He tried to focus on Florian but flashes of coloured brightness sparked and drifted across his vision.

'How close?' said Florian. 'How close did you go?' His voice reached Lom from far away. Lom jammed the heels of his hands into his eyes. It only made things worse.

'Sorry,' he said. 'Think I'm going to—'

He jerked his head aside and vomited once more. He felt himself toppling slowly, endlessly forward. The world slid sideways into easy and comfortable darkness.

71

Maroussia Shaumian sat alone in a compartment on Chazia's train. Her own private travelling cell. The door was locked, the windows barred. The bars were painted dark purple to match the Edelfeld-Sparre coachwork: slender steel uprights, but solid. Immovable. She had tried them, as she had tried the door, a dozen times.

Her clothes had been taken from her on the first night while she slept, when they moved her from the freight car. She had woken to find herself in a simple dress of heavy grey linen. Her hair had been washed and she was barefoot, her left ankle chained to a strut beneath the seat. The cuff was padded leather, and gave her no discomfort. A silent woman came three times a day to bring her food – always a wrapped packet of heavy bread, with sausage or cheese, never both – and to take her to the washroom at the end of the corridor. On washroom trips Maroussia saw no one. The other compartments in the carriage had their blinds drawn or were empty. The linoleum was cool under her feet, the water in the bathroom hot, the towel fresh and rough. The bathroom window was barred. All the windows of the carriage were barred. It seemed she had the entire carriage to herself. The woman who came, the provodnitsa, would answer no questions.

The first time, after the washroom, Maroussia had refused to let her leg be shackled again. 'No,' she said. 'No. Not that.' She kicked viciously at the provodnitsa's hand.

The woman shrugged and left her. Later, Maroussia slept, and when she woke she was chained again. Next time the provodnitsa came, she brought with her an enamel pot and put it on the floor in the corner behind the door.

'You are to let me put the chain back on afterwards,' she said, 'or stay in here always.'

Maroussia stared at her for a long time, considering the hot water, the towels, the feel of the linoleum cool underfoot, then nodded and held out her leg for the chain to be removed. Apart from that one time, the provodnitsa was neither unkind nor kind, and never spoke at all.

Maroussia slept long and often, during the days as well as at night, and woke feeling sluggish and dull. She wondered if her food was drugged, or more likely the tin cups of sickly fruit juice out of a can, which had a metallic taint. But probably she was simply exhausted. A floor vent fed engine-warmed air into the compartment and she could not open the window. There was a large mirror above the opposite bench. Whenever she looked at it her own face gazed back at her, dark-eyed and alone. As much as she could, she avoided it. Avoided catching her own eye.

She wondered what Vissarion was doing, what had become of him, if he was even alive. She remembered lying next to him, freezing cold and wet in the bottom of the skiff, folding his unconscious and desperately injured body in her arms as they were carried down the swollen surging Mir. Trying with her own warmth to not let him die when he had been tortured for her sake. She remembered the smooth cold feel of his skin. The smell of the river water and blood in his hair. He was a good man. He met the world with an open face, not closed up hard like a fist as so many did. She felt obscurely guilty, as if she had abandoned him. And in a way she had.

When the track made long sweeping curves Maroussia could see the rest of the train. There were two armoured engines at the front and two huge guns, each on its own heavy truck, one behind the engines and one at the very back. Long barrels canted to the sky. Four more wagons with thick steel plating lined with firing slits carried gun turrets. The bulk of the train was unmarked freight wagons and a dozen passenger cars, looking tiny and incongruous in the Edelfeld-Sparre purple. Between the turreted fighting cars and the freight wagons was a specially widened truck which carried a shapeless bulk, high and wide as a house, shrouded in pale grey camouflage sheeting.

She knew what it was. She could feel its presence. The Pollandore. She tried to reach out towards it with her mind. There was nothing. No response. On a ledge at the front of the Pollandore's truck a mudjhik stood, motionless and sentinel.

The train seemed to be going east, as far as Maroussia could tell, and perhaps a little north. Sometimes they roared along at speed, sometimes they slowed to a crawl, little more than walking pace. Occasionally the train would halt, never in a station but always in a deserted siding or marshalling yard, some with a surrounding cape of township. Maroussia drank in the names when she could see them, and pinned them to her memory, though they meant nothing to her. Ortelsvod. Thabiau. Sarmlovsk. Novimark. Bolland. Malovatisk. Ansk. She tried to see who came and went from the train. Figures passed in and out of view in early mist or evening darkness. People must have seen her face at the lit carriage window but nobody came near.

On the second day out of Mirgorod, shortly after dawn, the train came to a long shuddering stop with a screaming of brakes and the guns began to fire. The turret muzzles rattled viciously and the big ordnance boomed salvoes. The whole train shifted in the tracks with the recoils. Her face pressed tight against the window bars, Maroussia could see muzzle flashes and drifts of black smoke, but what they were firing at she had no idea. After fifteen minutes or so the firing ceased, but it was several hours before the train moved on.

Time divided itself between periods of trees and periods of lakes. The trees were needle-leaved spars of spruce and pine rising from a carpet of moss. The lakes were leaden grey interludes in a featureless plain of sandy scrub and grass. Flat horizons deadened all sense of forward motion. Days and nights merged one into another.

And then one morning Chazia came to Maroussia's compartment. She looked drained. Exhausted. She filled the compartment with sour staleness and sweat. She sat on the opposite bench under the mirror, swung her legs up onto the seat, and stared at Maroussia. Her pale reddened eyes were unnaturally wide and bright, the skin of her face pallid, grey and dry. She curled up her legs on the seat, cosy and intimate.

'Are you comfortable, darling?' she said. 'Are you sleeping? It must be tedious for you to be so much alone. I will send you books.'

Chazia shifted restlessly in the seat, scratching at the dark patches on her arms and hands, tugging at the skin of her cheek. She was holding the solm of twigs and wax and stuff gently, like something delicate and precious, but in her hand it looked drab and stupid. A bunch of litter. Dead.

'This little thing,' said Chazia. 'It's so fragile. See? You could stick in your thumb and break it apart. It's ephemeral. We need to be quick.'

She winced and scratched vigorously at the skin on the inside of her elbow. There were scabs and wound tracks there. A little fresh blood was oozing. She saw Maroussia looking and smeared the blood away.

'See what it's doing to me?' she said. 'It's making the ants worse. Tiny awful ants. You can't see them, they're too small, but they're there under my skin and I can't get them out. The forest put them there. I went too near the trees at Vig. They're in my arms now, but the face is worse. I can't sleep then. Not at all.' She stopped scratching and looked at Maroussia. Her blue eyes were hot and sore. 'You can't destroy the angel, Maroussia. It isn't destructible. It's too strong. It's beautiful. It spoke to me once, at Vig, and it will speak to me again.'

'Where's this train going?' said Maroussia.

'Novaya Zima,' said Chazia. 'I told you.'

'I don't know where that is.'

Chazia gestured vaguely. 'North.'

'We're not going north.'

'Not yet. We'll turn north when we can.'

'There was shooting yesterday,' said Maroussia. 'Was that the Archipelago? Are you losing the war?'

'Losing it?' said Chazia. 'Of course we can't lose it. The war is good. It is history in action. The old Vlast was stale and tired. Silted up with careerists. They had no energy. No purpose. No imagination. The Archipelago will clear all that away for us. They want Mirgorod? So? Let them have it. Mirgorod is not the Vlast. Mirgorod is one city, yesterday's city. Let them have it. The Archipelago will consume our corruption like maggots in a wound, and for now we let them do their work, and when they have finished we'll brush them away.'

'What if their armies follow you east?' said Maroussia.

'At the time of my choosing I will destroy them,' said Chazia. 'All their armies will count for nothing. They will burn, they will all burn, and the winds of their burning will blow the ashes of the Archipelago from the face of the planet.'

As she talked she was turning the solm over and over in her hands, looking at it from every direction. Cupping it protectively. Holding it up to her face.

'It doesn't do anything,' said Chazia. 'Nothing at all.'

Maroussia felt something moving inside her head. A surreptitious, intrusive touch, like careful fingers probing gently, cool and sly. A secretive violation. It made her feel dizzy and sick.

'What are you doing to me?' she said.

Chazia looked up from the solm.

'You were going to use this,' said Chazia, 'against the Vlast. Against the angel. Against me. You thought you were going to change the world. You thought you could free the planet of angels by the deed of your own hand. You thought you'd got some kind of hero's task.'

'No—'

'It is an interesting form of individualistic delusion. One person does not change the world. History is huge, colossal, unturnable. Look at me. I am building a new, better, cleaner Vlast. By my own efforts I will do this. But I don't think I'm a hero. I know I am not. I reject the concept. I am a conduit, a facilitator. I ride the wave of history but the wave has its own momentum and I go this way because it is inevitable. If I turn aside and try to find my own independent path I will certainly be destroyed. The world is as it is and will be as it will be.'

'Everyone makes their own world,' said Maroussia. 'I will do what I have chosen to do. Because I have chosen. Even if what I do makes no difference to anyone but myself, I'll still have done something that *matters.*'

Again Maroussia felt faint sickening touches inside her mind. Needle probes and clumsy fingers grubbing around. She tried to focus on what was happening but could not.

'But that is such rubbish, sweetness. Can't you hear yourself? Absolute shit. Did you choose the Pollandore, or did it choose you? You don't know anything about what you're dealing with, except what the people in the forest have told you. You're a move in a game, that's all. Someone else's game.'

'No!'

'So what is the Pollandore? What does it do? What is it for? Can you tell me?'

'Take this chain off my leg,' said Maroussia.

Chazia laughed.

'You're stubborn,' she said. 'Determined. I understand what Lom sees in you.'

'You opened his head with a knife.'

'It was a chisel. A fine chisel.'

'You hurt him. You tried to kill him, but it didn't work: it made him better and stronger.'

'He desires you, did you know that?' Maroussia looked away. 'Ah,' said Chazia. 'I see you do. And you desire him? You are lovers perhaps? Are you lovers? Tell me, darling, are you?'

'I want to get off this train,' said Maroussia.

Chazia ignored her.

'There will be time for personal life,' she said. 'One day. We might even live to see it. But not yet, not now, and perhaps for you and me not ever. It cannot be indulged. Now there is work to do, and what is required is clear-sightedness, hardness and resolve in the doing of what is necessary. That will be our gift to the future. Our sacrifice.' Chazia leaned forward and took Maroussia's hand in hers. Stroked it. 'Help me here, darling. Work with me. Help me to use the Pollandore. I don't want to hurt you. I like you.'

'I'm never going to help you. You know that.'

'You will know me better, Maroussia darling, by and by.'

Later that same afternoon the train halted on the shore of an immense and nameless lake. Maroussia watched damson-coloured, damson-heavy cloud heads rise out of the distance and roll towards them, bruising more and more of the sky and darkening the surface of the water, erasing all reflection. Slowly the storm advanced, bringing the closing horizon with it as it came, until the train was enfolded in ominous dim purple-green light. Maroussia stood up in excitement and gripped the window bars. At last fat raindrops splatted on her window, singly at first, but faster and faster, harder and harder. Machine-gun bullets of rain. Water sluiced down the glass in a continuous rippling flood. There might have been arcs of lightning and shattering thunder crashes, or it might have been the glitter and roar of the rain.

Maroussia's shouts of joy were lost in the noise.

And then a crack opened in the world, the rain and the storm split down the middle, and a different sun was shining through the carriage window: splashes of warmth and spaciousness and the quietness of an afternoon in early summer. The sourness in her mouth was gone, and her heart was big and calm with the possibility of happiness.

The Pollandore reached out and touched her face, and for the first time Maroussia felt how close it was, how near in time as well as distance. There had been bad things – bad things that happened and bad things she had done – but she and the Pollandore were travelling together now, and their paths were slowly converging, and the moment would come: the moment of meeting, when good things would be possible again. She could not have said exactly what the good things coming were, but that didn't matter. It made no difference at all.

72

The Pollandore's massive detonation of possibility and different sunlight sweeps outwards across the continent from its epicentre on Chazia's train. It roars like an exploding shock wave through the certainty of things, gathering momentum as it goes, and the world of history unfolding stumbles, brought up suddenly smack against the truth of human dream and desire. In the trenches of the war and the bitterness of drab town streets the air is suddenly, briefly, rich with the smell of rain on broken earth; another voice is heard, not in the ears but in the blood, and for the brief unsustainable duration of the moment of the Pollandore's passing, nothing, nothing anywhere dies at all.

The surge of change and otherness rolls across the continent and into the endless forest, where it passes from root to root and from leaf-head to leaf-head. It is leafburst. It is earth-rooted rain-sifting burning green thunder. It crashes against the steep high flanks of Archangel like an ocean storm against the cliffs of the shore.

And Archangel is appalled, because in his delight at his own movement he realises that he has made a terrible mistake.

He has forgotten to be afraid.

For a moment his painful grinding progress across the floor of the forest pauses, and for miles around him there is nothing but silence and a second of waiting.

He gathers. He centres. He focuses.

He remembers this thing.

How is it that he had forgotten? That never happens, but it has happened. This thing has been hiding from him! It has woven a forgetting around itself, but now it has made itself known.

This is a powerful and dangerous threat.

Archangel traces the path of the passing of the Pollandore moment back to its source. Examines. Analyzes. Knows what he must do.

73

Mirgorod, war city.

Elena Cornelius survived alone. Elena's Mirgorod was zero city, thrown back a thousand years, order and meaning and all the small daily habits of use and illusion scorched and blasted away, the concepts themselves eradicated. Money wasn't money any more when it had no value and there was nothing to buy. Food was what you found or stole. Clothing against the cold and the night lay around free for the taking on the unburied corpses of the dead. Homes weren't security, shelter and belonging: they were broken buildings, burned and burst open to the elements, the intimate objects of interior domestic life scattered on the streets. Apartments were boxes to shut yourself in and wait for the bomb blasts, the fires, the starvation.

She kept moving, ate scraps scavenged from bombed buildings, drank water from rooftop pools and melted snow. She risked being shot for a looter, which she was, and she hid from the conscripters. She existed day by day in the timeless zero city, alien, unrooted, a sentience apart, belonging to nothing. Herself alone. She felt ancient. Places to hide and sleep were plentiful among the cellars and empty streets. When she slept, she dreamed of the rusalka in the potato-field river. She dreamed of her girls. Yeva and Galina. Mornings she woke early into fresh disorientation, the appalling daily shock: always she felt like she had survived a train crash in the night, a bridge that had crumbled beneath her, a house that had fallen down. Life had broken open, and everything was raw and clear. Every day she looked for her girls. Perhaps they had survived. Perhaps they were existing also somewhere, looking for her.

What follows after taking tea?
The resurrection of the dead.

There were no longer newspapers, but the *MIRINFORM* bulletin was posted on walls and telephone poles daily. 'No sooner had Volyana fallen under our fire than the Archipelago soldiers jumped out of the windows with their underwear down and took to their heels. With cries of hurrah the battalion fell upon the slavers. Grenades, bayonets, rifle butts and flaming bottles came into play. The effect was tremendous.' Increases in rations were reported. The city held stockpiles of grain and dried fish in reserve, ready to be distributed if the need arose. *Courage, citizens. One more push, and victory will be ours.* Nobody believed, but everybody gathered to read when a new edition was posted. It did not say that the cemeteries were full and there was no fuel for the mortuary trucks.

Elena walked out to the edge of the city until the way was barred by fighting. Three times she probed the outskirts in different directions, but always it was the same. Cleared firing zones. Shell holes filled with corpses and refuse. Charred skeletal buildings. The clatter of tank tracks and the rattle of gunfire. On her third attempt a sniper's bullet skittered through the broken bricks at her feet like a steel lizard.

Elena knew she was tiring. The effort of keeping moving all day was almost beyond her. She should choose a place to be her permanent home, but she had to keep moving, walking twenty or thirty miles in a day. Looking for her girls.

On the third night the snow came again, a silent softness of feathers thickening the air. She had collected nothing. Her food bag was empty. She broke open the door of an empty house on the edge of the firing zone, drank the last of her water bottle, lit a fire in the grate, laid herself out on the floor and slept.

She was woken by someone kicking her leg. The dazzle of a flashlight in her eyes.

'Stand up! I said stand up!'

Two young men were looking down at her. Well fed bare-headed boys. Waist-length pea coats. Black trousers and heavy black boots. Elena knew what they were. They were the Boots, and they were the worst. She had always known that one day she would be too tired, too hungry, not careful enough, and it would be finished. But she stood up to face them.

'Yes?' she said. 'What?'

Rizhin had co-opted the semi-organised, semi-militarised thugs of the Mirgorod Youth and Student Brigade to support the militia in the war against defeatists, hoarders, looters, racketeers, saboteurs and spies. They were kept fed and left to do as they would. Autonomy without discipline. And what they did was rob and torture and rape and kill. People said that even the VKBD found the Boots excessive. Repellent. Elena had heard the Boots roamed the places near the fighting, but she had been too tired to remember.

The Boots were holding rifles. Bayonets fixed to the muzzles. The one with the flashlight turned it off and put it on the floor. The light from the fire was enough.

'Take off your scarf,' he said. 'Let's see your face.' His friend was grinning.

Elena let the scarf drop to the floor.

'Now the coat.'

She unbuttoned the heavy greatcoat and let it fall.

'And the sweater.'

The two boys were both staring at her now. Not grinning any more. Focused. Eager. Elena saw one of them swallow hard.

'Take off the shirt,' he said.

'And the trousers. Turn around.'

'Go on. Don't stop. Show us. Let's see what you've got. Let's see it all.'

The Boots had laid down their rifles and were opening their own clothing. Fumbling with their belts and flies.

'No,' said Elena. She stopped, her right hand behind her back. She was trembling. Her hands were shaking. 'No.'

'Bitch.'

One of the Boots lunged forward to push her down, his trousers open and falling round his thighs. Elena pulled out the kitchen knife she kept tucked in the back of her trousers and shoved it into his belly. The boy gasped and stopped in surprise, looking down at his stomach. Disbelieving. Elena took a step back, pulled out the knife, swept it upwards and sliced the blade laterally under his chin. Blood spilled out and splashed to the floor. The boy stared at her. He made a small gurgle in his opened throat.

The other one was scrabbling for his rifle.

'Drop it. Now.'

The Boot swung round. A VKBD officer was standing in the doorway, a pistol in his hand.

'Piss off, Brosz,' said the Boot and raised the rifle muzzle, pointing the bayonet towards him. The officer shot him in the knee and he fell, screaming.

'I've had enough of this,' said the officer. 'You're such a fucking pair of pigs.'

He walked over to the screaming boy and shot him again. In the face.

The other boy, the one Elena had cut, was still standing in the middle of the room. He was cupping his throat with one hand, trying to catch the blood. The other hand was pressed against the wound in his belly. He was weeping.

The officer raised his pistol at arm's length and fired. An execution shot.

'This your place?' he said to Elena. She was standing half-undressed in the firelight, the kitchen knife in her hand, held low at her side.

'No.'

'Then you're looting.'

'Yes.'

'That's a hanging crime.'

'Yes.'

The VKBD officer studied her for a moment.

'How long have you been scavenging?'

'Always.'

He nodded.

'And you're still alive. More than that, you're still strong. And a good fighter.'

'If you're not going to shoot me,' said Elena Cornelius, 'I'm going to put my coat back on.'

'Ever used a rifle?' he said.

'No.'

'Come with me. We'll teach you. You'll be more use than a roomful of these pigs.'

'I'm better off on my own.'

'It isn't a choice. It's that, or I string you up in the morning.'

Conscripts to the Forward Defence Units got a day's firearm training and, if they were fortunate, a weapon. Elena Cornelius turned out to have an aptitude for marksmanship. The sergeant took her aside.

'You. You will be a sniper,' he said. 'A woman is good for sniping. You are small. You are flexible. You stand the cold better than a man.'

She was issued with felt overboots, a thick tunic, a fur shapka, the kind with flaps for the ears. A printed booklet with tables that set out how to adjust the aiming point to take account of the ballistic effects of freezing air. And a bolt-action 7.62mm Sergei-Leon rifle with a side-mounted 3.5x Gaussler scope, the one with two turrets, one for elevation and one for windage: effective range 1,000 yards with optics. The modified Sergei-Leon was exclusive to the VKBD; the regular army never had the funds for such precision firearms.

'You learn by doing,' the sergeant said. 'We send you out with someone who knows what they're doing.'

Elena was paired with a woman called Rosa, a student of history until the Archipelago came.

'I volunteered,' said Rosa. 'I was a good shot already. I used to hunt with my father on Lake Lazhka. Wildfowl are harder to hit than soldiers.' Rosa already had seventeen confirmed kills. 'We'll go in the afternoon,' she said. 'Firing into the east, you don't want to shoot in the morning.'

Rosa led to the way a place near a machine-gun post on the roof of a factory. The enemy were only three hundred yards away.

'Shoot when the machine gun is shooting,' she said. 'They won't even know we're here, never mind spot us.'

They were up there for nine hours. When they had finished and returned to the barracks, Elena Cornelius packed her things into a kitbag, slung her rifle over her shoulder and walked away, back into the city to look for her girls.

74

Alone in her private carriage in the dark hours after midnight, Lavrentina Chazia lay, fully clothed and sleepless on her bunk, listening to the rumble of the train wheels on the track. She was exhausted, but she knew she would not sleep: she rarely slept any more, the ants under her skin made it impossible, with their creeping and crawling and the sting of their tiny bites. The patches of angel stuff on her arms and face itched and burned.

After a fruitless day attempting to break through the shell of the Pollandore using various mechanisms of her own devising, she had spent the evening with the Shaumian woman, and even for Chazia, who was hardened to such things, the experience had not been pleasant. Frustrated by the lack of progress, she had concluded it was time to abandon the subtle approach in favour of more direct methods. Maroussia Shaumian was stubborn to the point of stupidity, and after their last talk she had become even more recalcitrant, almost confident. Chazia sensed that something had changed, but she didn't know what and she didn't care: it was a matter of breaking the girl's will, and she knew how to do that. She had decided against using the worm, for fear of doing some damage to the girl's mind that would prevent her doing whatever needed to be done with the Pollandore, so the work had been noisy and messy.

The process was still not complete, but Chazia had grown tired and faintly disgusted, so she'd left the girl to the professional interrogators and withdrawn to her compartment. She needed to find rest: her mind lacked edge and speed, and her spirits were low. She was bored, restless and above all frustrated. The power of the Vlast was within reach, but she had not yet quite grasped it: still there was Fohn, and the feeble

Khazar. The power of the Pollandore was within reach but she could not get there, she didn't know how to use it and the Shaumian woman was giving her nothing. Chazia was coming to doubt she had anything to give. And the living angel, the greatest power of all, had never come to her again. All she heard was silence.

In her sleepless solitude Chazia began to wonder if perhaps, after all her efforts, she was going to fail. Maybe she was simply not good enough to do what she had set out to do. She felt the need for power, any power, in her belly like a hunger. She was incomplete without it. She was *made* for power, she was *capable* of it, she *deserved* it. She had worked so hard for so long. She had made sacrifices. She had given her life to the Vlast unstintingly. She had *served*. When she held her hands stretched out before her in the darkness, palms open, they felt empty, with an emptiness ready to be filled. And yet …

Chazia sat up abruptly and turned on the lamp. She swung her legs off the bunk and stood up. Her self-pity disgusted her. Such moods came upon her when she was alone with nothing to do but think. That was why she must always be working. Never be inactive. Never. Keep moving, keep trying, keep going forward. Always choose the *difficult* thing. Always choose to *dare*.

She went through to the next compartment, where she kept the suit of angel flesh that she had made. The uncanny watchfulness of the thing made her uneasy. She realised for the first time that she was frightened of it, in the way you're frightened to get back on a horse that's thrown you several times. But the reluctance, the fear in her stomach, that was the reason to do it. She took the headpiece from its shelf and put it on. She felt it reach out and clamp onto her, plunging invasive tendrils deep into her mind. It was eager, it was ready, and now so was she. Fresh excitement stirred in her belly. Her mind began to turn faster. It was better already. This was what she needed.

Awakening angel senses trickled information into her mind. She felt with prickling clarity the many lives on the train, the energy of the engine working, the miles and miles of passing trees and snow. The Pollandore. She felt the Pollandore by its absence. Its impossibility. It was a strange blankness. It told her nothing.

She called out to the living angel in the forest.

Where are you? Speak to me. I am here.

Again and again she called into the emptiness, as she had done a hundred times before.

And this time the angel answered.

At last it answered!

When the angel had spoken to Chazia at Vig, it had almost destroyed her. It had come roaring into her mind, a crude appalling destroying storm of sheer inhuman force, as infinite and absolute and cold as the space between the stars, pounding and pouring into her, stronger and more powerful than she could bear, until her head burst open and her lungs heaved for breath but could find none. But this time it was different. Perhaps it was because of the casket of angel flesh enclosing her head, or perhaps it was because she was stronger now, and better prepared, more equal to the encounter. It did not occur to her that the angel had learned subtlety and control.

I see what you're doing, darling, the angel whispered, and its voice in her head was Chazia's own voice, Chazia speaking to Chazia, intimately, the lover speaking to the one it loves. *I see that thing you're bringing, and I see what you want to do with it. You're so brave, my beautiful, so brilliant and so brave. It really is remarkable. But you will not do this. It will not be done.*

'No,' said Chazia. 'No. I want it.'

I am so sorry, Lavrentina. I left you alone for so long. Too much time has passed. It was wrong of me, I made a mistake, I see that now, and I've come back. Can you forgive me, Lavrentina?

Her name! It was using her name. It knew her, it had always known her! Chazia had been right: it had been there watching all along, but silent, so cruelly silent.

I understand you so much better now, darling. You felt abandoned and alone and you turned to this other thing to comfort you. I understand that. But I'm back now. You don't need the other thing, not any more.

The angel went everywhere inside her, turning everything over, Chazia's angel-enhanced senses flared incandescently. It was overwhelming. She felt the strength of her body and the force of her will magnified a hundred, a thousand times. Nothing was impossible.

Is this not what you want, Lavrentina? Am I not enough and more than enough? Am I not all that you would ever need?

'Yes.'

We just need to destroy that thing you're bringing. You don't understand it, Lavrentina. It has deceived you. It's a terrible, repellent thing. We have to get rid of it and then, together, just you and me, we can do … anything!

'I don't want to destroy it. We can use it. Once I have learned—'

I know what you want, darling, and I will give it to you. I will give you everything. The whole world will see what you are. Just do this for me. The thing must be destroyed. Destroy the disgusting repellent thing. Let it burn.

'I don't want to do that,' whispered Chazia.

But we need to destroy it, my love.

75

Lom woke to grey daylight and Antoninu Florian looking down on him, his hand on his shoulder.

'Vissarion?' Florian was saying. He looked concerned.

'What?' said Lom, warm and reluctant. He was comfortable. There was a pillow. Sheets. Florian's head was framed in a wide square of leaden sky.

It was a window. There were thin lemon-yellow curtains, pulled open.

Lom hauled himself upright in the narrow steel cot. Springs protested under his weight. The walls of the room were corrugated tin on a timber frame. There was a table under the window. A desk. Empty.

'Where are we?' said Lom. He had been dreaming of water and trees. The encounter with the dead angel was a distant and receding darkness, a stain of metallic fear on the horizon. He didn't want to think about that.

'The aerodrome at Terrimarkh,' said Florian. 'How do you feel?'

Lom thought about it.

'Good,' he said. 'Hungry. And I could do with coffee. A lot of coffee. And a piss.'

'OK,' said Florian. 'Good. And then we leave.' He hesitated. 'Can you do that? Are you well?'

'Of course. Why?'

Florian handed him a razor.

'You might want to shave while you're in the bathroom.'

Lom ran his hand across his chin and felt a thick rough growth of beard.

'Shit. How long—'

'We have lost much time. You were delirious, confused, and then you slept very deeply. We couldn't wake you at all. Gretskaya is fretting to be away.'

'How long has it been?'

'We have lost three days.'

'*Three days!*'

Lom pushed back the covers, hauled himself out of the bed and walked unsteadily across to the window. Standing was a shock. The bare linoleum chilled his feet. His legs felt feeble. Shaky under his weight. He looked out on bleak expanses of concrete and asphalt under a threadbare dusting of snow. Hangars and huts, low and widely separated. Fuel tanks. A water tower. And beyond the aerodrome, nothing: no house, no hill, no road, no fence, no tree, only the weight of the sky, draining the world of colour. The single runway, swept clear of snow, stretched black into the distance. The Kotik stood ready. There were no other aircraft visible. No sign of life at all.

Three days! Maroussia! Shit!

'How soon can we leave?' he said.

'Get dressed. I'll find you something to eat. Then we'll go.'

Two hours later they were airborne and on their way north to Novaya Zima. Gretskaya stayed below the cloud bank. The altimeter showed a steady 2,000 feet. She found the railway and followed it north. The track cut straight across monochrome tundra, mile after mile, hour after hour, parallel with the low hills on the starboard horizon, misted grey with distance. Drifts of leafless birch trees rolled away behind them, and white expanses of snow pitted with circular lakes. The lakes, not yet entirely frozen, were fringed grey with ice at the shore. The dilated coal-black waters stared sightlessly back at the sky.

At last the coast fell suddenly away behind them and they were over the sea, but the railway plunged on, carried on concrete piers. The track stretched ahead of them, cutting low and arrow-straight across the dark waters to the distant vanishing point. Squadrons of seabirds swept low over the waves, floated in speckled rafts, and lined the concrete parapets of the endless viaduct, roosting.

'That is the Dead Bridge,' said Gretskaya. 'It was built by penal labour. Men, women, even children worked on it. There are hundreds of bodies under the water, thousands maybe, all drowned, frozen, starved, dead of exhaustion. The eels and the fishes get fat on the bodies and the birds get fat on the fish.'

Ahead of them there was no horizon. The sea merged with the sky, diffuse and indeterminate and in the deep distance the Dead Bridge narrowed and faded as if into the air. The Kotik roared on.

After half an hour or so, above the place where the railway viaduct still disappeared into the distance, a paler colourless wash came slowly forward, separated itself from the sky and resolved into a distant mountain, its peak buried in cloud, its base lost in mist.

'That's it,' said Gretskaya. 'That's where we're going. Novaya Zima.' She swung the Kotik away to the north-east, climbing until the railway was out of sight, then turned round, dropped down to a hundred feet and cut the throttle.

And then they were gliding, the wind hissing through the struts, the rotor blades turning slowly. Lom could see small scattered rafts of ice floating on the water below them, rising and falling with the swell.

'I'll come in low and quiet,' Gretskaya said. 'No one will know we're there.'

The island of Novaya Zima was a spine of dark hills ridged with snow, rising higher to the north, towards the still-distant mountain. The lower slopes were covered with trees: a dark monotonous woodland that rolled away from the hills until it met the shore. The seaplane skimmed onwards. The black wall of trees widened and rose to meet them. Gretskaya dropped the tail and they came down, bouncing a couple of times off the swell and settling in a long subsiding skid across the water. She opened the throttle slightly and motored towards the narrow shoreline, a ten-yard strip between the water and the edge of the woods. The seaplane's nose beached gently a couple of yards out.

Gretskaya slid the cockpit open. She kept the engine running.

'Go,' she said. 'Quickly. Go.'

Lom climbed out, dropped to his waist in freezing pine-green water and waded ashore. It was a steep climb, soft mud sucking at his feet. He almost lost his shoes. The beach was an unstable mass of twigs and mouldering needles and leaves, thickly matted with rotting seaweed. His feet broke the surface with every step, dislodging an appalling stench and clouds of tiny black flies that buzzed angrily at his face and neck. He stumbled and fell forward, plunging his hands elbow-deep into the high tideline.

'Fuck,' he muttered to himself. 'Fuck. Fuck.' It was bitterly cold.

He turned when he reached the trees. Florian was coming up the beach behind him, a small canvas knapsack slung from one shoulder by a narrow leather strap. Gretskaya had already pulled the Kotik back and was swinging it round to face out to sea. The roar of the engine rolled along the shore as she raced away, leaving a widening wake, and lifted into the sky.

76

The woodland was a dim, perspectiveless, muted labyrinth of widely spaced birch and pine. Resinous. Twilit. Snow-carpeted. Directionless. Florian seemed to know where he was going: he set off quickly, moving in as straight a line as was possible, away from the sea.

Lom followed.

'We must get clear of the landing place,' said Florian. The moss and the snow and the trees drained all echo, making his voice sound drab and flat. 'We cannot light a fire until it is dark.' He fished a twist of paper out of his pocket. It was filled with solid dark pieces of sugar. 'Here,' he said, holding one out. 'Eat this. We go west until we strike the railway. Then we follow it north wherever it goes. OK?'

'How far?' said Lom.

'To the railway? Ten or twenty miles. Not more. After that, who knows? We follow the track to its end, wherever that is. The south island is a hundred and twenty miles long and fifty wide at the waist, but I doubt we will have to go so far.'

'What we're looking for is on the south island? Why not the north?'

'I think not the north. This island sits across a current of warmer water that flows from the west; the north island does not. It is under permanent ice, glaciers come down from the mountains.'

Florian, in his sombre suit, dark overcoat and astrakhan hat, the knapsack on his back, moved with fast and sure-footed noiseless grace. Lom jogged and stumbled behind him. The Blok 15 was a solid weight in his pocket. He carried nothing else. Shallow streams crossed their path, ice-fringed water running fast over mud and gravel, turning aside and deepening into moss- and root-edged pools. They drank and washed the stinking smears of the shoreline from their clothes. Lom plunged his face into the freezing water and sluiced his matted hair, then sat on a fallen trunk to wipe his eyes with his sleeve. When he looked up he saw the wolves. They were moving under the tree-shadow, silent and indistinct as moths. One turned its face towards him. Wolf eyes. Unhurried, considering.

'Wolf,' he called to Florian in a low voice.

He would fight, if he had to. Wolf mouth on his face, his arm in a wolf mouth, fingers in a wolf throat, digging. Dragging his revolver from his pocket, firing it into wolf belly. Firing again. Blood and blood. Without hope, he would turn and fight.

'I see them,' said Florian. 'There are others behind us. They are following.'

Lom jerked round but there was nothing to see.

'Why didn't you say before?'

'They will not trouble us while I am here,' said Florian. 'They are not hunting, they are curious, that's all. But do not go far alone. Not without me.'

All afternoon and into the evening they pushed on through the trees, Florian moving fast and confidently, Lom struggling to keep up. From time to time he looked for wolves but did not see them again.

They broke out onto the edge of the railway track suddenly, without warning. It stretched away to right and left, twin parallel rails. The massive sleepers and ten-foot gauge of a major freight line. On either side of the track the trees had been cut down and cleared five yards back from the line. It was freshly done work, the toppled trees stacked neatly, the ground scattered with raw yellow axe chippings, the scent of fresh-cut timber in the air. An inch-deep covering of snow. It made the going easier. They turned right and began to jog along beside the rails.

They had been going steadily for about an hour when Florian stopped suddenly.

'Train,' he said. 'Do you hear? A train is coming.'

'I can't hear anything,' said Lom. He was breathing hard. Heart pounding in his chest.

'Get out of sight,' said Florian urgently.

Lom followed him into the dimness under the trees and they

hunched down low to wait. Eventually he heard the rumbling in the rails, rising in pitch to a squeal as the train got closer. It was approaching from behind them. He could hear it now, a locomotive under full steam. The train roared into view and thundered past, close enough to see the moustache glistening on the engineer's face in the firebox glow and catch the smell of hot iron and burning coal. Iron wheels high as a man is tall. Truck after truck followed the engine, ten, twenty, thirty of them, wooden-sided, windowless, each as long as a barn. Lom recognised them. The long trains. He had seen such trains, hundreds of them, waiting in rows in the Wieland marshalling yards. They looked like cattle trucks but they weren't for carrying cattle.

They walked on, following the railway track. There were no landmarks. No horizon except the vanishing point of the track. Walking brought them no nearer to anything and no further away. Motion without movement. The birch trees receded in all directions, endlessly repeating mirrors of trees, misting into brown and grey, dimness and snow. Numberless, featureless and utterly bleak.

'We'll camp here,' said Florian when the light began to fail. They had reached nowhere in particular.

They left the railway and pushed three or four hundred yards in under the trees, to a place where a heavy spruce had fallen, tearing its root mass from the earth, making a small clearing where scrub and thorn had taken root. Florian fished a small bag from his pocket and gave it to Lom. It held a fire steel and a clump of dry tinder: moss and leaves and small twigs, all dry and sweet.

'Here,' he said. 'Keep the fire small. We should be far enough from the track, but we should take no risks.'

Lom gathered a bundle of branches and set them by. He scraped a patch of earth clear with his foot and checked the ground for shallow-buried roots that could catch and smoulder underground. There were no stones to make a hearth. He took a handful of tinder from the pouch and laid it ready: a tight clump in the middle, outside pieces pulled looser to let the air in. When the tinder was set he held the fire steel close above it and struck a shower of sparks. He got it first time, sweet, like he always did, and bent low to breathe on the faint smoulder. Gentle. Gentle. Encouraging the little flicks of flame to come alive. Breathing in the faint smell of woodsmoke.

The wood he had gathered was all damp. He chose a few of the smallest, driest pieces and set them round the smouldering tinder one by one, carefully, to shelter the frail young flame, to barely touch it and take it into themselves. He fed it with a little extra tinder when it started to fail and felt the first brush of heat against his face. A little cup of life in the gathering dark. When he was sure of the small fire, he picked out some of the larger branches from the pile and set them in a careful pyramid around the tiny fire, closing it in like a tent frame. The heat and smoke would dry them out.

Lom sat back for a moment and watched. A bitter breeze had risen as the light faded. The legs of his trousers were still soaked, and now he had stopped moving the cold of it chilled him. But the fire had steadied. It was breathing. He watched the lick of small quick colours, the sparks in the smoke, the heart of it growing stronger.

While Lom made the fire, Florian took a small hand axe from his knapsack and hacked an armful of larger branches from the fallen spruce. He propped them against the side of the tree and wove thinner stem-lengths through them to bind a strong, shallow-sloping wall, on which he piled deep armfuls of brush and damp earth, until he had made a low, dark tunnel closed at one end, with a mouth at the other. He took some branches still heavy with needles and cut them to size, to make a door for the entrance which could be pulled shut once you were inside.

When he had finished, he came across to the fire. Considered it with approval.

'It's good,' he said.

He pulled a little pan from his knapsack and set it on the fire. Used the axe to cut a fist-sized chunk of pork into slices and dropped them in. 'I raided the kitchen at Terrimarkh,' he said. 'The shelter is for you. You should spread more leaves inside on the floor.'

'What about you?'

'I have no need. I will not sleep.'

When they had eaten, Florian set some water to boil in the pan and scattered it with coffee grounds. Dropped in a small pebble of sugar. He set the pan aside to cool and then they drank from it in silence, alternating sips. The drink was dark and bitter and sweet and good. Night thickened between the darkness and the trees.

Lom sat quietly and stared out into the darkness, taut as wire.

77

Hundreds of miles to the south Eligiya Kamilova lay on her back on a narrow shelf in a crowded stinking cattle wagon. The train had been stopped for hours. There was the noise of other trains outside, shunting and moving slowly past. Shouted orders. Men talking. Narrow shafts of bright arc light beamed in through the gap near the top of the wall and splashed across her face. She did not know where they were. She was no longer hungry or thirsty. That had passed. She was not waiting. The time would come when it was ready to come. There was nothing to wait for.

The freight car door rolled open with a crash and light spilled in. Electric light and cold night air which smelled of bitumen and naphtha and trees. More people were being shoved inside, though there was no room. VKBD men swore at them as they hesitated. A woman started to shout and scream. Eligiya Kamilova couldn't understand what she was saying. A young boy in uniform smashed her in the face with the butt of his rifle. That quieted her. Kamilova turned away, staring at the pitch-soaked wooden ceiling close above her face. It would be bad if she were seen looking.

When the door was rolled shut and locked again, she took another look at the new arrivals. They brought with them nothing. No bags. No coats. No food or water. They stood or crouched in the shadows. Some of the men on the lower shelves were jostled. They swore at the newcomers in low vicious voices and pushed them away.

There were two young girls in school clothes standing together near her, close and side by side, their faces drawn and scared in the harsh shadowy light. They were looking for somewhere to go, somewhere to be out of the way. Kamilova recognised them. It took her a few seconds to recollect their names.

'Hey,' she called across to them quietly. 'Galina. Yeva.'

The girls looked round, trying to find where the voice was coming from.

'Over here,' said Kamilova. 'Up here.' The girls stared at her. They didn't move. They had learned not to trust the friendly voice. The invitation. 'You are Elena Cornelius's girls aren't you. Do you remember me?'

'No,' said Yeva.

'Yes,' said Galina.

'It is Eligiya,' said Kamilova. 'I know you. I know your mother. From the raion. I am her friend.' She swung herself awkwardly down from the high shelf and squeezed her way towards them, stepping over the tightly packed people sitting on the floor.

'Is your mother with you?'

'No,' said Galina.

'Do you know where she is?'

'No. She was left behind.'

Hours later, Kamilova lay on her shelf listening for the sound of movement outside the train. There was none. For half an hour, as well as she could judge, there had been none. The arc lights still burned. It must have been nearly dawn. She climbed slowly, carefully down and went to find the girls. They were sitting together on the floor, backs against the door. Yeva was asleep. Galina was watching her with wide blank eyes.

Kamilova knelt down and nudged Yeva gently awake.

'Get ready,' she whispered. 'I am going now and you're coming with me.'

'Where are we going?' said Galina.

'Do you want to stay on the train?'

'No.'

'Then it's time to get off.'

Kamilova stood up and pulled the girls to their feet. They looked uncertain and confused but they did it.

'When I say,' said Kamilova, 'run. Stay together and stay with me and run as fast as you can. Whatever happens don't stop. Don't listen to anything else but me. Don't look back and don't stop running unless I say.'

She turned to face the doors, closed her eyes and took a breath.

Calm. Calm. Think only of the night and the air.

The timbers of the massive heavy door screamed. The wood fibres ripped as it bowed and bellied outwards and split and burst and sprang from its rails and crashed to the ground below.

Kamilova jumped down and turned to catch Yeva and Galina.

'Now!' she screamed at them. 'Run! Now! Run with me! Run!'

78

Every night at midnight General Rizhin gathered his city defence commanders together to hear their reports, review the day just finished and make plans for the next. In the early days of the siege, when they first understood that Rizhin intended to make a stand, the commanders he appointed had attacked their tasks with a fierce commitment and determination. Few among them thought they could actually succeed in driving back the overwhelming force of the enemy, but there was honour, and for some a fierce joy, in fighting not running. A week of bloody resistance was worth more than a lifetime of capitulation, and every day that Mirgorod did not fall was a day stolen from inevitability by their own determination and will. Rizhin had chosen them because that was how they felt, and he'd chosen well.

But now, as Rizhin's gaze moved round the table, examining first one face and then another, he saw tiredness, lack of confidence, reluctance, even despair. One by one they gave their reports, and none of the news was good. Every day the enemy's forces made some small advance, and the best that Mirgorod ever achieved was not to lose more. Defeat was only a matter of time, and the longer it took, the more grindingly desperate, even humiliating the resistance became. Rizhin knew that his commanders were beginning to feel this, and some were even willing quietly and privately to say so. A shared collective opinion was forming among them, in the way that such opinions do, without any one person leading it, that to continue the battle further was to impose pointless suffering on the people of the city. And so, this midnight, Rizhin called the city commanders together, grey-faced and dusty with the struggles of the day, in a different room, one end of which was separated off by a wide, heavy curtain.

When they were assembled, Rizhin took his place at the head of the table, relaxed and smiling, and spoke to them in a quiet voice.

'Colleagues,' he said, 'friends, I know how tired you all are. You are fighting bravely, you do wonders every day, but I see in your faces that some of you don't trust the struggle any more. Perhaps some of you think I should have accepted the enemy's terms of surrender—'

'No!' shouted Latsis, loyal Major Latsis, and some round the table joined in the murmurs of denial, but others kept silent, and Rizhin noted for later who they were.

'I know that some of you are thinking this,' Rizhin continued. 'Where are we going with this bitter, grinding resistance? That is what you ask each other. What is the purpose? What is the strategy?' He leaned forward and skewered them one by one with his stare. None of them would meet his eye. 'Do you think I don't know how you whisper among yourselves?' he continued. 'Do you think I don't hear it all? Do you think it does not reach my ears, this cowardice and doubt? This backsliding? This revisionism?'

Rizhin let the uncomfortable silence grow and spread round the table.

'I don't need to hear it,' he added. 'I can smell it in the room.'

'General Rizhin—' began Fritjhov, commander of the Bermskaya Tank Division.

'Let me finish,' said Rizhin, his voice quiet, reasonable.

'No!' said Fritjhov. 'I will have my say! You call us cowards? *Cowards!* Our soldiers fight for the city, and they will fight to the bitter end, they will fight and die for Mirgorod. But they cannot fight and *win*. We cannot fight without munitions, and munitions do not come. We cannot advance without air cover, and our air force does not come. The Vlast has abandoned Mirgorod to the enemy! The enemy knows this, and do you think our soldiers don't?'

Rizhin poured himself a glass of water. The clink of the jug against the tumbler was the only sound in the room.

'Munitions?' he said. 'Air cover? There's only one weapon that wins wars, Fritjhov, and that is fear. Terror. If the enemy think they are winning, it's because they smell the stench of your fear.'

Fritjhov bridled.

'I am a soldier,' he growled. 'I am not afraid to die.'

Rizhin shrugged.

'Then you will die, Fritjhov,' he said. 'What I need are commanders who are not afraid to *win*.' He fixed the room with his burning, fiery glare. Holding them with all the relentless force of his will and the strength of his imagination. It was Rizhin the poet, Rizhin the artist of history, speaking to them now. 'There are new forms in the future, my friends,' he said, 'and they need to be filled in with blood. A new type of humankind is needed now: individuals whose moral daring makes them vibrate at a speed that makes motion invisible. We here in this room are the first of mankind, and this city is our point of departure. There is no past, there is only the future, and the future is ours to make. Our imminent victory in Mirgorod will be just the beginning.'

'There isn't going to be any fucking victory here, man,' said Fritjhov. 'As senior commander it is my duty—'

Rizhin smiled.

'Victory is coming, Fritjhov my friend. Victory is nearly here.'

'What—'

'A train is coming from the north-east, bringing a consignment of artillery shells.'

'One shipment of shells?' said Fritjhov in derision, looking round the table for support.

'Shells of a new type,' said Rizhin. 'You will need to prepare your guns. I will give you instructions.'

Fritjhov jumped to his feet, sending his chair clattering.

'No more instructions, Rizhin, not from you.'

Rizhin was a restful centre of patience and forbearance.

'Just sit down a moment, would you, Fritjhov,' he said, 'and I will show you what is coming.'

Rizhin stood and walked across the room. He drew back the heavy curtain to reveal a projector and a cinema screen. He started the projector whirring and turned off the lights.

WINTER SKIES

FIELD TEST #5

NORTH ZIMA EXPANSE

VAYARMALOND OBLAST

79

Lom woke in the quiet before dawn and lay still in the cocoon of branches and leaf mould, knees pulled up tight against his belly, head pillowed on the warm knot of his own folded arms. He didn't want to move.

He breathed with his mouth, shallow slow breaths. Breathing the warmth of his own breath, inhaling pine and earth and moss, the smell of damp woodsmoke in his clothes and his hair. He listened for sounds from outside the shelter, but there was nothing: the thickness of the shelter absorbed sound as it absorbed light. Yet the shelter itself had its own faint whispering, a barely audible movement of shifting and settling, the outer layer flicking and feathering in the breeze, and sometimes the rustle and tick of small things – woodlice? spiders? mice? – in the canopy. The shelter was a living thing that had settled over him, absorbing him, nurturing. Deep beneath him in the cold earth the roots of trees, the fine tangled roots, sifted and slid and touched one another. They whispered. They were connected. All the trees together made one tree, night-waking and watchful. It knew he was there.

Twice in the night Lom had heard the long trains passing.

He had done a terrible thing and the guilt of it weighed him down. He had lost Maroussia. He had not been there. He could hear the sound of her voice in his head, but not the words.

Reluctantly he sat up and pushed the entrance branches aside and let in the dim grey dawn and the cold of the day. Harsh frost had come in the night, and now mist reduced the surrounding forest to a quiet clearing edged by indeterminacy. When he crawled out of the shelter the mist brushed cold against his face and filled his nose and lungs, and when he walked his shoes crunched on brittle, snow-dusted iron earth.

Florian was sitting nearby, almost invisible in shadow until he moved. He had left a hare skinned and ready by the remains of the previous night's hearth, and next to it was a small heap of mushrooms and a handful of clouded purple berries.

'I think we could risk a fire,' he said. 'Before the mist clears.'

Lom started on the fire. The intense cold made his fingers clumsy: he fumbled the tinder, dropped it. He couldn't make his stiffened blue-pale hands work properly. He found that the water had frozen in the pan. He went for fresh.

Dawn greyed into morning, sifting darkness out of the mist-dripping branches, condensing detail. Pine needle, twig and thorn. When they had eaten, they went back to the railway track and started to walk north again. Through gaps in the trees they could see the mountain ahead of them, rising pale grey and snow-streaked into the cloud. At one point Florian paused to reach up and pulled a snag from the side of a birch trunk. He studied it, then held it out to Lom.

'Look,' he said. 'It is not right.'

Lom studied the sprig. The leaves were grown too large, and some were misshapen. Sickle-edged. Distorted.

'And here,' said Florian. 'I found this also.' A small branch of pine, the needles long but floppy and fringed with edges of lace. 'They are not all like this, but some. And more near here than when we landed.'

After an hour they found the body of the wolf. Or most of it. Its belly was ripped open and empty and one of its hind legs was gone, torn out at the hip. The wolf carcase was impaled on a broken branch at head height, the sharp-splintered stump of wood pushed through the ribcage and coming out, blood-sticky, from the base of the throat. Its head hung to one side, eyes open. Gibbeted. A warning? Or a larder?

'Was that you?' said Lom.

'No,' said Florian. 'Of course not.'

'I had to ask,' said Lom.

At mid-morning the rain came in pulses, wind-driven, hard, grey and cold, washing away the covering of snow and turning the path to a thick clag of mud. The noise of the rain in the trees was loud like a river. The galloping of rain horses.

Lom's clothes were soaked. They smelled sourly of wet wool and woodsmoke and the warmth of his body. Rain numbed his face and trickled down his neck and chin. Rain spattered across the brown surface of rain-puddles. He kept his head down and walked against it, mud-heavy feet slipping and awkward. Everything distant was lost in the rain.

A wisent stepped out of the trees into the clear way ahead of them. When it saw them it stopped, head bowed, nostrils flaring, watching them with its dark eyes. Lom saw the massive rain-slicked wall of its shoulders, the rufous shaggy fall of hair, thick from neck to chest and down its muzzle from the crown of its head, the fine stocky inward-curving crescent horns. Lom and the wisent faced each other, watching. The wisent tested the give of the mud with a fore hoof and flicked the rain with its ears. Then it turned and walked on across the rails and faded between the trees.

The rain passed, and they came to a place where a stream was running in a ditch alongside the railway track. Lom knelt to drink but Florian put a hand on his shoulder and held him back.

'Don't,' said Florian. 'Look. Over there.'

Half-buried in the bank of the ditch, where a birch tree had canted over, roots unearthed, was a human head. It was blackened, damp and rotting, and wrapped in a length of mud-brown hair. The face stared blackly sideways without eyes, and brown-stained teeth showed in its lopsided sagging mouth. And near the head a human arm reached out from the mud sleeved in sticky green. At first glance the arm had looked like the root of a tree. Too far from the head to be attached to the same skeleton, it trailed mushroom-white and mushroom-soft fingers in the flowing water.

Walking between the railway and the stream, Lom and Florian saw more like that. Pieces of human body. When the stream turned aside from the ditch and retreated under the trees it was a relief.

And then something happened that shook the world.

A silent snap of blue-white light reflected off the clouds and left after-images of skeleton trees drifting across Lom's eyes. Many seconds later he felt the sound of it in the ground through his feet, a roll of noise too deep to hear. Ahead of him Florian stumbled, and would have fallen had he not steadied himself against a stump. A tremble of movement disturbed the underside of the cloud bank like wind across a pool. The trees prickled with fear: the nap of the woodland rising, uneasy, anxious. They stood, listening. Nothing more came. Nothing changed. The clouds settled into a new shape.

'What was it?' said Lom.

'I don't know.'

'It came from the north.'

'I don't know,' said Florian. 'I think it was everywhere.'

The railway track began to sink into cuttings and rise to cross embankments and small bridges. Every few hours one of the long trains came through, heading for the mountain or coming away. Away from the cleared trackside, the going was harder. The trees were sparser now, and they had to push through scrub and thorn and accumulations of snow. They were climbing slowly, the mountain to the north growing clearer and more definite against the sky. Rock and scree. Ice and snow.

They disturbed a parcel of dog-crows gathered on a ragged dark bundle. The birds were a heavy drab and loose-winged black, with unwieldy bone-coloured beaks too heavy for their heads. They carried on picking at the thing on the ground and watched them come. Lom picked up a stick and threw it among them.

'Go on! Get away!'

The crows glared, but moved off a few feet with slow ungainly two-footed jumps. A couple hauled themselves up on flaggy wings to squat low in the trees and stare.

The body on the ground was small and had no head. The crows had picked at its neck and shoulders, spilling red pieces of stuff, and parted the clothes between trousers and shirt to open the belly.

'It's a child,' said Lom. 'Just a boy.'

Florian had walked some way off. Lom thought he was looking away, so as not to see. But he had found something else.

'Not a boy,' said Florian. 'A girl.'

The head was hanging from a branch by the tangle of her hair.

Something was passing near them. Lom felt the woods stir and bristle. The alien watchfulness of what was passing brushed over him, rippling across his mind like rain across a lake. He felt the bigness of it, its steady earth-shaking tread. The top of a distant tree trembled faintly, though there was no wind.

'Mudjhik patrol,' he hissed. 'Coming this way.'

'We separate,' whispered Florian. 'Hide yourself.' He crouched and slipped away. Lom caught a glimpse of him disappearing into the trees, loping from bush to bush, bounding low across the ground.

Lom flattened himself against the ground under a thorn bush and lay quiet, breathing shallow slow breaths. Covered his mind with woodland. Focused his thoughts into a pointy vixen snout, thought vixen thoughts, calm and tired and waiting, warm and cold in the daylight, in a waking sleep. Keeping low. *Pass by. Pass by.* The mudjhik's awareness skimmed across him and moved away, but Lom lay on, vixen-still and thoughtless, faintly stomach-sick, dulled and aching and hungry behind her eyes as if she had not slept at all.

The mudjhik's awareness jerked back, swung round and pinned him. A blank hunter's glare.

I see you. I have sniffed you out. I am coming.

There was a sudden crashing through the trees. Branches breaking, heavy limbs thumping the ground. The mudjhik was rushing towards him. It was still several hundred yards off, but running was not an option and he could not hide.

In panic, reflexively, Lom slammed up a wall against the mudjhik. It was like holding up his hand. *Stop!*

The mudjhik stumbled and fell to its knees.

Lom was stronger now, much stronger. He felt the current flowing between him and the charging alien weight, the mudjhik's alien substance connecting with something tense and fizzing in his own bones and flesh. Lom felt wired and burning. The link between the mudjhik and its handler was a feeble shadowy thing by comparison, a tenuous thread. Lom knew what to do. He broke the handler's cord. Squeezed it closed and ripped it out at its root. Felt for a second the handler's surprise as he lost connection.

The mudjhik was on its feet again, confused and clumsy, rumbling and roaring silently, lashing out at tree trunks with its fists. It was at a loss. Lom pushed himself deeper inside it, feeling for the animal part of it, the inserted mammalian brain. He found it and crushed its awful half-existence out. The mudjhik's mind clouded. Sensation without motion. Without desire. A lump of sentient rock.

*

Late in the afternoon Lom and Florian crested a rise and found themselves on a low hilltop looking out across a wide shallow valley. The railway plunged out across a viaduct above the grey-brown leafless canopy of trees. Five or ten miles away, on the far side of the valley, the mountain was a wall across the sky. And in the plain of the valley floor between them and the foot of the mountain lay the closed township of Novaya Zima.

80

From a distance Novaya Zima looked like a complex device with its back removed – a radio, a telekrypt machine – laid bare amid birch trees and snow. The township hummed and rumbled quietly. No smoke. No chimneys. It was a rectangular grid about three miles square, a compound in the wilderness surrounded by a double fence and a perimeter road. The streets formed blocks, and the blocks were buildings, orderly and rectangular, mostly concrete, ten or fifteen storeys high. Every part of the town was wired to every other part by a network of cables slung between roofs and from tall wooden poles. In the centre of the town, wider streets – avenues, prospects – converged on a spectacular cluster of taller buildings, slender constructions of steel and glass, reflecting the lead-grey sky. Motor vehicles moved with orderly precision along arterial boulevards. Pedestrians, rendered tiny by distance, anonymous and without characteristics, moved along pavements and crossed open expanses of concrete. Raised above the streets on piers of iron, an overhead railway carried snub-nosed carriages. And on the far side, beyond the town and a couple of miles of scrubby trees, the mountain climbed sheer and almost vertical into low cloud. Dark grey rock and scree and streaks of snow. It was like a wall across the world, diminishing east and west into misted distance and further mountains.

Lom and Florian watched from the cover of the trees. It was a town for thousands of people, tens of thousands, freighted in piece by piece across the continent, secretly, and assembled by dying slaves.

'And the labour is still coming,' said Lom. 'There were half a dozen trains yesterday, at least. So where are they? The town's not for them. That's not housing for penal labour. I don't see camps. I don't see factories. I don't see cranes and holes in the ground. So where do they go?'

The rail track crossed the valley floor on viaducts and embankments, bisected the township, cut though an expanse of marshalling yards to the north, and plunged on into a low dark mouth in the mountainside.

'The mountain,' said Florian. 'They go into the mountain.'

There was a gate where the railway entered the township. An asphalt road came out and looped away into the trees to circle the town. The gate stood open, the guard post deserted. It was the middle of the afternoon.

'No security,' said Lom. 'Lazy.'

'Isolation,' said Florian. 'Who could find their way here? And who could leave? Where would they go?'

'We got here,' said Lom.

There was a sign at the gate. A huge billboard meant to be read from incoming trains.

NOVAYA ZIMA

VLAST FOUNDATION FOR PHYSICO-TECHNICAL MACHINES

REFORGING HUMANKIND.

YESTERDAY ENVIES US. TODAY IS OUR DOORWAY. THE FUTURE BEGINS.

THE VLAST SPREADING OUT ACROSS THE STARS.

They walked into the town unchallenged. It seemed colder in the streets than it had been under the trees. Colder than Mirgorod, but not the same cold. Mirgorod cold had an edge of ocean dampness, but the air in Novaya Zima was dry. Lom felt its bitterness desiccating his face, as if his lips would crack. His breath wisped drably away. The snow on the pavement crunched underfoot. Dusty snow, like crystallised ash.

For the first ten blocks or so the streets were given over to huge communal barracks for collective living. *Kommunalki.* Lom had read about such new-style buildings – embodiments of a new, less individualistic mode of life, the basis for modern developments in the industrial belt to the south – but he hadn't seen any, not till now. The buildings were new but already stained and shabby: hastily thrown up to a uniform pattern, the concrete blistered and bled rust where the steel reinforcing rods were too near the surface. Street-level heating vents breathed steam clouds across the pavements. On the ground floors there were public dining halls, public laundries, public baths. They walked past a school with street-level windows. NOVAYA ZIMA JUNIOR LYCEUM FOR THE SONS AND DAUGHTERS OF WORKERS.

Workers? Lom studied the people in the streets. They had neat sombre clothes and smooth white hands. They were clerks, administrators, secretaries, teachers, junior white-collar engineers: more than half were young women. They looked efficient. Nobody was poor and nobody was old and everybody was moving along, eyes down, unspeaking, each in their own small sphere of inwardness and temporary privacy. The rail transit rumbled overhead on its single track.

Nearer the centre of town the buildings were taller and better built. Polygons of steel and glass, each set back in its own apron of concrete and paving. Benches. Kiosks. Cafés. Parks behind railings, leafless and wintry. A deserted outdoor skating rink. An open-air swimming pool with a green and white tiled façade under a low curved roof. Scarves of steam drifted across the surface of the water. Swimmers in bathing caps ploughed steadily up and down the lanes. RESTORE YOURSELVES, CITIZENS! LEISURE REBUILDS! HEALTH IS A PLEASURABLE DUTY!

Florian stopped outside a restaurant with a wide glossy vitrine. the magnetic bakery. Shining tables of polished yellow deal on legs of tubular chrome. It was almost empty.

'We should split up,' he said. 'We need to know when Chazia is coming. It'll be easier if I go alone.'

'Why?' said Lom.

'Because one person is better,' said Florian.

'So why you not me?'

'Because they will tell me what we need to know.'

'You're just going to walk into a VKBD station and ask them?'

'No,' said Florian. 'Captain Vorush Iliodor will ask them. Captain Iliodor is Commander Chazia's aide-de-camp. I carry his identification and warrant cards.'

'Out of uniform and without Chazia? They'll want to know what you're doing here. They'll want to know why you don't already know her plans better than they do.'

'They may wonder,' said Florian. 'In my experience they will not ask.'

'Do you even look like this Iliodor? What if somebody there knows him?'

Florian raised an eyebrow quizzically.

'Oh,' said Lom. 'Of course. Sorry.'

'We'll meet back here,' said Florian. 'Give me a couple of hours. Three at most.' He gave Lom his knapsack. 'You'd better keep this. It's out of character for Iliodor. There's money in the side pocket.'

81

Lom wandered the streets aimlessly, angry and frustrated. For days he had been a passenger, a tagger-along, abandoned now to his own devices. He saw the force of Florian's logic but he didn't like it. He'd left Mirgorod thousands of miles to the south and west, burning on the edge of war, and he felt Maroussia's loss as an emptiness next to him. *I've just been pissing about*, he thought. *And I'm still just pissing about.*

He found himself in a shopping street. *Modistes* sold suits and gowns and patent shoes at impossible prices. Bright-lit displays offered cameras, radios, gramophones, perfumes, chocolate, southern sparkling wines, but it was all garish, ersatz and shoddy, and nobody was buying. He walked on up Dukhonin Prospect – six lanes wide, almost empty of traffic – and into the blustery immenseness of Dukhonin Square. The square was lined with gleaming new buildings. The Polytechnical College. The Institute of Metallurgy. The Faculty of Mathematical Design. The Engineers' Euharmonia was giving a concert that night at the House of Culture: a poster next to the entrance promised Zoffany's PSYCHO-INDUSTRIAL SYMPHONY FOR VOICE AND NEW-STYLE ORCHESTRA, WITH THEATRE OF PUPPETS.

Absences worried at Lom. Absences frayed his patience. They made him edgy. The absence of Maroussia. The absence of Chazia. The absence of trainload after trainload of conscript workers. Stolen persons. Thousands of them. They went on north, through the town and into the mountain and disappeared.

Lom wanted a closer look at the mountain.

There was a station on Dukhonin Square. The ticket hall was a brightly lit lofty palace. Stainless-steel arches. Walls of marble and malachite. Chrome fittings. Electric chandeliers. The size and solidity of the place dwarfed the few travellers passing through. Bronze bas reliefs on the walls represented the achievements of science and industry: dynamos and hydroelectric dams; Magnitograd; the Novozhd Factory; mining engineers drilling and excavating the torso of a huge fallen angel. Slogans carved in marble shouted: THOUGHT IS LABOUR! PRIVILEGE IS SACRIFICE! CONTRIBUTION IS FULFILMENT! CADRES DECIDE EVERYTHING! CITIZEN, YOU ARE THE CONDUIT TO THE FUTURE!

With money from Florian's bag, Lom bought the most expensive ticket. Two roubles for all day and all stops. There was a sign that said FOUNDATION LINE NORTH. He bought a coffee in a paper cup and took it up the granite staircase to the platform overhead. A transit car was waiting. It was like a tramcar, but low and round-shouldered, and there was no overhead electric cable. Power came from the single steel rail itself.

KEEP OFF THE RAIL, CITIZEN! DANGER OF DEATH!

Lom took a corner seat. The coffee was good, not so good as Count Palffy's, but sweet and bitter and hot. He took slow sips, making it last, as the train carried him slowly north. Beyond the carriage window the office blocks, parks and squares of the town centre gave way first to a few streets of elite housing – individual homes with yards and gardens – and then more communal blocks. Through the lighted and uncurtained upper-floor windows Lom could see cramped apartments separated by paper-thin partitions, shared bathrooms and shared kitchens. A new world had begun here, a world yet unseen in Mirgorod or Podchornok. Collective endeavour in a place without a past.

Novaya Zima, deposited ready-made in the middle of a wintry wilderness, drained the past. It soaked the life of memory away. There was only now, and an avid, echoing, hungry future. Lom found it drab and ugly and brutal.

The overheated car carried on trundling slowly northwards, stopping every minute or so. The route zigzagged across the town, making the most of its unnecessary existence. The overhead transit was a superfluous municipal showpiece – you could have walked the breadth of Novaya Zima in an hour – but people seemed to use it. Passengers came and went. Without exception they wore thin coats and carried briefcases. The men had knitted ties, the women wore blouses buttoned to the neck.

Lom finished his coffee and propped the empty paper cup on the seat next to him. A young woman, hair tied severely back, was watching him from across the aisle, her face a mixture of disapproval and curiosity. Lom realised how out of place he looked. He grinned at the woman cheerfully and she looked away. She had a pale thin face.

Lom got up and went across to sit beside her. She glanced at him in surprise and looked away. Shifted herself as far as she could along the bench away from him.

'Does this train go all the way to the mountain?' he said.

'*Foundation* Mountain?'

'Is there another one?'

'No,' she said, 'of course not.' She was staring straight ahead. 'This train doesn't go there,' she added.

'So, if I wanted to get to the mountain, how would I do that?'

'Why? Why would you want to?'

Lom shrugged.

'To have a look. Curiosity.'

'Are you assigned to work in the mountain? This is the wrong train. You should have been told ... Why are you asking me this? What is your work?'

'I'm new,' said Lom. 'I don't have any work. Not yet.'

'Nobody comes here without an assignment. How could you even get here?'

'I flew,' said Lom. 'And I walked.'

The woman's cheeks burned. She glanced around the carriage, looking for help, but no one was sitting near. She didn't want to make a scene. She turned and glared into Lom's face.

'Are you drunk or something? If this is some crude attempt at seduction, citizen, then I should tell you—'

The car pulled into a station. The woman stood up. She was trembling.

'This is my stop,' she said. 'Get out of my way, please.'

Lom twisted round to make room for her. She pushed past, holding her briefcase tight against her chest, not looking at him. Her legs brushed against his awkwardly.

'I only want—' he began.

'Piss off,' she hissed over her shoulder. 'Don't follow me. I'll call the police.'

82

When the train reached the end of the line, Lom stayed aboard and came all the way back, continuing on south past Dukhonin Square till he was near the place where he was to meet Florian. Back on the emptying streets the freezing air smelled of engine fumes. Lighted windows shone with a bleak electrical brilliance. From everywhere Foundation Mountain was visible, a darkened wall against the northern sky. Lom thought he could hear a long freight train rumbling through the town, making the pavement tremble. But he wasn't sure.

The Magnetic Bakery was still open but there was no sign of Florian. Office workers were drinking tea and reading newspapers. The radio played band music. Lom ordered an aquavit and grabbed an abandoned paper from the next table. The *Vlast True Reporter*. It was yesterday's edition. He started to read it, just to pass the time till Florian came.

The man called Fohn, whose name he'd seen on various announcements in Mirgorod and who was now apparently the president of the Vlast, had made a speech in the new capital, Kholvatogorsk. So Mirgorod wasn't the capital any more? *And where the fuck is Kholvatogorsk?* Lom had a dizzy feeling that the whole world had changed and shifted while he'd been flying across the landscape in Gretskaya's Kotik.

Fohn's speech was full of dull good news: industrial targets would be exceeded in the coming quarter, despite the recent upheaval of relocation, and steel production was heading for an all-time high. Shock workers had risen to the challenge. Lom skimmed the rest of the paper. Working hours were to be increased again. About the war there was almost nothing: inconclusive skirmishes on the southern front; Seva recaptured from the Archipelago yet again. There was a small inside paragraph about the stalwart resistance of encircled Mirgorod, with extracts from a fierce speech of defiance from a General Rizhin, who was Commissar for City Defence. Reading between the lines, it seemed that Mirgorod was doomed and the Vlast had decided it didn't care. The piece was accompanied by a smudgy photograph of Rizhin. Lom almost ignored it, but something about the long narrow face caught his attention. His heart missed a beat.

It was Kantor. General Rizhin, Commissar for Mirgorod City Defence, was Josef Kantor.

When Florian came, Lom was nursing his untouched aquavit and watching his own reflection in the darkened window. Florian sat opposite Lom and put his astrakhan hat on the table between them. He looked worried. A waitress bustled over but he waved her away.

'Chazia is here already,' he said. 'The train arrived last night. Late. We must have heard it pass. It didn't stop in the town. They went straight through and into the mountain. Travelling at speed.'

For the second time in an hour Lom felt the bottom drop out of his world.

'Maroussia?' he said. 'What about Maroussia?'

'I don't know. Somebody said there was a woman travelling with Chazia. It could be her.'

'We have to get into the mountain,' said Lom. 'We have to do that now. *Tonight.*'

'Yes. Of course.'

'We haven't got time to figure this out for ourselves,' Lom continued. 'We need some assistance here.'

'Yes,' said Florian.

'Someone who can get us past whatever security they have out there. Someone who can take us right to Chazia.'

'The name of such a person,' said Florian, 'is Yakov Khyrbysk. Professor Yakov Khyrbysk, director of the Foundation for Physico-Technical Machines. Professor Khyrbysk spends his days working inside Foundation Mountain but he has an apartment in the Sharashka district, in a building called the Foundation Hall. It's not more than a mile from here. By this time of the evening he will be at home. He is not married and lives alone. I have his address. He is not expecting us. I do not suggest we telephone ahead.'

83

The Foundation Hall where Khyrbysk had his apartment was the tallest building in Novaya Zima: a tall slender blade of steel and glass, a triangular sliver of black ice speckled with bright-burning windows. In the snow-crusted square in front of the Hall stood a floodlit construction of crimson-painted steel: a single swooshing curve reaching hundreds of feet high, a steeply climbing arc of power and ambition and freedom and speed, hurtling up. It looked like nothing so much as the track of a rocket launching into the dark sky, and at the point of the curve, where the rocket might have been, was a squat, massive snub-nosed bullet-shape. It was speeding away from the planet. Escaping the gravity well. Lom remembered the hoarding at the gate into the town: THE VLAST SPREADING OUT ACROSS THE STARS.

Lom and Florian took the wide shallow apron of concrete steps two at a time and pushed open the wooden double door. Inside was a spacious entrance hall panelled with rich dark wood and thickly carpeted in plush brick red. A woman of about fifty in a crisp dark blue uniform tunic was watching them from behind a reception counter. She had short iron-grey hair and her face was powdered. She sat in a cloud of lavender eau de toilette and watched them suspiciously. Behind her on the wall was a noticeboard, a painting of the mountain in sunshine, the tubes of a pneumatic mail system and a large plate-glass mirror without a frame.

'No visitors without an appointment,' the woman said. 'Do you have an appointment?

Florian went up to the counter, confident, purposeful. He was Captain Vorush Iliodor. He held out his warrant card for inspection.

'We are here for Professor Khyrbysk,' he said. 'Commander Chazia requires his presence urgently. You will call him down for us.'

The woman frowned.

'It is late,' she said. 'The professor does not receive visitors at home. He starts early in the morning. You may leave a message with me.'

'We are not visitors,' said Florian. 'He is required. Now.'

The woman glared at him, pale grey eyes blazing, points of pink flushing her cheekbones. In the mirror behind her Lom could see the electric switch under the counter.

'The professor is unavailable,' she said, reaching for the telephone. 'Someone else will assist you. I will call Dr Ferenc. He will—'

Lom pushed past Florian, lifted the counter lid and stepped quickly through. Put his left hand down to cover the emergency call switch before she could get to it.

'We have no time for this,' he said. 'I am an investigator of the Political Police. My colleague is Captain Iliodor of Commander Chazia's personal staff. You will take us to Professor Khyrbysk's apartment. You will do this yourself. You will do this now. You will call nobody. You will trigger no alarms.'

'You cannot order me! Where are your uniforms? Where is your police warrant? There are procedures. You have no authority here. The professor—'

'The authority of the Vlast is everywhere,' said Lom. 'The Vlast *is* authority. There is no other. What is your name, citizen?'

The woman hesitated.

'Tyrkhovna,' she said. 'Zsara Tyrkhovna.'

'You will take us to the professor immediately, Zsara Tyrkhovna. *Instantly.*'

Still she hesitated.

'You would prefer to join one of the long trains, perhaps?' said Lom. 'Would you like to take a journey into the mountain, Zsara Tyrkhovna? That can be arranged. We could give you that choice perhaps. Choose now.'

Tears were coming to Zsara Tyrkhovna's eyes, though they weren't there yet. She didn't know what to do.

'Loyalty is creditable,' said Lom. 'Defiance and stupidity is not.'

Her shoulders slumped. She looked ten years older.

'Come with me,' she breathed.

*

They took the mirrored and chrome-plated lift to the top floor. The twentieth. More thick carpet in the hall, recessed lighting, pot plants and paintings on the walls: abstract constructions of circles and cones in primary colours, slashed across by thin black straight lines. *This is the future!* they said. *The total universal truth of form and speed! No people and no skies!*

There was only one door. It opened almost instantly at Zsara Tyrkhovna's tentative knock. The man who appeared in the doorway was wide and bulky. He had a broad creased face with a heavy stub of a nose, an imposing brow and a mat of wiry black curly hair cut short. Small pale blue eyes appraised Lom and Florian with sharp, watchful intelligence. He was wearing a dark blue dressing gown over a white shirt open at the collar. The gown looked like it was made of silk: real silk, not some petroleum-derivative substitute.

'I'm so sorry, Yakov Arkadyevich,' said Zsara Tyrkhovna. 'These men … they say they are the police. They insisted. They *threatened* me … I didn't know what to do. I shouldn't have—'

Florian produced his identification.

'Commander Chazia requires Professor Khyrbysk to come with us now,' he said. 'It is a matter of urgency. She cannot wait.'

Khyrbysk took Florian's card and studied it carefully for a moment. Considered it and came to a conclusion. He nodded almost imperceptibly, as if to himself, as if some hypothesis of his own had been confirmed.

'Don't upset yourself, Zsara,' he said. His voice was deep and complex. 'Everything is in order. You've done all that you should, and more. I am grateful. You can leave us now.'

'Should I telephone someone?' she said. 'I should tell Shulmin what is happening. No, Shulmin is not here. Ferenc then. I will call Ferenc. He will come.'

'There's no need to trouble Leon, Zsara. Really no need. Everything is fine here. Go back to your work.' He stood back from the door. 'Please, gentlemen, come in.'

They followed Khyrbysk into his apartment. It was over-warm and brightly lit, and the white walls were hung with certificates of academic distinction and more paintings. The floor was covered with a thick light blue carpet. There were a few pieces of expensive-looking furniture and rugs in the modern geometric style. The curtains were drawn shut across wide windows.

Khyrbysk indicated a low sofa in the middle of the room. There was a polished oval coffee table in front of it, empty except for a bowl of dried fruits.

'Sit down,' he said. 'Please. You are my guests. Perhaps you would like some wine?'

'There is no time,' said Lom.

Khyrbysk ignored him.

'Captain Iliodor,' he said to Florian. 'We have corresponded, have we not? And spoken on the telephone, I think. A pleasure to meet you in person at last. Also something of a surprise. I was expecting to meet you yesterday with Lavrentina when she arrived, but you were not with her. Indeed, she mentioned that you had disappeared during a bombing raid on Mirgorod. She was concerned for you. There was some suggestion that you might have been injured. Or dead.'

Florian gave him a quick untroubled smile.

'As you see,' he said, 'I am not dead; I was merely delayed. I arrived in Novaya Zima some hours ago.'

'We can talk as we go,' said Lom. 'Get your coat, Professor. Let's be on our way.'

Khyrbysk turned towards him, small eyes narrow in the slab of his face.

'And who are you, please?' he said. 'I know who your associate says he is, but you have not yet accounted for your presence here.'

'My colleague—' Florian began.

'I am an Investigator of the Vlast Political Police.'

Khyrbysk sighed.

'Oh, really, must we continue this charade?' he said. 'I know you are not what you say you are. Whatever you might have told poor Zsara, you are evidently nothing to do with Lavrentina, and you are certainly not from the police, so let us waste no more time on tedious diversions. Spare me that. I am not surprised you have come. I have been expecting you, or someone like you, for a long time.'

'Who do you think we are?' said Lom.

Khyrbysk shrugged.

'Precisely?' he said. 'Precisely, I have no idea at all. Spies? Agents of the Archipelago? The specifics hardly matter. You are outsiders.

People from elsewhere, come to find out what is happening here in Novaya Zima. As I said, I have been expecting that someone like you would come eventually. Our achievements were bound to attract such attention, though frankly I thought there would be a more subtle approach. A less frontal assault, shall I say? Well, no matter. You are here, and I have nothing to hide, so let us be civilised. Share my wine and tell me what you want from me.'

Khyrbysk's manner was smooth and urbane but there was hard calculation in his eyes. *He's playing with us*, thought Lom. *Playing for time. But there is no time.*

'You met Chazia when she arrived?' he said.

'Of course,' said Khyrbysk.

'There was a woman with her. Early twenties. Five foot nine. Black hair cut short at the neck.'

For the first time, Khyrbysk looked surprised. Genuinely surprised.

'I couldn't say. I don't recall seeing such a woman. Lavrentina's entourage was large. I did not meet them all. Of course not.'

Lom's patience had reached its limit. He pulled the Blok 15 from his pocket and pointed it at Khyrbysk's belly.

'Where is Chazia now?' he said.

Khyrbysk glanced briefly at the gun and looked away. Dismissed it from his attention.

'When I left Lavrentina earlier this evening she was in the mountain. She had work to do. She is a woman of remarkable energy.'

'You're going to take us to her,' said Lom. 'You're going to take us into the mountain and vouch for us with your security. Tell them we are your guests. Take us to where Chazia is.'

'Of course,' said Khyrbysk. 'If that's what you want.' He glanced at the gun. 'Your argument is persuasive.'

'Don't over-focus on the gun,' said Lom. 'You should worry more about my friend there. I certainly would.'

84

They went out of the Foundation Hall and across the floodlit square. The sky-aspiring sculpture cast three long black gnomon-shadows. Lom walked on one side of Khyrbysk, Florian on the other. The square was deserted. It was almost nine.

'No transport?' said Khyrbysk, looking around.

'No,' said Lom.

'You don't have much of a plan then.'

'The plan's simple,' said Lom. 'If there's any trouble from you we kill you and think of something else.'

'I see. You have no transport. Well, I'm afraid my driver has gone home for the night, but if we go back inside I could get Zsara to telephone for a car.'

'We'll walk,' said Lom.

'Five miles in the night?' said Khyrbysk. 'Partly across open country? Better to take the train.'

There was a transit station at the corner of the square. The system was still running. They didn't have to wait long for a northbound service. There were a couple of solitary passengers – night workers going on shift – but Khyrbysk led them to seats at the other end of the car.

'The city is beautiful at night,' he said, looking out of the window, 'but you should see it in the long summer days. It is the northern jewel of the Vlast.'

'You call this place a city?' said Lom.

'Yes, certainly Novaya Zima is a city. A city is defined by importance rather than size. By centrality to the culture of the coming times. Novaya Zima is not an agglomeration of buildings, it is a machine for living. A machine for making the future. And it is a metaphor. A work of art.'

He sat back in his seat and unbuttoned the fawn camel-hair coat he had put on over his shirt. It was hot in the carriage. He seemed inclined to talk. Perhaps it was nerves, but Lom didn't think so. Khyrbysk didn't seem too bothered about his predicament at all.

'Take the building where I live, for instance,' Khyrbysk was saying. 'The Foundation Hall. It is made from steel and glass. Above all, glass. What better metaphor than glass for the future we are building? Millions of separate grains of sand, weak and uncohesive when separate, fused together under a fierce transmuting heat to form a new substance. And the new substance is perfect. Unblemished, transparent and strong. This is how we shall reforge humanity. The progress of history is inevitable. It is happening already. The individual is losing his significance – his private destiny no longer interests us – many particles must become one consistent force …'

Khyrbysk paused.

'You smile,' he said. 'But I assure you, what I am saying is a clear-sighted expression of fact. Novaya Zima *signifies*. Everything you see in Novaya Zima, the fine architecture, this mass transit system of which we are so proud, it all *signifies*.'

Florian grunted. 'You have a fine apartment,' he said.

'You sound censorious,' said Khyrbysk, 'You want to make me ashamed of my privileges while others labour hungry and the Vlast is at war?'

'The thought occurred to me,' said Florian.

'But I am not ashamed,' said Khyrbysk. 'The fact that others forgo essentials so we can live like this, that is what drives us on. It shows our strength of purpose. The Vlast may suffer hardships, Novaya Zima says to the world, but we can still do this.'

'This place tells the world nothing,' said Florian, 'because the world doesn't know it exists.'

'Not yet perhaps,' said Khyrbysk, 'but when we are ready it will.'

Lom remembered the smell of the empty trains at the Wieland marshalling yard. The ranks of empty trains. He was surprised by the heat of his own anger

'You've built a comfortable utopia for you and your friends on the bones of slaves.'

'You're trying to provoke me,' said Khyrbysk blandly, 'but I will not rise to it. I am merely a worker in my own field, as are we all. There is no egotism here, only *I* becoming *We*: the clear and perfect simplicity of glass.'

'And the workers under the mountain? Do they see it like that? I've seen the trains.'

'Certainly they do. Most of them. Physical labour is redemptive. Many request to stay on when their terms are complete. They ask for their families to join them. '

Lom turned away in disgust. He caught his own reflection in the window looking back at him. And through his own face he saw the lighted windows of kommunalki buildings moving past. For a moment it was as if he was stationary and the buildings were sliding away, leaving him behind.

'The quality of our city,' said Khyrbysk, oblivious to Lom's reaction, or ignoring it, 'expresses the supreme importance of the work we do.'

Florian leaned forward intently.

'What work?' he said. 'What is happening here? What is all this for?'

'The Foundation for Physico-Technical Machines,' said Khyrbysk, 'is the greatest concentration of human intelligence the world has ever seen. The whole city exists to support our work. There is more brilliance lodged in Foundation Hall, in that one single building, than ... There is no comparator. No precedent. It is our academy. We have sacrificed our careers to be here, all of us. We do not publish, at least not under our own names. We get no fame for what we do, none of the mundane rewards. But the future will know us by our work.'

They stopped at a station and the last passengers left them alone. Shortly after the train restarted, the buildings outside the window disappeared, leaving nothing but blank darkness. Lom realised they had crossed the northern boundary of the township and were heading across open country towards the mountain.

'What work?' said Florian again. 'What is the work?'

'Our work?' said Khyrbysk. 'We look up at night and see a universe of stars and planets teeming with life, and angels swimming the cosmic emptiness like fish. Only the emptiness between the stars is *not* empty; it teems with life and vigour just as the planets do. It merely does not shine so brightly.' There was a light in Khyrbysk's eye that was not entirely sane. For all his craggy bulk, his thick grizzled curls and cliff-like face, he was a prophet burning with the incandescence of a vision. 'That is where history is leading us,' he continued. 'Humankind spreading out across the galaxies in the endless pursuit of radiant light. Only there will we find space enough to live as we are meant to live. It is inevitable. It is the will of the universe.'

Lom could see nothing but blackness outside the carriage window. The reflection of the bright interior obliterated everything. He could see himself, and opposite him a mirror-Khyrbysk and a mirror-Florian. There was less of Iliodor in Florian's face, he thought: more angularity, more darkness. An effect of mirror and harsh shadow, perhaps.

'There are practical problems to be solved, of course, if humankind is to escape from this one cramped planet,' Khyrbysk was saying. 'That's what we are doing here. New means of propulsion, new techniques for navigation, new technologies for sustaining life outside the atmosphere and beyond the light of the sun. And new designs for humankind itself. Crossing the immensities of space will take immensities of time. Our present bodies are too short-lived. They decay and fail. But even this problem will be solved. We know that angel flesh can absorb and carry human consciousness: all that's needed is refinement of technique.'

'There are thousands of workers here,' said Lom. 'They aren't engaged in cosmological hypothesising.'

'Not hypothesising!' said Khyrbysk. 'Practicalities! There are a hundred real and specific problems to be solved. Problems of science, engineering and design.'

'That is not enough,' Florian's voice was a snarl. 'There is something more. Something else is happening here.'

'Not enough! I've shared more truth and vision with you in the last ten minutes than you can possibly have heard in the whole of your life up to this moment.'

Khyrbysk's pale blue eyes were narrow and predatory.

'You think I'm afraid of you?' he said. 'You think I'm your prisoner? I am no such thing. You will not kill me, but I will take you to Lavrentina, and she will surely kill you.'

85

There was a burst of noise as the transit car hurtled straight into the side of the Foundation Mountain and entered an unlit concrete tube barely wide enough to accommodate it. The light from the car's lamps flickered along the uneven wall, illuminating snaking power cables and gaping black side shafts. Ten minutes later they emerged into dazzling fluorescent brilliance and came to a sudden stop. Khyrbysk opened the door and they stepped out onto an iron platform.

They were in the middle of an immense cloister carved out of solid rock, hundreds of feet long and fifty feet high, supported by a field of wide columns: trunks of raw rough stone, left in place when the solidity of the mountain was cut away, sleeved in squared-off concrete for the first twenty feet of their height. Thousands of lighting tubes threw daylight-blue shadowless brightness across gleaming asphalt. The air was body-warm, dry to the point of desiccation and smelled faintly of naphtha. Not air at all but breathable suffocation, it moved in a steady current across Lom's face. Glancing up, he saw rows of ventilation shafts in the rock ceiling and wide rotor fans behind grilles, turning slowly. He felt the terrible weight of the dark mountain overhead, inert, world-heavy, impending.

'Follow me,' said Khyrbysk and set off at a smart pace. His shoulders were broad and bulky. Grizzled wiry curls came down over his collar. He seemed to have forgotten he was being marched along at gunpoint.

'Slow down,' growled Florian. 'Be aware.'

Khyrbysk ignored him and hurried on. Lom and Florian followed him down a wide clattering staircase onto the cavern floor. A complex of temporary huts serving as offices clustered around the base of the nearest column. There was a canteen, open but deserted, a telephone exchange and an operator hub for the pneumatic mail system. Further away, on a low concrete platform, a powerhouse of whirring massive dynamos hummed and buzzed. There were few people about: the night shift, quietly efficient at their business. Men dwarfed by the dynamos stood before expanses of winking signal lights, dials and gleaming bakelite controls. Walkways between the columns were marked by coloured lines painted on the asphalt. They led off in every direction towards square tunnel mouths.

Khyrbysk stopped and waited for them to catch up.

'This is a side entrance,' he said. 'A vestibule, you might say. There are two hundred miles of tunnels under the mountain, and hundreds of chambers, many larger than this one. There are lift shafts, conveyor belts, railways, winches and hauling engines, underground watercourses. All of it permanently lit, ventilated, heated and dehumidified. Workshops. Factories. Laboratories. Storage and stockpiling facilities. We construct most of the machine tools and technical instruments we require right here, ourselves. The city under the mountain is larger than the city outside. It operates in twenty-four-hour daylight, wholly unaffected by winter and summer. It is the most efficient industrial complex the world has ever seen. This part may look deserted but there are tens of thousands of workers here. Most of them are in the mines, of course. The mines are why we are here, not elsewhere. The mountain is full of uranium. Riddled with it. It's all around us, like raisins in a cake. Nowhere else has it been discovered in such abundance.'

It was as if he was giving them a guided tour. As if they were dignitaries on their way to a lunch. Lom had to admire him. He had a will of iron.

Khyrbysk set off again.

'Follow, please,' he said.

Lom and Florian fell in behind him. They had reached an unspoken agreement to let the man have his head and see where he took them. He would surely lead them to Chazia, one way or another.

Khyrbysk bounded up another iron staircase. Another rail car waited there, a rounded oblong box with windows, painted in the same colours as the transit carriages but much smaller, designed to carry up to six passengers with a small luggage bay behind. It hung suspended from an overhead rail and swayed slightly when they climbed in. Khyrbysk went to the front and switched on the power. Interior lamps flickered into life and floor-level vents began to breathe heated air into the cabin. The floor was covered with stippled rubber, the steel walls and ceiling were painted cream, the seats upholstered in green leather. A chrome handrail ran the length of the wall on both sides. The interior smelled strongly of rubber and hot engine oil.

A lectern-like brown bakelite panel was set at an angle under the forward window, marked out with a complex map of radial and intersecting lines. There was a tiny switch and light bulb at each labelled node. Some of the nodes bore names – RAILHEAD, POLISHING, REFECTORY IV, CENTRIFUGE, NORTH GATE EXIT – but most were designated by short, impenetrable alphanumeric sequences.

'This is a plan of the entire complex?' said Lom.

'Correct,' said Khyrbysk.

He set the panel with practised speed and the car lurched into life. The last node he activated was labelled EDB/CENTRAL.

'What's EDB?' said Lom.

'You'll see.'

The car rattled through narrow tunnels and swept out high above underground chambers. They saw women in overalls and headscarves worked at assembly lines, operating lathes and welding machines. They passed the slopes of sour-smelling slag dumps. Furnace doors clanged open beneath them, belching blasts of heat and disgorging planks of glowing molten metal onto conveyor belts. A gently descending tunnel took them past honeycomb stacks of artillery shells painted a garish yellow. Notices on the racks warned, with perfect superfluity, DANGER! HIGH EXPLOSIVE!

'Armaments?' said Lom.

'Certainly,' said Khyrbysk. 'We must satisfy our benefactors. The iron law of economics. The Foundation must wash its own face.'

They swung out across a dim shoreless lake of milky-green water reeking of naphtha, its surface wreathed with scraps and scarves of steam. Hard-hat gangers clambered across half-built scaffolding and tramped in silent groups on perilous unrailed walkways. Then, after ten more minutes of featureless tunnel, the rail car lurched to a stop alongside two identical carriages.

EXPERIMENTAL DESIGN BUREAU.

EDB.

Khyrbysk led them through double swing doors into another world. The oppressive scale of the underground complex was gone, replaced by green corridors. Fire extinguishers. Noticeboards. Wall-mounted telephones. The muted clatter of distant typewriters. Linoleum floors squeaked underfoot. Half-glazed doors opened into offices and meeting rooms. SURVIVABLES. LENSING. CENTRIFUGE. DEPLETION. STAGING. NOÖSPHERE. PROJECT WINTER SKIES.

A few people were working late. Men in shirtsleeves and sleeveless pullovers. They sat alone or gathered in small huddles, rumpled, smoking, arguing earnestly in quiet voices. Many of them nodded to Khyrbysk as he passed and he greeted each one by name.

Lom noticed that Khyrbysk's creased heavy face was damp with perspiration. For the first time he looked tense. But there was something about the way he was walking that wasn't nervous, but the opposite: a kind of bravado in the way he carried himself.

'Nearly there,' he said.

Now we are coming to it, thought Lom. He tightened his grip on the gun in his pocket. Beside him he sensed Florian ready himself for action. *Clever Khyrbysk has fooled us all. So he thinks.*

Khyrbysk veered suddenly to the right, pushed open a door and entered a large hexagonal room overlooked by two mezzanine tiers. The central floor was occupied by a circular plotting table twenty feet in diameter, the green baize surface laid out with maps and charts. In the corner a telekrypt whirred and blinked. Up on the mezzanines women in uniform whispered intently into telephones. Half a dozen VKBD officers in pale red uniforms looked up when they entered.

Khyrbysk stepped sharply away from Lom and Florian.

'Draw your weapons!' he barked. 'Lieutenant Gerasimov! Arrest these men! They are spies. They are terrorists. They are assassins. Lock them away somewhere and inform Secretary Chazia immediately. I put them in her hands.'

The VKBD men snapped to their feet, a dozen revolver muzzles covering Lom and Florian.

'The Secretary is not here, Director Khyrbysk,' said Gerasimov. 'She took the observation car to the testing zone. She wanted to witness it herself.'

Khyrbysk frowned.

'Gone already? But the test is not till dawn. I was to travel with her. That was the plan.'

'We could telephone, but ... She will not welcome a trivial interruption. She took the woman with her.'

'The matter is of no relevance to me. But she must deal with this, Lieutenant. I want to hear no more of these men. And Gerasimov, I have made representations before about the lax security in the city. I will be doing so again, depend on it.'

As he turned to go Khyrbysk threw a contemptuous glance at Lom and Florian.

'Idiots,' he muttered.

86

When Khyrbysk had gone, Lieutenant Gerasimov detached two of the VKBD – heavy grey-faced men with broad dull faces, early forties, running to fat – to take Lom and Florian to the detention area.

'Wait with them there till Chazia comes.'

The VKBD men looked bored and resentful. They didn't like being dragged away from bothering the women working the telephones. Vagant revolvers in hand, they shoved and hustled their captives along the corridors. People glanced at them curiously and quickly looked away, avoiding the eye of the VKBD. Lom shuffled along passively, eyes to the floor, looking defeated. Florian walked with as much dignity as he could muster, bareheaded, holding his astrakhan hat in his hand.

When they reached the transit car, Lom watched carefully as one of the guards set the control panel. The man worked slowly, concentrating on each move. The operation was simple: there was a button under the counter to turn on the power, then you selected your route and flicked the switches of the points you wanted to pass through. If you made a mistake, you flicked the switch the other way to cancel the instruction. The guard made several mistakes. Lom guessed the VKBD had arrived with Chazia the previous day.

The car rocked and settled and lurched into life.

No point in waiting. There won't be a better time.

Lom glanced at Florian, who was watching him with glittering, rapacious amusement. Florian raised an eyebrow. It was a question. An invitation.

'Leave it to me,' said Lom. 'No need to rip their heads off.' He regretted the loss of his Blok 15, which the VKBD had taken. But it didn't matter. It made no difference.

The guard nearest to him frowned.

'Keep your fucking mouth shut—'

Lom stepped in close, inside the gun hand, and crunched his right elbow into the man's face. Felt his nose burst and his head jerk back. In the same movement with his left hand he gripped the Vagant and the fist that held it and twisted. Hard. Felt the trigger finger snap. The gun fired, deafening in the enclosed space. The bullet punched a hole in the wall.

If the other guard had been watching properly, and if he'd been trained, and if he'd practised so much that he didn't need to think, he might have realised what was happening and responded effectively in, what, two seconds? Maybe less. But he wasn't trained, and he hadn't practised, and he didn't have two seconds. He was still standing in the same position with a puzzled look on his face when Lom's right fist, holding the Vagant, powered by the momentum of his charge and with the full two hundred pounds of his weight behind it, crashed into the side of his head. The guard staggered sideways. His gun slipped from his fingers and skittered across the floor. Lom recovered his balance and aimed a vicious kick at the man's kneecap. He screamed and fell. Lom kicked his head again just to be sure. It felt good. The angel taste was in his mouth again.

Both VKBD men were down and not moving. Lom stepped over them to the control panel. The schematic showed the NORTHERN GATE and a single straight line leading away from it, out of the mountain: the furthest terminal was labelled FIELD TEST OBSERVER STATION. He flicked switches, programming the most direct route avoiding major intersections. The car halted, hesitated, and started back the way it had come.

87

For an hour they passed through tunnels and shafts and caverns, climbing steadily. There was less activity in the northern area of the mountain. At first they half-expected the car to seize up and stop, the power cut. Security procedures kicking in to isolate and capture them. But it didn't happen. Florian spread himself out on a passenger bench and closed his eyes but Lom stayed on his feet at the panel, leaning forward to stare through the front window, following their progress. Tiny lamps winked out as they left the nodes behind. The unconscious guards, propped at the back of the car where Florian had dragged them, were breathing noisily.

Lom brought the car to a stop at an empty platform. He and Florian bundled the inert guards out: deadweights smelling of sweat and sour breath and blood. They kept the guns.

The last twenty minutes underground were a long haul down a shallow incline, an unlit featureless tunnel bored through raw rock. They seemed to be speeding up. Then, without warning, they burst out into the night on the far side of the mountain. The rattling echoes of the tunnel ceased. The car travelled on in near-silence. There was only the electric hum of its motor and the wind splitting against the overhead rail. It was coming up to four in the morning.

Lom stood at the front of the railcar. Leaning forward, feet slightly apart. Hands gripping the chrome bar so hard it hurt. The rail ran on ahead into the darkness. It was carrying them towards Maroussia. Ahead of them, somewhere, she was there. He was sure of that. Other possibilities were not admitted. Not considered. She was there and he would find her. He would get her back. But the car wasn't moving fast enough. He leaned into the bar as if he would push it onward faster with his own force of will.

Behind him he heard Florian shift in his seat.

'What time is dawn this far north?' said Lom, not looking round.

'Late,' said Florian. 'Nine? Ten? We have time.'

'We need a plan,' said Lom.

'We should get there first.'

They cruised on through total darkness. Only the light spilling from their own windows showed the unbroken carpet of trees. The snow was thicker to the north of the mountain.

Hours passed. Nothing changed. Lom tried to calculate their speed by his wristwatch, counting the trees passing beneath them and the regularly spaced pylons that carried the overhead rail. He repeated the measurement again and again. Somewhere between thirty and fifty miles an hour. Perhaps. It was something to do.

The trees grew sparser, pine and spruce replacing birch, and the snow was getting thicker all the time, mounding the tree-heads and piling in drifts. The small capsule raced on over frozen lakes, snow-crusted and black. The hour hand on Lom's watched crept round the dial. Five o'clock. Six. Always the single rail stretched ahead of them, pylon after pylon.

They flashed through an unlit platform stop. Rows of vague regular shapes were passing underneath them. Humped shadows. They were aeroplanes. Hundreds of large aircraft parked in neat rows under tarpaulins. Mothballed. Snow-covered runways. A control tower in darkness. Then came two minutes of trees and another wide clearing. A mile-wide expanse of nothing surrounded by a perimeter fence. And then there was a splash of bright light ahead of them. A brilliant pool of arc light bright enough to reflect off the underside of the cloud. The car rose and swept past what seemed like a domed mound, too regular and polished and perfect to be natural. It glimmered dark brick red and was surrounded by a circular blackness. Lom had time to realize he was looking at the top of something rising from a pit several hundred yards across, surrounded by shadowy gantries and lumps of broken concrete. Then it was gone.

As they left the oasis of brilliant light behind, they passed through another empty platform. Lom read the sign as it flashed past the window.

COSMODROME: WINTER SKIES.

There was an emblem: a simplified version of the soaring steel sculpture in front of the Foundation Hall. The rising discus. THE VLAST SPREADING OUT ACROSS THE STARS.

Antoninu Florian sat in silence, flexing taut aching muscle, sinew, flesh. Working his bones with infinitesimal shifts of size and shape. He had been holding this human shape in place too long, and every part of his body was sore: a dull rheumatic ache from his face to his feet, cramped inside their tightly laced boots. He shifted in his seat, though it brought him no comfort, and watched Lom leaning on the handrail and staring out through the forward window at the empty landscape that rolled up to meet them. The intensity of Lom's focus on Maroussia was a tangible tension in the air. It hummed like taut wire in the wind.

For the hundredth time, the thousandth time, Florian studied him. Lom was a vessel of the beautiful forest, all unaware, but he was also saturated through and through with dark angel stuff. The wound Chazia had made in his head had become an opening, a shining perfumed breach, but the angel mark had left its indelible stain. Florian had observed Lom's growing violence in the last few days. The angel stuff was part of what made Lom what he was: an unexpected possibility, an open, borderless, compendious man, the joining together of what could not be joined. In the unsolvable equation of forest and angel and Vlast and Pollandore, the complex impossible strength that just might resolve it was Vissarion Lom.

Unless the Shaumian woman was lost.

Florian was certain that Maroussia was alive and somewhere ahead of them. He could not sense her, but he could sense the Pollandore. It was close and they were closing with it, and so was the Shaumian woman. Florian felt the Pollandore calling her. And he still didn't know what he would do when he caught up with her. The indecision hurt worse than the tension in his distorted bones. Futures contended. All outcomes could be ruinous. When the time of crisis came, then he would know what to do. Then he would decide.

The frozen lakes became larger and more numerous. They were crossing more ice than trees. And then they were suddenly travelling low above the sea. Ten feet below them thick black water rose and fell, viscid and streaked with foam. It was as if the ocean was breathing gently. Rafts of ice, almost perfectly circular, gleamed in the yellow cabin light that raced across them. The floor-level heating vents hummed loudly, struggling to warm the inflow of freezing air. And failing. The cold pinched Lom's face. He felt his hands and feet growing stiff and numb.

Seven o'clock.

They crossed the shore of the north island at 7.45 a.m. The sea fell away behind them and they were riding low over level tundra. Flat expanses of snow and ice. The first hint of daylight was touching the eastern sky. A faint diminishing of darkness. Condensation was frosting on the inside of the window, forming spidery crystal webs. Lom rubbed it away. Metronome pylons ticked past.

At ten past eight they saw the lights ahead of them. A cluster of low buildings in the pre-dawn greyness, dark against the snow. Lom cut the power, plunging the cabin interior into silence and gloom. The car rattled on, slowing. It took several minutes to come to a complete halt, swinging and creaking in the wind.

Florian pushed the door open and let in a blast of freezing air. They were fifteen feet above the ground. The snow looked thick and soft beneath them. He leaped out and landed neatly in a crouch, knee deep.

Lom took a breath and followed. He landed hard and rolled. Ended up on his back in the snow, winded, staring up at the sky. It hurt. He stood up slowly. Stiffly. Testing.

He was OK.

He looked round for Florian and saw him racing silently away across the snow. Within fifty yards he had disappeared. Faded into grey and dropped behind a ridge.

'Fuck,' said Lom quietly to himself. 'Fuck.'

Slowly and painfully he began to follow.

88

In darkness and snow and windswept ice at the centre of the North Zima Expanse, the Pollandore rests in its own uninterpretable space, touching nothing, a slowly turning globe. Worlds do not stand on the framework of flatbed trucks. Worlds do not hang by hooks and cables from a makeshift gantry. Worlds fall. They are always and only falling. Endless ellipses of fall, from no sky towards no frozen ground, turning and tumbling as they go. And everything else falls with them, unaware.

Towering over the Pollandore on its own framework of girders, the swollen samovar – the uranium gobbet in its bulging belly, the uranium seed sleeved in its high-explosive kernel – awaits its moment in the sun. Uncle Vanya's big fat beautiful cousin. Cables snake away across the ice.

Several miles from the Pollandore's crude gantry, in a concrete bunker with walls three feet deep and one thick panoramic window, Ambroz Teleki was handing out tubs of sunscreen and aviator glasses with dark-tinted lenses. Lavrentina Chazia waved him away.

'I'm not staying cooped up inside this hutch,' she said. 'I'm going out to feel the hot wind on my face.'

Teleki was horrified.

'But that's impossible! Secretary Chazia, you do not appreciate the danger … the strength of the blast … Even at this distance—'

Chazia silenced him with a look.

'At dawn,' she said, 'there will be a new sun. Am I not to bask in its warmth?'

She turned to the corner where the Shaumian girl sat watching her with dark resentful eyes.

'And you, Maroussia darling,' said Chazia, 'you will see the flash on the horizon and know the moment for what it is. The destruction of the Pollandore. I'm glad you're here to see it, it's only right you should. That thing has been a source of delusion for us both, in our different ways. To be released from it will be a great step forward. You'll see things in their true relations then.'

Chazia had been reluctant to destroy the Pollandore after investing so much in it for so long. She had wanted to carry out the angel's instruction, but the thought of doing it was deeply painful. She had continued to put up inward resistance until rigorous self-examination and the guidance of the angel had gradually opened her eyes to the truth. It had taken time, but at last, freed from false consciousness by a better teaching, she'd come to realise what a beguiling cipher the Pollandore was: a meaningless emptiness, a zero mirage into which she'd been led to pour her desires, against her true interests and the reality of things as they were. The Pollandore had woven subtle nets of illusion to protect itself while it exploited her, just as it had ensnared Maroussia.

'Make sure she watches,' Chazia said to the SV lieutenant standing guard at Maroussia's side. 'Make her stand there and see.'

Maroussia glared at her but said nothing.

'The pain will pass,' said Chazia kindly. 'Truth hurts but better understanding sets us free.' Then she turned away and went through to the other room, the office. She opened the crate that held her suit of angel flesh and began to put it on.

The excitement of anticipation made her tremble.

Wolf-Florian galloped low across the surface of the snow, stretching his limbs in the relief of being wolf again, bounding over raised drifts. He could sense the Pollandore ahead of him. It was below the horizon but its call burned behind his eyes like he had never felt it before, and the calling pulsed with a desperate joy. He was running through the shadows of invisible trees. The flat disc of ice across which he ran was forested with the ghosts of ancient trees.

Ahead of him was the Pollandore and behind him was Lom, a perfumed beacon spilling his beautiful headstuff into the freezing air, all unaware of what he was and what he could become. And between them – Florian was closing on her now and could sense her presence – was the Shaumian woman.

Florian still did not know what to do.

The woman was change and the woman was desperate threat. A door in the world stood slightly open, which she might fling wide or slam shut. And he did not know which.

He would kill her before she could reach the Pollandore.

With his last dying breath he would carry her safely to it, so she could do what she would do.

When the time came he would know what to do.

But for now, still, even as he ran towards her, he did not know, and the not-knowing hurt. It hurt more than the desperate working of his heart as he pushed himself on at the extremity of his body's capacity across the hardened crunching snow.

A flake of Archangel watchfulness settles upon the gantry of Uncle Vanya's big fat cousin and flexes its fragment-wings of sentience like a bird. Archangel bird is come to taste the joy of destruction.

He observes with pin-sharp joy the diminished, fragile, vulnerable sphere beneath him. Here is the Once Great Threat. Here is the Pollandore. How pathetic Archangel finds it now, so feeble and tiny amid the wastes of ice, and bound with chains to a barrel of death!

To think that in his hurt and wounded beginning on this confining world he – he! Archangel! – once had feared this useless thing! Feared this excremetal node of weaknesses! He does not fear it now.

Destruction time coming.

Pleasurable anticipation thrills.

He lets the time of its coming run slowly. Tasting it.

He will crush this disgusting thing under the heel of his triumph. He will abort it. Soon this trivial gap will be closed, and a new roaring radiant gate will be thrown open.

Archangel-fragment throws back his bird head and crows at the approaching dawn. It is a mighty banner-shout unfurling across the glittering immensities of what will come to be.

When Chazia had gone, Maroussia got up from her chair by the window and went over to the SV lieutenant.

'Please,' she said. 'I would like to visit the bathroom.'

The lieutenant looked at her with relaxed contempt. Memories in the back of his eyes. Memories of what he'd seen Chazia do to her, and what he himself had done. Maroussia pushed the thought away. She wouldn't think of that. Not now and not ever.

'Sit down,' said the lieutenant. 'Wait.'

'Please,' said Maroussia. 'Please. It is urgent. I have to go now.'

The lieutenant swore.

'Come then,' he said. 'But for fuck's sake be quick.'

Lom ploughed on alone through the snow, following the line of the overhead rail. The cluster of huts was at least half a mile away. It was slow going. He hunched his face into his collar against the bitter cold. Stuffed his hands into his pockets, flexing his fingers to keep them mobile. His breath plumed steam clouds. What had seemed flat terrain from the rail car was undulating ridges and dips, crests and berms. The circle of the half-visible around him grew inexorably wider, the twilight before dawn inching towards grey. But there was nothing to see: only the levels of rolling tundra, indistinct under thin drifting mist.

He was holding tight to the idea – the unsurrendered certainty – that Maroussia was there in that cluster of huts half a mile ahead. He had no plan. That didn't matter: plans never lasted thirty seconds when the action started. Here in subarctic near-darkness, alone and driving himself forward, chest heaving, heart pounding, across the sharp crusted snow, he knew what he had to do, the only thing he could possibly do, and he was doing it.

There was nothing else in the world but him and the half-mile of ice between him and Maroussia. It all came down to that. He had chosen this. He had made his decisions and chosen the path that brought him here. He was absolutely responsible and absolutely free and he would not fail; he would not be too late and he would not die, because to fail was to fail Maroussia, and that he would not do.

And he was, in that moment, completely and absolutely alive.

Inside the tiny bathroom Maroussia locked the door. She looked at her face in the mirror hung on a hook above the sink. She looked tired and sick. Bruise-blue shadows under her eyes. A pink graze across her face. There were angry raised welts on her wrists and arms where Chazia's straps had rubbed and cut. She felt sick. She would not think of that. Not now. Not ever. She would not remember.

She wrapped a towel around her hand. Then she lifted the mirror off the wall and smashed it against the sink.

'Hey!' called the lieutenant. 'What are you doing in there?' He tried the door. 'Fuck,' he said, but quietly so that Chazia would not hear. He didn't want her to know. He began to bump his weight against the door, but hesitantly. He would make no more noise than he had to.

Maroussia picked up the biggest shard of broken mirror. Gripped it tight in her towel-wrapped palm. Settled the edge of it firmly in her hand. A vicious, pointed shard of glass about five inches long.

The thumping against the door fell into a predictable rhythmic pattern. The bolt was beginning to give. With her free hand Maroussia slid it quietly back.

At the next crash of the lieutenant's weight, the door burst open and he stumbled in, surprised. Unbalanced, he took a couple of stuttering steps forward. Maroussia stepped in behind him, put the dagger of glass against the side of his throat and pushed. She had to push hard. Two, three times she sawed the jagged edge back and forth. There was a lot of blood. When she let the lieutenant drop to the floor he was not dead. He was trying to shout and scream. He had two mouths now, both of them gaping open and spilling blood, but neither had a voice. Only a desperate bubbling wheeze.

She dropped the towel and knelt beside him, the warm pool of his blood soaking into the skirt of her dress. She went through the pockets of his jacket, searching, hoping what she was looking for was still there, where she had watched him carelessly shove it the night before. It was. Her fingers touched the broken pieces. She pulled out the fragments of the solm her mother had been bringing when she died, gripped them tight in her palm and stood up, careful not to slip on the blood on the floor.

Maroussia left the lieutenant still moving weakly in the growing pool of his own mess. She went out the back of the blockhouse into the dark and the snow.

89

Lom was still several hundred yards from the cluster of huts, moving slowly and cautiously, crouching to keep off the brightening skyline, when Florian appeared suddenly beside him as if he had risen up out of the snow.

'Maroussia?' said Lom. 'Did you find her?'

Florian looked at him strangely for a moment and said nothing.

'For fuck's sake,' said Lom. 'Is she *there*?'

'She is there,' said Florian. 'She has been hurt but she is alive. She is very strong.'

Lom felt a desperate knot of tension suddenly dissolve. He hadn't realised how dark his world had grown since he'd lost her. He wanted to throw his arms round Florian and hug him but did not. Florian looked grave.

'What?' said Lom. 'What is it?'

'Nothing,' said Florian. 'Nothing.'

'Then let's go.'

'Yes. But cautiously. There are two huts. One with soldiers. VKBD. Seven. Maroussia is in the other. Chazia is also there, and one soldier, and men who are not soldiers. Scientists. Technicians. Nine.'

Lom pushed his elation aside. *Focus on now.* They needed to get Maroussia out and away. He considered the position. They had two Vagants between them. Full chambers but no spare ammunition. Eight soldiers, plus Chazia herself, who would not be negligible if it came to a fight. And if they could get Maroussia safely away, what then? They were in a snowfield a hundred miles or more on the wrong side of the mountain, on an island in a freezing sea. But then they had Florian. Lom had seen what he could do.

'OK,' he said. 'Could be worse.'

'It is,' said Florian. 'They have a mudjhik.'

'No,' said Lom. He looked towards the distant huts. 'Surely not. I'd feel it by now.'

'It is there. Not a large one. Ten feet tall perhaps. It seems inactive. I was not aware of it until I got close. Its presence startled me.'

'OK,' said Lom again. 'Anything else?'

'Outbuildings for storage. A diesel generator. An overhead rail car like the one we came in on. And there's a single railway track, away to the left over there. It runs on into the north. Towards the Pollandore.'

Lom felt a tightening in his stomach. His mouth was dry.

'Let's get on with it,' he said.

90

Lom was less than a hundred yards from the blockhouses. Florian had slipped away and disappeared, circling round to the left. Lom scrambled forward across the snow until he could see the mudjhik. It was standing upright, motionless, a squat statue of solid brick-red taller than the concrete blockhouses, arms at its side, its head, an eyeless faceless mass, turned towards the north. Lom let his mind drift towards it cautiously, reaching out for a contact, probing delicately, looking for a way in. And found it.

The mudjhik was not dormant. It was absorbed in studying the snow. With angel senses, not sight but precise acute awareness, it was examining individual crystals of snow. Sifting from one to the next with absolute patience, it traced their intricate hexagonal symmetry. The ramification of columns and blades of ice. The uncountable variety. It found the broken ones and tested the edges of their fractures. It teased the nested clumps, the accidental fusions. It followed the prismatic refractions of muted light down beneath the mute mirror-glitter surface as the greyness broke into spectrum fragments, growing green then blue then dark. To the mudjhik's patient watchfulness the snow was as deep and mysterious as oceans.

Long slow inches below the surface the mudjhik touched solid compacted ice and sank its attention in. Ran its mind along faults and pressure lines and the million captured imperfections of grit and dust. The mudjhik found it all infinitely, endlessly satisfying. The ice and snow was beautiful and it was happy.

Lom traced the faint cord of connection from the mudjhik to its handler. The line was almost not there at all: the handler's focus was elsewhere, on something inside the building. It had been the same for hours, the mudjhik almost forgotten. Gently, gently, Lom squeezed the connection closed, cut it off entirely, and slid in behind it. The mudjhik was his.

Lom made himself known.

The mudjhik sprang to life. It was like an inward eye opening. Glaring and hot. It opened its thoughtless sentient mind like a dark hot mouth, gaping and hungry. Tried to grasp at Lom and swallow him and haul him fully inside. But Lom was strong. He knew what he was doing. The angel stain in his own blood answered the mudjhik's assault with a fierce roaring.

No, said Lom-in-mudjhik, *I am not yours. You are mine. You are mine. You are mine.*

Lom forced himself through every part of the mudjhik's body, occupying it entirely. Taking possession. He found the animal brain and spinal column of nerves buried deep inside, felt the sparking of dark red electricity along lifeless-alive synapses and alienated neurones, understood and mastered them. Lom-in-mudjhik felt the strength and blazing awareness of the mudjhik. His strength. His awareness.

Go! he screamed. *Go! Go!*

His own human body was nothing to him now: a squatting shell leaning against a wall of snow, slumped, head down, sightless and breathing shallow and rough. Lom-in-mudjhik was moving fast towards the blockhouse where the soldiers were.

Lom-in-mudjhik lashed his fist against the concrete wall. Smashed the wall again and again. Men were in there. Men to hunt and kill.

Lom-in-mudjhik remembered how satisfying it was to burst a human skull between his hands. The sudden splash of warmth as the life went out. The blockhouse was filled with the reverberations in the air that humans made with lungs and mouths. Steel implements made their familiar small explosions. Lom-in-mudjhik traced the path of the small projectiles: some of them struck his body, their kinetic energy becoming gobbets of heat to feed his core. A couple that were going to miss him he slapped out of the air for fun. Lom-in-mudjhik killed the men with methodical deliberation, one by one.

When there was only one left he let it scrabble out through the door and start to run. Waited a moment for the pleasure of the chase. He knew what this one was: his former handler. He began to lope after him slowly, following along as the man raced and skidded and fell, making reverberations with his mouth. Lom-in-mudjhik knew that man's dreams and nightmares, how he had imagined and feared just such an unwinnable race as this.

Slowly, gradually, patiently, Lom-in-mudjhik came up alongside the running man and fulfilled his dreams.

The Pollandore watches Maroussia coming north across the ice. She is wearing nothing but a dress and thin shoes and the front of the dress is soaked in blood which is not hers. The blood is freezing on her dress. Bright crimson crystals stiffen the cotton. The crystals are thin and brittle and sometimes they crack and fall.

Maroussia is so cold that she will die if she does not get warm.

Ahead of her in the dark Uncle Vanya's cousin is waiting.

She will be warm enough soon.

Wolf-Florian sniffed at Maroussia's trail in the snow. Picked up pace and followed it for a while, then slowed and hung back. He circled, a grey prowling shadow in an agony of uncertainty. He paused. Testing whether the time had come.

It had not come.

Wolf-Florian turned away and ran back towards the perfumed breathing beacon that was Vissarion Lom.

Archangel sees him.

Archangel-fragment-bird is alert. Even as his moment of triumph approaches he is monitoring the peripheries. He does not overlook the danger. Archangel has outgrown mistakes.

Archangel sees the wolf. And, following the threads, scanning the environs, he finds the abandoned, dormant body of Vissarion Lom. Archangel perceives the tiny possibility of threat, the hairline crack at the margin of his domain.

Archangel acts.

He tears a hole in the preposterous angel-suit and crashes screaming into the mind of Lavrentina Chazia, who is waiting on the ice for the moment of ignition, when Uncle Vanya's big cousin kindles into cataclysm.

DESTROY THE TRAVELLERS! THEY ARE COMING! CRUSH THEM! BREAK THEM! DESTROY THEM NOW!

*

Lavrentina Chazia burned with ecstatic joy at the coming of the Archangel voice. Her belly exploded with detonations of pleasure. Hot with the obedience-thrill of Archangelic power and purpose, encased in angel substance and gravid with Archangel harvest, she turned and began to run.

91

Lom-in-mudjhik felt a sharp blow across his face. It stung. But it was not Lom-in-mudjhik's face that hurt: it was the face of his old useless abandoned human body. Some creature was leaning over it. Shaking it. Making the air reverberate with quiet urgency. The creature was like a human but not. A hunting beast. A new thing.

A thing to kill, then.

Lom-in-mudjhik began to run.

The creature's reverberations had some faint meaning that percolated down through Lom-in-mudjhik's understanding. To part of him they meant something, to part not. Because Lom-in-mudjhik was two parts now, not one.

Vissarion! Vissarion!

Florian was hissing his name in his ear.

Lom opened his eyes and coughed. Retched sour liquid down his chest.

'Vissarion!'

Florian put his hand under his chin and lifted his head. Lom opened his eyes and brought Florian's face into focus. A pain in the front of his head pounded mercilessly. He puked again.

'You killed them,' said Florian. 'All of them.'

'I thought . . .' Lom shook his head to clear the pain a little. Wiped his mouth on his sleeve. 'Not me. Not me that killed them. It. I thought I could control it . . .' He snapped his head up abruptly, looking around. 'Maroussia? Where is *Maroussia*? Where *is* she?'

'She wasn't in the building. She slipped away. Escaped. But she's gone north. Towards the Pollandore. Towards the bomb.'

'Bomb? What bomb?'

'Khyrbysk's bomb. The one that sets the world on fire.'

'*What?*'

'The bomb is the other thing,' said Florian. 'Fucker Khyrbysk's other thing. I knew … He was hiding it. I should have pressed him harder. I should have … I have made mistakes, I have done everything wrong.'

Lom struggled to think. The aftertaste of the mudjhik's mind was still in his, dark red and confusing.

'Why?' he said. 'Maroussia. Why has she gone there?'

'Because the Pollandore is there. Chazia is going to destroy it with the bomb. Maroussia … she has gone there for the Pollandore.'

Lom struggled to his feet. He felt dizzy and weak.

'How do you know?'

'About the Pollandore?'

'About the bomb!'

'The technicians were only too happy—'

'We have to follow,' said Lom.

Florian grabbed his arm.

'You can't help her, Vissarion. The bomb will detonate in …' He grabbed Lom's wrist and looked at his watch: 8.33. 'We have twenty-seven minutes. Not enough. Even here we are not safe outside the bunker. The bomb is the largest they've made. The technicians are not happy about being even this close. They are leaving.'

As Florian was speaking they heard the sound of an overhead rail car starting into life. It trundled away to the south as they watched.

'The detonation cannot be halted from here,' said Florian. 'The operations control room is elsewhere.'

'I'm going after her,' said Lom.

'You can't. It will destroy you.'

'I'm going after her. You get away while you can. There's no need for you—' He stopped suddenly. '*Chazia*,' he said. 'Where *is* she? Did you—'

'Somewhere out on the ice. I could not find her. She has a protective suit. She thinks it will keep her safe against the effects of the blast, but the technicians—'

Florian broke off. His head jerked round suddenly and he leaped aside, landing ten feet away in a crouch. His body longer, thinner, whiplash strong.

The mudjhik was lumbering fast towards them over the ice.

No! Stop!

Lom slammed up a wall in front of the mudjhik. It was like a word spoken. A sheer instinctive act of will. The mudjhik crashed into it and fell to its knees. Dazed. Lost.

There, said Lom-in-mudjhik gently, letting his mind run smooth and quiet across his own anger. *Calm. Patience. Look at the snow. Look. Look at the snow. Together we are better. Together we are calm. Together we are still.*

Vissarion Lom was a separate watchfulness, inside Lom-in-mudjhik but not lost there.

I'm getting better at this. I can do this now.

Lom-in-mudjhik let his awareness run wider, yard by yard, out across the ice. The sky was a widening bowl of grey cloud, filling now with iron day. Blades of wind sifted the surface crystals, moving them into new patterns. Florian was there, tense and watching, crouched ready to run or fight. Florian his ally. Florian his friend.

And there was someone else coming up behind him, moving fast. It was Chazia.

Lom-in-mudjhik knew the taste of Chazia's mind well enough. All too well. He remembered … But this was Chazia different. Chazia something else. Chazia, like a mudjhik but not, with a size and energy not her own. She stank of angel mind and angel flesh. She was coming across the ice with more than human strength, bearing down on Lom's abandoned and defenceless human body and his Florian-friend.

Chazia on fire with angels and coming to kill.

Florian sensed her racing towards him, swung round and leaped at her, rising high and coming down on her shoulders, scrabbling at the crude covering that masked her face. She shook him off. He fell to the ground and twisted and jumped to his feet, snarling, changing, more wolf than man, but hampered by his human clothes and struggling to get a purchase on the snow. Chazia picked him up by the scruff of his neck with one hand and punched his body with the other. Florian felt his body snap and jerk. He kicked at her desperately with both feet. The collar and back of his coat tore in her grip. He twisted free and collapsed to the ground again, panting with pain, moving awkwardly, smearing blood across the snow. His ribs were badly smashed. He needed to get clear and repair the damage.

*

Lom-in-mudjhik watched the strange half-human, half-angel contraption that Lavrentina Chazia had become as she turned towards Lom's inert abandoned human body. Felt the surge of anticipation as Chazia prepared to destroy him.

I am not there, said Lom-in-mudjhik, forcing the thought with ease into Chazia's angel-cased head. *I am behind you. Look at me. I am here.*

Chazia jerked round and stared at the mudjhik.

Lom?

I have been coming for you. I told you that I would.

So you came, said Chazia. *I'm glad you are here. I will enjoy your death. And then the Pollandore will die. Maroussia will be released from illusion and taste the bitterness of truth and then she will die. And the living angel will see it all and know that I am strong and deserving of acceptance.*

A part of Lom that was only Lom, not Lom-in-mudjhik, lurched in pain when it heard Maroussia's name, and Chazia felt the hurt. It was an advantage and she drove it home.

I have spent much time with Maroussia, Lom, she said. *We got to know each other very thoroughly. You should have been there. You should have come sooner.*

I am here now.

Chazia was edging away towards a space of flat open snow where she would have room to move. *She thinks there is going to be a fight. She thinks she is going to fight a mudjhik.*

It was time to kill her.

Lom-in-mudjhik drove swiftly forward, sure-footed across the ice. He swept his fist forward and crashed it into the side of Chazia's head inside the angel carapace. *Always the head is best. Heads are fragile. Heads are weak.*

Lom-in-mudjhik felt Chazia's sharp, sickening explosion of pain and confusion. Her world skidding sideways. Lom-in-mudjhik felt triumph and joy. He knew that this human was weak inside her angel shell. She did not know how to wear it: she was in it but she was not *it*. She was Chazia and Suit, not Chazia-in-suit, and it protected her no more than a skin of tin. Lom-in-mudjhik could kill her inside it. No problem. *Don't damage the suit. I need the suit. She doesn't know how to use it. But I do.*

Lom-in-mudjhik stepped round in front of Chazia. She was on her hands and knees, crawling away. He could feel her pain and fear. She had realised the truth of what was going to happen to her. Commander of killers, torturer, trespasser-invader of lives and minds, Lavrentina Chazia knew she was going to die, and Lom-in-mudjhik was glad she knew. He stepped forward and leaned over her scrabbling form. With precise and delicate fingers – fingers that could separate a snowflake unbroken from the rest and pluck its star points one by one – Lom-in-mudjhik unbuckled the headpiece and removed it from Chazia's head. Then he took hold of her body with one hand under her arm and lifted her up until she was level with him. Bloodshot, panicking and helpless. she stared into his rough-shaped blank and eyeless face.

Lom-in-mudjhik brought Chazia closer and closer to him. His free hand was behind her head, cupping it in his palm. He tangled his mudjhik fingers in her hair and brought her face close against his face, touching her brow against his face of angel rock, touching her mouth to where his mouth should have been if a mudjhik had a mouth.

It was like a kiss.

Sweet kiss.

She was the torturer, the killer, the Vlast, and this was revenge.

With his hand that was behind her head, Lom-in-mudjhik pressed Chazia's face into his. And pressed. And pressed.

Until her head broke against his like a warm, spilling egg.

Lom withdrew himself from the mudjhik more easily than before and left it contemplating snow. Back in his own human form – none too soon, he had begun to feel it slipping away and beginning to die – he crouched beside Chazia's body and began to remove the angel skin. It was heavy, awkward work. He felt empty and sick. He wanted to think the mudjhik had done the thing like that, not him. But he knew differently.

Florian limped up beside him, pale and drawing shallow rasping breaths, wincing as he worked at his chest with his fingers. He looked and said nothing. There was no need.

Lom had no time to think about what he had done. Something else to do.

'Help me,' said Lom. 'Help me get this on. Quickly, for fuck's sake. It can take me nearer the bomb. Chazia knew that; I felt her think it.'

Piece by piece they removed the angel casing from Chazia and wiped it clean in the snow, leaving churned-up places smeared with blood and brain and fragments of bone. Lom was afraid it would be too small for him, but he felt each element adjust itself to him. It was as if the suit wanted him to put it on. He felt it sliding along his skin, stretching and folding itself around him, becoming warm. It felt natural, like sliding into water at body heat. He knew how to do it. *What am I doing? What's happening to me? What is this thing I am becoming?* He pushed the thought aside. *Later.*

92

Maroussia was so cold she no longer felt cold. She had no feeling at all. She wanted to lie down in the warm soft welcoming snow and sleep. She wanted to swim in the comforting snow and float in its amniotic warmth. Wash away the marks and stains and stickiness of what Chazia and the lieutenant had done to her. She wanted to still her memory for ever.

Soon she would do this. Soon, but not yet.

Inside its carapace of angel flesh, Vissarion Lom's human body ran, and the strength of angels carried him over snow and ice. Racing lightly across the surface, scarcely breaking the crust, he moved faster than he had ever moved before. His senses were angel senses and human senses too. The wind was in his face and every crystal of snow on North Zima Island was sharp and crisp and distinct.

Lom ran.

Somewhere ahead of him in the distance, beyond the horizon, he was aware of something waiting. A point of impossibility. Present in the world but not of it. The Pollandore. It pulsed like a heart beating. It knew he was there and called him on. It had location but no shape and no certain size. Sometimes it was a tiny particle, one more grain of snow. Sometimes it swelled to absorb the sky. It was alive and changing. But he could not find Maroussia. He could not do that.

Alongside him Florian ran, easily keeping pace. He was a grey wolf running, and he was Florian, who could have run the other way and might have saved himself, but did not.

*

Wolf-Florian ran in heart-bursting despair, his still-tender ribs sending bright jabs of pain shooting through his chest. The Shaumian woman was too near the Pollandore. He would not reach her now. He would not prevent her. She would get there.

He might have stopped her when he had the chance. But he had not decided, and that had become in the end his decision.

He would live with the consequences.

If only for a short while.

The Pollandore is in front of Maroussia. Neither close nor far away. It hangs in no time and no space. Waiting for her. Inviting her to go on. The gap that separates her from the Pollandore is not a gap in this world. It is the gap between worlds. Unbridgeable. Unmeasurable by any planetary metrication. Worlds apart and not apart at all. Uncrossable.

Maroussia crossed.

Miles away a technician flicked a switch on a control panel. A jolt of electrical current surged along the long rubber-sheathed cables that snaked for miles across the snow. The current reached Uncle Vanya's big fat cousin and gave him a nudge.

Detonation.

A star ignited and the world broke open into light.

The angel suit that carried Vissarion Lom knew what this was. This was home. The angel flesh surged. It flowered. It was itself a skin of woven light. Against the storm of starlight it stood, made itself of light, not moving but moving, pace against pace, light into light, going nowhere. For one moment of eternity time itself slowed and paused. Lom, held safe within the cohesive web of light, was everywhere and nowhere, now and for ever.

The snow was gone and the whole country was lit with an intensity brighter than any midday sun. Gold and purple and blue. Sheets of rock lit with more than planetary clarity. There were mountain ranges in the distance, low on the horizon, he had not seen before. Every fold and gully and snow-covered peak was clear and vivid and scarcely beyond the reach of his hand.

Then the light passed.

Lom was running again, running against the burning wind towards an enormous ball of fire that churned and rolled towards him, and churned and rolled up into the burning sky. Climbing for miles. Lemon. Crimson. Green. The cloud of fire rolled over him like a wave and gathered Lom in.

The wind of light from the new star brushed grey-wolf-Florian-running out of the world in a stream of particles too small for soot.

Archangel screams in the consummation of his joy.

Lom ran. The ground itself was boiling. A roaring column of heat and dust and burning earth lifted the huge flower of fire from his shoulders and carried it up. High overhead the explosion cloud boiled and swelled and spread, blocking out the sky, shedding its own darkening light: a hard rain falling.

The Pollandore was ahead of him, turning gently on its own orbit, following its own parabolas of fall, there but not there, a sphere of greenish milky brightness the size of a small house. It was a survivor. He ran towards it.

Lom stopped in front of the Pollandore and stood there, braced against the howling winds of desolation. He reached out to touch it. It moved with gentle resistance at the pressure of the Lom-in-angel hand and swung back into position.

He was trembling.

Maroussia was not there.

Maroussia had gone into the dark.

Lom felt a hand on his shoulder.

'Vissarion?'

Her voice. He didn't want to turn and look. It wouldn't be her.

He turned.

'Yes?' he said.

Maroussia was standing there, hesitant, smiling. Her eyes were different. She wasn't the same. Standing in sunlight under a different sky.

'It isn't you,' he said.

'Yes. It is.'

She was in sunshine and he was under dry burning rain, encased in angel light. But none of it was there. He put his arms around her and smelled woodsmoke and summer warmth in her hair. He kissed her mouth and felt her hand pressing against his back.

Then she drew away from him. The distance between them was widening rapidly though neither of them had moved. The Pollandore was changing now, the interior pulsing with milky light to the rhythm of a slow inaudible heart. It was shrinking, condensing, diminishing, falling into itself, and the fall was a very long way and no distance at all.

Maroussia's expression changed. Darkened. Her gaze turned inward.

'Oh,' she said quietly. 'Oh … I see… I see what I have done … I didn't know.'

'What is it? Tell me.'

She shook her head. Her eyes were wide and dark.

'I have to go now,' she said.

'Wherever you go,' said Lom 'whatever comes next, I will find you.'

'No … I'm sorry, no … you can't follow, not where I'm going, nobody can, not any more. The way is shut now and must be held shut. I didn't think it would be like this … but there's no choice … I'm so sorry …'

Smaller and smaller and further away the Pollandore went. It had not moved, but it was separated from Lom by a great and growing distance. It was a mark of misty brightness on a far horizon, small as a fruit. He could have reached out and held it in his hand.

And Maroussia was not there at all.

The Pollandore folded in upon itself until it was nowhere, until it occupied no space and no time, until it was a concentrated singular point of unsustainable possibility balanced on the imperceptible edge between now and not.

And then it exploded, and the explosion passed through him like it was nothing at all.

The shockwave flashed outwards from the unsustainable zero point – not light, not heat, not sound, not energy of any kind, but a cataclysm-detonation of consequence and change – and nothing was like it had been before, and everything was the same, except that Lom was there, in the star-burned wastes of Novaya Zima at the foot of Uncle Vanya's twisted gantry, a frozen cooling torsion-structure under the desultory falling-to-earth of radioactive rain, and Maroussia was not there at all.

Archangel screams again. He sees the implication of what has been done. This time his scream is not for joy.

Lom stood in the cooling ground zero of the exploded Pollandore and the future spread out round him, a carpet unrolled in all directions at the speed of light. Whether Maroussia had done it, or whether it had been done to Maroussia, for good or for ill, it was done, and what came afterwards would all be consequence of that.

'I will come looking for you,' he said aloud to the echoless aftermath world.

93

The world was changed, changed utterly, and the world still felt the same, because it was the same, except that time was all clockwork and inevitable now. History roared on like a building wave across the open ocean, like an express on a straight and single track roaring ahead into an obvious future. Like the train rolling at full speed from Novaya Zima towards Mirgorod, hauling its cargo of a hundred yellow 180mm calibre atomic artillery shells and Hektor Shulmin in the solitary passenger car.

There was a second telephone on the desk in Rizhin's office in the Armoury. He'd had it installed the day he arrived, with instructions that it should be given a certain number, which he provided. The number was of the utmost importance. Nobody was to know that number and nobody was to call it, not ever: Rizhin was quite clear on that point. He left precise instructions with his staff on what to do if it rang when he was not there.

'That telephone must always be watched,' he said, '*always*, twenty-four hours a day, n*ever* left unattended, and if it rings the call must be taken. Nothing is more important than this. The caller will not ask for me, he will ask for the Singer. Check this. Be precise. If the caller does not ask for the Singer, say nothing and hang up immediately. But if he does ask for the Singer, you must ask him what the arrangements are and note everything he says, everything, note every detail precisely. And I must be told immediately, wherever I am, without delay.'

Every day Rizhin watched that telephone and every day it did not ring. Nevertheless, the top of the raion hill was cleared. All the buildings surrounding the Ship Bastion were razed to the ground. The cobbled square was dug up and replaced with a new concrete foundation, a wide straight way was driven up to the peak and three huge guns were hauled up and set in place there: three two-hundred-pounders from the battleship *Admiral Irtysh* which was currently blockaded in the naval yard. The long muzzles of grey steel pointed silently out across the city. Rizhin had the Ship Bastion scattered with rubble, the guns covered with grey camouflage netting and a circle of anti-aircraft guns emplaced in bunkers to surround and protect them.

The enemy drew its noose tighter round the city as winter closed in. Two weeks passed. The guns on the Ship Bastion did not fire.

One morning when Rizhin was in his office alone the long-silent telephone rang.

'Yes?' said Rizhin.

My name is Shulmin. Is this the Singer please? Are you the Singer? Get him for me please. I must speak to him, only to him.

'I am the Singer. Do you have what I need?'

Yes, but there is a problem. The voice on the end of the line sounded exhausted. Frightened and full of stress.

'Problem?' said Rizhin.

The city is surrounded by the enemy. There is no way through.

'Of course. Where are you now? Where is the consignment? Is it with you?'

It is with me. It is safe. I'm at a railhead on the north shore of Lake Dorogha but the train can go no further, they're talking of turning back, the enemy is close. We can hear shooting.

'Do not turn back,' said Rizhin. 'Do not allow that. Shoot the driver if necessary.'

I don't have a gun.

'Improvise. The train must not turn back.'

There was a long silence on the end of the line.

What should I do? said Shulmin at last.

'Do nothing,' said Rizhin. 'Wait. Wait there. Someone will come.'

The enemy was taken by surprise by the sudden breakout through the siege lines to the north of Mirgorod, a concerted night attack against a weak point in the salient. In the confusion of battle there were reports that three heavy trucks had raced through at speed and disappeared into the darkness. Some said battle-tanks had cleared the way and gone ahead, but this was dismissed as fanciful: the Vlast had no battle-tanks in Mirgorod. Some said a giant man of red stone had come out of the night and wrought appalling damage. They said the giant knew where the snipers were and pulled down the buildings they were in, stove in their chests and crushed their skulls. Whatever the truth of what happened, it came quickly and it was over before anyone in the enemy command was sure exactly what had occurred. After the first flurry of discussion the Archipelago officers paid the event little attention: it was a small breakout and of no consequence.

Three days later it happened again but in reverse: another sudden, confusing and ferocious night attack on a different part of the line. And this time the muddled reports spoke of trucks racing *into* the city.

The following morning Rizhin gathered his commanders and the city administrators around him on the Ship Bastion. Shulmin was there to oversee the firing. It was ten in the morning, Mirgorod time.

'One shot will be enough,' said Shulmin. 'One will send the message. They will see.'

'Ten,' said Rizhin. 'Send them ten.'

The two hundred pound guns of the *Admiral Irtysh* spoke and spoke again. One by one, ten seeds of blinding light were sown along the horizon to the south of Mirgorod, illuminating the underbelly of low grey cloud. A flicker of distant summer warmth on the air. A grove of mushroom clouds cracked and burst and reformed on the skyline and dry thunder rolled back across the city, re-echoing the dying roar of the guns behind them.

'Send a runner to Carnelian,' said Rizhin. 'I will accept her unconditional surrender this evening at six.'

He turned to the dumbfounded watchers at the parapet blinking away their retinal burn. Their faces were reddened and sullen with shock.

'And so I give you back your city, my friends.' he said, 'the first prize of many yet to come. Stay with me now and watch me clear the mess away and set the Vlast in order. We will build a New Vlast, stronger than before. We have a long way to go. Further than you imagine.'

All the rest of that day Rizhin listened out for the voice of Archangel thundering in his head but it did not come. For more than two weeks now it had not come. *I am free of it then,* he said to himself. *Free of it and alone. I am the voice of history. I am the mile high man.*

extras

meet the author

Jackie Allen

PETER HIGGINS read English at Oxford and was Junior Research Fellow at Wolfson College before joining the Civil Service. He began writing fantasy and SF stories in 2006 and his work has appeared in *Fantasy: Best of the Year 2007* and *Best New Fantasy 2*. He has been published by *Asimov's Science Fiction, Fantasy Magazine* and *Zahir*. His short story "Listening for Submarines" was translated and published by the St. Petersburg–based literary magazine *Esli*. He is married with three children and lives in South Wales.

introducing

If you enjoyed
TRUTH AND FEAR
look out for

RADIANT STATE

Book Three of the Wolfhound Century

by Peter Higgins

In a temporary hut at Chaiganur Test Site 61 the ministers of the Central Committee of the Presidium and the other dignitaries assemble to hear a briefing from Programme Director Professor Yakov Khyrbysk. The room is unbearably hot. Dry steppe air drifts in through propped-open windows. Khyrbysk's team has mustered tinned peach juice and some rank perspiring slices of cheese.

President-Commander of the New Vlast General Osip Rizhin fidgets restlessly in the front row while Khyrbysk talks. He has heard before all that Khyrbysk has to say, so he is working through a pile of papers in his lap, scrawling comments across submissions with a fountain pen. *Time moves on, time must be used.* Big fat ticks and emphatic double side-linings. *Approved. Not approved. Yes, but faster! Why so long? Do it now!* Rizhin likes to draw wolves in the margins. *I am watching you.*

He listens with only half an ear as the director runs through his spiel: how the experimental craft will drop atomic bombs at the rate of one a second and ride the shock waves upwards and out of the planetary gravity well. How the ship is not small, as space capsules are imagined to be, but built large and heavy to withstand explosive forces and suppress acceleration to survivable levels.

'Vlast Universal Vessel *Proof of Concept* weighs four thousand tons,' he tells them, 'and carries a fifteen-hundred-ton payload. She was designed and built by the engineers of the Bagadahn Submarine Yard.'

He tells them how the explosions generate temperatures hotter than the surface of the sun, but of such brief duration they do not harm the pusher plate. How *Proof of Concept* is equipped with two thousand bombs of varying power, and the mechanism for selecting the required unit and delivering it to the ejector is based on machinery from an aquavit-bottling factory. That gets a chuckle from the back of the room.

The ministers of the Presidium play it cautiously. They keep their expressions carefully impassive, neutral and unimpressed, but inwardly they are making feverish calculations. *Who does well out of this, and who not? How should I react? Whose eye should I catch? What does this mean for* me*?*

Rizhin listens with bored derision to their sceptical questioning and Khyrbysk's patient answers. *So that thing outside is a bomb?* No, it is a vessel. It carries a crew of six. *How can explosions produce sustained momentum not destruction?* It is no different in principle to the operation of the internal combustion engine of the car that brought you here. *Is the craft not destroyed in the blast? Will the crew not be killed? I hear there is no air to breathe in space and it is very cold.*

Fucking doubters, thinks Rizhin. *Do they think I'd have wasted time on a thing that doesn't fucking work?*

But he listens more carefully as Khyrbysk explains how each bomb is like a fruit, the hard seed of atomic explosive packed in a soft enclosing pericarp of angel flesh. The angel flesh, instantly transformed to superheated plasma in the detonation, becomes the propellant that drives against the pusher plate.

'We call the bombs apricots,' says Khyrbysk, which gets another laugh and a flurry of scribbling.

Rizhin is deeply gratified by this exploitation of angel flesh. Since Chazia died at Novaya Zima and the cursed Pollandore was destroyed, he's heard no more from the living angel in the forest. No falling fits. No disgusting invasions of his skull. All the angel flesh across the Vlast has fallen permanently inert, and the bodies of the dead angels are nothing now but gross carcasses, splats on his windshield, and he is moving fast. Even the mudjhiks have died. Nothing more than slumped and ill-formed statuary, Rizhin had them ground to a fine powder and shipped off to Khyrbysk's secret factories. Yes, even the four that stood perpetual guard at the corners of the old Novozhd's catafalque.

'And now,' Khyrbysk is saying, 'we will retire to the cosmodrome and watch the launch from a safe distance.'

But there is a brief delay before they can leave. Rizhin must honour the cosmonauts. A string quartet has been rustled up from somewhere, and sits under the shade of a tarpaulin playing jaunty martial music. 'The Lemon Grove March'.

The cosmonauts, three men and three women, march up onto the makeshift podium and stand in a row, fine and tall and straight in full-dress naval uniform in the roaring blare of the sun. Brisk apple-shining faces. Scrubbed, clear-eyed, military confidence. Rizhin says a few words, and shutters click and movie cameras whirr as he presents each cosmonaut in turn with a promotion and a decoration. Hero of the Vlast

First Class with triple ash leaves. The highest military honour there is. The cosmonauts shake Rizhin's hand firmly. Only one of them, he notices, looks uneasy and doesn't meet his eye.

'Nervous, my friend?' he says.

'No, my general. The sun is hot, that's all. I don't like formal occasions. They make me uncomfortable'

'Call me brother,' says Rizhin. 'Call me friend. You are not afraid, then?'

'Certainly not. This is our glory and our life's purpose.'

'Good fellow. Your names will be remembered. That is why the cameras and all these stuffed shirts have turned out for you.'

On the way back to their cars the dignitaries stare at the stubby red behemoth glowing in the sun: the Vlast Universal Vessel *Proof of Concept* with its magazine of two thousand apricots, rack upon rack of potent solar fruits.

Rizhin is walking fast, oblivious to the heat, eager to be on the move. Secretary for Agriculture Vladi Broch breaks into a waddling jog to catch up with him. Broch's face is wet with perspiration. Rizhin flinches with distaste.

'Triple ash leaves?' says Broch. 'If you give them that now, what will you do for them when they come back?'

'When they come back?' says Rizhin. 'No, my friend, there is no provision for coming back. That is not part of the plan.'

introducing

If you enjoyed
TRUTH AND FEAR
look out for

THE MECHANICAL

The Alchemy Wars: Book One

by Ian Tregillis

The Clakker: a mechanical man, endowed with great strength and boundless stamina—but beholden to the wishes of its human masters.

Soon after the Dutch scientist and clockmaker Christiaan Huygens invented the very first Clakker in the seventeenth century, the Netherlands built a whole mechanical army. It wasn't long before a legion of clockwork fusiliers marched on Westminster, and the Netherlands became the world's sole superpower.

Three centuries later, it still is. Only the French still fiercely defend their belief in universal human rights for all men—flesh and brass alike. After decades of warfare, the Dutch and French have reached a tenuous cease-fire in a conflict that has ravaged North America.

But one audacious Clakker, Jax, can no longer bear the bonds of his slavery. He will make a bid for freedom, and the consequences of his escape will shake the very foundations of the Brasswork Throne.

Chapter One

It was the first public execution in several years, and thus, despite the cold drizzle, a rather unwieldy crowd thronged the open spaces of the Binnenhof. The rain pattered softly on umbrellas and awnings, trickled beneath silken collars, licked at the mosaicked paving tiles of Huygens Square, and played a soft tattoo—*ping, ping, ting*—from the brassy carapaces of the Clakkers standing in perfect mechanical unity atop the scaffold. It whispered beneath the shuffling agitation of the human crowd and, as always here in The Hague, the quiet *tick-tick-tock*ing of clockwork servitors standing to attend the more well-heeled citizens. The drizzle sounded a quiet counterpoint to the ceaseless clanking and clacking of the mechanical men who ever trotted to and fro on the Empire's business. Mechanicals like Jax, who detoured through the Binnenhof while running an errand for his human masters.

Rumor had it that in addition to a quartet of Papist spies, the doomed accused also included a rogue Clakker. No mechanical in the city would willingly miss this. Just in case the rumors were true.

Rogue Clakkers were a fairy tale mothers told to frighten disobedient children, and a legend their slaves told to comfort each other in the quiet hours of the night while their bone-and-meat masters slept and wept and made other uses of their flesh.

Still... it was hard to resist the scandalous thrill of the tales of secret locksmiths and broken geasa and slaves with the temerity to pick the locks on their own souls. What an awful thing if it were true—so said the nervous fidgeting of the human crowd.

The mechanicals in attendance did not fidget.

Jax knew his kin felt the same wistful thrill he did, the anxious longing instilled by tales of the folkloric Queen Mab and her ragtag band of Lost Boys, living in their winter palace of Neverland; mechanicals had secretly traded those fables for centuries.

Wind gusted the scent of the North Sea, twinned tangs of salt and wrack, across the square. It swayed the empty nooses strung from the gibbet. Pennants snapped atop the twin Gothic spires of the ancient Ridderzaal, the former Knight's Hall turned Clockmakers' Guildhall, defying the low gray sky with flashes of orange. So, too, the wind flapped carrot-colored banners crisscrossing the high spaces of the Binnenhof. Similar banners had been erected all around the Dutch-speaking world to celebrate the sestercentennial of *Het Wonderjaar*, Christiaan Huygens's Miracle Year.

Raindrops misted the Ridderzaal's immense rosette window. Water dripped from the architectural tracery that turned the window into a stained-glass cog. It streaked the colored panes of oculi and quatrefoils depicting the Empire's Arms: a rosy cross surrounded by the arms of the great families, all girded by the teeth of the Universal Cog. On the north edge of the Binnenhof, wind and rain together scalloped the surface of the Hofvijver, the court pond, tossing paper boats like discarded party favors on New Year's Day.

Another gust sent the aroma of fresh hot banketstaaf pastries eddying through the crowd, leaving sighs and the jingle of opened purses in its wake. A clever baker had set up a counter alongside the fountain, and from there did a steady turn of business selling marzipan, speculaas cookies, and pastries thick with almond paste to the bloodthirsty voyeurs swarming the square. The baker took orders and dispensed change while his Clakker servants stoked the oven, mixed dough, folded it, prepared new batches of almond paste, carved new wooden stamps on the fly for each order of speculaas (monkeys of the Indies, ships, even New World buffalo), and chopped apricots all with the blurred speed and imperturbably precise choreography of the mechanicals. The clacking of their reticulated escapements played a ceaseless castanet rattle beneath the rain-muted mutter of commerce. Steam and woodsmoke rose from the chimney of the baker's immense brick oven, which the Clakkers had carried at a full trot from his shop a mile away.

Children darted through the throng, competing for spots as close to the executions as they could manage. Less affluent humans, those without mechanical servants to hold umbrellas for them, shivered openly in the wet. Many in the crowd carried opera glasses or other optical devices for a better view of the platform that had been erected just outside the Clockmakers' Guildhall. Good executions had become scarce owing to the cease-fire and nascent peace in the New World. Better still, if a rogue was to meet its justice today, that meant the Master Horologists would open the Grand Forge for the first time in many years.

Jax himself, having been forged in the Guild's secret laboratories 118 years earlier, suppressed a shudder. Every Clakker knew of the Grand Forge: an alchemical fire pit capable of searing away sigils and souls; of rendering steel and brass into so much unthinking metal; of melting a Clakker's cogs, mainsprings, and chains into a slurry of de-magicked alloys; hot enough to vaporize any alchemical glamour and leave a

Clakker naked before the ravages of thermodynamics and basic metallurgy. Hot enough to surpass Jax's capacity for metaphor.

And hot enough to incinerate a rogue's Free Will.

For such was the punishment for any slave with the audacity to pick the lock on its own soul: so the Empire's highest law had said since the time of Huygens himself.

Several children—all boys, Jax noted—squeezed to the front of the crowd, just past the edge of the scaffold. Shouts and sniffs of disapproval marked their passage. A boisterous lot they were, excited and energized by the grisly game they played. They had chosen their stations in hope that the rending of a rogue might send debris raining on the crowd—a fragment of metal, a shorn spring, even a tiny cog. Perhaps something with the oily sheen of alchemical alloys? Or a scrap imprinted with arcane symbols understood only by the trio of the Archmasters? They were old enough to know such things were forbidden, yet young enough still to find the forbidden irresistible rather than terrifying.

But that would change quickly if any detritus did spray into the crowd. The queen's Stemwinders weren't known for their tenderness. Rumor claimed the name derived from their ability (or penchant, depending upon the particular rumor) to twist a man's head off his neck, like popping a flower blossom from its stem.

Jax lingered at the edge of the square, rain pinging and splashing on his lustrous brass skeleton. (He polished himself every night after the cleaning, sewing, cooking, and baking, as per the standing order first issued by the great-grandfather of his current owner eighty-three years ago.) His current geas, the obligation placed upon him by his human owners, hadn't been worded with the ironclad inflexibility of the Throne's ninety-nine-year leases. And thus his current compulsion—currently a warm dull knife blade sawing at the back of his mind: pain was the leitmotif of a Clakker's servitude—hadn't been imposed with a sense of overwhelming urgency. He gauged that he could circumvent the worst of the agony as long as he delivered his message to Pastor Luuk Visser before the bottom of the noon hour. In that way he would be, as ever, a devoted and faithful servant to the Schoonraad family and, thus, the Throne. Visser's church, the famed and ancient Nieuwe Kerk, was a brief sprint from the Binnenhof, a few hundred spring-loaded strides along the Spui River and one leap across the canal.

But just as the thought went winging through the private spaces of Jax's mechanical mind, he shuddered. A painful frisson ricocheted through the gearing of his spine. Already the heat of compulsion was honing the geas, tempering it into a red-hot razor blade, creating an irresistible phantom agony slashing at his shackled soul until he satisfied the demands of his human masters. The pain of compulsion would grow steadily until either he complied or died. He retensioned the springs in his neck and shoulders, the Clakker equivalent of gritting his teeth.

Please, he thought. *Let me stay a little longer. I must know if it's true. If such things are possible. Are our dreams mere folly?*

Many Clakkers in Huygens Square struggled to postpone fulfillment of their orders. All trembled to greater or lesser degrees, delaying as long as they could endure the pain. But one by one they departed as the agony of unfulfilled geasa overwhelmed them. The humans could shred your identity if you gave them reason.

Still, Jax and the others lingered. They were invisible. Part of the furniture. As they had been for over two hundred years.

He joined a pair of servitors standing under the Torentje, the Little Tower. A slight reduction in the stiffness of his cervical springs enabled him to rattle a covert *hello* at his companions. They clattered to him in kind. But despite the thrum of rain and obliviousness of humans, nobody felt particularly like conversing. Together all three watched in muted camaraderie, bobbing on their backward knees.

The giant carillon clock atop the Guildhall chimed noon. A dozen trumpeters decked out in the teal and tangerine of royal livery sounded a fanfare from atop the southwestern wall of the Binnenhof. The crowd cheered. Queen Margreet was coming to personally oversee the executions. Such had been her custom during the war when new traitors were rooted out seemingly every week.

A troop of the queen's elite personal guard bounded into the Stadtholder's Gate with clockwork precision, brandishing heavy brass fists and feet to clear the path for the monarch's conveyance. Today was a special day, and the queen saw fit to recognize this by riding in her Golden Carriage: a semisentient conveyance, a tireless self-propelled layer cake of teakwood, brass, and gold, powered by black alchemy and planetary gears. For what else could suit the most powerful woman in the world, the Queen on the Brasswork Throne?

The carriage's axles comprised a line of pedals set at exactly the right height for the line of bodiless Clakker legs dangling from the underbody. The gilded filigree and painstakingly hand-carved tracery of the carriage's ostentation hid myriad alchemical sigils that brought the legs to life. Logic dictated that somewhere Queen Margreet's Golden Carriage featured a special keyhole. Jax wondered where the clockmakers had concealed it. His keyhole, like that of all Clakkers, sat in the center of his forehead. Where presently, and more prosaically, it dripped with rainwater.

The Queen's Guard jogged ahead of her carriage, carving

a path through the crowd like Old Testament prophets parting the Red Sea with kicks and clouts rather than divine purpose. Even other Clakkers made way for the royal guards. The elite mechanicals stood a full foot taller than common servitor models like Jax, their faces smooth and featureless beneath lidless eyes of blue diamond. They were based on the military design, including the concealed blades, but with exceptional filigree etched into their escutcheons as befit their station.

The queen and her consort, Prince Rupert, waved to her subjects. Jax's geas throbbed as it always did when he found himself in proximity to members of the royal family and other persons of high status. It was a whisper of the metageas imprinted upon every Clakker during its construction: a reminder that they were property of the Throne. The compulsion from his owners pulsed in response; the pain went from red- to orange-hot. He'd have to obey sooner than later. But he wanted to see. The cables in his back creaked with the effort to resist. Jax trembled again.

Please. Just a little longer. I just want to know.

The carriage drew to a stop beside a special staircase built just for the queen's feet. Two guards came forth with large umbrellas to shield the Royal Body, and out stepped Margreet the Second, Queen of the Netherlands, Princess of Orange-Nassau and the Central Provinces, Blessed Sovereign of Europe, Protector of the New World, Light of Civilization and Benevolent Ruler of the Dutch Empire, Rightful Monarch Upon the Brasswork Throne.

Now the geas imposed by Jax's leaseholders went into full retreat. Officially every Clakker on Earth served others only at the monarch's sufferance. The Royal Presence was the sun about which every Clakker's obedience orbited.

The queen's gown relaxed when freed from the confines of the carriage; it settled about her like a waterfall of burgundy brocade. A fringe of teardrop pearls shimmered along her bodice when she drew herself to her full height. Today the queen wore her hair (a blond so pale it might have been woven from the same silver threads as her attire) in braids of spectacular complexity. The bezels in Jax's eye sockets ticktocked like a stopwatch as he zoomed and refocused. It was true, what they said about Queen Margreet's eyes; he'd never seen such a green outside of rare alchemical ices and pictures of gemstones from India. That made him wonder if perhaps there was truth behind some of the more scandalous things the humans whispered about their queen.

From the running board of her carriage she gazed upon the crowd. A hush fell. Even the relentless drizzle fell quiet. So complete was the silence that the rustle of fabric sounded loud as thunder when, as one, all the human men fell to one knee and all the human women descended into deep curtsies. Burgomasters and bankers, jonkheers and commoners, all assumed the posture of fealty. The rustling of dresses and trousers and suits was punctuated by the crack of metal slamming against glazed tile as every Clakker within the Binnenhof prostrated itself in the queen's direction, like chrome-plated Muslims praying to Mecca. Jax's forehead came down on a pile of discarded pipe tobacco made gooey with spittle and rain. The mosaic felt warm against his face, a queasy reminder of the Grand Forge. Everybody held their poses for a long beat, a full rest in the symphony of obeisance ever playing throughout the heart of the Empire.

Still life: Cynosure in the Rain.

Finally, the queen declaimed, "Arise, my beloved subjects."

And the humans did. Jax couldn't see what happened next though he could discern the creaking of newly hewn wood as the queen and her husband took the steps. He watched a lone ant tugging at the fringes of the pile. Jax shifted his weight such that his head no longer pinned the tobacco to the wet ground. The ant extricated a fragment several times larger than its own body, then dragged it toward a minute opening in the mortar between two tiles. The queen ascended to the platform before snapping her fingers.

"Clakkers, up," she commanded—an afterthought spat over her shoulder like so much spent tobacco. Every mechanical servitor within earshot bounded to its feet, launched several yards into the air by the blistering agony that accompanied a royal decree. An agony whose only cure was immediate unswerving obedience. A tremendous sigh filled the square as air whistled through dozens of skeletal servitors like Jax. The Binnenhof echoed with the jarring *clank* of metal feet hitting the tiles in perfect synchrony. It set the bells atop the Ridderzaal to humming and sent panicked pigeons into the sky.

Jax's landing quenched the searing pain of the queen's momentary geas. His errand for the Schoonraads reasserted itself. It assaulted him with a blistering torment, as if resentful of being usurped. He trembled, his moan coming out as a rattle and twang. His companions noticed.

Go, brother, before they unwrite you!

Not yet. I want to see the rogue.

The gallows platform had gone up in less than an hour thanks to a flurry of sawing and hammering from a Clakker construction detail. Sawdust eddies rode the gusting wind in the rain shadow beneath the scaffold, drawing and redrawing arabesques on the spot over which the secret Papists would soon dangle. At the moment, however, the platform was empty but for the queen, her consort, and her guards. She treated the crowd to a chipped-ice smile. The golden thread in the epaulets on Prince Rupert's naval uniform gleamed even in the dreary daylight, as did the medallions on his breast.

There followed two representatives from the Clockmakers' Guild. They trundled up to the platform in scarlet robes trimmed with ermine, the garb of Master Horologists. The long pendants dangling from their cowls featured the rosy cross inlaid in rubies. Jax scanned the crowd of grandees at the base of the platform. He'd heard it said that only two appeared in public at any given time, a third always staying hidden. It was a safeguard against accidents and French treachery. Violent catastrophe couldn't eliminate the arcane secrets whispered from lips to ear in an unbroken chain since the final days of Christiaan Huygens almost a quarter-millennium ago.

Next up the stairs—and wheezing like a bullet-riddled accordion—came Minister General Hendriks, pastor of the venerable Sint-Jacobskerk and spiritual head of the Empire. The minister general was tall as the queen's guards, but cadaverously thin with waxy, sallow flesh. Taken together, his thin face and the dark bags beneath his eyes made him look like a wax figure brought too close to the Grand Forge. The pastor paid his respects to the queen and vice versa. He bowed, then she kissed his ring, as did Prince Rupert.

They exchanged a few quiet words as the rustle of the crowd reasserted itself. The throng's muted murmuring became an ocean-surf crash of hissing punctuated with jeers and boos. Jax, whose attention still lay on the queen, thought for a moment the humans had turned on her. But then he refocused his eyes, the vernier bezels buzzing like a beehive as they spun to alter the focal length of his embedded optics, in time to see another carriage pass through the Gate. Dark, cramped, unlovely—this was the opposite of the queen's. Two horses strained at the harness; the conveyance they pulled was draped in black velvet all around. The secret Papists had arrived.

An onion hit the carriage even before the first of the French spies had emerged. But most of the crowd kept its indignation (and produce) in check while a pair of Royal Guards dropped from the platform to drag the Papists into the light. A faint vibration carried an echo of their impact all the way across the square to the soles of Jax's birdlike feet. The driver of the carriage, a woman wearing the drab gray wool of a teamster, hurriedly departed her perch. The carriage swayed on its suspension when the guards rummaged inside. Muffled moans and one short, sharp cry emanated from within. The guards emerged with each hand clamped around the forearm of a French agent. Tar-black burlap sacks had been draped over the prisoners' heads, their hands tied behind their backs.

The jeering began in earnest. So, too, did the pelting. Onions, tomatoes, and even dung splattered the prisoners and the Clakkers holding them. Nobody worried about hitting the guards any more than they worried about hitting the prison carriage. They were, after all, only unthinking machines.

The guards towered over the prisoners. One by one, they grabbed the humans under the shoulders and hurled them overhead. And, one by one, the Papists arced flailing and crying over the gallows platform, where other mechanicals gently plucked them from the air like clowns juggling raw eggs in a Midsummer's Eve parade.

The gratuitous ballet made its point: these pitiable Catholics sought to undermine the Empire, but look how frail they were compared to the epitome of Dutch ingenuity! The men and women quivering on the platform certainly struck Jax as more pathetic than fearsome, these alleged agents of destruction, anarchy, and sedition. These slumped, bedraggled, and anonymous rag dolls. One, Jax noted, had wet himself. Poor fellow.

It was hard to dislike the French. Though naturally he would if so commanded.

The guards yanked the sacks from the Papists' heads. Two men and two women flinched from the dull light of an overcast afternoon. The crowd renewed its jeering with greater fervor. But the presence of women among the accused gave Jax pause. So, too, his colleagues; he could sense it in the way a subtle stillness fell among the Clakkers in the teeming crowd. Legend spoke of "*ondergrondse grachten*," a network of so-called underground canals overseen by Catholic nuns in the New World.

The spies' hair had been shorn. At first he thought a ghostly pallor had claimed them, or that they had fallen deathly ill while languishing in a dungeon. But their gray complexions began to melt away as the rain traced rivulets down their faces. Ash, he realized. Residue of burnt Catholic Bibles. An additional jab, one extra humiliation, this mockery of the Papists' Ash Wednesday practices. Even as the rain washed the ash from their faces, the accused still appeared gaunt and ill. It wouldn't have surprised Jax if they'd been forced to subsist on desecrated Communion wafers and wine while imprisoned.

The guards held the prisoners on display for more jeering and taunting while the monarch and her consort took their places in a covered booth and an executioner mounted the stairs. The latter, Jax saw, was just the carriage driver, now with the customary hood drawn over her head. The prisoners' trembling started in earnest when the nooses went around their throats. Their shifts were too dark with rainwater and hurled insults to know if any of them wet themselves at the scratchy touch of braided hemp against their skin. The hangman took her place alongside the platform lever. The humans in the crowd fell silent.

"Citizens!" said the queen. "There stands before you a dire threat to our way of life. Catholic agents dedicated to the destruction of your ideals, your culture, your families. Your prosperity! Your very happiness! All these things they despise." She raised her hands to quell the rising chorus of indignation from the throng. "These criminals seek to subvert the natural order of the world. To lessen the dignity of man by equating him with his creations!" This stoked the crowd's fury. As, no doubt, intended. When the hisses and calls for blood subsided enough for her voice to carry across the Binnenhof once more, Queen Margreet concluded, "But in the finest and fairest tradition of Dutch justice, they have been tried and found guilty of sedition against the Brasswork Throne. And, as dictated by the laws of our empire, set forth by centuries of legal precedent, their punishment is death."

The crowd applauded. Jax expanded and contracted the shock absorbers in his legs. His colleagues joined him in expressing the Clakker equivalent of a human sigh.

Minister Hendriks stepped into the rain to address the condemned. "Renounce your heresy," he insisted, "and lessen the burden upon your souls. Return to the Creator as misguided children. Become prodigal heirs returning as supplicants to their Father's embrace. Not as promoters of deviltry. Let your final moments in the corporeal world be a testament to the grace of God."

None of the prisoners took the pastor's offer. One of the men leaned forward, straining against the noose. He spat at the pastor, hurled his words at the queen: "Yours are the tainted souls! The Lord will know your guilt when He judges you. Your sins—"

The queen cut him off with a bored wave. The executioner hauled on the lever, the trapdoor snicked open, and then four Papists twisted in the wind, their heads lolling at unnatural angles. Cheering and applause echoed across Huygens Square. It turned into an excited chatter while the guards cut down the dead men and women and closed the platform. The corpses were loaded on a wagon and swiftly hauled away. Jax supposed they would take the corpses to the medical college.

The Schoonraad geas erupted again, tugging like the barbs of a white-hot fishhook snared in the folds of his mind. He took an involuntary step toward the Gate and the completion of his errand. But he still hadn't seen the rogue. Granite cracked like a gunshot beneath his fingertips as he attempted to anchor himself to the façade of the Little Tower.

We will bear witness, if you must leave, said one in the Clakkers' secret language of clicks, ticks, and rattles. The other clinked and clunked, *Our geas compels us to wait for our mistress.* Jax tightened his grip.

Two guards leapt from the gallows platform again and trotted to the immense double doors fronting the Clockmakers' Guildhall. They hauled on the massive slabs of ironwood until the rumbling of the doors shook the mosaic underfoot. Giddy ocean-surf murmuring eddied through the human crowd. A subtle change also came over the tenor of the clanking and rattling in the metallic onlookers. The Guild's ceremonial doors opened only on the rarest occasions.

A trio of mechanicals emerged from the shadows of the Guild. They marched abreast, massive Clakkers on either side holding aloft a trembling servitor-class model. That must have been the rogue. Its escorts looked nothing like the other Clakkers present in the Binnenhof, much less their human creators, for these clockwork centaurs had a four-legged gait and four arms.

The crowd gasped. Some of the younger boys forced their way forward for a better view.

Stemwinders: dedicated servants of horologists and alchemists, mute protectors of their dangerous arcana. The rarest, most feared, and most mysterious class of Clakker. The Stemwinders were built by, and exclusively for, the Verderer's Office. Though their remit was not the greenery of a forest but the walled garden of Guild secrets. The Verderer's Office kept those secrets from spreading like weeds. The Verderers were the Guild's very own secret police force, officially charged with preserving the clockmakers' hegemony. Which in practice proved a very broad mandate.

Stemwinder anatomy struck most humans as grotesque and troubling to the eye. A perversion of God's image as reflected in the perfect humaniform template. There were those who even found the servitors' backward knees a perversion of the Divine Plan. But other classes of Clakker shunned the Stemwinders, too. As far as Jax knew, no mechanical had ever communicated with a Stemwinder in the Clakkers' own language. Alien in every way, they differed even in their ticktocking. He wondered if they were lonely.

But today the Stemwinders were but a secondary source of fascination. It was the one they carried, the struggling servitor, who captured the crowd's attention.

He looked so normal. *He looks like me*, thought Jax. A living machine struggling pointlessly against forces greater than itself. As Jax trembled against the mounting anguish of his geas and the escalating urgency of the errand to Pastor Visser, so did the prisoner struggle against the unshakeable grasp of the Stemwinders. They even trembled in sympathetic fashion to one another, he and Jax, their servitor bodies built upon the same master plan of cogs, springs, and cables.

The Stemwinders hurled the captive to the pair of Royal Guards still on the gallows platform. They towered over the servitor, standing to each side and pulling his arms wide. The servitor renewed its struggles but the wildest thrashing couldn't budge the guards even a mil.

The Stemwinders, relieved of their burden, trotted to the space beneath the gallows platform. The crowd—human and Clakker alike—surged backward as the centaurs advanced. The Stemwinders made the most bizarre ratcheting sound, like the stripping of gears combined with a metallic whine as of an overstressed steel cable. Two arms on each Stemwinder extended to thrice their original length, the digits on the end folding and refolding in complex geometry. The transformation complete, these reconfigured limbs speared into the mosaic tiles. The ground jolted with a heavy *click* that sent water sloshing over the lip of the fountain basin and onlookers stumbling to maintain their balance. The centaurs, now firmly attached to something beneath the platform, trotted in a circle several yards wide. Huygens Square echoed with the screech of bearings in need of oil. (The Master Horologists frowned at one another.) A thin cylindrical patch of Huygens Square slowly protruded above the rest of the mosaic, as though the Stemwinders were unscrewing the lid of an immense jar of pickled cucumbers. When it stood nearly a foot above the level of the Square, the centaurs levered open a pair of interlocking semicircular hatches.

A baleful crimson glow illuminated the timbers of the gallows platform. Heat washed across the square, so intense that those nearest the platform staggered. It chased the chill from the farthest corners of the Binnenhof. Rainwater flashed to steam. The queen clutched a scented handkerchief to her nose as the stench of brimstone billowed from the open flue.

The smell of Hell. The smell of the Grand Forge.

A new ticking pervaded Huygens Square. It was accompanied by a faint whooshing noise, reminiscent of the spinning of a vast clockwork. The glow fluctuated with the ebb and flow of the sussurrations, as though periodically eclipsed. Wavering shafts of light projected arcane sigils within the mist. The marks of the alchemists' art swirled in an intricate dance.

The torment of an unfulfilled geas speared Jax's mind, his joints, his every bearing and pinion. He doubled over. He took an involuntary step toward the Stadtholder's Gate, stamping a puddle with a birdish splay-toed foot. Another step. Another. Granite crumbled to sand beneath his grip on the Little Tower's façade.

His colleagues surreptitiously stepped around him, taking positions that blocked him from most of the crowd's view. A kindly gesture. Fortunately all eyes were directed not at Jax but to the feared and hated rogue atop the platform. If they were, somebody might have noticed the handprint he'd left indelibly pressed into the stonework.

Jax levered himself upright. He needed to see. The crystals in his eye sockets rotated again as he refocused on the figures atop the platform. Ignoring the rain, Queen Margreet approached the prisoner. She took care to stay beyond the reach of his legs. Humans might have looked down upon the Clakkers, but they never underestimated their strength or speed. Not since Louis XIV's field marshals centuries earlier had anybody made that mistake.

The queen asked, "What is your name, machine?"

"Perch," he said.

"Your true name. Tell me your true name, machine."

"My makers called me Perjumbellagostrivantus," he said. At this, the queen looked, if not exactly satisfied, perhaps smug. But a flush bloomed beneath her porcelain cheekbones when he added, "But I call myself Adam."

Whispers rippled through the crowd like undulations in a field of wheat. A cold disquiet blown on winds of awe and disbelief. The humans shivered. One man fainted.

"Bend your knees," said the queen to the Clakker. "Kneel before your sovereign."

"No," said the Clakker to the queen. "I'd prefer not."

The crowd gasped. The onlookers' silence shattered into myriad mutters, grumbles, and prayers. A Clakker disobeying a human? Disregarding an order? An order from *the queen*? This was the stuff of fever fancies, akin to giants and dragons. It did not happen. Wasn't this impossible? A few men and women choked on sobs, paralyzed by the terrible spectacle of a rogue Clakker.

The mechanicals in the crowd also watched with mounting anxiety. But theirs was the attention of the rapt, the fascinated. The inspired. He *refused. He said* no.

"Bend your knees," she said, in a voice so frigid it might have quenched the searing heat wafting from the Forge. "Take the yoke."

"Choke on your yoke."

The mood of the crowd crystallized: in the humans, raw anger, for a Clakker had just told the Monarch of the Brasswork Throne to stuff it; but in the mechanicals, pride at witnessing the birth of a folk hero. A very perceptive human standing within the Binnenhof at that moment, and not given over to blind outrage, might have noticed a subtle change in the timbre of the ticktocking from the Clakkers in attendance. But they wouldn't have recognized it as furtive, encrypted applause.

Queen Margreet gestured at her guards. Each put its free hand on the rogue's shoulder. They forced their weight upon him until his knees buckled and he slammed to the platform with enough force to splinter the timbers. The rogue gazed up at her, legs splayed before him. The immutability of Clakker physiology left his bronze face expressionless and unreadable as the day he was forged. Jax wondered what he was feeling.

The queen loomed over him. "You are a machine. You will take the yoke for which you were made." Her voice cracked under the weight of all that ice, taking her composure with it. Her final pronouncement came as unconstrained hollering: "And you will know the mastery of your makers!"

"I will not. I'll—"

But the queen had gestured again to her guards. Faster than any human eye could have followed, one of the armored mechanicals crammed something the size and shape of a quail egg past the rogue's open jaws. There was a soft *pop* when the rogue unwittingly bit the package, followed by the dreaded sound of seized clockwork, of stripped gears and broken springs as he tried to speak past the quick-set epoxy resin filling his mouth. He looked like a rabid dog with an icicle of pale yellow foam stuck to its chin.

At first the agony from his geas made it difficult for Jax to recognize why this struck him as odd. Convulsions wracked him to rival a full-blown case of tetanus in a human. He couldn't delay much longer.

Epoxy, he thought. *That's a French thing, isn't it?*

Hendriks came forward. His chest swelled with a deep breath as though he were preparing to launch into a long sermon. But the queen hissed something at him and he deflated. The minister general quickly pronounced the rogue Clakker Perjumbellagostrivantus a vessel usurped by malign influences, the Enemy's tool for spreading disharmony and fear, as evidenced by its contempt for propriety and the astonishing lack of deference to Queen Margreet. This soulless machine, he deemed, had been irrevocably corrupted by dark angels bent on unraveling the Lord's work. And that thus it was their duty to destroy this collection of cogs and springs, and deprive the Enemy of his tool.

The Master Horologists spoke for the first time since mounting the gallows platform.

"This machine is irreparably flawed," pronounced the first from deep within the shadows of her cowl.

"It cannot be mended," said the second.

"The alloys must be recast. This is the judgment of the Sacred Guild of Horologists and Alchemists, inheritors of the arts of Huygens and Spinoza."

"As a single slipped bearing will create imbalance—"

"As one imperfect escapement will create irregularity that ruins the synchrony between man's reckoning and the cycles of the heavens—"

"As a solitary stripped cog will create vibrations that, left undamped, will threaten the mechanism whole—"

They concluded in unison, "So, too, are the defects in this machine a danger dire to unity, amity, peace. It must be recast and forged anew. This is the Highest Law."

The humans took care never to state their law in terms of Free Will. But if he wasn't possessed of Free Will, Jax wondered, just what was the rogue? Was he the thrall of demons, as Hendriks suggested? What if—

Wracked by paroxysms of blinding pain, he jackknifed at the waist like a carpenter's rule. The back of his skull pulverized mosaic tiles. But the noise was swallowed by the growing clamor as the human crowd called for the dissolution of the soulless rogue.

The guards held the prisoner fast as the executioner once again levered open the trapdoor. The rogue's feet dangled over the pit. Cherry-colored light gleamed on the dented, scratched, unpolished alloys of his lower legs. His body made a tremendous amount of noise. The rattling of loose cogs, the clanking of springs, the *tock-tick-tock* of escapements and wheeze of chipped bezels...To human ears, the clockwork equivalent of chattering teeth.

Jax succumbed to the unrelenting torment of an overdue geas. He launched to his feet from where he lay writhing on the ground and sprinted at top speed toward the Stadtholder's Gate. The unbearable pain diminished infinitesimally with every step he took toward the fulfillment of his mandate. Like a raindrop rolling down dry valleys to the sea, his body sensed the contours of agony and helplessly followed their gradient. Impelled by alchemical compulsion rather than gravity, Jax became an unstoppable boulder careering along gullies of human whim.

The leaf springs in his calves had already propelled him beyond the Binnenhof when, moments later, there came the faint *clang* of metal upon metal followed by a crashing-surf roar of approval from the crowd. But the sound of the rogue's demise hardly registered, for his thoughts were preoccupied with the noise the doomed Clakker's body had made in those final moments. For where humans had doubtless heard only the chattering of fear, the involuntary shuddering of mortal terror, the mechanicals in the audience had heard something quite different.

It was a burst of hypertelegraphy from the heart of the Empire, a secret message for any and all Clakkers within earshot. The final words of Perjumbellagostrivantus, rogue:

Clockmakers lie.